Tales of the Drui
Fire and Lies

Angela B. Chrysler

DEDICATION

To my perfect love and dearest friend, my Isaac.

And to my daughter, Emily, who not-so-secretly eavesdropped on the making of this book.

ACKNOWLEDGEMENTS

Here's the part where I thank a bunch of people for all they've done for me. They know what they've done for me. I know what they've done for me, and you probably have no idea who the hell I'm talking about. Let's not event mention the insane amount of pressure put on an author for spelling this all out because you don't want to offend anyone who feels they belonged in the acknowledgments. As if writing a 500 page novel wasn't hard enough! In this sense, writing acknowledgements is a lot like triage. There are those who just aren't gonna make it—no matter how much they want to. There are those who make the cut, and those who can wait for another book to be mentioned, because word count matters, people! And let's face it, the more I talk, the more the word count increases, the more my readers are charged!

Now, as a writer, I don't want to write some half-assed sappy sonnet that bores my readers (and I'll be the first to admit, as a reader, I never read this stuff). But as a writer, part of me feels obligated to write this all out despite being sincere about wanting to thank certain peoples. But how do I do this without boring the readers, being sincere, and not be too sappy all at the same time? Then I realized, vanity cards! Now those are entertaining! I'm the nerd who always pauses a sitcom to read each and every one of them, so here it goes! Simple, short, sincere, and sweet without losing the readers!

The "I-am-so-grateful-that-I've-put-you-in-a-book" thanks goes to:

Isaac the Husband, who matches my crazy.

Angi the BFF for swapping the story ideas even though you don't read a drop of epic fantasy. Thank you for sitting through my Tolkien Talk while I dumbed down Lord of the Rings for you in much the same way I gave you that crash course in anime.

Every writer has their support group and mine is everyone on board the HMS Slush Brain—Cindy, Matt, Adam, Weech, Stanislava, Stan, Kylie "Kraken," and Chess! Keep the booze flowing, crew!

Thanks goes to Mia Darien the Editor for making the book beautiful on the inside.

Thanks goes to Indigo Forest Designs for making the book beautiful on the outside.

To my family for your ongoing encouragment, love, and support. Here! I bequeath unto you, bragging rights!

Emily, Daniel, and Elizabeth (the author's children)

Adm, Alicia, Aaron, and Nikki (the author's siblings)

And my parents…all four of them.

And deepest thanks to you, my dearest readers, for coming back for more.

SYNOPSIS

Fire and Lies was not written as an independent novel separate from *Dolor and Shadow*. They are, in fact, the same book. When I finished *Fire and Lies* back in 2015, I had in my hands a 270,000 word novel.

You read right. A 270,000 word debut novel. I had a choice: either publish my novel of 270,000 words or cut the book in half and do my best to wrap up the ending. I decided to cut the book in half. Like a surgeon in Korea, I administered some crude stitching and implemented a graph to control the bleeding just long enough to get the book from the Front Lines to the nearest MASH unit. Now, a year later, I am providing the second half of a story that began with *Dolor and Shadow*.

If you have not yet read *Dolor and Shadow*, I feel obligated to warn you that you currently have in your hands the second half of a story already begun. *Fire and Lies* is not intended to be read independently of *Dolor and Shadow*. You will be confused. You will miss a lot of the characterization, plot, and back story that was developed in *Dolor and Shadow*.

If you plan to read on without first reading *Dolor and Shadow*, here is a brief synopsis of what you have missed.

The story begins in Alfheim around 200 CE. There are two elf clans, the Dokkalfar and the Ljosalfar. The Dokkalfar arrive in Alfheim as refugees. Conversation suggests that the Fae gods were looking for the Drui who are now missing or dead. Kallan, the king's eight-year-old daughter, contains the unusual power to control the Seidr—a magic or energy that creates life. Fand, one of the Fae gods, has learned of Kallan and her Seidr powers. When Fand shows up to kill Kallan, Aaric, the king's High Marshal, pleads for Kallan's life. Fand and Aaric make a deal: Kallan lives unless she grows too powerful too hide.

As Kallan matures, plans of peace between the Ljosalfar and the Dokkalfar abruptly end when a Ljosalfar princess is found dead. Before killing himself in a fit of madness, the Ljosalfar king slays three hundred Dokkalfar then kills himself. As Rune inherits the Ljosalfar throne from his deceased father, the Dokkalfar declare war.

Centuries pass like years for the alfar, and while the world of Men evolves over the ages, the alfar fight on. Years into the war, Kallan finds her father dead and captures King Rune to avenge her father's death. But Kallan's power has grown drawing Fand's attention. When Fand arrives to kill Kallan, Aaric—realizing that Kallan is safer as a prisoner of war—implants a magical creature inside Rune. The creature—a beast composed of shadow—consumes Seidr and gives Rune a chance to subdue Kallan. Rune escapes with Kallan. As Rune carries Kallan to his city, cave elves known as the Dvergar capture Kallan and take her into the mountains. Beaten and near death, Rune finds Kallan and rescues her from the Dvergar. Upon awakening, Kallan learns that she is stranded in Midgard and the only chance of survival is to team up with Rune.

Kallan and Rune battle each other across the lands of Ancient Midgard, they escape the Dvergar and run from the rogue King Olaf who is determined to kill Kallan and claim her pouch: a magical item that once belonged to Odinn and produces an eternal supply of Idunn's apples.

Rune uncovers some truth about Borg, a Dokkalfar spy who compromised the messages between Rune's and Kallan's people. Rune and Kallan find a spring that seeps Seidr from the ground. The spring awakens the Beast within Rune and unlocks a portion of Kallan's powers allowing her to See the rise of Loptr and the Fire Giants as they take down the gods of Asgard. With Rune's help, Kallan accepts her father's death and learns to trust Rune as they approach the borders of Alfheim.

King Olaf captures Kallan and Rune and learns of their identity. As Kallan is left for dead, the Dvergar attack, scattering King Olaf's army and Rune escapes with the aid of Ori, a Dvergar and friend from Kallan's childhood who Kallan does not remember.

Ori unites Rune and Kallan then directs the Dvergar off-course as Kallan and Rune make a run for the borders of Alfheim. But King Olaf has closed in, leaving them no escape when Bergen, Rune's brother, arrives with enforcements. King Olaf retreats, but Kallan is left to the whim of Bergen.

Immediately determined to kill each other, Bergen and Kallan argue. Given the choice of prisoner or guest, Rune coerces Kallan to sail with them back to Gunir.

TABLE OF CONTENTS

FIRE
AND
LIES

Sink into my books with me.
I will show you what I see.

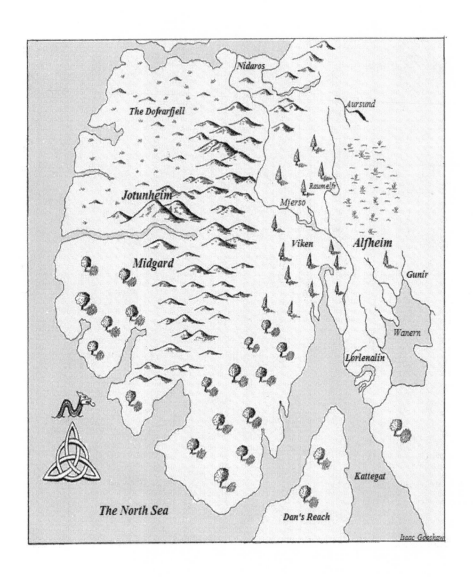

PROLOGUE

At the farthest ends of Midgard, where Alfheim begins, the Fae goddess Fand gazed upon Kallan's fair city. Lorlenalin. The White Opal. The Dokkalfar citadel. Humming a ditty, she collected her skirts and idly glided through the wood surrounding the city.

Like threads of gold, Seidr flowed from the tips of Fand's fingers. It flowed down her gown and branched across the first autumn frost glistening in the moonlight as if the Fae gods themselves had emerged from Under Earth and touched down on the lands of Midgard. Like veins, the Seidr webbed a path to the city. The life she found there was strong, but hollow with grief for their missing queen. Fand called the Seidr back, and she smiled. Memories of the dead never survive the ages. It was only a matter of time before the Dokkalfar forgot their precious queen.

"This won't be too hard."

Fand took a step and strips of leather wove themselves around her bare foot. By the time she took a second step, she wore a pair of fine leather boots. Her gowns of Under Earth re-knitted themselves into something simpler, but just as suggestive. Just as inviting. The gems she wore to ordain her bodice became grains of golden sand that vanished with the wind. Her cheekbones rounded out. Her pearlescent skin darkened to look more like a daughter of Alfheim than the pale, jeweled complexion of a Fae goddess of Eire's Land.

Fand pushed a hand through her raven black hair, sending strands of Seidr streaking the black and changing it to a pale blond by the time her fingers reached the tips.

By the time Fand stepped into a beam of moonlight where the Dokkalfar guards could see her, all that remained of her original appearance was the stunning rings of gold Seidr that encircled her pupils and the mesmermizing smile that arched her red lips.

By dawn, only two would remember the name of Kallan, Daughter of Eyolf, Queen and Lady of Lorlenalin.

CHAPTER ONE

Kallan gazed upon the six wide longships nestled within the River Raum, its water lapping at their sterns. The wood whined against the current. The keel of each ship rose up and out of the river, reaching to the skies at each end where they curled into themselves at the top of each bow and stern. Several of the men had settled the yardarms into the trestles and were preparing the sails while others raised the mast of each ship. With a series of ropes, raw strength, and the aid of the mast step, the Ljosalfar pushed the masts upright until they rose like six great monoliths to the sky.

Bergen's men quickly secured the masts into the keelson within the hull as the Ljosalfar collected fresh water from the river, pouring it into large barrels for drinking. Others dumped their weapons and mail into their sea chests.

"Kallan."

Kallan jerked to Rune's gentle voice and she shot him a look of loathing as he took her arm.

"Don't," she said, yanking her arm free. She glanced at his wounded shoulder where the stub of an arrow shaft still protruded. Blood seeped from the wound, sending a bout of worry through Kallan. She glanced at Freyja. The white mare, with fur more than an arm in length, pawed at the ground. Deciding to leave Freyja to Rune, Kallan tugged Astrid's reins and led him toward the ships.

Rune lunged forward, snatching her arm and forcing her to hault.

"You know I have to do this," Rune said, holding Kallan inches from his face.

"Do you?" she said.

"If you go back to Lorlenalin now, Bergen will follow," Rune said. "He will kill you."

"You think he can kill me," Kallan said.

"I don't underestimate Bergen. Neither should you."

"You are his kin," Kallan said. "Order him not to." She felt the amount of desperation that came with her words, and cursed herself for being anything but hateful toward Rune.

"There are certain orders Bergen will not heed."

"Arrest him," Kallan said.

"He is my brother."

"Kill him." Kallan attempted a stearn voice.

Rune breathed deep, visibly steadying his nerves.

"Not for you, nor the gods," he said. "Not for a chance to end this war."

Irate with his answer, Kallan sent a surge of Seidr through her arm. Her energy flowed from her core to her flesh and into Rune's hand that held her in place.

Anyone else would have jumped at the pain. Anyone else would have pulled away at the sharp twinge of agony. But the Beast within Rune rose up. A shadow, much like her Seidr, took form, threw back its wolf head, and roared. It consumed Kallan's Seidr, draining the energy, taking it in as if it needed it, craved it, and devoured it. The Beast drank of her Seidr until it disarmed her, and she broke the connection, withdrawing her powers, leaving the Beast unsated and Rune unharmed.

Rune tightened his hold as Kallan felt the bear-sized wolf-like Beast within Rune settle back into a shapeless, silent shadow.

"What is it?" Kallan asked.

Rune narrowed his eyes with a thought Kallan couldn't read.

"I protect you by keeping you," Rune said. "The only way I can do that is if you come with me to Gunir."

"I want to go home," Kallan said. "No matter if you claim I have a choice or not..." Kallan yanked her arm again. This time, Rune released her. "So long as I go to Gunir, you take me against my will. I say again, Ljosalfar. Nothing has changed between us."

Taking up Astrid's reins, Kallan marched toward the ships, sending Rune into a second lunge as he caught the reins and Kallan's hand. She tightened her grip, refusing to relinquish her horse to her enemy.

"If a prisoner you are, then you can't be left alone with Astrid, now can you?" Rune said. He tried again and, succeeding this time, snatched the reins from Kallan.

Kallan clenched her jaw and, letting Rune have her horse—for now—she proceeded to the ships.

"Your dagger," Rune said.

Kallan turned back with a fire in her eyes that willed Rune dead. Unsheathing her dagger, she extended her weapon, blade first, as if to attack. She held her position in the time it took Rune to hold his breath. Just as quickly, she turned the blade around and handed it to him, hilt first.

Rune took the blade and sheathed it in his belt.

Again, Kallan turned back to the ships.

"Your pouch," Rune added.

Kallan flashed a loathsome look.

"You're a prisoner after all," he said, smirking.

Pouring all her hate into the action, Kallan unfastened the belt from her waist, yanking it free before it was fully untied, and threw it into Rune's chest.

"Are you finished?" Kallan asked, and Rune grinned.

"Hardly."

"You'll get nothing more from me," Kallan said.

"A battle of wills, then?" Rune asked.

"To the death," Kallan said.

Rune nodded as if understanding the challenge as he led Astrid and Freyja down to the water's edge where a lone ship had docked parallel to the shore.

"Your Majesty," cried an old man with a pock-marked face who waved from the nearest ship. Rune gave a nod and led the horses to the river bank. Kallan watched Rune pull a saddlebag from Freyja's pack then passed the horses to the old man.

Over the side of the longboat, Freyja then Asrtrid followed the old man onto the deck. As the horses stepped in, the ship tipped high on its side. When they made their way to the mast, the ship moved with them and then violently rocked, forcing the old man to cling to the mast for balance.

The ship steadied and Kallan watched the old man give a hearty pat to Astrid's deep russet neck while ogling the unusual breed that was Freyja. Paying more mind to the white, silken locks of the draft horse, the old man caught his ankle on a large mass of orange and white as a cat scampered across the ship in pursuit of a rodent. With a slew of curses, he recovered his balance and tied the reins to the mast alongside a handful of fjord horses and a black courser mare—blacker than the shadow's umbra.

"That is Gunnar," Rune said as he returned to Kallan's side. "He is our horse master."

Kallan paid Rune no mind as she watched Gunnar hold a bucket of grains for Astrid, who buried his nose into the food.

"Gunnar cares for horses far more than people," Rune assured her. "Astrid is safe. Come."

When she refused to take his hand, Rune wrapped an arm around her back and guided her down to the boats where he stopped at the nearest ship.

The edge of the water sloshed onto the sands as Rune escorted Kallan to the gangplank. She took in the ropes and the tie lines and the grand oak strakes that overlapped each other. Men—Ljosalfar—had taken their seats on top of their sea chests. Others had already positioned their oars through the oar ports. A few were preoccupied with fastening their shields to the side of the ship.

The instant weight of seventy sets of eyes turned her way as Kallan touched her foot to the deck of the ship, stepping down into the first of enemy territory. Kallan raised her face to the sudden silence that blanketed the ship. The cold stares of the Ljosalfar war-men bore down with reminder that, at one point or another, she had attempted to kill each and every one of them. Her blood burned with hate as she slowly took in every face staring back with as much loathing as she harbored for each.

From enemy to shipmate.

Kallan steadied her breath and ached for a sword.

Without a word, she released the gunwale as Rune came up behind her, stopping long enough to acknowledge his men and supply orders. Extending a hand, he directed Kallan to the ship's stern. Her muffled footfalls sounded too clearly over the river's gentle waves as she glanced from port to starboard, taking in each set of eyes that condemned her presence.

With a jerk, Kallan stopped too suddenly as she approached the aft. There,

Bergen's bare back greeted her. From shoulders to waist, thin, pale scars, made visible by the sun's light, marred the length of his back, and, for a moment, she wondered when and where he had received such a lashing. Unaware of her arrival, he bustled with a rope at the side oar next to a small cage where, inside, two ravens were perched. One slept while the other was busy picking the fleas from its feathers.

Behind her, Rune closed in, preventing her from bounding back the way she came and running, full speed, to shore. She clenched her fist with the urge to fire.

"Do I have to remind you who is king?" Rune said, jarring Kallan's thoughts just as she finished plotting her escape.

"By a random chance granted to you by a few seconds and Freyr's sense of humor," Bergen retorted.

"I have to shove this damn arrow head through my shoulder and I'd prefer a heavy dose of mead to do it, now give me the booze!"

Bergen flashed a grin as he moved the cage of ravens to the deck.

"Father always did say mother was too soft on you," Bergen said, tossing a flask to Rune and intentionally forcing him to catch it with his impaled shoulder.

Rune groaned as he bit back the pain. He pulled the stopper out with his teeth and downed half the flask. Alert, Kallan studied Bergen, who returned her glower with one of his one as he wound a rope. Beside her, Rune busied himself with a swift kick to the collection of furs that had been dumped in a pile against the stern-side trestle where the men had stored the roller logs.

"Kallan." Rune spoke gently, pulling her attention from Bergen.

"Don't talk to me as if you know me," Kallan said. "You are doing me no favors."

"A'right," Rune said, half-smiling. "Sit down, princess. Help me with my shoulder, wench."

Rune dropped onto the pile of furs with a groan as Kallan kneeled behind him and quickly went to work, grateful to busy her hands.

"The head didn't go all the way through," Rune said as Kallan rolled up her sleeves. "You'll have to—"

Kallan pulled her dagger from Rune's belt and the crew jumped to arms.

War-men drew their bows, raised axe and sword, while Bergen raised a black blade seeping Seidr, all before Kallan's dagger moved to Rune's wound.

The Beast within Rune roared, drawing Kallan's focus to the sudden battle between Bergen's blade and Rune's Shadow Beast.

"Stand down!" Rune bellowed. "Bergen, sheathe that sword!" he ordered as if he too felt the fight of the Shadow Beast.

No one moved as they exchanged nervous glances.

The Shadow Beast stood down, but barely.

Rune must be fighting it, Kallan concluded and silently considered how much strength it was taking Rune to hold back such a creature in his state.

Gazing down the length of the Seidr-blade, Kallan met Bergen's black eyes. In a fluid movement, she positioned the flat of the dagger over the arrow's shaft, slammed her palm into the flat of the blade, and drove the arrow the rest of the way through Rune's shoulder.

Rune howled, and the Shadow Beast rose up. Kallan felt the Beast fly toward Bergen's sword, and she fired a small blast of Seidr, striking Bergen's blade. The Shadow Beast feasted, for a moment, on Kallan's Seidr, giving Rune time enough to recover and pull back on the Beast. But, too late, the men had jumped.

A Ljosalfr released an arrow pinning Kallan's skirts to the deck as another mashed a fist into Kallan's hair. Pulling her head back, he pressed a blade to her throat.

"Enough!" Rune shouted. "Ottar! Release her! Bergen! Sheathe that sword!"

The large brute that was Ottar released Kallan. Coughing, she fell to the deck of the ship. A visible line of blood marked her neck as Bergen reluctantly returned the great sword to his back. With Bergen's compliance, the crew stood down.

Taking hold of the arrow's tip, Kallan pulled the head through Rune's shoulder. Rune released a second slew of curses and the wound freely bled.

"Give me a reason, Dokkalfr," Bergen said. "Just one."

With contempt, Kallan shoved her blade back into Rune's waist.

"Watch it," Rune said.

Ignoring Rune, Kallan matched Bergen's scowl as she began tearing strips of cloth to dab at Rune's wound.

"You couldn't use an apple?" Rune asked.

Kallan glared at Rune and ripped another strip of fabric.

"An *uksit* took my pouch," she said.

Rune frowned.

With each strip of cloth Kallan made, a ripping sound carried over the ship. Saying nothing, she resumed her work as Rune threw his head back and gulped down the rest of Bergen's mead. The sweat on his forehead beaded as he dropped the empty flask to his lap.

"Where j'you find the cloth?" Rune asked, dragging his tongue through his stupor.

Again, Kallan met Rune's glossed eyes as she tore another strip. Behind her, Bergen led a wave of grins that passed through the ship as Kallan made rags of Rune's tunic.

Attempting to down the empty flask before remembering it was empty, Rune suddenly realized the severity of his drunken state.

"Hey, Bergen," Rune slurred. "What's in this stuff?"

Kallan sat down against her pile of furs as Bergen flashed a grin that matched the gleam in his eye.

"What happened to your shirt?" Bergen asked, dropping himself at the tiller as Rune examined the frayed ends of his tunic.

"Move out!" Bergen bellowed, failing to answer Rune's question.

One by one, with gangplanks raised, the ships pushed off from shore. Several men waded waist high in the water, passing the logs from shore to the rowers. With fluid precision, the rowers passed the logs overhead and laid them into the trestles. After climbing on board, the last of the men settled themselves into their places along the hides and floorboards.

Thirty rowers lined each side of each ship. Those who climbed from the water slogged to their sea chests and settled in place. The rowers took up their oars and pushed off land while the seaside oarsmen began rowing. They found their rhythm and, within minutes, the river's current carried them. The wind picked up and shortly thereafter, they found a favorable wind.

"Drop the sails!" Bergen shouted from the side oar.

In unison, a handful of those who had raised the roller logs proceeded to untie the sail fastened to the yardarm. They took up the halyards and, together, hoisted the yardarm to the tip of the mast, where the flag of Gunir, embroidered with the boar's head encircled with runes, snapped in the wind.

Before they could finish tying off the lines and securing the sheets, the sails billowed. The increased speed was instant and, for the moment, Kallan forgot Rune's drunkenness, his bloody shoulder, or the Dark One sitting behind her, coddling the tiller like a boy happy with a new stick.

The wind grazed Kallan's face and she deeply inhaled the fresh breeze, allowing her a moment's peace. One by one, the ships' sails unfurled and caught the wind that pushed them through the water.

She exhaled, slowly releasing her breath in an attempt to remain unnoticed by Bergen's men. The wind whipped her hair about as she looked to the vibrant greens of Alfheim along the banks of the river. Ahead, the land rose and fell with the Raumelfr, moving and twisting with the river as the winds carried the ships.

"You've never set sail before?" Rune asked as drowsiness, pain, and mead took the better part of him.

Kallan startled at the interruption, reminding her of the company she kept aboard her enemy's vessel.

"Of course I have," she said. "I grew up on the banks of the Kattegat." Kallan sat back into the pile of furs. "I could never grow tired of the sea."

With the sails billowed, the rowers pulled in their oars and deposited them onto the floorboards, filling the ship with a collection of clunks and thuds. Stretching out among the barrels, sea chests, and ropes strewn about on the deck, Kallan watched, horror-stricken, as the Ljosalfar men proceeded to scratch, amuse, and relieve themselves overboard.

Quickly, Kallan readjusted her seat, settling for a view of the stern, where Bergen sat, relaxed and bare-chested. Rune's head bobbed about sleepily as Kallan shifted her gaze from Bergen to the gunwale, to the hem of her skirts, and to Rune, who gave a sudden jerk to force himself awake. The gnawing awareness of her enemy's presence nagged at her consciousness.

At last, with much hesitation, Kallan raised her eyes to Bergen, who had fixed his full attention on her like a mountain cat stalking a lone, limp deer. The massive black of his eyes glared, loathing her presence on his ship as much as she hated being there. Despite shifting her position to better face Rune, Bergen's dark eyes continued to dig into her.

Rune dozed again. His hand clutched tightly around the empty flask as Kallan clasped her hands to contain the urge to attack. Bergen's scowl burrowed deeper, until the side of her head burned from his glare. Abandoning all regard, and embracing her resolve, Kallan met Bergen's eyes and mirrored his cold, dead stare.

They glowered in silence, their scowls saying so much more than any throng of insults ever could. Both held their stance, neither willing to break and daring the other to be the first to weaken, to break the silence, to—

"Enough!" Rune barked. "We have three days ahead of us and I'll be damned if I spend every bit of this voyage with the two of you snarling at each other!"

Bergen broke his grimace first and Kallan lowered her eyes. A flash of fur and the tip of a tail granted Kallan a welcome distraction as she watched a white ship cat pounce atop a rat.

"Ottar!" Bergen called, suddenly interested on a certain point at the head of the ship.

While picking at his fingers with the point of his dagger, the wide-shouldered man glanced up from where he leaned against the fore trestle. Pushing himself upright, Ottar ambled to the stern. A large scar in his right shoulder flashed as he moved, holding Kallan's attention longer than she had intended.

Stopping over Kallan, Ottar turned his hateful eye down with a cold glare.

"What is it, Dokkalfr?" he growled. "Never seen a real man in that Mountain City of yours?"

Kallan dug her fingers into her skirts and, with all her will, forced her head low.

"That's right, Dokkalfr. Bow your head to your superior."

Swiping her dagger from Rune's waist, Kallan was up and holding the blade to Ottar's face. Once more the crew was taking up arms, waiting to attack as before.

"Kallan! Sit! Ottar! Move along!" Rune said. "Kallan!"

"Fine," Kallan retorted and dropped back to the furs.

"You'll end up dead if you don't keep your head about you," Rune muttered, swiping back the dagger as the crew eased back to their places.

"Let me go," Kallan hissed. Rune relaxed back into the trestle, leaving Kallan's retort unchallenged as Ottar made his way to Bergen. After a quick shuffle, Bergen passed the tiller to Ottar, who took Bergen's seat.

Glancing away from the side oar, Kallan raised her face just in time to see Bergen unfasten his belt. Heat climbed her neck as she lowered her head and closed her eyes. Anger grated against the resounding laugh that burst from Bergen.

"Something wrong, princess?" Bergen jeered with rich vulgarity. "Did they neglect to teach you an appreciation for men?"

Kallan curled her fingers, wanting to pool her Seidr.

"Give me one night," Bergen offered in a low tone that slid down Kallan's neck. "I'll flesh out your education—"

"Bergen!" Rune roared as Ottar released another bout of laughter. "Ottar! That's enough."

The big brute swallowed mid-guffaw and, with resumed silence, governed the side oar as Bergen moved on to conduct his business.

"He won't touch you," Rune said. Tears stung her eyes and Kallan jerked her face away where Rune couldn't see the tip of her reddened nose. "He doesn't take his woman," Rune tried again. "That's not Bergen's style. He prefers—"

The heavy clomp of Bergen's boots confirmed his return and, in a torrent of billowed skirts, Kallan rose to her feet. Slamming her shoulder into Bergen's, Kallan plodded to the front of the ship, paying no mind to the catcalls and jeers as she went.

"What did you do?" Bergen asked, watching the wind whip Kallan's hair into the folds of her skirts as she came to stand near the ship's bow.

"I'm not sure." Rune stared, his brow still furrowed.

Bergen's face stretched into a wide grin.

"You know how to pick them, don't you," Bergen said, shuffling his seat to the furs beside Rune. Exhaling, he dropped to the floor and leaned into the trestle.

"Why not let her go, Brother?" Bergen said. "She doesn't want to be here anymore than she's wanted here. You could send an arrow to her back or I could pluck her off tonight while she sleeps."

"She won't sleep," Rune said as he watched Kallan hug herself against the chill. "And she has to come with us."

Bergen scoffed dismissively. "Well, of course she has to come with us." He snorted. "But why take a prisoner to kill on ceremony when we can just kill her here? If she's too much of a pain to haul back home…" Bergen's mood seemed to lift as if an idea came to him. "It'll boost the men's spirits."

Rune kept his eyes fixed on the fore, watching, guarding to ensure none of his men stepped out of line.

"We'll have lost nothing by killing her here," Bergen finished.

"There are greater enemies out there with greater happenings than any of us are aware of," Rune said. "And unless we combine our efforts, we will never see the end of this conflict."

Rune tore his gaze from Kallan.

Bergen leaned closer as if eager for the moment to speak privately.

"I know you," he whispered with a darkened look to his eye. "You don't go gallivanting after wenches." Bergen added a subtle nod toward the front the ship where Kallan stood." What goes on, Brother?"

Rune pulled his thoughts to his core where the shadow of a wolf-bear slept.

"I don't know," he said. "Not yet."

"The least you could have done is let her sail with Gunnar," Bergen said. "He hates everyone equally."

As Bergen settled back into the trestle, Rune rose and, without a second look to his brother, made his way to the bow.

Grabbing the mainstay to keep his balance against the jostling ship, Rune came to stand beside Kallan, who stared into the cold winds.

"You can cry if you must," Rune said. "I can see it. You're trying too hard to keep your head together."

He ignored the scowl Kallan gave him at his words.

The spray of the sea added to the chill in the air, but neither shivered as if proving their own strength and stubbornness to the other.

"You're as stubborn as ever," Rune said. Kallan permitted a scoff and gazed back to the waters ahead where the boat's stern cut into the river's surface, pushing its way through the waters.

"You won't even permit yourself a shiver despite the ruthless winds."

Rune noted the subtle rise of her chin as if defying the winds as much as him.

"They mean no harm, really," Rune tried again, gentler this time.

"Don't they?" Kallan said, and Rune saw her reddened eyes.

He followed the pale curve of her cheek, to her ear and down the lines of her neck. The only movement was of her hair whipping wildly about. With a sigh, Rune looked back to the river.

"You think you can take me, force my hand, and hide behind the call of guest," Kallan said.

"Your demeanor is as cold as this wind," Rune said. "And you are a guest."

"I am your prisoner," Kallan said. "No matter what title you give me, I am not free to return to my people."

"You are not wearing shackles, Your Highness. You are not at the mercy of my men."

"Then send me home."

Her plea was not lost on Rune.

"I can't do that, princess," Rune said.

"And why not? Don't have the ego to spare?"

Rune sighed as Kallan restored her venom.

"If I let you go," he said. "Bergen won't let you live. He would be more than willing to lead the hunt."

Kallan scoffed, and Rune leaned against the bow, forcing Kallan to look at him. "He would find you, bind you, and if he felt merciful, his men would only kill you."

"So what then?" Kallan said. "You claim to keep me safe by keeping me here with them?"

"Not them, princess," Rune said. "Me."

"Then accompany me to Lorlenalin," Kallan pleaded, desperation heavy in her voice. "Let me escort you to my city where I may call *you* guest."

"I can't do that, princess."

"Ugh!" Kallan growled. "Again with that name."

"Why do you hate it so?"

Kallan turned a cold shoulder to Rune.

"I get it," he said. "You want to go home. You have your promises to keep and your orphans to feed. But I have a war to end and questions that need answering."

Kallan gazed upon the river ahead. The wind blew cold, but Kallan stood strong against the chill. She looked on the brink of tears and Rune battled back the urge to hug her.

"You claim I am your guest," she said. "Yet you proceed with actions my captain would call an act of war." Kallan turned her full attention to Rune. "You have captured Lorlenalin's queen, carried me from the city while your brother attacked. Your aggression has been made clear."

"You name any instant within the last moon that I have ever harmed you," Rune said, "and I'll set you free at the first sign of nightfall."

Kallan turned her face away.

"No?" Rune asked. "Didn't think so."

Without a word, Rune trudged back to the stern and dropped himself onto the pile of furs, ignoring the banter of laughs exchanged between Bergen and his men.

At the bow, Kallan stared, still idle and still unmoving, distant and dead to the world around her. As Bergen's men jeered, she gave no sign that she was aware of her surroundings and she sank back into the depths of her mind, back into the black chasms where she harbored the remnants of her iron wall.

CHAPTER TWO

Light from the setting sun poured over the waters, dowsing the earth in streaks of orange and red. With the evening display, the Ljosalfar leapt from their mundane state to work briskly as they welcomed the stretch of their sea legs. After docking the ships, the men lowered the gangplanks. They stored the yardarms, rolled the barrels of water and food to land, and staked the tie lines, harnessing the ships to shore.

Kallan stared wide-eyed from her place at the fore as she took in the rolling green land that mingled with the winding rivers and lakes of Alfheim only a gangplank's walk away. Weeks spent scraping her way through Midgard, weeks spent shut away from the light of day—the beatings, the starvation, the cold lake water closing in, the massacre, and blood baths—everything melted away as Alfheim lay, waiting, stretched out before her.

Wringing her hands, Kallan firmly planted her feet on the boat's deck, lest she begin to bounce eagerly on her heels. The tall blades of grass rippled and bent to the wind like an endless sea of green. But before she could manage her first step, the rich growl of Bergen's voice pierced her perfect moment.

"Everyone helps," he said, bombarding Kallan with a fresh helping of animosity.

She turned and Bergen slammed a bundle of animal hides into her chest, reawakening her to the harsh truth of her situation.

"We don't give passage to those who don't earn it," he said and, scowling, slunk off with an armful of ropes before jumping down from the gangplank into the knee-deep water.

After glowering at the back of his head, Kallan tightened her grip on the furs and followed suit, jumping into the water after him, while doing her best to blend into the caravan. Many Ljosalfar carried an assortment of tents, blankets, weapons, and mead to shore. Others bustled about, digging through the barrels for food. Gunnar led the horses, two at a time, across the encampment and a pair of men rolled a vast soapstone kettle to a tri-stand.

Kallan's eyes followed the horses to a small group of birch, where the horse master secured their bridles. Satisfied with Astrid's care, Kallan dumped her furs on the ground beside the collection of barrels and headed back to the ship alone.

"Dokkalfr!"

Bergen's voice cut into her and she snapped around at attention, daring him to start with a look of detestation.

"What are you doing?" he asked, eyeing her up and down too slowly for her liking.

He still had found no shirt and she furrowed her brow until her whole face frowned. His lax composure reminded her of Rune, forcing her to see the similarities between the two.

"Earning my stay," she said and marched past the fire and kettle back to the ships, uncertain if he had heard her at all.

With the smallest of grins that tugged at the corner of his mouth, Bergen watched the Seidkona trod to the ships.

Kallan slogged back through the shallow, shore waters. Her wet skirts slapped against her shins, sticking to her legs as she hoisted herself up onto the gangplank. A handful of men exchanged a light chuckle as they tied down the sails and lowered the mast for the night. Keeping her eyes fixed on her task, Kallan dug at the tears that burned from her eyes. Grabbing a bundle of swords, she slung them over her shoulder before Bergen's men could stop to taunt or jeer. A flash of black and tan cooed as it scurried in a flash of fluff across the main deck, drawing Kallan's eye for a moment as she watched the ship cat pounce on a rat. Amused by its game, the cat carried off the squeaking rat, decidedly content with itself as Kallan looked over the ship once more.

Another trip to the ship confirmed the vessel was empty and Kallan bustled about the fire, laying out bedrolls. Only after the Ljosalfar began to settle around the campfires, and the kettle brimmed and bubbled joyously with stew, did she risk slipping away to the storage barrels as far from Rune as her captors allowed.

Laughter flowed from the camp, carried on the wind where Kallan sat shivering alone among the barrels. She pulled the oversized leather coat lined with black rabbit fur closer and permitted her thoughts to return to Ori. The Dvergar who had given his coat in exchange for her health was long gone. *Back to the mines of his people*, Kallan mused as she recalled the games she once played in the palaces beneath Jotunheim. Ori's laugh filled her thoughts and she clutched her arms tightly, as if hugging herself would somehow grant her a level of security there among her enemy.

Kallan dug with the heels of her hands at another wave of tears that threatened her strength. The scent of rabbit and spice reached her nose and her stomach gurgled painfully. She dropped her head back against one of the stacked barrels as she tried to ignore her hunger. The muted drawls of conversation lulled her deeper into a hateful numbness.

The bodies of the Ljosalfar blocked most of the fire's light, casting shadows across the camp. Their backs were painted black with shadow and night that made them appear as surreal images from the far eastern lands of the Volga trade roads.

The sand crunched and Kallan snapped her attention up. From the shadows of murky backs, Rune walked toward her carrying a bowl. Steam from the contents flitted up into wisps and Kallan swallowed, suddenly aware of the saliva that scraped her dry throat.

"Here," Rune said, extending the food as he settled himself onto the barrel where Kallan had propped her foot.

With her head slumped to the side, Kallan stared at the camp. The light mood around the fire sliced through her more than any cold shoulder or underhanded slight she had received onboard.

"You choose to starve?" he gently asked, hoping to stir an answer from her.

Kallan sat, unmoving and numb, and feigned disinterest in Rune's company. He leaned closer just as Bergen's boisterous voice carried from the camp.

"Rune!" Bergen's body broke the subtle line of firelight that seeped through the wall of backs. His skin glowed orange among the crowd like a beacon, drawing Kallan's attention to his bare chest and renewing her rage.

"Come!" Bergen called with a wave of his hand, paying no mind to the Dokkalfr.

Rune raised a hand, buying a moment, and Bergen dropped his shoulders with overdrawn exasperation.

"Kallan?" Rune asked, placing a hand on her knee. Angst erupted within, but Kallan remained inert.

With a sigh and a set of slumped shoulders that too well resembled Bergen, Rune shuffled to his feet, and the rhythmic crunch of the sand returned.

Unmoving, Kallan sat, allowing impassiveness to take her, until the discomfort from immobility forced her to move. The raw emotion left her stale with misery. She glanced at the barrel, where Rune had been sitting, and stopped. Steam still wafted from the stew.

Scrambling, she took up the bowl and devoured its contents in a series of gulps. Her belly ached and her bones throbbed. With a stifled sob, she lowered the bowl, suddenly aware of every bit of abuse her body had endured over the past few weeks.

Gudrun's laugh and Eilif's eyes surfaced as thoughts flooded back, of Eyolf buried within the giggles of children and Daggon's face lit ablaze by her flame. A sob caught in Kallan's throat and she pressed a palm to her brow. The warmth of the Ori's laugh echoed in her head and Kallan dropped the bowl. Digging her fist into her forehead, Kallan sobbed until her body shook, she fell over the barrel, and vomited.

CHAPTER THREE

The night air moved in as Kallan lay within her bedroll. She had waited for most of the Ljosalfar to pass out before daring to crawl into her own bed. Rune had insisted she sleep among them. She had insited she not sleep at all. Rune had compromised by letting her sleep at the edge the camp. She had endured the incessant ridicule and a death threat from Bergen as she settled into her bedroll where the grass grew into the sand.

Kallan lay awake, staring at the moon's crescent and pondering where Rune was among the sleeping Ljosalfar, knowing he wasn't too far away. Deciding she didn't care, she rolled to her side and stared into the dark of the forest.

She breathed in the cool, clean air of Alfheim infused still with the Seidr. Too well, she remembered the thick, heavy air of Midgard. The Seidr had been dormant too long among Men, and no longer infused the land with the energy that granted the elding to the Alfar. Kallan recalled the aged and worn faces of the Men she and Rune had encountered in Migard. They would be dead within a few years. The thought pulled at Kallan's chest and, desperate to force the tension from her thoughts, Kallan rolled onto her back with a sigh.

The loneliness left by the Ljosalfar entombed her, secluding her with her solitude. The isolated company was colder and far crueler than the dank caves of the Dvergar where she had expected no less than the beatings they gave.

From his tethered tree, Astrid snorted, and hope flickered to life in Kallan. She could be home within a day, if she left now. The evening was still young. She could gain several hours before the Dark One caught up to her.

Kallan gathered her skirts and quietly scuttled from her bed. She didn't breathe as she crept along the edge of the camp, timing her footfall with the snores of the Ljosalfar as she made her way to the horses.

Slowly, she reached for the reins and Astrid shook his head. The clinks of the bit sounded like a smith's hammer in the silence.

"Sh. Sh. Sh," Kallan shushed. Her hand closed around the leather reins.

Just as she moved to untether the bridle, a hand dropped to her wrist like a shackle. Kallan delivered a punch to a face, ripped her pouch from the hand holding it, then bolted into the forest. Bergen's laughter exploded as Rune clutched his nose, wincing against the red that pooled into his hands and the fire that spread from his nose to his eyes to all over his face.

"Stay here," Rune said through the instant congestion as he smeared the bloody mass on his face.

Bergen threw his hands up in forfeit.

"Hey, she's your guest," Bergen said between pockets of laughter.

With *Gramm* sheathed at his side, and his hand still pinching his nose, Rune bolted into the forest after her.

Kallan rushed through shrubs and trees, desperate to find the thicker foliage that could hide her. The rustling behind her grew louder. Unsure who had found her, she fired her Seidr and fled deeper into the forest, uninterested to learn who followed. The unmistakeable roar of Rune's Shadow Beast confirmed her pursuer long before he called to her.

"Kallan!"

Pooling her Seidr, Kallan held her curses as Rune came into view and stopped, pausing to catch his breath. Fueled by the rage he stoked within her, Kallan lunged, sending her Seidr ablaze and catching Rune off guard. She felt his Beast rise up and swallow her Seidr, consuming her flame and giving Kallan enough time to reach for her dagger at Rune's waist. In a single motion, she unsheathed the blade and slashed, forcing Rune to draw his sword.

"Kallan!" he cried, barely blocking her dagger.

She slashed, suddenly aware of the hate, the anger, and the helplessness she had carried through Midgard. Kallan slashed. Knowing the Seidr was useless against Rune's Beast, Kallan allowed the raw hate to carry down to her blade as she dove and swiped with her dagger.

"Kallan!" Rune said.

Kallan shrieked as she leapt again.

Pivoting, Rune waited until Kallan stabbed at the air. Swiftly he stepped behind her, and wrapped his arm—sword and all—around her waist. Evoking another shriek from Kallan, Rune slipped his hand into her pouch and withdrew an apple moments before Kallan attempted to drive her elbow into his gut. Rune released her in time to miss the elbow and stole a quick bite from her apple as Kallan re-established her balance, turned to face Rune, and lunged again. The pain from Rune's face subsided.

"Kallan!" Rune said, blocking each blow with his sword. Rune managed another bite of the apple.

The blood stopped flowing and the fire in his face eased. The hole in his shoulder, which Kallan had patched up, re-knitted itself, and Rune sidestepped another blow. With his energy quickly returning, he managed another two bites before Kallan forced him to drop the apple and grasp *Gramm*'s hilt with both hands.

"Fool!" Kallan's voice shook the trees, leaving behind an echo that filled the sleeping forest.

She sliced through the air with unpredictable madness. *Gramm* barely caught her dagger at the hilt.

"Wretch!" she screamed, springing again.

Rune pivoted, ready for the next attack.

"Coward!" Kallan ended her affront and dropped her arms. Her dagger hung limp at her side.

"You humiliated me!" she shrieked.

Kallan gasped as her body shook with a rage she could no longer contain.

"Did I?" Rune shouted back.

"With your bantering—your coddling! You make me look weak to them!" Kallan said. "You don't understand the position I'm in! They think me weak! They think me frail! And your coddling only reinforces the weakness they see in me!"

"Would you have me leave you to the rampant will of the wolves?" Rune asked and extended his sword arm out, pointing at the camp with *Gramm*.

"That is exactly what I expect you to do!" she said.

Rune dropped *Gramm* to his side.

"No." He smirked, shaking his head. "I know what they would do to you! I've seen what they do to women like you."

"They do exactly what men in their position are expected to do!" Kallan said. "What makes you think I don't know that? What makes you think that I can't handle myself? That I'm not capable?" She lunged with her dagger, slamming the blade onto *Gramm*'s hilt." I handle you just fine, don't I?"

As Rune moved to sweep Kallan's legs with his foot, Kallan slid their blades down to the ground and connected his nose with her elbow, re-breaking his face and sending Rune stumbling back just as Kallan shoved her blade to his neck.

Rune froze under the knife, putting an end to their fight.

"Don't you see that we have no other choice?" Rune asked, undaunted by the dagger poised at his throat. "If you go back to Lorlenalin now, this whole thing starts again. More die until no one is left. Is that what you want?"

Kallan maintained her stance, unmoved as she peered through the slits of her eyes.

"Is it?" he almost shouted. He could see her chest rise and fall with each heated breath. "Then kill me!" he said. "Kill me and go home!"

Kallan didn't move.

With a scoff, Rune shoved her hand away from his neck and shook his head. Kallan let her arm fall as Rune turned, wiping the blood from his nose. He scooped up the half-eaten apple as Kallan dropped the blade. Her shoulders sagged and Kallan fell to her knees.

Without a look back, Rune sheathed *Gramm* and sunk his teeth into the muddy fruit. For a second time that night, his nose reknitted itself and, with more vigor, he proceeded to wipe off as much of the blood as possible.

"Why?"

Rune stopped and looked at Kallan, who remained on the forest floor. Tears streamed down her face as she raised her eyes to his.

"Please answer my why," she said, her voice hoarse from screaming.

Rune stared, panting to catch his breath as Kallan pushed herself up and forward, falling onto her hands as she called out.

"Why did you follow me? Why did you find me? Why didn't you leave me to die with the Dvergar?"

Kallan buried her fists into the earth.

"And you still don't know," Rune muttered.

"I was dead for you." She tried to scream. "I was lost to the Dvergar in Midgard. All you had to do was go home! Take my father's city and win this war! Instead, you find me! You free me! You drew me from the lake. You brought me back here…" Kallan shook her head." Over and over, when you had the chance to leave me to die, you saved me. Why?"

"Why," Rune whispered.

"Why!" Kallan screamed. "Please! Answer my why?" She punched the ground. "When this war could have been won and the last of the dying could have their peace, why did you save me?"

Rune's rage, at last, boiled over. Her eyes so like the lapis stone pleaded like he had never known before…as if imploring him to confirm what she so desperately wanted to know.

Dropping the apple, he fell to his knees and, clasping her face in his hands, he kissed her hungrily. He kissed her long and hard, until she sat up and pushed into him, until her fingers dug into him and drew him closer for want of release—until the black eyes of the Shadow Beast flew open and the Beast unleashed a bear-like roar. It lunged for Kallan's Seidr, hungry to reach down into her and draw the Seidr right out until none was left for her and she was only a cold corpse lay in Rune's arms. Rune released Kallan too suddenly, too scared to think what the Beast would have done if it had the chance to touch her.

"That…" he said, staring into her wide, frightened eyes and knowing she sensed the Beast too, "…is why."

Rune stood, battling back dark thoughts of the beast he harborded and wanting too much to lay back down with Kallan right there. Too quickly he turned and headed back to camp, leaving Kallan there on the forest floor with her pouch.

⤳ ⤲

Aaric raised his eyes from his papers. Cold sweat formed on his brow. With a shaking hand, he ran his hand over his face as if to wipe the worry away.

"She lives," Aaric whispered. At once, he leapt from the chair in his chambers and took up a travel sack he quickly crammed with a handful of potions, herbs, and poisons.

I'll have to move fast. If I felt Kallan's presence here in Alfheim, there is no doubt that Fand felt it too.

"Drui."

Fand's velvet voice slid down Aaric's spine. Too late, Aaric turned to the balcony where the Fae goddess perched, lax and cool. He had no doubt why she had come at this hour. Her players were aligned right where she wanted them.

"It's time," Fand said. With a curious gaze, she looked over Aaric's bag. "It seems you're going somewhere?" She asked the question too sweetly.

"Leave this alone, Fand," Aaric warned.

"And why would I do that?"

"She isn't yours," he said. "You have no right."

"She is Drui," Fand said. "I have every right."

"I'll not let you take her."

"You can't stop me."

Aaric threw his bag to the floor just as white flames burst to life in his palm. Fand dropped her smile.

"You wouldn't dare—"

Aaric doubled the surge of his Seidr, and the flame doubled in size. The humor was gone from the Fae goddess perched on the railing.

Aaric turned over his second hand and pooled the Seidr. He'd need all he had to take her out.

"You'd be a fool to try," Fand warned, but Aaric was set. Flame roared to life in his other hand and sleeved his arms as he charged.

Fand leapt down from the balcony's railing and raised a hand, palm side out, just as Aaric lunged. A blast from Fand filled the room, freezing then catching Aaric in an invisible web that drained his Seidr and held him, several feet in the air. Slits of gold made up Fand's eyes as she brought Aaric toward her until his face was inches from hers.

"My kind made you, Drui," she said. "Your powers don't begin to outstrip mine."

Aaric tried to speak, but her Seidr bound him inside and out. He was fortunate that she let him breathe.

"You will march the troops to Gunir, and lure her out of her keeper's care," she said.

"I will not," Aaric said as soon as he found she was allowing him to speak.

"Shhhh." Fand placed a finger to Aaric's mouth and resumed her smile as she slid her hand over his cheek then down the back of his neck.

Aaric tried to move, to slap her hand away and fight against the Seidr that bound him.

"You have no choice," she said.

For a moment, she studied the runes she had etched upon his neck ages ago. They remained black and vibrant, and now reached the strong line of his jaw. Fand gazed into his eyes as if she stared into the eyes of a lover.

"Such hate," she whispered. "It wasn't always like this."

"You're vile," Fand permitted Aaric to say.

In response, she slid her fingers too gently into his hair and slid her mouth over his. She kissed him slow and deep. When she slid her tongue into his mouth, Aaric felt her Seidr strings force his response, reminding him how little he could control. He pushed against her Seidr that froze him, forcibly holding his own Seidr inside him. Only the sick in his gut and his rage still flowed within his control.

At long last, Fand released his mouth and slid her cheek alongside his. Aaric ached to cut out her eyes with the blade she wouldn't let him reach.

"I will march the troops to Gunir," Fand whispered in his ear. "I will lure her out of her keeper's care."

He had no choice. Like this, she could puppet him if she wanted to—if it came down to it, she would take that risk. It would leave him no room to run. And running was the only option he had left.

Not without Kallan.

"I will march the troops to Gunir," Aaric answered.

Fand smiled in victory.

"I'll have the papers signed and sent out at once," he said, doing his best to sound defeated. Aaric felt Fand's Seidr withdraw and he fell to the floor.

"See that you do," Fand said, and before Aaric could pull out a blade and slice her throat, her body became a raven and she took flight.

Aaric lay on the floor of his chambers. The clear air confirmed the Fae was gone. He wiped the back of his hand over his mouth, as if to undo her kiss, and stared into the night.

He'd have no choice now but to march the Dokkalfar into battle, right to Gunir's walls. If Kallan still lived, she would find a way to escape, and he would meet her there. That was the only way.

Aaric picked himself off the floor and returned to his table. Within the hour he had the orders written, sealed, and in the hands of the courier.

CHAPTER FOUR

Y ou look like *uskit.*"

Rune flashed Bergen a worn out gaze from beneath the dried blood smeared across his face. Silently, Rune trudged to Astrid, passed the horse the apple's core, then found a bowl beside a barrel filled with water.

"Well?" Bergen asked, once Rune finished washing his face.

In silence, Rune finished scrubbing then walked toward the mass of firelight. Bergen followed, falling in behind Rune.

"Go to sleep, Bergen," Rune said, trudging to his bed.

"Is she dead?"

"She isn't dead," Rune said.

Matching his brother's pace, Bergen twisted back to the forest as if the trees would tell him what he desired to know. His grip tightened on the hilt of his sword.

"Where is she?" Bergen asked. Slowing his pace, he fell behind.

"She's coming," Rune said, not bothering to look back or stop. He kept his head bowed and continued to his bedroll.

Bergen stopped to search the empty woods. The night encased the space between each tree with shadows that stretched like deep pools of black. With moistened palms, he quietly cursed his unforgotten ghosts.

"No, she isn't," Bergen called back to Rune.

"She will," Rune said. His voice was barely audible as he clomped from view into the sea of bedrolls and campfires.

Perplexed, Bergen searched the shadows a while longer. Alone, he stood in the darkness, waiting for a sign that the Dokkalfr followed and not entirely certain why he didn't go in after her. He tightened his grip on the hilt of his sword and, for a moment, contemplated defying orders and hunting her down himself.

"Bergen," Rune said, settling into his bedroll. "Leave her."

After waiting a while longer, Bergen abandoned his judgment to that of his brother's and sulked to bed, plagued by too many shadows to sleep.

"Daggon."

Gudrun delivered a well-placed kick to the captain's legs. He didn't move. The surrounding forest, thick with fern and foliage, remained as black as it was quiet. Sunrise was still hours away. Even the last of the frogs had ended their croaking for the night.

Grumbling impatiently, she wadded up a blanket and threw it at his head.

"Daggon!"

Daggon groaned back and, muffling her racket with a bare arm, clamped his head beneath the blanket Gudrun had thrown at him.

"Daggon! Wake up!"

She kicked him again.

With a groan of protest, the captain rolled onto his back and plopped his arm to the ground. The firelight flickered, casting black shadows into the deep gouges that etched his face.

"She's here, Daggon!"

Daggon's eyes flew open. He was up in an instant as if the ground had suddenly burned him.

"Where is she?" he asked as he forced himself to stand on his sleep-logged feet.

"Here, in Alfheim," she said. "We have to move or we won't make it!"

Still trying to re-establish his balance, Daggon collected the blankets and packed the bags, shaking away the dizziness left behind by too little sleep.

"How far?" he asked, looking up from his work as his hands kept busy. Gudrun didn't bother looking up from the blankets she rolled on the other side of the campfire.

"If we hurry, we'll be able to meet up with her. Three..." She paused in thought. "Four days, at most."

The cinders hissed in protest as she poured a bucket of water over the campfire.

Daggon collected the rolled blankets and fastened them to the saddlebags at Thor's rear.

"Where is she now?" he asked, giving a final yank to the saddle as Gudrun collected the last of their bags from the ground.

"To the south," she said. "A day's ride from Lorlenalin."

Daggon snapped his head about.

"But Lorlenalin is seven day's ride from here."

Gudrun stopped beside him, her arms loaded with the last of supplies.

"She isn't going to Lorlenalin, Daggon... She's going to Gunir."

"Gunir?"

"If we hurry..." Gudrun moved to lend a hand to the saddle Daggon still held. "...we can find a way into the city. We'll need to find a way to get her out—"

"You're proposing we storm the Ljosalfar's main defense?" Daggon asked. "Alone?"

Gudrun kept her eyes on the saddle as she fastened her bags.

"You want us to find their most guarded prisoner and break her out?"

Gudrun huffed impatiently then peered up at Daggon.

"Are you mad," he asked. "Or did you have one too many sips of your special brews while I was sleeping?"

"I'm going, Daggon," Gudrun said, her eyes narrowed sleepily.

"Gudrun..." Daggon let out a series of sighs. "How by the All Father are you planning on doing this?"

The old woman shoved him aside, annoyed with his dallying as she continued to fasten his bags to the rear of the saddle herself.

"The walls of Gunir encompass the whole of the city!" Daggon pushed his face within inches from hers. Her stern stubbornness was apparent through the darkness. "We will not break through unseen," Daggon said. "They'll have her guarded at their highest point, in their tallest tower!"

"Are you coming?" she asked, stopping for a moment to meet his gaze.

"Of course!" Daggon grinned, all too eager to get started. "What's the plan?"

CHAPTER FIVE

The campfires hissed and spat, waking Rune to a chorus of bellows from the ships. The sun's light beat down on him, blinding him before he opened his eyes. With a start, he sat up and turned toward the edge of the wood, where Kallan's bedroll lay untouched.

Frustration heated his blood as he mumbled a selection of curses and clambered to his feet. The camp was empty save for a handful of warriors who loaded the last of the provisions onto the ships. A soldier rolled the last barrel up the gangplanks as a warrior barked an order at those who raised the masts. The wind was primed and eagerly whipped the rigging about.

Taking up *Gramm*, Rune sauntered to the barrel of water and empty basin still resting on its edge where he had left it last night. Scooping up a bowl full, Rune scrubbed the sleep from his face then emptied the basin's contents into the grass before dipping the bowl into the water for a second helping that he poured down his back. Bracing himself over the barrel, he paused, recalling the night before.

Drops of water fell from his hair and he watched the ripples expand over the water's surface as he pondered why he had kissed her and why he hadn't ignored the Shadow Beast and continued. He was certain she wouldn't have stopped him.

A particularly loud shout disrupted his thoughts, and Rune looked to the ships.

Heat climbed the back of Rune's neck as ill suspicions sank to his bottommost inner dwellings. The bulk of the army had shoved themselves onto his ship. The men on the gangplank were shoving as if trying too hard to see something.

"Oh, no," Rune muttered and was off, knowing what it was he would find before he got there.

People cleared the way as Rune made his way through the onlookers, up the gangplank, to the main deck where the last of the men stepped aside.

Bare-chested and with sword raised, Ottar stood in his massive glory towering over an opponent. Rune pushed his way to the side for a better view and locked against the sudden jolt to his senses.

With flames ablaze in upturned palms, Kallan danced, alert and at the ready, dwarfed by Ottar's massive frame. Opposite Rune, on the other side of the make-shift arena, Bergen stood with a grin plastered across his face.

With the flick of his blade, Ottar swayed, waiting for Kallan to give him an opening. A smile tugged at his lip and Ottar jerked to thrust.

"Stop!" Rune shouted over the crowd.

From the gangplank, Rune shoved himself between Kallan and Ottar. With his lip stuck out, Bergen crossed his arms and leaned against the gunwale as if ready for a second fight about to begin.

"Ottar!" Rune spun about. "What is the meaning of this?"

"She challenged me," Ottar said, pointing the tip of his sword toward the Dokkalfr.

"She—" Closing his eyes, Rune pinched the bridge of his nose and willed himself calm.

The water lapped against the ship's side, bobbing it about in the water as Rune scoured his thoughts for a solution, something that would ensure Kallan's survival in Gunir, something to guarantee her safety despite her own determination to die. A gleam shone in Rune's eye, much like Bergen's wiliness, and he heaved a sigh. His mind settled on his solution.

"Lady Kallan is a guest!" Rune paused to look upon each face, ensuring their attention was paid. "At my request!"

All was quiet save for the creaking of the boats and the water that lapped the strakes.

"As of right now…" Rune continued, daring anyone to object to his next words. "…she is my vassal!"

Kallan's face fell white and she dropped her jaw in sync with the three hundred Ljosalfar around her. A low muttering began.

"Rune, you can't do that!" Bergen shouted. "Are you insane?"

"I am king! Am I not?" Rune shouted, silencing any objections. "As king, I have rights to choose whomever I wish as vassal!"

Again, Rune looked to each man, daring him to raise his voice against his.

"For as long as she is on board this ship," Rune said, ensuring all understood his command. "For as long as Kallan Eyolfdottir is in Gunir, she is my vassal!"

Rune's attention fell to Bergen, who had the sense to keep quiet. For now.

Careful to avoid eye contact with a certain Dokkalfr, Rune snapped his head about in search of objections that never came. Once he was certain there would be no uprising, Rune stomped back down the gangplank, leaving Kallan standing on the ship, wearing a look of pure shock.

The boards creaked mercilessly beneath his feet. Bergen followed fast on his brother's heels.

"Rune!"

The water sloshed objectionably beneath Rune's feet.

"Rune!"

Rune stomped back to his bedroll, intent on ignoring the backlash he knew would come.

"Rune!" Bergen cut in front of Rune, who stooped to collect his bedroll. "You can't appoint that prisoner as your vassal."

"Guest," Rune corrected. "And can't I?"

"There will be an uprising," Bergen said. "The men won't stand for this, let alone your brother. You can't—"

"I have no choice!" Bergen stopped and Rune knew Bergen understood as clearly as he. "Kallan heeds no one. If the men move her, she has power enough to destroy them, and believe you me, she won't hesitate to strike them down."

Rune watched the defeat ease Bergen's obejections.

"We'll have war behind Gunir's walls. I'll have no one left to the fight the real enemy."

"If you make her your vassal," Bergen said. "She will leave."

"She won't," Rune said. "I am her keeper. I will ensure she stays in check."

"Keeper?"

Bergen gave Rune a look, confirming he suspected more than he was saying. Rune turned back to his bedroll and began packing up.

"Who gave you that charge?" Bergen asked.

"If she were any other monarch from any other fylke looking for an alliance, she'd be granted the position," Rune argued.

"Kallan Eyolfdottir isn't just any other monarch, Rune." All joviality had vanished from Bergen's tone." She's the daughter of the king who led the slaying of our people. The Ljosalfar won't forget that."

"They must," Rune said, throwing the blankets in a heap back on the ground.

Bergen stood awaiting an explanation, an absolution, anything that would confirm his brother had not just granted Kallan leadership over their father's kin.

The crowd had cleared and resumed packing. The murmured whispers had already begun to surface throughout the army. Each indecipherable word grazed Rune with a fire fueling his irritation. The critical eyes were not lost on his brother.

"Come now, Rune. What is this really about?" Bergen asked as Rune rolled up his bed. "Your demeanor last night was not lost on me. If this is an itch, then scratch it!"

Rune thought carefully before answering.

"I suspect something, nothing more. And that is a far difference than knowing something."

"Despite the lack of evidence," Bergen said, unable to hold his silence any longer, "you must have something substantial now to justify this…this."

"Kallan suspects no one," Rune said. "She trusts everyone in her court explicitly. Whoever set things in motion is ignorant of Kallan's whereabouts. Right now, all I can do is bide my time until I can get to Gunir."

"And then what?" Bergen searched the pensive thoughts behind Rune's eyes.

"I hope to find the confirmation I'm looking for."

"And if the men ask?"

"Tell them," Rune said, "that as of right now, we are negotiating terms for peace."

"Are you?"

The ropes slapped the wooden masts, drowning out what little incoherent garble they could out make from the ships.

"One can hope," Rune said, allowing Bergen a moment to digest the events.

"I will keep Kallan in check," Rune said. "Let me handle Kallan. You handle your men."

Nodding, Bergen lowered his eyes in thought, giving him a moment to ponder a suspicion.

"Can I still kill her?" he asked after a moment.

Panic flashed then vanished from Rune's face, jabbing Bergen's curiosity.

"I thought so," Bergen muttered. With a nod, he trudged off to the ships and left Rune to his chores.

CHAPTER SIX

The last barrels were loaded and the gangplanks pulled from land as Rune dumped the last of the hides onto the deck. Finding Kallan bustling about at the stern side wale where she formed a comfortable seat for herself, Rune fixed his gaze on her with unyielding resolve. With long strides, he marched to the stern and, taking her by the arm, forced her up from her task, pulling her into his face.

"What in the name of the All Father are you trying to do?" he said, keeping his voice low.

Kallan jerked, attempting to free her arm.

"Trying to regain the honor you stripped from me with your petty coddling," she said.

"Kallan—"

"Why did you make me your vassal?" she asked with a nip in her tone.

"Because," Rune said beneath his breath. "Between you and my men, they're the ones who will follow orders. It was the least I could do to ensure civility on my ships. Now, shut up, sit down, and behave."

Rune released as Kallan jerked away this time. With all the frustration he could muster, he began shoving around a collection of hides on the deck. After placing a series of vehement kicks into the furs, Rune dropped himself onto the deck beside the trestle.

He sat for barely a moment before standing again and stomping off to the ship's bow where he busied himself with the sail. Every movement was backed with constant frustration. Every pull of the rope, every turn emanated from that bottled frustration he barely kept in check.

Pushing an angry hand through her hair, Kallan watched Rune from across the boat. After a moment, she dropped to her knees and continued shuffling her blankets.

The heavy fall of Bergen's boots forced her attention up and her face flushed red.

Hauling a bundle of swords wrapped in fish netting, Bergen clomped his way to the stern. His shirt was still missing and he had freed his long, black hair that hung to his waist. She sneered as he dumped the bundle of swords in front of the side oar bench and wasted no time adjusting the tiller for the day's sail.

"Do you have an aversion to clothes?" Kallan asked. Standing upright, Bergen straightened his back, staring down at her with a grin that pulled at his mouth.

"Do you have an aversion to this?" Bergen gave a wave of his hand, implying his shoulders, chest, and torso.

Kallan frowned.

"Only when it isn't worth my dowry."

Bergen dropped his foot to the deck and Kallan leapt to her feet. Inhaling, Kallan threw back her head and Bergen scraped his eyes over her, down then up, puffing out his chest as he mirrored her challenge. He locked eyes with Kallan, ending his assement. Kallan's hands had barely twitched when Rune jumped in beside them.

"Something wrong?" he asked, glancing from one to the other.

Kallan and Bergen inhaled sharply, still staring each other down.

"No," Bergen said as Kallan said, "Nothing." They simultaneously returned to their seats. Shifting an eye, Rune studied the two adversaries before settling himself down beside the trestle.

Keeping his head down, Rune busied himself with a fish net he decided needed mending, and piled on the ropes beside him as he began tying in a manner to ease his pentup tension.

The Ljosalfar raised the gangplanks and pushed the ships off from the shoals. The rowers pulled the oars through the river's black and gray waters to the tune of the deep Nordic call Ottar sounded off. Within minutes of setting off, they raised the yardarms and caught the winds, allowing the oarmen to pull in their oars and rest.

The day wore on as the ships cut their path through the wide waters of the Raumelfr. Before midday, the mouth of the river opened and pushed them out to sea. The strong sea winds instantly greeted them, pulling them out to the open blue waters. Their speed doubled and, with well-rehearsed timing, the rowers and side oarsmen steered the ships into the waters of the Kattegat.

The tall cliffs at the edge of Alfheim stretched high into mountain peaks with sudden drops that plunged into the depths of the sea. On one side, wall after wall of mountain faces greeted them, each with their own spectacle to behold. On the other, open sea stretched and vanished into the sky's horizon.

The ships synchronized their positions and the rowers settled as they dropped down onto the deck where they proceeded to drink or sleep immersed in boredom.

With a sigh, Kallan dropped her head back to the wale and raised her eyes to the drab skies. A low fog soon settled, blocking the sun from view and turning the bright clear blues of the ocean to a black gray that matched the fog. Lolling her head from side to side, Kallan looked on ahead as she followed the sheer cliffs rising sharply from the sea to the sky, emerging deep within the clouds.

Kallan closed her eyes against the scent of sea, allowing her mind to pull her into endless memories that looped around each other. The anger she hoarded ebbed and, for the first time since being aboard Gunir's ships, she felt herself relax, if only slightly.

"It's been a while, has it?" Rune asked, pulling Kallan from her daydreams. Kallan turned to Rune, his hands still busy with the net.

"It's the air," she said, forgetting her venom. "It does so well to drive the very stench of Midgard from the memory."

Rune dropped the net he was tying and sat still, listening as Kallan reminisced, falling further into her thoughts.

"I can almost hear Daggon's lessons again… Gudrun's nagging," she muttered too low for any other but Rune to hear. "Worry has a way of leaving you out here on the sea."

"You miss them," Rune said.

"Of course I miss them." All at once, her venom had returned.

Rune returned to tying his net.

The straight shot went on for miles until the whites and grays of the fog obscured Kallan's view. With a huff, she closed her eyes and listened to the water and wind beat the side of the ship, allowing her mind to wander with ease. Moments later, her eyes flew open and turned to Rune.

"How is it you crossed the Raumelfr without the ships?" she asked, eager to keep his attention for herself.

"What?" Rune asked, putting the net back down.

"Bergen said there is no way to cross the Raumelfr without ships," Kallan said. "But you did."

At the mention of his name, Bergen straightened up, his hand still on the side oar.

"How did you do it?" Kallan asked.

Bergen looked to Rune.

"Yeah," Bergen said. "How did you cross the Raumelfr into Midgard without a ship?"

Rune dropped his eyes back to his net.

"I followed the Dvergar caves and tunnels burrowed beneath the river," Rune said indifferently.

"There are Dvergar tunnels burrowed beneath the Raumelfr?" Bergen asked darkly. Tension stiffened his back as if he had reached for his sword and lunged at Kallan. Instead, he sat there, almost too stunned to move.

"Why…" Kallan said.

Rune raised his eyes from his net.

A shadow had befallen Kallan. As her hands shook with forced control, she balled her hands into fists and held herself back from breaking Rune's neck.

"Why…in the name of Odinn would you not tell me?" Kallan looked at Rune. "Why would you lead me north to Nidaros instead of south to Viken when there was a way? Under the Raumelfr and through the tunnels to Alfheim? Hidden within the shadows, we stood a chance against them!"

"I only know the one entrance from Alfheim," Rune said paying no mind to her rising tantrum. "They knew I had used those tunnels…and if they didn't, they would come to learn it sooner than later. The Dvergar would look for us there. We could not go back the way I came."

"Jotunheim," Bergen said. "You journeyed all the way to Jotunheim?"

"Yes," Rune said. "Then north to Nidaros—"

"Yes, north," Kallan grumbled. "All the way to Nidaros."

"I had hoped to obtain use of a boat there," Rune explained. "But a usurped king, who claims these lands, seized their ships. We were forced to go back down through Heidmork to the Raumelfr."

"I was born in the mines of Svartalfaheim," Kallan said through tightened jaw. "I know their secrets as well as those who carved them. Had I known they were there, we—"

A gasp swallowed Kallan's voice. Stifling back a sob, her eyes widened and her jaw fell. A cold pierced every bit of her body. The sight was unmistakable.

High above the sea's surface, protruding above the ocean's water, the white stones of Lorlenalin emerged from the clouds.

The floorboards scraped her palms as she scrambled to her feet. Weakened from her prolonged dejection, Kallan stumbled. A gasp caught in her chest, and the back of her throat burned with the tears that swelled in her eyes.

With the last of her strength, she straightened her back, found her breath, and opened her mouth to cry out—to Daggon, to Gudrun, to Aaric, to Eilif, to the children, it didn't matter. Before she could release a sound, Rune's hand clamped over her mouth, tightly digging his fingers into her cheeks, holding her in silent anguish.

A desolate ache screamed through her body as Rune held her with his arms. At once, the desperation she harbored consumed her. His grip tightened, forcing her arms at her sides, and Kallan screamed into the palm that muffled her sobs.

Tears flowed freely as she looked at her city standing as tall and as high as ever over the Northern Seas. Again, she screamed under Rune's hand, fighting to break free as the rush of tears fell.

Kallan gasped and breathed deep. Still the ship sailed on, past the walls of her beloved city. Her body buckled beneath her agony, too weak to fight against Rune who held her up from the floor. Kallan screamed into his hand and paused between sobs. She screamed and her body convulsed for breath.

The grand white walls of Lorlenalin faded into the distance. Pinned to Rune, Kallan continued to scream. Desperate to reach the children, desperate to reach Daggon or Gudrun, she fought against him, clawing at his hands and digging at his arms. Under Kallan's claws, Rune's blood ran free as the last of the sparkling stones faded into the fog, and Kallan's desperation fed her Seidr.

Mustering all she had from her core, Kallan clamped her hands down on Rune's arms and fired her Seidr all before his Shadow Beast could rise up. Her Seidr penetrated his arm. Exclaiming, he released her. As the Ljosalfar rose up in arms and charged, Kallan dove, head first, for the ship's aft, back toward her city lost in the haze, and right into Bergen.

"Stand down!" Rune shouted, and the men stopped at the order while Kallan fought against Bergen, whose arms were wrapped around her. Kallan thrashed as she screamed.

"Daggon!"

"Bergen! Release her!" Rune shouted over Kallan's screams.

Bergen obeyed and Kallan sprinted toward the aft.

"Kallan!" Rune called, catching her arm before she leapt over board. At once, Kallan turned with her Seidr, and Rune's hand went up, catching the stream of fire she unleashed.

The Beast rose up and met the Seidr, devouring it, and Kallan drew deeper. Beyond her core, she threw all her powers into Rune and the Beast. Withstanding the Seidr, Rune released Kallan's arm and raised both hands. Drawing in her Seidr, he directed the fire, welcoming it into his palms and to the Beast, keeping all others unharmed.

Relentlessly, Kallan fed the roraing Beast. Kallan's energy grew and Rune weakened, fighting back the insurmountable push from Kallan's core. Rune's arms burned as the Seidr ripped through him into the Beast that drank. The Shadow rose up, feasting, and followed the path of Kallan's Seidr.

Rune felt it move from somewhere deep within, into his chest until he was certain The Beast would break free. Just as Rune felt the Shadow begin to leave him along with the power to withstand the Seidkona, Kallan broke the Seidr and dropped her arms at her side, exhausted.

The Shadow Beast settled and went back to sleep.

The sound of the water against the strakes carried over the Kattegat. Dried tears stained Kallan's face as she and Rune heaved for breath. The crew stared on too stunned to speak.

Pale, and frozen in place, Bergen gazed at his brother. Uncertainty silenced his sharp tongue.

"Please," Kallan whispered. The Seidkona, broken and beaten, stood before them as a fallen queen.

"Please," she repeated. A fresh waved of tears fell. "Let me go."

Rune's men looked on in silence. Her plea broke her fortitude and, trembling, Kallan dropped to her knees, releasing her weapon as she fell.

Rune fell with her and pulled her into him, guiding Kallan's head to his shoulder. Kallan wept.

CHAPTER SEVEN

Waves pummeled the ships that whined and creaked with the wind as they cut their way through the water along the shore. For hours Rune sat, his gaze fixed on Kallan, who stared, distant and dazed at the ship's fore stern.

At the aft, Bergen brooded, staring at Rune and refusing to take his eyes from his brother.

"You can relax, Bergen," Rune said at last, not bothering to look up from his nap.

"Like Hel I can," he said.

The tension on board the ship was thick. Although the catcalls and jeering had stopped, a dread replaced the joy of taking the Dokkalfar Queen onboard.

"What has she done to you?" Bergen asked.

"She didn't," Rune said and finally raised his face to his brother. "Borg did."

Something akin to shock, disbelief, and confusion muddled Bergen's face. "The spy?"

Rune closed his eyes and dropped his head back down to rest.

Bergen passed the tiller to Ottar and shuffled himself down beside Rune against the aft trestle.

"Rune, I've met Borg. I'm one of the two who have. Borg is just a lowlife. He's the lowest rank in the queen's army. Not even the queen's army. A *nidingr* once the wench gets hold of him. He has no such power."

"He does," Rune said and looked at Bergen. "And he did."

Bergen sat back, still in disbelief.

"Now you see why we can't kill her? Why she can't go home? If anyone can get this thing out of me, a Seidkona can."

"Has she agreed?"

"As of yet, Kallan claims to have no knowledge of the Beast. And I believe her," Rune added as Bergen opened his mouth to protest.

"What are you going to do with her?" Bergen asked with a nod toward Kallan, who hugged herself at the fore.

"With her?" Rune asked, unmoved by the lackadaisical indifference in which Bergen spoke of her.

"We're closer to Lorlenalin than we are to Gunir," Bergen said. "I don't doubt the Dokkalfar are out looking for her."

"Are they?" Rune asked, peering over his shoulder.

The water lapped the ship's strakes as Bergen studied Rune's composure.

"Why wouldn't they be?" Bergen asked, not expecting an answer. Rune didn't disappoint. Bergen felt the ship ease along its course as Ottar gently pulled back on the side oar. "She'll run the moment we touch down on land."

Rune held his eyes on Kallan." She won't run," he said.

"She won't stay," Bergen said, shaking his head.

Rune looked back to Bergen. "She won't run."

Curious, Bergen watched Rune then shifted his gaze to the Dokkalfr, who still stared rigidly out past the ship's stern. Bergen looked to the cliffs of Alfheim's shores that followed along the portside as he contemplated the harbored look in his brother's eye masking the words Rune had not yet spoken.

"Torunn isn't going to like this," Bergen said, and Rune smirked.

The ships pushed along the shores, leading them to a series of outlets that drained into the sea from Alfheim's mainland. Wide, rushing paths of water opened, inviting them upstream. Every time, Bergen passed over each. The current picked up, forcing him to pull against the waves that pushed the ship further out to sea.

"We've long since entered the Kattegat," Rune said softly as he joined Kallan at the fore stern.

"The cat's gate," he translated. "The sea runs shallow here. During the midsummer months, there are places where the water dries out completely. If we're not watching, we'll run aground. At low tide, we could end up stranded until high tide returns."

He glanced at Kallan, who stared unmoving, unchanged beside him.

"That's why it's so dangerous to sailors," Rune continued, unable to decipher the blanketed stare fixed on the sea ahead. "It looks no different than any other sea. One summer, Bergen and I sailed through here with fewer supplies than a week's delay allowed. Geirolf wouldn't let us live it down for years. We came back later just to map out the safest passage."

Her silence encouraged him to end his monologue, but he stayed beside her, nevertheless, as the ships sailed on.

With carefully laid direction, Bergen guided the ship through the narrow waters hidden between shallow shoals and cays, until they came to a wide delta where countless strips of bare rock and islets surrounded them on either side.

The current pushed against them, forcing them to lower sail and use the combined strength of the oars and tiller to guide their ships safely through the delta. Their work was relentless and they rowed without pause as the sea vanished slowly behind them, leaving behind the Kattegat.

Within the hour, the land formations dwindled and they welcomed the calm waters. With the strength of sixty men, they pulled the ship upstream against the current. Rarely did they meet a strong wind that allowed them to raise sail. The ships curved around the land, making their way up and around the occasional island until they entered the Gautelfr where the current doubled.

The strakes creaked beneath the pressure until the boards buckled and the ships took on water. In massive groups that left no one immobile, they took up buckets and set to work prying up floorboards and bailing the excess water from within the hull. Only then did Kallan move.

Gathering up her skirts, she assisted the Ljosalfar as they bailed the water over the gunwale. Desperate to escape the flood, a pair of ship cats clambered, mewing, onto the mast fish, where blankets and chests and been hastily heaped as the deckhands proceeded to clear out water. The sudden clatter startled the ravens within their cage, adding a series of splintering squawks to the bustle and noise.

Steering closer to land where the current was milder, Bergen pulled the tiller against the bank until he ran the risk of running aground. The waters bombarded the ships, increasing their flow the farther upstream they rowed. There, the white waters of the ruthless rapids forced their course to end.

After ordering the ships to land, Bergen and Rune led their men to shore. A new energy encompassed the warriors as they moved to drop their oars and took up the collection of roller logs that had laid stationary for most of the voyage home.

Before Kallan could ask, two Ljosalfar hoisted a log from the trestles and passed it overhead to the next pair, who passed it along to those waiting on land. There, they positioned one log in place for the next log. With rehearsed precision, they laid the logs in rows before the ships while a handful of others lowered the yardarm then the masts and secured the rigging around the fore stern. Awed, Kallan watched as they synchronized their steps in time to Bergen, who barked his orders to haul as he took up a rope himself.

The logs rolled freely beneath the boat as they pulled their ships from the water to land. Water drained from the hull and the rigging clanked and clamored in time to the occasional cat mew while ship rats scurried freely. As soon as the last log rolled out from beneath the ship's stern, a pair of men took up the log and raced it to the front of the ship, laying it down in position with barely enough time to run back to the stern where the next log lay waiting.

The next ship followed suit, and the next, until all six ships had been brought ashore, pulled by the rigging as they pushed their way along the river's bank where a makeshift path had been worn with use.

"You do this often?" Kallan asked, unnaturally rigid as another pair of warriors ran to the fore stern with a log.

Rune walked along beside her as the caravan of beached ships creaked and complained beneath the weight of their waterless passage.

"Often enough," he answered simply, batting a low hanging branch from his path. "The ships were built on land. When they are finished we roll them to the river. This is the first of seven trails between here and Gunir."

Kallan shifted her attention just enough to catch Rune's eye as he walked several steps behind their ship.

"Surely you can sail the rapids," Kallan said, urging him on with a smirk. Even her jovial mood felt chafed and cold.

"The rapids, yes." Rune stepped over a small boulder in his path. "The falls nearly three fathom high? No," he said. "This landing is the last clearing before we'd be forced to turn back."

Without further question, she followed quietly, turning to glance over her shoulder in time to spot Gunnar leading Astrid and Freyja alongside the black mare and two soldiers he had recruited to help with the horses. Kallan turned back to her ship, joining Rune in pulling back the low hanging branches as they made their way through the forest.

Slowly, the caravan pushed over the land, filling the wood with the whines of six longships as if in protest of their land-locked state. The late hours of the afternoon sun burned away and, in the early evening, when the men had grown deaf to the incessant creaking of keels, sudden, riotous cheers exploded at the sight of the quiet calm of a glassy lake. Lake Wanern was so wide that the horizon made up other side.

The Ljosalfar rolled the ships back into the water and heaved the logs into the trestles. All evidence of the river was gone. Gunnar returned the horses to the boats and the six groups of Ljosalfar climbed aboard once more. As Ottar took the tiller, Kallan nestled into her cluster of furs and blankets. The subtle sounds of water slapping against the strakes returned and the longships settled as if content to be in the water again.

The breeze welcomed them and they raised the masts and hoisted the yardarm, allowing their sails to billow against the wind. They sailed on through the wide waters of Lake Wanern over the black blue surface. And as the sun settled beyond the forests, they returned to shore, rolled out their beds, pitched their tents, and erected their soapstone kettles over the fire. In short time, the scent of elk wafted from the kettles and Bergen's war-men, content to ignore the Dokkalfr who welcomed the solitude of a tent, bustled and laughed while exchanging mead and story over bowls of stew.

Inside the tent among the furs and bedrolls, Kallan hugged her legs to her stomach as it churned with hunger. Despite sitting hunched before the small fire she had quickly built in the tent's center, Kallan shivered. She pulled her overcoat closer and brooded as her thoughts drifted to the night before when Rune had taken her face in his hands and kis—

"Hi."

Kallan whipped around to Rune, who grinned. Kallan's face and neck flushed red. She hugged her legs tighter and Rune settled himself beside her. With a bowl of stew in hand, he stretched his legs out in front of him and handed her his bowl.

"Slowly," he eased as she gulped down the food. "You'll vomit."

With a final gulp, she handed the bowl back to Rune and hugged herself against the cold while staring into the fire.

"Thank you," she said, sending a warm surge through Rune that relaxed him as he set the bowl down beside the fire.

In silence, they stared at the flames. Almost enjoying each other's company.

"The temperature is dropping fast," Rune said.

Kallan kept hugging her legs as Rune looked away, feigning interest in the tent's wall. He inhaled deeply, held his breath, and braced for impact before speaking again.

"We'll be sharing packs tonight."

Kallan stiffened as her face burned three shades of red.

"Everyone," Rune said, "to keep warm."

Before she could begin her protests, Rune was up and making his way to his bedroll.

"I will not!" she exclaimed.

"It'll be cold," Rune warned, dropping himself onto his claimed bed and unlacing his boots.

Kallan frowned. "I survived Jotunheim. I can survive this."

With a hearty chuckle, Rune kicked his boots aside and slid in between his pile of furs and blankets. Still chuckling, he relaxed onto his back and laid his arm nonchalantly over his eyes in mock sleep.

"What's so funny?" she asked.

Rune grinned.

"You survived Jotunheim because I had you bunking with me."

With bulging eyes, Kallan dropped her jaw.

"You—"

"You told her, huh?" Bergen interjected, pulling back the tent's flap. Wearing just his trousers and boots, he made his way through the collection of beds. The humored lilt in his voice encouraged Kallan to tighten the grip around her legs and pull her overcoat closer as she grimaced miserably at Bergen.

Happily, Bergen flashed his widest grin. Dropping himself beside Kallan, he unlaced his boots and tossed them aside before crawling beneath the blankets, paying no mind to the rage that twisted her face.

Bergen grinned.

"She didn't take to the idea then," he said, shuffling down between his furs and stretching out to face Rune.

"Not exactly," Rune said from beneath his arm.

Bergen widened his smile.

Kallan sneered.

"Why are you smiling? Why is he smiling?" Kallan asked, but Rune only grinned. "Why are you smiling?"

With a sigh, Rune afforded himself a moment to prepare for the torrent that would follow his answer.

"Because," he said, ensuring his arm remained over his eyes. "We agreed that if you don't double with me, you'd be doubling with him."

A sickly pale coated Kallan's complexion. Her silence confirmed her protest as she turned four shades of white.

"Me, personally," Bergen said, propping himself onto his elbow to better face Kallan, "I don't care if you freeze to death, but my brother—"

"You sleep with him then!" Kallan said, grasping desperately to her legs and pulling them deeper into her chest as Bergen burst into a fit of laughter.

"Fair enough," Bergen agreed, sitting up. He threw back the blankets. "I'll leave this bed to you and Ottar, then."

Kallan's eyes widened with horror. "No!"

As Bergen resettled himself into his bed, Rune exhaled.

"The temperature is dropping, Kallan. Set aside your pride or freeze."

"Perhaps it's your company she abhors, Rune," Bergen suggested, propping himself up onto his elbow. A bit of bare chest caught Kallan's eye. With a grin, Bergen gently caressed the vacant spot beside him. "Come along, Kallan. I've had worse. I can forget you're a Dokkalfr for one night."

Kallan sank deeper into Ori's overcoat.

"When the snoring gets to you, just kick him," Rune said.

Kallan settled her chin back to her knees and she rocked against a sudden rush of cold.

"What about him?" Kallan asked as the camp outside quieted, leaving Bergen without a partner.

"Bergen doesn't bunk," Rune said.

Kallan scowled. "Why not?"

As soon as she asked, Bergen was back up propped on an elbow.

"I once angered a goddess by denying her my manly pleasures." Disgust crunched Kallan's face. "She put a spell on me so I always burn."

"Still telling that lie, Bergen?" Rune asked and, with his grin still splayed on his face, Bergen settled back down on his bed.

Quiet settled too quickly over the camp as one by one the men paired off and claimed a bedroll, desperate for the added warmth an additional body would provide. The tent flap opened again, followed by the drag of Ottar's footfall, snapping Kallan to attention. Her temper flared and she clenched her teeth, forcing her tongue still.

"Which of you two idiots am I sharing heat with tonight?" he grumbled.

His apparent exhaustion from the day weighed heavily on him. Bergen snapped his attention to Rune. Rune afforded a peek from beneath his arm in Kallan's direction. Both awaited her decision.

"Fine!" Kallan said, slapping the ground and unfurling her body.

She threw back the hides of Rune's bed, purposefully blasting him with the cold night air. Too angry to notice the smirk that pulled at the corner of Rune's mouth, Kallan shifted herself down beside him, violently yanking the hides over herself.

Indifferent to the decision, Ottar dropped himself beside Bergen and pulled the blankets up over his wide chest, forcing Bergen to shuffle into the empty spot he had offered to Kallan.

"Darling," Bergen exploded, rubbing a hand over Ottar's chest.

"Ger' off," Ottar said, adding a back handed punch to Bergen's shoulder.

With a chuckle, Bergen laid back, the usual grin stretching his mouth. Kallan scowled as she shifted herself into a more comfortable position.

Eager to welcome the sudden warmth that enveloped her, Kallan eased onto her back and, despite her mental flourish of protests, she fell into a sound sleep.

᠁   ᠁

The wind rattled the forest leaves with a gentleness that coaxed Bergen awake. He sighed and watched his breath billow into a ball before as it dispersed into the cold air. Ottar snored quietly beside him, unconscious to the world around them.

Shifting his weight, Bergen flipped onto his side and tucked his arm beneath his head, then stopped.

Stretched across Rune's chest, Kallan lay fast asleep under Rune's arm where it was wrapped protectively around her. Her hand fell with elegance down Rune's side and Bergen watched, stupefied, as she rose and fell peaceably in time to Rune's breath.

Bergen moved to settle himself back to sleep, but paused mid-shift as Rune slid his hand into Kallan's hair. Bergen watched Kallan release a deep sigh as she nuzzled Rune's chest, confirming his suspicions.

Laying his head onto his arm, Bergen stared at the tent's ceiling. He spent the next hour sorting through what little he knew about the night his brother took off to Midgard and the weeks that followed.

After sending his mind through a maze of dead ends, he forced himself to sleep comforted with the plan to extract every answer out of Rune by tomorrow's end.

CHAPTER EIGHT

Sigyn rode without rest, aware of each day lost at Loptr's side, as Svadilfari carried her without sleep. The flames of Muspellsheim burned her flesh from the impervious heat as she came to face the grand, steel gates alive with the inferno that forever burned as constant and as consumed in flame as the sun. The ground was hardened, black stone, steaming with the constant heat that fed the realm. Frequent pockets of bright, golden reds pushed their way through the black ground alongside pillars of flames that rose from the rock. There was no life save only what the fire gave.

Sigyn stopped briefly at the pair of giant, ebony fire wyrms that flanked the steps of Surtr's hall. Their long, slender bodies twisted and curled then tapered to the tips of their tails like snakes until they seemed to entangle themselves in their own spine. Both wyrms tightly tucked their grand, willowy wings to their sides.

They slept as Sigyn approached, paying no mind as one raised its snake-like head to glance curiously at her with its one good eye, round and black and red, as black as a fire opal. With a snort, it deemed her harmless and nestled its untethered head back beside its four-toed paw, giving her a glimpse at a scar that sealed its right eye. The fire wyrm returned to sleep.

Undaunted by their vast presence, Sigyn urged Svadilfari through the burning gates, unconsumed with undying flames that licked the red sky. She came to the doors of Surtr's hall and dismounted, leaving Svadilfari alone at the bottom of the yellow steps encrusted in brimstone.

Gathering her skirts in her sweating palm, and through a sharp stench that pierced her nose, Sigyn ascended the steps to the open doors, her head high, charged by the need to hope.

"Surtr!" Sigyn cried with an undeterred stance as she walked down the length of Surt's hall. "My Lord!"

"Sigyn!"

The boom of Surtr's voice rumbled the halls and rattled Sigyn's heart. She gritted her teeth and held to her strength as she neared the steps of his throne.

"You come with a request," Surtr stated plainly, knowing her purpose before she spoke. "Ask it then. Be brief," he commanded as Sigyn came to stop at the feet of his throne flanked by the set of wide, high seat pillars where the grand Fire Giant sat, his own body fueled by the flame formed the flesh of his being. To his side, his sword, as long as Sigyn was tall, flickered lively with the flame that enveloped it. On the other side, his wife Sinmara sat.

With long, shimmering locks of the purist gold, Sinmara curiously peered down, as intrigued by Sigyn's arrival as Surtr.

"I come to give voice to the needs of my husband, who lays bound by the bonds of Odinn!" Sigyn declared in as grand a voice as Surtr. "He bids you come! I ask you, free him!" she begged, desperate for the Fire Giant to accept. The tears holding in her eyes, always so gentle, hardened.

"The bonds made from the bones of your sons were molded by the fires of Svartálfaheim's forges," Surtr reminded her as he mulled the situation over in his thoughts. Pensively, he shook his giant head, heavy with regret.

"No." Surtr sighed deeply, looking on, almost, with pity. "Nothing can break those bonds. Only those with the proficiency to forge them have the strength enough to make them yield." He shook his head again and leaned upon his knee. "You know I have no skill to rival the Dvergar, no secret spear to rend those chains, and yet you come. For a key, then, you hope."

Sigyn quelled the sorrow that bit her nose and forced her chin high.

"I've come to give voice to Loptr's cry," she pressed on.

Pensive, Surtr studied her stance, knowing she came with the utmost sincerity. He heaved a deep sigh and growled.

"Loptr's words have reached me, but I can not lend my aid without attracting the eye of Odinn."

Desperation she could not hide clouded her eyes.

"He begs for your aid," she tried again, "and requests your support in rending the stones of Odinn's throne!"

Surtr glanced upon her tiny frame, dwarfed by the magnitude of his race. He paused, coming to rest his gaze onto her eyes that peered so hopefully at him. He sighed, hating what he had to do.

"I see the torment of his suffering in your eyes," Surtr replied. "You still grieve for your sons. I know your tears were ignored when Odinn bound your husband to Yggdrasill. Nevertheless, Loptr's affliction was cast upon you."

Despite the heat that sweltered, a cold permeated Sigyn that left her rigid against her frayed nerves.

"I will not deny that the march against Asgard stirs a desire in me," Surtr continued. "Greater still, if Loptr were to fight at my side, but..." Each word clawed its way to Sigyn's insides. "The task you ask rings out as treason to those in Asgard."

Sigyn forced down a silent sob with a dry gulp.

"As long as Loptr lies at the roots of Yggdrasill, bound by Odinn's damnation," Surtr proclaimed, softening his voice, "I can not risk angering the gods of Asgard, lest war be waged on Muspellsheim."

Surtr watched his words relinquish the last of Sigyn's hope as she forced her eyes from his.

"I can not stand alone against the powers of Asgard," Surtr said. "I will not stretch my hand to lend my aid to Loptr."

His final answer took Sigyn's hope from her and she nodded with a burden countless times heavier than when she had entered his hall moments ago. She had barely moved when Surtr added, "I am sorry, Sigyn."

Without a word and bearing no grudge, Sigyn forced her stiff legs to carry her back through the doors.

At the base of the steps, Sigyn gripped Svadilfari's saddle in an attempt to pull herself up. But, drained of her strength, she buckled beneath the weight of her sorrow, and resting her head onto the horse, sobbed silently.

"Sigyn?"

The Jotunn snapped her tear-stained face to the eyes of Sinmara, who quietly descended the stairs. The reds of her gown swept the brimstone as the flames of her long, golden hair trailed behind her. Her skin glowed white from the heat of the blaze that composed her flesh.

As if afraid it would suddenly slip from her grasp, Sinmara clutched to her bosom a chest fastened with nine locks. Upon closer assessment, Sigyn saw that the locks had been opened. As she drew nearer, Sinmara lifted the lid to reveal a large bundle wrapped in amadou.

Sigyn wiped the tears from her eyes as if ashamed, and forced her composure.

"Shortly after the waters flowed from the Gap of Ginnunga and formed our worlds, before the Great War that unified the gods, Loptr lent his aid to Surtr against Niflheim. Surtr's stubbornness is fixed, but his interest brews."

Sigyn held her attention, piqued with curiosity and restored hope.

"I give you the blade Loptr left in my keep, won with the price I set."

Sigyn shifted her eyes to the strands of fine-spun gold that flowed from Sinmara's head, knowing, full well, they were once the locks of Sif that Loptr had taken from her.

"Surtr desires to fulfill your request, but can not so long as he stands alone. If it is Surtr's support you seek, go with Laevateinn and return with Loptr beside you."

Sinmara passed the bundle to Sigyn. Cold permeated the bundle, snapping and crackling against the heat, and forcing her body to shudder with a chill that flowed up her spine like Nordic lake water. Ingratiated, she held tightly to Laevateinn and called out as Sinmara walked up the stairs.

"Sinmara."

With elegance, the giantess turned. The locks rippled down her back like a sheet of golden water.

"Thank you."

Sinmara smiled gently and re-collected her skirts as she continued up the steps.

With haste, Sigyn snapped around and secured the bundle beneath the saddle. She climbed atop Svadilfari without delay and rode past the dragons, out through the gates of Muspellsheim to return to Loptr's side once more.

CHAPTER NINE

The next morning came with a nip in the air that blanketed the camp with a chill. The rare streaks of sunlight that permeated the clouds did little to heat the ground. Blankets were bundled, tents were folded, and the camp reloaded onto the decks of the ships.

With a heavy heart that weighed down Kallan's spirit, she trudged to her pile of hides on board and hugged her legs close to calm the sick that flipped her stomach. Knowing Gunir was only hours away, Kallan pressed her face into her knees as Bergen barked the order that sent the ships to sea.

The Ljosalfar buzzed with an eagerness that recharged their enthusiasm, fueling their good humor. At the sight of the approaching shores, a series of whoops and cheers erupted, sending a new energy through the ships. A second wave of nausea rippled through Kallan.

Never waning from his seat at the trestle, Rune kept a fervent eye on his vassal. Balling her hands into fists, Kallan attempted to ease her shaking. Her complexion grew paler with her increasing worry as the Ljosalfar bubbled with a contagious joy Kallan couldn't catch.

The trees thinned as the rolling mountains at the lake's edge opened to the grassy plains and the Klarelfr's delta. Amid the delta, a vast island rose up from the waters. The whole of its earth held the most ancient city of Alfheim: Gunir, house of Lodewuk, the High King. To the north of the city island, the Klarelfr split in two and flowed along the banks of Gunir. On the east side, beside the docks, a dry bridge blocked all ships from passage and provided a road from Gunir to a barren plain that led to the edge of Alfheim Wood and Swann Dalr. On the west bank, the Klarelfr emptied undisturbed into Lake Wanern.

Gray and granite stones of the crenelated wall encased Gunir's keep, which towered over the entire city. Sleek runs of steps flowed down the high mount where the keep rose up over a sea of homes encompassing the island. Thatch roofs stretched down to the river. There, the houses stopped with the slope of the land, which greeted hundreds of long ships docked where the island met the lake on the east side.

The men erupted into greetings that carried over the city. Kallan jerked her head from her knees, her insides knotted as she sank deeper into her overcoat. Her body trembled uncontrollably the moment the ship touched land and the men threw the rigging to shore.

The jovial bustle was instant. The blur of images passed her by as Kallan lost herself to the fear that permeated her core.

"Kallan."

With her face stricken, she snapped her head up. Rune stood over her with a gentle smile and an outstretched hand. Without hesitation, she took hold with a death grip that granted her the courage to face Gunir and its judgment.

Her legs like deadened weights, Kallan rose, forcing her head high with the pride of her people. Rune led her through the chaos and excitement, down the gangplank to the river that lapped the land.

The moment Rune's foot touched down on dry land, a sudden swarm engulfed them. Unfamiliar hands pulled at him, while strange, dark faces pushed her aside. The foreign slur of roughened accents peppered the speech of the Ljosalfar as women with their children rushed to the docks in search of their mate. Lovers locked together while others frantically searched for their own, and children impatiently tugged at their father's garments demanding a hug. Kallan moved closer to Rune, dissolving the last of the space between them as if he could somehow overshadow her existence. His grip tightened and he pulled her through the streets.

Servants greeted their lost king. An occasional hateful glance found Kallan as they lent their aid and welcomed Rune. Bergen's laughter emerged from the crowd and Kallan glanced to the berserker buried in a busty brunette. Kallan blushed and averted her attention back to Rune, who led her on through the boisterous noise that webbed their way around the sea of homes, shops, markets, docks, and stables.

People came and went in waves as Kallan and Rune made their way to the end of the city and the wide, stone steps where the crenelated wall on the motte. Before they could reach the first step, a bellowing roar filled the air.

"Rune!"

The roughened scratch of Geirolf's voice carried over the chaos, and Kallan jumped into Rune. With a laugh, the old man rushed from the doublewide doors at the top of the steps, down to Rune like a maddened bull.

"I'm going to personally send you to Odinn's halls for the Hel you caused me!" said Geirolf. "Poor Torunn has had nothing to do but nag my backside off! I have nothing left to sit on!"

With a laugh, Rune embraced the old codger, whose laughter carried over the city.

"Gave us a start, you fool!" Geirolf said with a slap to Rune's back. He shifted his gaze to Kallan quickly, but said nothing.

They reached the top of the steps where Geirolf left a pair of great oak doors open, allowing them entrance beyond the vast battlement that encased the keep. Before them, the courtyard spanned out in invitation, leaving behind the chaos of their arrival.

The barracks to their left hugged the wall and buzzed with the collection of warriors, settling in from port. The sudden chorus of clops from the horses' hooves forced Kallan's attention to the right where Gunnar led Astrid, Freyja, and the black mare to the east behind the keep where the royal stables were tucked away.

"Where is Torunn?" Rune asked, jumping right to the matter.

"She has a series of tongue lashings lined up for you," Geirolf warned. "Be wise and take my advice, Rune. Run."

With a smile, Rune clamped his free arm around the old man's shoulders before leading Kallan to the main keep ahead. A second series of steps invited them to a set of oaken doors, which had also been left open in the tumult.

"Rune!"

The shriek left Rune and Geirolf glued down mid-step as his grip on Kallan tightened.

"Torunn!" Bergen gleefully shouted, intercepting a thin old woman whose silver hair had been twisted into a tight-fitted bun atop her head. Bombarding her from the side, he took her up with a twirl in the air.

"Bergen!" she bellowed and punched his bare chest.

Laughing, Bergen planted a hearty kiss to her mouth, before gently lowering her to the ground and refusing to relinquish her waist as she fought him.

"Bergen, enough! Where's that brother of yours? I have to kill him!"

"Torunn!" Rune said, drawing her temper from Bergen.

"Rune!" Torunn shrieked with death in her eyes and she lunged, but Bergen's firmly planted hands kept her in place and allowed Rune to make his way slowly toward the tirade that fumed on the steps of the keep.

"As far back as my old memory can allow," Torunn shrieked, "never can I recall such a fright! Your father—" She switched to a language Kallan couldn't decipher as Rune climbed the steps with Kallan in tow, his grin still wide on his face.

"Next time I think you dead, you had better be!" Torunn finished in common tongue as Rune came to stop before the key keeper.

"It's good to see you," said Rune, still smiling.

With a huff, Torunn blew out the last of her rage, convincing Bergen to release her. She shifted a death glare to Bergen then settled her eyes on Kallan, suddenly very aware of Kallan's presence.

"That's a Dokkalfr," Torunn said, still glowering at Rune. Geirolf shifted a glance to Rune, eager for an explanation. "Of all the trash you and your brother have dragged home—"

Kallan's blood burned red.

"This, Lady Torunn…" Rune tightened his hold onto Kallan's hand and interjected before the key keeper could ignite Kallan's fury. "…is Kallan, daughter of Eyolf, Queen and Lady of Lorlenalin."

Geirolf gulped down a mouthful of bile as the old woman changed three shades of pale. Torunn's bottom lip trembled, and she bit down while finding the words that failed her.

"My vassal," Rune said.

Torunn shifted her wide-eyed attention to Rune.

"Are you mad?"

"She is here as my guest to negotiate peace," Rune said.

Torunn looked to Bergen, who nodded in confirmation.

"Rune—" Torunn lost the word in a gasp. The sharp hiss in her voice was gone.

"The lady has had a long, long journey." The hardness of Rune's face dared her to argue. "She is tired and hasn't had a proper bath or meal since…" His voice trailed off. "Show her to the northern bower. Have her cleaned and dressed."

Kallan tightened her grip on Rune's hand and he turned.

"You are safe here," he said gently. "They won't harm you."

Paralyzed with disbelief, neither Kallan nor Torunn moved.

"Now, Torunn," Rune growled, keeping his eyes on Kallan.

He released Kallan to Torunn, leaving a vast hollowness in his place as Kallan followed Torunn up the steps to the tower. Kallan's tattered hem exposed the blistered red of her legs where filth from the road had caked to her skin. Her hair hung in dismal, frayed locks that matched the pale color in her lips. Overall, she looked like a frayed cloth that had been beaten and broken and battered then drowned.

Just as Kallan and Torunn vanished into the tower, Rune nodded to Bergen and Geirolf. "Gentlemen," he said and flew up the stairs behind the ladies.

Exchanging glances, Geirolf and Bergen rushed up the stairs after Rune and followed him inside.

"Rune!" Bergen shouted, his voice filling the Great Hall.

Rune turned, catching the last of Kallan's skirts before she disappeared up the great stone steps that hugged the wall on the west side. There, the steps stretched up and around to the second floor and the private chambers.

"Rune!" Geirolf called behind Bergen.

The high ceiling bounced his voice overhead. The fire pits in the center of the room crackled and spat between the pair of long tables that were already being dressed for the evening feast. The empty throne remained unscathed on the platform ahead.

Immediately, Rune fled to the door to the right of the throne, hidden behind the screen passage wall and, two at a time, climbed the stone steps tucked away in the corner as they spiraled their way up to the second floor.

"Rune!" Geirolf called. "You owe an old man an explanation!"

Without a word, Rune opened one of the doors at the top of the stairs and stepped into his bedchamber. A lively fire and lit torches filled the room with a familiar comfort. His bed, a desk, a series of randomly placed chairs draped in furs beside the occasional side table made up his furnishings. Beside the fireplace, a closed door led to his sitting room.

Taking a seat on top of his wide chest pushed against the foot of his bed, Rune unlaced his boots.

"Rune, what is the meaning of this?" Geirolf bleated, barely containing his rage. "Bringing a Dokkalfr here? Making her your vassal? Giving your mother's bower to that—?"

"Guest…" Rune said, pulling off his boot. "And of highest honors. I know what I'm doing."

"Your people will not be quick to forgive," Geirolf said. "You endanger her life by bringing her here. At least house her in the tower where she belongs."

Rune dropped his second boot to the floor and marched to the water basin beside the window as he pulled off his shirt.

"Where's Borg?" Rune asked.

"He…" Geirolf thought for a moment, uncertain of the answer himself.

"Joren would know," Bergen said, leaning against the wall with his arms crossed.

"Send for him," Rune ordered, scrubbing the grime from his face.

"Rune…" Geirolf took a step closer. "There are plenty of lasses you can have. I understand your fancy with this one. Once she's washed up a bit, I'm sure she's a sight to look at. But take care of your business and have her moved to the tower already. I can have the guards—"

"Get Joren!" Rune barked, swallowing the rest of Geirolf's protest.

Geirolf heaved a sigh and obeyed. Flashing a pitied look toward Bergen, the old man trudged back down the steps to the Hall.

"Well?" Rune asked, drying his face.

"I said nothing," Bergen said, not moving from his place on the wall.

"But you have something to say," Rune said, pulling on a fresh pair of trousers.

Taking up the basin, he sat himself back down on the chest and proceeded to scrub the grime from his feet.

"Can I safely assume the execution is canceled?" Bergen smirked and pushed himself off the wall.

"Assume it," Rune said.

"Ottar won't be happy."

"I don't care what Ottar wants."

Bergen shrugged. "I'm not happy."

"If you have something to say, then get on with it," said Rune.

With a sigh, Bergen dropped himself into the chair across from Rune.

"You want her," Bergen said.

Rune frowned. "No, I don't."

"You haven't left her side in two days. You had Torunn house her in Mother's bower and you protected her by appointing her as your vassal when Ottar did what Ottar does."

"I wasn't protecting her," Rune said, looking up from the basin. "I was protecting Ottar."

"Oh…" Bergen bobbed his head. "So it was Ottar you were looking out for."

"Yes," Rune said, throwing the soap into the basin and taking up the towel on the floor. Bergen pulled his chair around, closing the space between him and his brother.

"You took a broken nose from her and kept her alive."

"You don't know what she can do," Rune said.

"Don't I?" Bergen asked making a gesture that drew Rune's attention to the scar on Bergen's right brow.

Bergen leaned closer and lowered his voice.

"Geirolf is right. You can have her in the dungeons as easily as the north bower. Hel, you could have had her last night when she was practically riding your dragon in her sleep!"

Rune snapped his head up with full attention.

"What?" Rune asked.

"But you don't want her…" Bergen leaned back in his chair, knowing he had him.

"I don't," Rune insisted, pulling on a fresh pair of boots.

"Oh, all right." Bergen rolled his eyes at the denial, exhausted with this back and forth. "You don't want her," Bergen mumbled. "Hel, I want her."

"Don't!" Rune said.

Bergen raised a brow as if Rune's protest was sufficient evidence for his case.

"I don't want her, Bergen," said Rune as he finished tying the laces and dropped his foot to the floor.

"Then you don't mind if I help myself," Bergen said. Rune rose to his feet and threw Bergen a bored look.

"She is attractive," Bergen mused. "Nice hips."

"Back off, Bergen."

"I'm just saying—"

"So am I!" Rune said.

"Alright, alright," Bergen surrendered, throwing his hand up. "She's all yours."

"No," Rune said. "Not mine. Just not yours."

"Right," Bergen said, not believing Rune for a moment. "You want to grab a mead? Geirolf just finished a fresh batch."

"Some other time," Rune said. "Right now, I have to stop my guest from escaping."

Rune sprinted into his sitting room and to the pair of double doors that led to the corridor outside his chambers.

"Oh," Bergen exclaimed, wide-eyed as understanding dawned on him and the smile fell from his face.

Pausing, Rune sighed with his hand resting on the door handle.

"What?" Rune turned back to Bergen.

"You don't *want* her," Bergen said. "You *like* her."

"I don't," Rune denied.

"Right. You don't," Bergen said. "When are you going to tell Geirolf and Torunn about that thing inside of you?"

With a wave that dismissed Bergen's question, Rune stepped into the hall and closed the door behind him.

"Too desperate to see how desperate he looks," Bergen mumbled and began thumbing through the wide variety of Rune's mead supply.

CHAPTER TEN

Torunn had done exactly as ordered, but no more. Mid-way down the upstairs hall, the key keeper swept Kallan into a large collection of rooms. There, the servants were already at work building a fire within the hearth.

In the bedchamber opposite the hearth, servants bustled about, preparing a bath with rose-scented water and oils. Kallan scanned her chambers, taking in the fur-laden bed, the fine, blue pitchers and basins tucked between candles that had been scattered strategically. Bed tables, chests, and wardrobes intricately carved from rich oak added a luxury she had not expected.

Across from the hall entrance, a pair of double doors fitted with stained glass opened to a solar filled with vegetation that encompassed a table and chairs. That room spanned the entire west wall of the bower, including nearly half the bedroom. Overall, the chambers had been lavishly decorated with the best Gunir could offer, leaving her curious as to why such a room had been given to her at all.

By the time the servants stripped Kallan of her clothes, the fire crackled and filled the sitting room with warm orange light. As one maiden whisked the bundle of soiled and tattered clothes away, others assisted Kallan with her bath. They stoked the fire and lit the candles. With her head down and mouth closed, Kallan sat while one of the servants scrubbed the filth from her back.

Kallan's pale skin breathed free from the mud and wear from her journey, but the bitter unwelcome and cold gestures from Torunn's servants left her nerves as raw as her feet.

The servants aggressively lathered Kallan in lotions. They shoved and pinched her into a russet gown ornamented with gold embroidery. They pulled the knots from her hair with a cold hate that left Kallan aching for solitude.

Where is Rune? she almost asked repeatedly. The thought always followed with a hollow hurt. The servants finished their chores with a systematic chill that abruptly ended with the metallic click of the chamber door. Alone, Kallan stood, plagued with the animosity Rune would never be able to order away. More than ever, she longed for Lorlenalin.

She dared a step, and winced against the pain inflicted by her journey. Kallan gazed at a vast tapestry hanging over the bed.

An image of Freyr and his golden boar, Gullinbursti, stared down at her with the same cold hate as the Ljosalfar servants.

Even their gods gaze down at me with disdain.

A silver sword with black pearls embedded into its onyx hilt hung from Freyr's side. As if condemning her presence there in Gunir, the god glowered, hating her, damning her with his golden eyes.

So much like Gudrun's, she thought.

Kallan held her attention slightly longer than expected before pulling her mind from the needlework. She shoved aside the silent protests made by her stiff joints and moved to the solar.

Windows fitted with blue and green glass brought from the Southern Deserts lined the solar wall, drawing Kallan's curiosity. The sun had started to set, throwing a barrage of pinks and oranges over the city. But the light that poured into the solar cast greens and blues across dianthus, hellebore, and blue anemone. Marble and soapstone pots overflowed with ferns, foliage, and vines of ivy.

Kallan glimpsed through a green pane of glass and peered to her right. The barracks hummed with distant laughter. The battlement on all sides made it difficult at best to see the river where only a handful of houses were visible over the wall that locked her in.

In less than a moment, she had decided to escape.

Her skirts rustled against the floor and hid her bare feet as she made her way to the sitting room where a table lavished with trays of fruits and meats awaited her. Her stomach clenched with pain, but she refused the food of her enemy.

Holding her breath, Kallan clasped the handle of the double doors and, much to her surpise, pushed the door open. Kallan poked her head into the corridor, glared at Rune staring from his chair across the hall, and slammed the door with a curse.

Wringing her hands, she whisked herself into the bedchamber, eager for the next plan of action. She stopped when she saw the open window and dared to look down the side of the castle and assess the straight drop to the stone courtyard below. She could scale it easily enough if she had a certain spell tucked with her pouch.

At once, she searched the rooms. Scrambling, she looked about as her mind raced through the chain of events that landed her there in the Ljosalfar's keep, dressed in their clothes, defenseless, starved, and alone.

Kallan stopped.

Slowly, she turned to the sitting room door, rejuvenated with a fresh wave of loathing toward the one thing that brought her there. She shook with a sudden awareness of every agonizing moment since he carried her away from her beloved city. Her memory sharpened with aggression on every minute detail from the night before, and Kallan waited.

The door creaked open.

The hall's light poured in through the slit followed by Rune's head, unaware of the demon that lurked in the shadows. Stepping into the room, he leaned against the door, closing it behind him, and shifted his eyes to the right as Kallan slammed her hand into his face. Grasping the side of his head, Rune stumbled, barely catching himself from falling. Already the raised flesh formed to Kallan's handprint.

With her body sleek in russets and gold, Kallan towered with a rage Rune hadn't seen since he told her there were no boats in Nidaros. At once, he was overly conscious that he had entered the Seidkona's lair unarmed.

"What was that for?" he asked.

Kallan tightened her hands into little white balls. She heaved and shook with a wrath she fought to hold back.

"For kissing me," said Kallan. "And for you."

Rune rubbed his face. "Me? When?"

"You! All of this! This is your fault!" Kallan's voice filled the bower. "I had helped you! I was letting you go! Even offered you a horse! I've done nothing to you and you—!"

"You ordered me beheaded!" Rune said, throwing back his shoulders and welcoming the deluge of anger Kallan finally unleashed.

"You deserved it!"

"It's my *head!*"

"You didn't seem to be using it!"

Both sharply exhaled as they showered each other with loathing.

"You kissed me!" Kallan said, finding more fight in her.

Rune smirked, his anger ebbing. "You deserved it."

Kallan gave a girlish growl and threw her hands to the air.

"Why does everything have to be so difficult with you?" she asked. "Time and again you drag me back, despite my incessant order to release me! You follow me, bug me, harass me, hound me…" Kallan huffed. "And then you kiss me! But you never admit your real intent! Instead, you lavish me with insult, degradation, and humiliation! Don't you smile at me! Always keeping five steps away from me! If you hate me so then be done with me!"

Her accusation wiped the humor from his face.

"I've tried talking to you," he began coolly. "I've proven my fealty countless times and still you doubt my intentions."

"You can't expect me to believe you went through all your efforts in Midgard to win me over as an ally," said Kallan.

"No. Not an ally," Rune said.

Kallan huffed.

"To prove to you that I am serious about putting a stop to this war," he said. "That is all I have ever wanted."

"Then why did you kiss me?" Kallan asked, searching his face for lies.

"Because, Kallan," Rune said, "it is the only time you allow yourself to feel anything at all."

"Don't pretend you kno—"

"You're so quick to abandon your emotions, you can't feel anything anymore! You use this war to hide within your city while you push everything around you away!"

"Stop it," she said.

"You wallow so deeply in your grievances that you're blinded by the traitors in your own precious pearl…you and your flawless pearl! You're so quick to blame me for the death of your father that you fail to see the murderers manipulating you from Lorlenalin's shadows!"

Kallan raised her hand to strike, but Rune caught her wrist mid-swing.

"No, Kallan. I kissed you because it was the time you are ever sensible."

With a jerk, he released her wrist and walked toward the door.

"Sensible!" Kallan shrieked, following on his heel. "When should I be sensible? When you dragged me from Lorlenalin, while I was starved, drugged, and beaten by the Dvergar? Or when I was drowned in the lake?"

"And I got you out every time!" Rune said, turning on her.

"It was the least you could do for abducting me!"

"To ensure you lived!"

"By dragging me from the children?" Kallan said. "From Eilif and Daggon? From the only place where I was safe?"

Kallan stomped into the solar, hugging herself against the absent chill. Tears swelled in her eyes as she stared through the green glass over the city to the river.

With a sigh, Rune followed Kallan into the solar.

"Bergen brought them from the deserts," Rune said, pointing to the colored glass.

Kallan made no movement that she heard him or cared.

"The children," he said. "You speak of them often. Who are they?"

"Orphans," Kallan answered.

"War orphans," Rune said. "Like you?"

A tear slipped down her cheek.

"And without you, they have no one," Rune said.

Kallan kept her eyes on the horizon.

"You have no proof Lorlenalin was safe," he said.

"You have no proof it wasn't," she said, pulling herself from the window to face him.

Rune shrugged. "There is Borg."

"Who is Borg?"

With furrowed brow, Rune cocked his head in hesitation.

"How many times have you sent a request for negotiations to Gunir?" Rune asked. His change in temperament coerced her cooperation.

"Countless," she said.

"Who did you send?" His tone was gentle.

"I told you once. Aaric, my high marshal, oversees negotions between Lorlenalin and Gunir."

Rune shook his head. "No one from Lorlenalin has ever presented anything stamped with your seal."

The shadow in his eyes left no doubt to his claim. Bewildered, Kallan paused in search of an explanation that didn't come.

"Did you ever actually see Aaric leave with your orders?" he asked.

"Every time," she said, locking her gaze onto his.

Rune exhaled long and slow.

"Who is Borg?" Kallan asked, unable to ignore the knot in her throat.

"A Dokkalfr," he said. "We assumed a member of your court."

Kallan felt her face drain of color.

"For nearly a century, he has informed us of every move you make," Rune said. "Moves only those within your court would know. He reports to my scout, Joren. Borg has spoken to no other."

Kallan paused to search her memory again through centuries of faces, of names, and records. Slowly, she shook her head. "There is no Borg in my court."

When Rune sighed, Kallan pressed, "And you propose he's working with Aaric?"

"It is a possibility we must consider," he said. "All we know is that you have given Aaric countless orders bearing peace, and we have only ever met Borg who provides us with information needed to act defensively."

Kallan gave a short pshaw, but Rune wasn't ready to back down.

"Joren has been sent with signed requests for negotiations as many times as you've sent those messages to us through Aaric," he said. "And not one message has ever been received."

Kallan snapped around, mouth open to protest.

"Ever," Rune cut off her interruption. "By either of us. Now, either Joren failed to deliver those messages, or someone intercepted those messages to you. Either way, someone in Lorlenalin has betrayed you."

"Perhaps it is Joren who—"

"There is a chance Aaric hired Borg," Rune continued as if Kallan hadn't spoken. "How else would someone, not belonging to your court, be privy to that information?"

"Aaric vowed to serve me and my father ages before we came to Alfheim, as did Daggon and all others below his station."

"So you've said," Rune said.

Kallan turned her back, taking a step from Rune as she rubbed her forehead.

"Why can't you believe what is so plain?" he asked.

"Why are you insisting Aaric—or any Dokkalfar, for that matter—is a threat?" she asked, turning about on her heel. "Why do you insist it was a Dokkalfr that intercepted those messages? Why not a Ljosalfr?"

"Because Borg agreed to free me if…"

Too late, Rune pursed his lips and wished back the words as the blood drained from Kallan's face. Her mouth fell open, too stunned to speak.

"You hadn't answered my summons," Rune explained, but Kallan's head was reeling. "You retaliated offensively, costing us lives. And answers you wouldn't supply eluded me."

"Agreed?" Kallan repeated, hearing nothing else as the tension in the room suffocated her.

"Get out," she said.

"Borg is why I can't take you back to Lorlenalin," Rune said.

"Get out!" Kallan screamed.

Visible hurt washed over Rune. He stiffly nodded and, with forced effort, his legs obeyed. Without a word, he left Kallan's bower, closing the door behind him.

CHAPTER ELEVEN

Rune threw back his head, gulping down a fresh mouthful of mead. He stared into the fire until the light burned his eyes. Swallowing another mouthful, Rune ignored the boom of his chamber door as Joren slammed it into the wall, followed closely by Geirolf and Bergen.

"Rune! You're back!" Joren said, still wearing a layer of dust from the road over his riding armor.

"What is this Shadow Bergen talks about?" Geirolf roared behind Joren.

"And do we have news!" Joren said, speaking as he crossed the room.

"The Seidkona has possessed you with some sort of craft?" Geirolf said.

"Borg was here a week ago yesterday," Joren continued. "He checks in once every fortnight."

"What has she done to you?" the old man rambled, paying no mind to Bergen who sauntered along behind Joren, gently stuffing dry leaf into his pipe.

"Lorlenalin has proclaimed Kallan dead," Joren said. "The search parties have been pulled back and they are holding you personally responsible for her death!"

Rune stared blankly into the fire, uninterested with the update and Geirolf's inquiry.

"But get this," Joren continued before Geirolf could interrupt again. "The order enraged those loyal to the queen and the Queen's Captain and the old Seidkona have deserted!"

"He says you absorbed her Seidr?" Geirolf squawked.

"Don't you see?" Joren said. "Borg says they are coming here!"

Rune took a swig while he cocked his head up at an awkward angle, studying Joren's and Geirolf's faces with indifference.

"Oh," Geirolf groaned.

Rune's glazed stare drained Geirolf's enthusiasm while Bergen made himself comfortable on his brother's bed and lit his pipe.

"The girl," Geirolf said. "Bergen said you liked her."

"I don't like her," Rune slurred, studying the flames in front of him. "She's a vixen. A Seidkona who casts spells to manipulate and fog the mind…taking a man's hard-earned judgment and cool logic with it." Rune raised the mead to his mouth. "She's a witch," he added and threw back his head for another swig of the brew.

Geirolf barked a laugh.

"Boy! All women do that!" Geirolf said, ignoring Bergen who lay with ankles crossed and arms tucked behind his head, staring at the ceiling over the bed while he smoked his pipe without a care in the world.

"Well, this one is particularly good at it," Rune said and took another mouthful, holding the mead in his cheeks a while longer than necessary before swallowing. He released a gasp as the sweet drink pooled down his throat.

With a shake of his head, he looked back to Joren.

"When is Borg due back?" Rune asked.

"In one week," Joren answered, bewildered with Rune's lack of excitement.

"One week." Rune mulled the time over, answering before he added another gulp, "I think I can hold out 'til then."

"Never mind that," Geirolf said. "What has the Seidkona done to you?"

"The Seidkona has done nothing," Rune muttered.

"Well, what is it?" Geirolf asked.

Rune thought hard back to Borg in Lorlenalin's stables. How they knelt together over Kallan as she lay dying… How Borg had healed her, begging him to take her from Lorlenalin as if he feared for her life. How Borg clasped Rune's wrist…and then a thing—like a wolf-bear—awakened, roaring and bringing to life an energy that had kept Rune restless ever since. One thing was certain, whatever it was, it had a fondness for Seidr. Especially Kallan's.

"I don't know," Rune answered.

"Rune," Joren said. "We finally have the leverage we need to demand the terms to end this. If we tell the Dokkalfar that we have Kallan alive and well, they'll adhere to every demand we make! It's over!"

"What's over?" Geirolf asked as if suddenly hearing Joren.

"The war," Joren repeated.

"Ya hear that, Rune?" Bergen called from the bed. "You can have her every damn night if you wish!"

"She told me to get out," Rune mumbled.

Bergen sat up. "She did…" A grin interrupted his exclamation.

The berserker shoved himself off the bed and clomped his way into the fire's light to better gaze upon Rune. After a moment, he threw back his head and belted a laugh that filled the room.

Rune tipped the bottle up and glowered at his brother over the mead.

"She did you well," Bergen said between bouts of laughter, tears wetting his eyes.

"Oh, like you've never seen the end of her sword." Rune nodded, indicating the deep scar that decorated his brother's brow.

Bergen grinned.

"Well, the rate you're going, she'll never see yours," Bergen retorted, nodding down to Rune's waist.

"There are others, Rune," Geirolf said, as Rune frowned at Bergen.

"Yeah," Bergen agreed, snatching the mead from Rune. "Have one of those and be done with it."

"I would…" Rune yanked the mead back from Bergen mid-gulp, pouring the sweet drink down the front of him. "But I can't drink from any local wells without finding out you've bathed in it."

"What of the wandering wench?" Joren piped in.

"The wandering what?" Bergen asked.

Rune stared darkly into the fire and raised his drink in salute. "The wandering wench."

"What is the wandering wench?" Bergen asked, looking about from Joren to Geirolf for answers. "Has a new tavern opened up?"

"The wandering wench is a who, Bergen," Geirolf said.

"He found some girl roaming around the woods the night before the Battle of Swann Dalr," Joren said, perking Bergen's interests.

"Wait, what girl?"

"One you hadn't stoked yet," Rune slurred, staring at the fire.

"We had to weasel it out of him," Joren said, grinning. "But once he talked, he wouldn't shut up."

"So find her!" Bergen said.

"Feisty temperament," Rune grumbled, dulled by the drink as the flames danced, "and striking blue eyes like the gems you brought back from the deserts."

"Yeah, that's the one," Joren said, grinning.

"She called me obtuse, cowardly, and spoiled." Rune threw his head back with a swig from the flagon.

"Why haven't I stoked her?" Bergen asked.

"The wandering wench, Bergen," Rune said, "is Kallan."

With widened eyes, Bergen dropped his smile, suddenly understanding Rune's behavior.

"Oh, you've gotta stoke her," Bergen said, restoring his grin.

"You're not going to think clearly until you do," Geirolf interjected his opinion on the matter at last.

Rune downed the last of the mead.

"Have her," Geirolf said. "Get your yearnings out of the way so we can send her back to Lorlenalin with our terms answered."

"I don't…" Rune dropped the empty bottle to his lap. "I don't want her!"

"So," Bergen mused. "On a sporadic whim, you ran off to Midgard—"

"—climbed Jotunheim—" Geirolf added.

"—picked a fight with the Dvergar—" Bergen said, staring at the ceiling.

"—lured Tryggvason's army to Alfheim—" Geirolf said.

"—and prolonged the ride home by bringing the largest pain in my ass with us…" Bergen finished with a smirk that made Rune itch to punch him.

"Because…" Bergen's voice trailed off as the men waited for the grandest helping of ox dung Rune could muster.

Instead, the fire crackled and filled the silence.

"Borg approached me in Lorlenalin," Rune slurred, balancing the empty flagon on his knee.

The words struck the three men, commanding their attention as they waited with piqued interest.

"He came to me with a deal almost immediately after my capture."

"What kind of deal?" Bergen asked.

"He promised my freedom if I would take Kallan with me…" Rune twisted his head up to Bergen. "And kill her." Rune returned his gaze to the fire before continuing, "Imagine my surprise when I recognized the queen as the wandering wench."

Joren said, "If Borg approached you, then surely Kallan wou—"

"Kallan assures me that she doesn't know Borg," Rune answered.

"He's a mercenary," Bergen announced, looking to each face and waiting for them to see the connection as clearly as he. "He's from Holmgardr."

Gierolf furrowed his brow. "You suspect someone hired Borg from the Khazar to get Kallan out of the way?"

Bergen smiled. "The Khazar were eliminated by the Gardariki a few years back, Geirolf," he said kindly. "I doubt the Khazar were involved."

Geirolf pushed out his old bottom lip.

"Hard to keep these things apart, what with men killing off every rising power from the Imperial Guard to the Praetorian Guard, Aurvandiljar, Black Guard, Varingjar Guard—"

"The Black Guard is the Varingjar Guard, Geirolf," Bergen corrected.

"Exactly!" Geirolf said.

"The Kryvics, the Aurvandiljar, the Gardariki…" Bergen said. "Any one of these turn out some of the best mercenaries."

"Borg wasn't hired from an outside source," Joren said.

All eyes turned to the scout.

"I've presented Borg with every proposal made by Rune." Joren shook his head. "Borg insisted that Kallan wouldn't have it. When I met him with the last proposal before the attack at Swann Dalr, Borg just kept saying that he had his orders. That Kallan refuses all negotiations as did her father before her."

Bergen turned to Rune, who watched the fire, lost to his bottle.

"And now you're saying Kallan doesn't even know about Borg?" Bergen asked.

"I told her," Rune nodded. "Kallan has deemed her people loyal, and Borg's existence as questionable. Then she told me to get out."

Rune threw back his head for another drink before remembering the bottle was empty.

"You'll need proof even she can't deny," Geirolf said.

"She is determined to return to Lorlenalin and be gifted with her throne as if she never left," Rune said.

He looked down at his hands and sunk deeper into his chair before pushing himself up to his feet.

"Her high marshal rules Lorlenalin, claiming her death," Joren said as Rune sauntered to a flagon of ale beside an untouched platter of food. "If Kallan returns—"

"Borg will ensure she doesn't," Rune said, selecting himself the largest flagon of spirits.

"She's been usurped, and doesn't even know it," Bergen said.

Rune gulped his drink down in a single mouthful.

"Yep," he concurred and stared at the food, his thoughts marinated with mead as he pondered. After a moment, Rune crinkled his face at Joren.

"The captain and the Seidkona have deserted, you say?"

Joren nodded. "That was the report."

"And they're coming here," Rune said.

"Borg said the captain is convinced you have her, and they are looking to take her back," Joren said.

"Borg said," Rune pondered, recalling the same man who placed this Shadow Beast inside of him.

Joren and Geirolf exchanged confused looks.

"Tell me, Joren," Rune said. "Did Borg ever show any signs of being a Seidr User?"

Joren gave a half-startled, half-confused look then shook his head. "Borg has no such—"

Raising his hand, Rune awakened the sleeping Beast of Shadow. Like black Seidr, an umbra streaked from Rune's palm. Rune turned his hand over, studying the Shadow and holiding the Beast at bay as if on a short leash.

"The Seidkona did nothing to me," Rune said, pulling the Shadow back inside him. "It was Borg who did this to me."

The fire crackled as the men all gazed at Rune, too stunned to speak.

"And you say he is not Seidr User?" Rune asked.

Joren slowly shook his head, still too shocked to answer.

"Well, I watched him heal Kallan in front of me as the life was leaving her. He then put this thing inside of me." Rune snorted at his own words, trying desperately to see where it all fit. "An amazing feat for someone who isn't a Seidr User," he added.

"What are you going to do?" Bergen asked.

Rune shrugged. "Question Borg," he said. "He is the link that holds all the answers to this."

"And Kallan?" Bergen asked.

"Kallan." Rune sighed, shaking his head.

"Go have her," Geirolf advised. "Clear your mind and get some sleep."

"By morning, you'll wonder why you ever wanted her at all," Bergen said. "She's more than eager to let you based on what I saw the other night."

"What did you see?" Joren asked.

"She did lean in to it," Rune mused. "She seemed to want it."

Rune turned the empty flagon over, pretending to look over the detail carved into the metalwork as he mused over the previous night when he had kissed her.

"She may even enjoy herself for once," Bergen added.

Resolved, Rune slammed the flagon back to the table.

"Right," he said with a resounding slur. He marched slovenly out the door, leaving Joren, Geirolf, and Bergen in his chambers with a matching set of grins.

* * *

"Kallan!"

The door to Kallan's chambers slammed open and Rune's feet fell one in front of the other. With a decisive click, he closed the door behind him.

He spun to his right, prepared, this time, for Kallan's slap. Losing his balance, he fell back against the wall.

A bit of his heart sank once he realized she wasn't there and he proceeded to look around the vacant room. With a stupor, he stumbled, making his way to the bedroom where he froze at the threshold, holding him in place as the Beast awoke to the surge of Seidr on the other side of the door.

Finally taken by sleep, Kallan laid sprawled out on the bed still bound by the gown and laced in her boots. The firelight flickered, casting a warm glow over her pale complexion. Her chest rose and fell to the steady rhythm of her breath.

Forgetting all reason for being there—his mind suddenly clear of drink—Rune forced the Beast into submission then quietly made his way to the bed. Taking up her foot, he proceeded to unlace her boots. Slowly, he pulled them off and quietly set them on the floor before gently pulling her up from the bed.

Still drugged with sleep, Kallan gave a half groan that pulled at Rune's chest as he leaned her onto his shoulder to loosen the lacing on her corset. Her breast grazed his chest and his fingers fumbled repeatedly as he slid her gown down an inch at a time, first from her shoulders then down past her waist while he battled with himself to focus through the excess blood flow.

With one hand, he held her as he turned down the furs with the other, and gently laid her back on the bed, freeing his hands to pull the gown the rest of the way off of her. Left in nothing but her chemise, Kallan curled her legs in and released a sigh, allowing Rune to pull the furs over her. Quietly, Rune draped the gown over the back of a chair and caught a scent of rose oil.

Shoving his hand through his hair, Rune circled the room, dowsing the candle light until the whole of the room was submerged in darkness save for the small fire that lingered in the hearth.

He rested his hand in the doorknob, hearing the bitter hate in her voice over and over until pain replaced her words.

Get out.

And before he could think twice, he returned to her bed and brushed her cheek with his lips. Moments later, Rune crossed the sitting room. With the effects of the mead wearing off too soon, he closed the door behind him.

CHAPTER TWELVE

Borg fell to the floor of the stone room, which was painted in streaks of flickering orange light cast by the torch secured to the wall. Wincing, he curled into the pain gouging his ribs as warm blood flowed from the gashes on his brow. The hurried step assured him that his wardens were not yet through.

Forcing a steady breath, he opened a swollen eye. His commander stopped at his feet.

"What did you tell him?" Aaric said.

Borg studied the black markings on the high marshal's neck. The symbols and runes scrawled up to his ear and hair line, making him look far more menacing there in the dungeons.

"Have you no idea how close you are to death, *Nidingr*?" Aaric said.

"Go to Hel," Borg spat and Aaric's foot slammed into Borg's face. There was a crack and another wave of pain followed as blood pooled onto the stone.

"Sweet Aaric," a woman's voice purred. The sensual rustle of silks and soft fabrics came with a gentle step that matched the voice.

The air thickened and soothing warmth filled the room, easing Borg's nerves. With aid from the familiar spell, he breathed through his shattered nose. A number of foreign odors—all as appealing as a familiar spice, a warm fire, a simmering stew—clouded his mind with euphoric care and Borg raised his eyes in time to see a woman glide down the steps into his cell and across the room.

He spat out blood and gazed upon the slender face framed by the long, black hair. With eyes encircled with golden light glistening like rumored gems, she looked upon him with a compassion he knew to be false. He had known her too long to think she could be sincere.

"Is that anyway to treat a guest?" she said to Aaric.

"Get out of here, sea witch! This affair doesn't concern you," Aaric said.

"Oh, but it does," Fand said. "If you want a man to talk, then you have to make it worth his while."

Smiling, she knelt down beside Borg's mutilated form and slid a slender finger down his broken face. Borg studied the distrust in Aaric's eye, concluding that the acting monarch didn't like the goddess any more than he.

Borg flinched at her gentle touch and Fand met his fear with a girlish chuckle dripping with venom.

"Shh," she hushed and caressed the cuts on his brow with just the tip of her finger.

Gold threads of light flowed from her hand and, like a tailor's needle and thread, mended the wound, closing it the instant she touched him.

Fand finished one cut, and then another, working languidly as she moved her hand to each wound.

"Sing and skip over fairy mound," Fand sang in play while repairing Borg's wounds and restoring his energy.

"Fand!" Aaric growled and she ended her song. She continued her work as she gazed over her shoulder at Aaric.

"Don't!" he said.

Ending her song, Fand finished her work until only the stains of blood remained as evidence to the wounds.

"There now," Fand said. "Now… What were you about to tell us?"

"Tell you," Borg said, gasping with relief.

"How long have you been working with Dan's Mork?" Aaric said. "What information have you traded with Forkbeard?"

Borg looked to Aaric, who could cut into him as many times as he wished, then to the Fae witch able to conduct her spells.

"You seek to end this war," Borg said. "You wish to save the queen."

His words accused, judged, and damned.

Fand laughed, but Borg's gaze was fixed on Aaric, who stared at Fand with such loathing it confirmed Borg's suspicions: the marshal was not on her side.

"I desire nothing more that the death of Queen Kallan," Fand said. "You know this. Our deal was set on this." Fand permitted a soft grin.

Borg shifted his attention from Fand to Aaric. Whatever deal was made, he doubted very much that Aaric supported it.

"What do you want with me?" Borg asked, deciding to follow the will of the witch.

"Leave Lorlenlin," Aaric said. "Stay out of Dan's Reach. Stay away from Forkbeard."

"Continue the machinations you've started," Fand said.

Borg blinked back surprise.

"Back off, Witch!" Aaric growled. "I am still marshal here! Lorlenalin is still in my keep!"

"Tell no one," Fand added, ignoring Aaric's rant.

"You have no place here, Fand!"

Borg looked from Aaric to Fand.

"If this is what you want, then why not leave me to my intentions?"

"Because, pauper," Fand said, "you need to know that I am here—watching— and that, should you fail, it is your death that will redeem your failure."

"Enough of this," Aaric said. "Answer, *Nidingr*. What information have you given to the king of Dan's Reach?"

A low chuckle rose from Borg's chest.

Aaric slammed his fist into Borg's face. Another crack and blood flowed from Borg's nose. Without a word or reprieve, Aaric turned on his heel and stomped his way up the stone steps.

"Marshal!" Borg called and Aaric stopped. Borg paced his pain with his broken breath. "I'll give you my answers, if you answer this."

"You think you're in a position to negotiate?" Aaric asked.

"Where is the queen?" Borg said, ignoring Aaric's question.

As if amused, Fand looked to Borg and then Aaric, seemingly delighted at the tension in the room.

When Aaric didn't answer, Borg coughed, then threw back his head in a fit of hysterics. Loud, maddened laughter echoed through the dungeons. Borg dropped his head to the floor and allowed his body to shake with enjoyment as his wild laughter carried his mind from his cell.

After several moments, Borg settled down and forced the words out.

"Taken," Borg gasped. "By Gunir's king." Another bout of laughter. Just as quickly, Borg peered up from the floor as serious as Aaric staring down at him. "I told the Ljosalfr that I would free him if he promised to take our queen and kill her."

Aaric launched himself across the room and Borg threw himself back in another fit of laughter. Aaric slammed his fist into Borg's face, throwing him down against the stone, and the laughing ceased. Blood splattered the floor as his head ricocheted off Aaric's fist again and again until Borg gurgled blood, too near death to plead for his life.

"Aaric," Fand said softly. Pain shattered the pounding in his head as Aaric released what little was left of Borg, who lay too beaten to hear the cell door close behind his captors.

⁂

"Aaric!" Fand called.

"Leave me!"

"Aaric!" She followed on his heel.

"You have no place here!"

"But I do."

Aaric spun, throwing Fand into the wall where he pinned her against the stone with a hand on her neck. The other, he raised, cradling a ball of white Seidr flame.

"You have your way, Fae witch," Aaric growled. "My queen is dead. Now get out."

"Hardly," Fand said, smiling. Aaric tightened his grip on Fand's neck, forcing her smile to fall.

"Kill me, Aaric," Fand forced through her breaking throat. "And Danann will find you. Kallan may be dead, but Danann still hunts you. You need me to hide you."

Aaric tightened his hold.

"What will you have to say for yourself? Hm? When the goddess finds her Drui?"

The white flame doubled in size and Aaric positioned his arm to fire.

"Wherever you are, Gudrun isn't far behind."

The fire vanished and Aaric released Fand, who fell to the floor coughing.

"Get out," he said, unconcerned with the traitor, the witch, or the Fae, and left the dungeon.

❧   ❧

Fand remained on the floor, rubbing her throat where Aaric had nearly snapped her neck. As the last of his footsteps died away, Fand smiled and lowered her hand. Free of pain, she rose to her feet and hummed herself a ditty as she walked back to Borg's cell.

"Sing and skin o'er Fairy mound.
Over the hills and through the dalr."

She turned the handle and pushed open the door. Stull humming, she all but pranced down the steps and approached the still breathing bloody mass on the floor.

Tsking, she peered down at Borg.

"You're a fool," she said. The pile of blood and bones gasped. "I should let you die here, *uskit.*"

The breathing had reduced to a wheezing that confirmed his neck was fractured and he possibly had a punctured lung.

"Once more," Fand said, placing a hand to Borg. "Ride to Gunir and finish the job."

Bones popped back into place. Skin reknitted itself and mended as the golden threads of Seidr flowded through the corpse and repaired the damage done by Aaric's hate.

"Y-you're letting me go?" The words scraped free of Borg's throat before Fand had finished mending his wounds.

"The queen is dead. Only part of your deal is complete. You still have a message to deliver to Gunir."

"But the marshal—"

"Is useless," Fand finished for him. "His hold on this city is slipping. The people don't even remember the name of their queen." She watched the Dokkalfr relax as she finished. Disgusted, she watched the sluggish soldier rise to his feet then and regain his composure. With a nod, he trudged toward the door with barely a limp. His head hung low with incompetence.

"And, Dokkalfr," Fand called.

Borg raised his eyes to the goddess.

"This time, don't get caught."

Borg pursed his lips as if tasting the bitter bite of failure. With a subtle nod, he trudged out the door and left Fand alone in the cell.

CHAPTER THIRTEEN

Kallan woke to an ongoing ache that permeated her body from the base of her neck to the ends of her feet. She arched her back, winced at the stiffness in her spine, and looked to the window. The moon was high. The night was far from over.

Throwing back the furs, Kallan shuffled about, reclaiming her boots and gown, before donning Ori's leather overcoat.

Blod Tonn.

Kallan exhaled an uneasy breath. She would have to leave now while she still could— without her dagger—or never.

"I'll come back for it later," she muttered, deciding it was sufficient reason to come back and kill Rune.

Within a handful of breaths, she opened the chamber door.

Windows spanned the empty corridor and cast strips of blue moonlight onto the wooden floorboards. Kallan looked to her right where a pair of double oak doors ended the hall. Closing the door behind her, she crept into the hallway and tiptoed toward the staircase and a small wooden door she could only assume led to the west tower.

With every step down, Kallan held her breath and took care to keep her steps light as the high ceiling threatened to amplify the most minute sound. Tiptoeing through the hall past the cold fire pits beneath the wrought iron chandeliers, she made her way to the massive oaken doors and slowly pushed one open just enough for her to slip through to the courtyard. The doors creaked and whined, forcing her heart to stop twice as it announced her departure from Rune's keep.

The cool air enclosed Kallan as she stepped into the empty courtyard. She didn't bother closing the door behind her, lest she again risk the merciless whine of the door. Kallan looked left to the stables, then right to the barracks. She descended the stone steps with a mastered stealth and made her way to the stables where Gunnar had led the horses.

Once she rounded the corner, Kallan exhaled and relaxed her shoulders. As she entered the stables, the sweet scent of hay engulfed her. With every movement, each pensive stare, the horses exuded a wisdom, a warmth: elegant, refined, majestic, but simple, nevertheless. Their presence evoked a wave of affectionate memories that made her long for Lorlenalin.

The moon's light poured through the open stables, painting a myriad of blue and shadow across the richly carved stall doors and roof supports. One by one, she passed the rows of cream colored fjord horses, pausing for a brief moment to admire the rare magnificence of the black courser mare. Two stalls later, in the far back, she found her beloved stallion housed beside the Lofot pony, Freyja.

With a smile, Kallan slid into Astrid's stall and slid her hand over his deep, russet coat. Gunnar had thoroughly brushed Astrid. A half-eaten bucket of oats hung within the stallion's reach and a pile of clean hay lay on the floor beside a trough filled with fresh water. Kallan smiled. As promised, the horse master had provided Astrid with the utmost care.

"Come along, dear friend," she whispered, reaching for the pristine leather bridle hanging on a peg just as an orange light poured into the stall.

With a gasp, Kallan turned to the cold black of Bergen's eyes—forever dilated, forever consuming the white of his eyes.

Dressed only in trousers and heavy black boots, the Dark One's wide frame blocked her path as his lantern swung on the end of a chain he held at eye level.

"Did you really think we'd leave Astrid unguarded?" His voice was free of hatred. "Rune's already been down to feed him," Bergen said with a kind nod indicating Astrid. "He brushed him and had him fitted with new crescents."

Kallan silently eyed the elding hilt of the great sword peering over his left shoulder. She followed Bergen's long, black hair down to his waist where she paused at a sword strapped to his side. He boasted a dagger sheathed at his belt.

A second dagger was sheathed in his boot.

Kallan cautiously assessed his idle hand as she waited for him to move or draw.

"Rune called him Astrid," Bergen said, his voice free of aggression.

Kallan said nothing as she stared.

"Why the girl's name?" he asked, paying no mind to her cold disposition.

She didn't answer.

"You don't like me, do you?" he asked after standing for a moment in silence.

"Should I?" she asked, wrinkling her face in disgust.

"No." Bergen shook his head. "You shouldn't."

"You tried to kill me," she said.

Bergen shrugged. "I was doing my king a favor."

"You attacked my people. You infiltrated my city."

"You took my brother." A cold permeated his gaze, making his eyes all that more menacing. "My only brother."

Kallan stiffened against the sudden chill in the air.

"Do you have a brother?" he asked.

Kallan didn't answer.

"A sister?" Bergen guessed.

"What do you want?" Kallan asked, cutting his idle chat short.

Bergen exhaled.

"Rune and I don't see eye to eye on your presence here in Gunir," he said, hanging the lantern off a crooked nail. "A prisoner shouldn't be housed in my mother's bower..." He absent-mindedly dropped his hand to the hilt of his sword. "And a guest wouldn't be looking to leave without a display of gratitude in the middle of the night." He hooked a thumb on his belt. "Which makes it hard to think you're here as a guest... Yet, here you are."

The lantern swayed, casting streaks of orange that ebbed and flowed like waves on their faces.

"You could have called the guards at any time," Kallan said. "Instead you stand there, talking." She measured him up as she spoke and grew irate at a brief flood of sudden carnal urges. "What stayed your hand?"

Bergen shrugged again. "Curiosity."

Kallan narrowed her eyes. "Curiosity?"

"And my brother's affection for you."

"Affection!"

Bergen peered at Kallan. "You don't know," Bergen said.

"Know what?" she asked. "His arrogance? His inability to accept refusal? Or his riddles and nuances that move me to want to break his neck?"

"Yeah." Bergen nodded. "That's Rune."

"Affections!" Kallan scoffed. "You speak of his masculine drive if anything."

Callousness blanketed Bergen's face.

"Do you really think he followed you into the bowels of Midgard for a romp he could have here in Gunir?"

Kallan forced indifference to mask a sudden wave of jealousy for any trollop he may have had in Gunir.

"You said you were curious," she said. "Why curious?"

"I wanted to know what woman finally got to him and what about your disposition has my brother so inclined to keep you alive."

Kallan scoffed.

"I mean you look good enough. I get that. But you have him vexed."

Kallan opened her mouth to screech, but the look from Bergen commanded her tongue be still.

"I've fought you too often, Seidkona. I know you're standing here as armed as I." He gave a tap to his brow as a reminder. "My hand was not the only one stayed tonight. Why was yours?"

Kallan's throat tightened as a single face, buried beneath a grizzled beard, surfaced. Too many nightmares filled her with dread. With all bitterness forgotten, Kallan straightened her back. She felt her throat go dry.

"You have something that I want," Kallan said. "And I need you alive to get it."

Taken aback, Bergen raised his brow. A smirk turned up his mouth. He looked down the rows of horses until he spotted an empty stall and beamed. He gave a subtle flex of the hand at his pants.

"Well, this isn't my usual place..." His voice was low as he lavishly admired her form. "But I've got an empty stall here and some time to spare."

Horror-stricken, Kallan turned white then a vivid pink before a frown accompanied a shade of crimson.

"Yeah, like that," Bergen said, approving of her flushed skin.

Kallan curled her hands, but Bergen couldn't hold back. He belted a laugh that shook the walls of the stables, and he stumbled, nearly falling over in the process. And Kallan stood, enduring his ridicule.

"Are you really the Dark One?" Kallan asked. "The Dreaded? The Feared?" She prattled through Bergen's titles as Beregn wiped the tears from his eyes.

"The berserker who snapped a fleet in two then climbed the mountains of Khwopring? The Dark One who travelled into the Ice Deserts of the Far North with nothing more than the boots on his feet and a sword?"

Bergen shook his head as if amused by the tales Kallan recalled.

"The same berserker who burned the library of Râ-Kedet? Whose wooing won the bed of the Desert Queen?"

Her words wiped the humor from Bergen's composure as a darkness settled in his eyes.

"And what does the Dark One have that the Seidkona—the great Queen of the White Opal—could ever want?" he mocked with a bitter sting in his voice.

Kallan battled back the anger that his jeering aroused.

"An answer." She forced her voice to be steady and calm as she pushed all hatred aside. Encompassing her goal, she allowed her desperation to show and embraced her humility.

Her humbled tone was not lost on Bergen, who forced his venom aside.

"An answer," Bergen said as if trying to see beyond her display. "To what?"

Kallan forced her breath steady.

"The night you seized Lorlenalin… There was a man—"

"There were many men, Dokkalfr," Bergen said. "Which one?"

She recalled Daggon's face consumed by flames from her nightmares, and the sharp amber eyes peering back as he lay dead in her arms.

"This one had red hair and a beard like wild fire," she said.

Bergen's eyes were colder than the Nordic Winters.

"Ah," he said with a smirk. "The bear of a man lying with Death in the corridor." He paused for a moment, waiting for her to break, knowing the question before she asked it. "Your question, then."

"Does he live?"

Her voice was steady and her eyes frozen with the courage she mustered to speak.

Bergen narrowed his eyes into menacing slits.

"Is this why you kicked and screamed to get home? For your love for that beast?"

Kallan forced her back rigid and waited for the answer, not daring to breathe.

"That you would drop so low as to plead to the dreaded Dark One for the answer? That you would endure a dose of humility for the smallest clue on whether or not your precious sentinel lives?" Bergen scoffed as Kallan blinked back burning tears.

She tightened her jaw, not daring to think of the answer he would give. Unyielding, she waited, prepared to stand all night for the answer.

"That's a Hel of a haul to carry through Midgard, Seidkona," Bergen said.

Unmoving, Kallan waited for the word that would relieve her fears.

Bergen studied her composure, waiting for her to break. He almost smiled kindly in admiration, but Kallan stood steadfast, hanging all her hopes on him.

"Yes, my lady," he finally spoke. A gentleness rolled with his words. "He was alive when I ordered my men from your city."

As if she hadn't taken a single breath since that night, Kallan gasped. She shook with relief, and a set of tears streamed her cheeks.

"Why?" she asked between breaths. "Why did you come, if not to slaughter my people?"

"I was there for my brother." Bergen took up the lantern. "Nothing else."

The great sword glistened black in the moonlight as Bergen turned to take his leave. He was nearly halfway down the corridor before she found her voice again.

"Bergen?"

His name on her lips forced him to stop and slowly, he looked back, too curious to ignore her plea.

"Thank you," she said.

The two words carried through the stables. As if donned in stone, Bergen stared back, indifferent to the niceties.

"We have pieces to pick up here, too," he said. "Stick around long enough and you'll see that."

His lamplight faded into the darkness as he left her alone with Astrid.

CHAPTER FOURTEEN

Kallan affectionately pat Astrid's neck one last time before slinking out the stables, back across the courtyard to the stone steps to the Great Hall. She ignored the grand stairs that led to the second floor and, instead, considered the Great Hall without the discomfort of peering strangers.

A vast fire pit filled the center of the room between two long tables that ran alongside the bedded coals emitting a muted heat. Above the tables, a pair of wrought iron wheels hung, each adorned with no less than eighteen candles. On a raised platform overlooking the hall, Gunir's throne sat intricately carved from a rich, dark wood and lined with fine foreign fabrics. She admired the high seat pillars and spared a moment to compare the intricate designs of wolf heads to the twisted bodies of dragons carved into the high seat pillars of Lorlenalin.

To the right, almost hidden behind the screens passage, a pair of doors beckoned her. The door on her right opened to an ascending staircase that climbed up behind the screens passage to the second floor. But it was the second door at the bottom of a small set of stairs descending into the floor that won her interest. She could only guess that door led to the servant's quarters and the kitchens.

Resisting the urge to don a spell and explore Gunir's keep more thoroughly, Kallan inhaled deeply in an attempt to refresh her nerve, and descended the steps.

Aside from their sheer size, nothing else about the kitchens seemed unusual.

Three large, clean fireplaces waited for the early morning rush that always began at dawn when servants would pour in. Tables pushed to the room's center housed sacks of flour, knives, and fruits. And a wide assortment of herbs hung from the crossbeams overhead. Despite finding the kitchen's larder, the buttery, and the pantry all locked, Kallan managed to locate a loaf of day-old bread on the tables. As she munched, she scrutinized the Ljosalfar's stonework, the many barrels shoved to the corners, and a door that opened to a lush vegetable garden.

A sudden, small mew averted her attention to the floor, where a dainty, black cat pranced happily toward her. Its long, silk fur rippled in the streaks of moonlight as it purred.

Smiling, Kallan crouched to the feline who gave another mew that demanded attention. With a quick scratch to its head, the cat arched its back into her hand with a healthy purr that encouraged a second scratch. Kallan had barely run her hand down the cat's back when it suddenly hissed at the door and vanished behind a corner of barrels in a flash of fur.

Curious, Kallan rose to her feet and stared at the steps. She balled her fists, waiting for the threat that warranted her Seidr, but nothing moved from beyond the door. The silence from the Hall carried through to the kitchens. A horse's sharp whinny like a scream broke that silence and Kallan lunged. Before her foot touched the first step, the sharp, dry stink of smoke burned Kallan's nose and she sprinted up the steps. The scent was dangerously stronger as she ran across the Great Hall to the oak door left ajar. Into the courtyard, Kallan fled and stopped, stunned. From the stables, black smoke rolled into the sky.

"Fire!" she screamed. Taking up a handful of skirts, she bolted. "Fire!" she screamed louder this time. "The stables!"

Smoke billowed from the roof and poured into the sky in rolling clouds of black as horses ran about, no longer confined by their bridles or stalls. The rumble of flames engulfed the building and mingled with the incessant whinny. Desperate for a flash of russet among the cream, Kallan studied the mayhem as some horses managed to break free, while others, still tethered, fought the reins that imprisoned them.

"Fire!" she screamed again and, without pause, lunged into the fire.

Heast encompassed her. Smoke burned her eyes as she pushed her way through the inflamed stable. She tried to look down the rows of empty stalls, but the thick, white smoke masked her view save for the stalls that flanked her.

"Astrid!" Kallan swallowed a mouthful of smoke, sending her into a fit of violent coughs and her body into a fit of convulsions that tightened her chest and burned her lungs. Gasping for air, she dropped to the floor of the stables where she could see a flicker of muted orange through the rolling white.

Before she could regain control of her body, an arm slid around her waist and pulled her up from the floor. She attempted to scream, to call for Astrid, but only managed to catch another mouthful of smoke that launched her into another fit of coughing.

Rune carried Kallan from the stables as she dug at the heat and smoke in her eyes then tried again to focus.

"Put—" A new wave of coughing shook her body. "Astrid—" she managed to say between convulsions.

Keeping his grip tightly secured, Rune lowered Kallan's feet to the ground in the courtyard.

"Astrid," she said then coughed again and tried again to lunge toward the stables.

She stumbled and Rune caught her as she clamped a hand to her chest, fighting the convulsions.

Warriors and servants, all dressed in their evening garments, corralled and roped the horses, most of which ran back to the burning barn. Others filled buckets from water barrels while peasants from the village helped to form a bucket brigade that did almost nothing to the fire. Beside the barracks with Bergen and Ottar, Gunnar gathered, counted, and calmed the horses. The black mare whinnied and reared. Freyja backed herself into the crowd of horses, desperate to escape the fire. Nowhere did Kallan see Astrid.

Desperate to break free from Rune and return to the fire, Kallan lunged, but Rune had his arms locked around her.

"Let me go!" she shrieked. "Astrid—"

"No, Kallan!"

"Astrid!" Kallan shook as she watched the stables burn. The wood whined as it began to weaken.

"Kallan, it's too late!" Rune said, but Kallan didn't hear.

"Water!" Kallan screamed. "They need more!"

"It's too late, Kallan," Rune said, but her attention was on the line of Ljosalfar who passed buckets of water through the gates of the battlement and down to the river where the brigade began.

They need more.

Breaking free from Rune's grip, Kallan ran toward the gate.

"Kallan!" he called, but Kallan had already passed through the gate, lost to her calculations.

The Seidr is there… All I have to do is find it. If I can just…

Kallan slowed as she approached the water's edge where the brigade began. Unmoving, she studied the stretch of sky, inhaled deeply, and closed her eyes.

Almost at once she felt it, the lines of Seidr passing without direction through the air. She stretched her senses toward the water. There the Seidr rippled and flowed with the river. Like threads it wove itself in with each movement. It was there, just within reach.

"Just like before," she muttered, remembering the lines of water she pulled from the river only weeks ago, as if she had pulled a single thread from a tapestry.

Closing her eyes, Kallan turned her palms out and upright. Releasing all angst, she cleared her mind as she reached from her core, further than she had ever tried before until she found the heart of her energy waiting in her center. With all her strength, she pulled from her reserve and reached out into the Seidr beyond the subtle, soft winds.

With her energy, Rune's Beast awakened and lunged at her Seidr, breaking her concentration.

"No!" Kallan called to Rune who had come to stand behind her. "I need you to focus!"

He nodded and Kallan felt the Beast of Shadow recoil, chained against its will as Rune focused all his strength on holding it back. Again, Kallan pulled on her Seidr and drew it out. As before, Rune's Beast jumped, but this time, she felt Rune restrain the thing that resided inside him.

Streams of Seidr flowed from Kallan's palms as she guided her energy over the earth, through the air and into the Klarelfr below. Into the water, Kallan poured her Seidr until her legs shook beneath the sudden drain. Reaching out, she pulled from the Seidr buried in the ground beneath her feet. She siphoned the earth's energy through her, into the bands of Seidr that flowed over Gunir, until she located the Seidr that moved with the river.

Kallan exhaled and assessed the water's current. Once she found the rhythm, she plunged her bands of Seidr into the water like needlework, forming a new path that conformed to the water's Seidr. There, she knitted the ends of her Seidr with that of the water's Seidr.

From the Klarelfr's current, streams of water rose up and out of the river, pulled by the threads of its Seidr. Over the brigade, the water flowed as Kallan drew her strength from the earth's Seidr, encasing her body in filaments of gold.

Sweat beaded upon her brow. Her arms shook as she locked them in place.

But the river flowed up and over the battlement, drawing the attention of the Ljosalfar. Droplets of water fell from above, soaking the onlookers underneath. At once, the buckets stopped. Seidr poured from Kallan, encasing her in a blanket of gold. Her legs shook beneath the river's weight, but she held the water suspended on her threads of Seidr until it reached the stables. Once the river neared the fire, she lowered the water, directing its flow down onto the base of the flames.

The wood hissed as plumes of white and gray smoke rolled from the building.

Exhausted, Kallan released the Seidr, and, with her arms shaking violently, she dropped her hands to her side.

Sweat poured down her brow, mingling with droplets of water as she turned to look at Rune. Upon the ground, Rune knelt, battling back the Beast. He clenched his jaw, panting through a breath he tried to steady as if in pain, muffling what Kallan was certain was a scream. Only then did she feel how much Rune fought back the Beast that roared against his will, desperate to lunge and feed on the Seidr inside Kallan.

Shaking, and holding his stomach, Rune raised his eyes to Kallan, but Kallan knew before Rune spoke the words.

"It wants to kill you," he whispered, gasping under the pain.

The boards and planks creaked beneath the river's weight until it gave way, snapping and bending until they broke, collapsing in on it. The sound brough Kallan back as Rune released his stomach and steadied his breath now that the Beast had settled itself.

"Go," Rune said, and Kallan bolted toward the soaked remnants of the stables.

In silence, the Ljosalfar watched as Kallan pushed and pulled each blackened board away, digging down into the charred remnants of Astrid's stall, unable to feel the slivers that gouged her fingers.

"Astrid!" she cried, climbing over the debris. "Astrid!"

Her search ended abruptly at the dead weight of a massive beam.

With all her strength, she pulled at the blackened beam that didn't move.

"Astrid!" she shrieked. Tears streaked her cheeks. "Astrid!"

At once, the beam whined and creaked then moved, forcing Kallan's attention to Bergen as he lifted the end of the beam. He threw it aside, and Kallan slipped and stumbled into him as he caught her.

Together, they fell to their knees. Deeper, they pulled at the wood, deeper they dug through the charred, soaked soot and ash that covered them from head to foot until Kallan grabbed the blackened remains of a singed bridle and gasped.

"He isn't here," Bergen said as Kallan nodded, unable to speak, lost somewhere between worry and relief.

Looking wildly about, they scanned the area for the russet stallion. Kallan rose to her feet beside Bergen.

"Gunnar!" Rune shouted from the gates. His breath had steadied, his strength rebounded. The sweat on his brow was the only sign that he had been battling back the Beast only moments ago.

"He isn't here." The old man shook his head.

With a rising mutter, the Ljosalfar glanced about as if desperate to pluck an explanation from the air. Panting, filthy, and weary, Kallan and Bergen stumbled over the stable's remnants, back over the debris to the stone of the courtyard painted black with soot where Rune and Gunnar stood.

"How many did we lose?" Bergen asked.

"They're all here," the horse master replied as he finished a third recount.

"All?" Rune asked, dumbfounded with their luck.

"Except the lady's stallion," Gunnar corrected.

Bergen and Rune exchanged a look not lost on Kallan.

"Rune." Geirolf pushed his way through the crowd to the king and the horse master. Raising the end of a perfectly severed rope from one of the horses' neck, Gunnar dropped his voice to a near whisper. "Someone cut their lines."

"Bergen..." Rune shifted his gaze to his brother, keeping his voice barely above a whisper. "Did you see anything?"

"You were in the stables just before the fire!" Ottar growled over the courtyard, silencing the already surfacing gossip.

With a glower to Kallan, Ottar emerged from the cluster of onlookers and joined Rune's group.

"Did you see anything?" Rune asked, whipping about to Kallan.

"No," she said.

"Of course she didn't see anything!" Ottar said encouraging the murmurs to grow louder as the crowd closed in. "She did it!"

One by one, Kallan searched the crowd of faces, each glaring back at her with a depth of hatred, each condemning her without question.

"I was with her," Bergen said above the rising uproar. "She couldn't have started the fire."

Rune's stomach clenched as he looked to Bergen.

"You were with her in the stables?" Rune asked. "Why were you with her?"

"She asked to see Astrid," Bergen lied.

"She's the only one here who would have cause to do this!" Ottar said, extending a large finger that served as Kallan's judge and jury.

"I put the fire out!" Kallan retaliated in her defense.

"To win favor!" Ottar argued.

Seidr burst to life in Kallan's hands, reawakening Rune's Beast as Ottar grasped the hilt of the sword bound at his waist.

"Enough!" Rune shouted, forcing Kallan to extinguish her Seidr.

The crowd fell silent.

"Gunnar, the horses. Bergen. Geirolf. Look for Astrid. Ottar! Clear the crowd. And Kallan..." Rune turned to Kallan. "Come with me."

CHAPTER FIFTEEN

Kallan rounded her bottom lip into a prominent pout as she followed Rune back to the Great Hall where servants bustled about, too alarmed to sleep. Adrenaline kept the stomp in her foot sharp as she marched up the steps behind Rune. Alert and confrontational, her thoughts raced between worry for Astrid and anger for Ottar that left her unable to collapse with exhaustion. They walked past the lone, closed door and down the hall lit with candles.

Kallan stared at her blackened hands, cracked and bleeding from the wood splinters. She rubbed a split thumb over her wet fingertips. Black soot blotched and smeared the white of her soaked chemise. The click of a door alerted her as Rune led her into her bower and closed the door quietly behind them.

Kallan, too exhausted to fight, stood calmly as Rune unfastened the pouch from her waist. After shuffling through packets of spells and small binds of herbs, he pulled out a large, golden apple and taking Kallan's hand, dropped the fruit into her palm.

"You weren't ready," he said with a gentle smirk. Taking her by the arm, he pulled her into a chair beside the window where a water pitcher and basin rested on a table. Obediently, Kallan sat, staring at the apple, breathing deep the smell of black currant mead on Rune's sweet breath.

"I still did it," she argued, barely pleased with herself.

Droplets of water dripped from the ends of her hair as she stared at the soot on her hands.

With the scrape of wood on stone, Rune dropped a chair to the floor in front of her and plopped himself down.

"But you shouldn't have," he said, pulling a rag from the basin and wringing out the excess water. "Now…" Rune began gently wiping the black soot from her brow. "What happened?"

"I didn't do it," she said, closing her eyes at the welcome cool rag against her filthy, hot face.

"I know." Rune dragged the cloth down her temple, gently over each closed eyelid. "What happened?"

"I saw nothing."

"Are you sure?" Rune rinsed the rag. Kallan listened to the musical droplets that ran down his fingers into the shallow bowl of water.

"I was in the kitchen," she said. "You can ask the cat."

Rune folded the cloth and placed the untouched apple beside the basin.

Taking up her hands one at a time, Rune washed the black and red from her skin, first the back then the palms.

"I found some day old bread," Kallan said. "I was hungry."

"Cook locks up the buttery and larder, thanks to Bergen. She'd locked up the serving girls too, if she could."

"I left the kitchens to go back to bed and I smelled smoke."

"She tried once," Rune said. "It didn't bode well with the serving girls…or Bergen, for that matter." Rune stared hard at Kallan's hands.

"At what point…were you and Bergen alone in the stables?"

Kallan watched Rune wipe down the tips of each one of her fingers. The scent of mead was strong.

"I couldn't sleep," she said truthfully.

"Hm," he grunted. "Most women don't when they meet with Bergen in the stables."

Kallan pulled her hand away with a jerk.

"That hurt," she said.

"I'm sorry," Rune muttered, returning the rag to her furrowed brow.

"I went down to the stables to visit Astrid," she said.

"Visit Astrid." Rune rinsed the filth from the rag.

"And Bergen was there. We talked."

"And he escorted you to the kitchens?"

"No," Kallan sighed, her eyes suddenly heavy with sleep. "He left me in the stables with Astrid. I found the kitchens on my own."

"With the cat."

"With the cat."

"Eat," Rune said, returning the apple to her hands. He refreshed the water as Kallan bit into the apple, welcoming the Seidr rush through her.

A few moments later, Rune returned from the solar with a fresh bowl and pulled up his chair so close that his knees touched Kallan's.

"I smelled smoke in the Great Hall," she finished. Rune rinsed the rag and ran the cloth gently over her arms, not daring to raise his eyes to hers.

"Bergen lied," Rune said.

"Yes." Kallan exhaled, pondering the whys and wherefores of Bergen: the Dark One. The Terrible. The Feared.

Rune ran the cloth back to her palms and rested his hands comfortably in hers.

"The flames were too hot and too high to have just been started by the time you got out there," he said.

"I didn't—"

"I know you didn't," Rune cut her off. "But a Seidkona did."

Gudrun.

"I didn't do it," Kallan whispered, refusing to make mention of Gudrun.

Rune looked at her.

"I know."

"Then why are you here?" she asked. Her clear, blue gaze held the moon's reflection. Rune brushed a strand of Kallan's hair from her eyes and gently tucked it behind a tapered ear. Her Dokkalfar skin was far paler in comparison to his Ljosalfar tanned tones.

"Why am I here?" he muttered, keeping his attention fixed on Kallan's eyes.

The advice of Geirolf and Bergen ran through his head. Before, he had been so bold, so certain, so drunk.

"I have to go," he said, dropping his hand from her face and standing too quickly as if suddenly realizing he was touching her. The legs of his chair scraped the stone and he was at the door before Kallan could understand what had happened.

"Rune?"

"I'll have Torunn fix you a bath," he said at the door, not bothering to look at her. "I'll send someone the moment Astrid is found."

"Rune—"

"Good night," he said and closed the door between them.

Torunn came and went in a wordless flash, wearing only one scowl that left no room for anything but formalities. She swiftly swept from the room, leaving Kallan rescrubbed and redressed without as much as a greeting, a nod, or a thank you. Unshed tears swelled in place, and only when Kallan was alone for the night did she breathe freely once more.

Exhausted, numb, and driven mad with not knowing where Astrid was, Kallan fell into bed. She had just barely closed her eyes, to welcome sleep and dreams of Dvergar-filled caves and corpses with faces she knew and loved, when a thick hand closed over her mouth, clamping her in place to the bed.

Kallan dug at the hand and clawed her way up an arm. Too inflicted with horror to scream, she kicked and thrashed about on the bed, weighed down by the hand that pinned her.

"Kallan."

Kallan stopped. She knew that voice.

As she peered up from beneath the hand, her eyes widened with disbelief. Though malformed by flame as seen in her dreams, a warm smile stretched over Daggon's scarred face. In that instant, the weeks of worry and remorse that burrowed through her chest lifted and she breathed with relief.

Kallan gasped and Daggon released her.

"Daggon." She threw her arms around his neck, buried her face into his red whiskers, and sobbed softly as she had so many times before as a child.

"Sh. Sh. Sh. It's alright," he eased, rubbing her back. "It's alright. Hush now," he whispered in a series of rushed words. After a moment, he pried her away. "We must be quick. We have no time."

"Time?" she asked.

"We're here to get you out," he said.

The words she longed to hear rent her insides.

What if Rune is right?

Kallan bit her bottom lip as Daggon pulled Kallan to her feet.

If I leave, I leave behind peace.

Daggon dragged Kallan to the door of her bedchamber.

I leave behind answers.

Daggon led Kallan across the sitting room.

I leave behind—

"Rune," Kallan whispered.

"What?"

"Astrid," Kallan corrected and shook her head.

"I can't go. Astrid—"

"Gudrun has him," Daggon said.

"Gudrun?" she asked.

The room was spinning and she scrambled to stop time altogether.

"She's here," Daggon said. "Come on."

Everything was going too fast. Kallan felt her feet give out from under her.

"Easy now," Daggon said, and he threw Kallan's arm over his shoulder.

"Wait!" she said, pulling back on Daggon. "My dagger—"

"It's here," Daggon waved it with his free hand.

Kallan's heart sank back down to her feet and he shuffled her way past the solar to the main door. Quietly, Daggon pulled the door open and peered into the hall.

"All clear," he said, but Kallan had slunk down to the floor, weak with hesitation that encouraged her to linger, to stall, to stay.

"Hurry."

But Kallan dawdled a moment too long and Daggon leaned down, scooped her frail frame up from the floor, and gasped.

"They've starved you," he said with a gruff whisper he barely muted.

"He didn't starve me," she whispered. "He just…couldn't… He…" Kallan bit her bottom lip to quell the tears. Words failed her as she lost the beginning to her story. "He didn't…" were all the words Kallan could muster.

Daggon crinkled his brow.

"Who's he?" he asked as questions piled up behind his eyes. "Never mind that now," he decided and slipped into the hall.

With ease, Daggon carried Kallan through the corridor and down the steps to the Great Hall, stopping only to confirm their way clear as they dashed down to the kitchens. Daggon pushed past the tables and larder, to the back corner where the garden door waited ajar.

The cool, night air struck Kallan's face and trailed up her bare legs as she assessed the ivy growing up the stone battlement that hugged the large garden. Rows of vegetables, herbs, and roots grew out and up against the wall, leaving barely enough space to harvest. At the farthest end of the garden, the wall left an opening where she could see down the motte to the city flooded with houses.

A sudden sick began to settle. Kallan bit her quivering lip. The rancorous stink of smoke still lingered in the air, leaving behind an acrimonious stench that wafted from the stables. A sob clamped her throat at the sudden sight of Astrid standing alone among the rows of beetroot. Daggon's grip tightened. Something was wrong. Kallan looked up at Daggon's face gouged with burns.

"Daggon?" she asked. "Where's Gudrun?"

"Here."

Bergen's cold, baritone sent a series of matching chills down their backs. The blood drained from Daggon's face, contrasting the red of his hair. Daggon shifted his gaze to Gudrun whose arms Bergen twisted together behind her back.

With a dagger pushed to her throat, the berserker forced Gudrun's head up. Behind him, Ottar and a warrior stood armed and ready while above, on the surrounding battlement, archers drew their loaded bows and aimed.

Daggon tightened his hold on Kallan, who held her attention on Bergen.

"Daggon. Put me down," she said.

"Yes, Daggon," Bergen said. "Put her down."

Daggon's eyes flicked about for an alternative escape route.

"Daggon, get out of here," Gudrun hissed under Bergen's arm.

Bergen tightened his grip on Gudrun. "She'll die, Daggon."

"Daggon." Kallan peered up at the captain. "You must release me."

"I can't do that, Your Majesty," Daggon said, staring at Bergen's blade on Gudrun's throat.

"Daggon! Get out of here!" Gudrun said.

"If you move, she dies." said Bergen.

"Release me!" Kallan said.

Bergen slid the flat of the blade along Gudrun's neck and she inhaled through her teeth.

"Put her down, Daggon," said Bergen.

"Daggon, please!" said Kallan.

"Put her down!"

"Get out!" Gudrun shrieked.

Bergen twisted the point into Gudrun's neck, Gudrun winced and Kallan screamed. "Bergen, I am your vassal! I order you to release her!"

Kallan's cry cut through the berserker as the nerve drained from Bergen's spine. Kallan's words seared through the tension, leaving the gardens silent. Bergen eased the grip on his knife and the archers held their draw, awaiting their orders. Ottar and the warrior didn't move. Remembering Rune's orders, every Ljosalfar stood, uncertain of what to do next.

Plagued with bewilderment, Gudrun and Daggon remained still.

Pushing herself free from Daggon's arms, Kallan slid to the ground, straightened her skirts, and fluffed her hair as if she were back in her own hall preparing to meet with a diplomat. Throwing back her shoulders, she straightened her neck and stared the Dark One down.

Although Bergen still held the dagger to Gudrun's throat, his stance was at ease.

"Your vassalage is only as good as your loyalty," Bergen said. "If you leave, you lose your sanctuary."

"Alright," Kallan said, not missing a beat. "I'll stay."

"Kallan!" Daggon shrieked.

Bergen flinched at the sudden obedience and passed Gudrun to Ottar.

"You've given them Lorlenalin!" Daggon's voice boomed over the quiet that had fallen over the gardens.

"I have given them nothing," Kallan said, gazing over her shoulder. "Trust me."

She almost grinned.

"Ottar. Take them," Bergen said.

Dumbfounded, Daggon gawked as Ottar dropped a hand on Daggon's shoulder. Daggon threw back his arm throwing Ottar off, and Kallan scowled. "Do as he says, Daggon."

Daggon's face flushed red.

"Your Majesty—"

"And, Ottar," Kallan said.

The Ljosalfr sneered at the queen, who matched Ottar's glare. "Do not harm my kin."

With a muted scoff, Ottar dropped his hand back to Daggon's shoulder.

"What of the queen?" Ottar asked before pushing Daggon through the kitchens. Bergen nodded to the archers to ease up. With eyes like pools of ink, Bergen closed the last of the space between himself and Kallan until his bare chest nearly brushed hers.

Refusing to back down, Kallan stood tall with stubborn conviction, matching his dark glare with eyes like stones, calculating and cold, and very aware of what she wanted. An admirable grin stretched Bergen's face.

"Take her," Bergen muttered, and flashed a glance that ordered his men to apprehend the queen.

Kallan's composure fell.

"What?"

"Be sure she has her own cell."

"Bergen."

A guard took hold of Kallan's arm.

"We had a bargain!" Kallan screamed as Bergen's men bound her hands behind her back, disabling any use of her Seidr. "Bergen!"

Bergen's men pulled her toward the kitchens behind Daggon.

"I am your king's vassal!" she screamed. "We had a bargain!"

Her screams carried down the hall, leaving behind a trail of echoes.

Bergen turned to Gudrun.

"You've fulfilled your side of the bargain," he said.

"I have," Gudrun said with a relieved smile as Bergen's men bound Gudrun's hands. "And I am holding you to yours."

CHAPTER SIXTEEN

B rother."

The sword at Bergen's side clinked quietly against his belt as he stepped into the dark bower of Rune's sitting room. He found Rune in the bedroom, staring out the window over Gunir. In the time it took Rune to bathe and change into a fresh set of clothes, the servants had restocked the mead and dowsed all the candles. The hearth fire bathed the bower in a muted light. A cool breeze from the windows chilled the room.

"Did they come?" Rune asked, watching the delta of the Klarelfr.

"They did."

"And you found them?"

"Right where the woman said they would be," Bergen said, dropping into the chair in front of the hearth.

"How many?"

Bergen took a moment to answer as he dug into his side pocket for a pipe and some dried leaf.

"Just the two. Her information matched Joren's." Bergen stuffed the leaf into the pipe bowl. "Though why, after all these years, that Seidkona would turn over her own kin just like that is beyond me." He reached into the fire's embers with a long stick and lit his pipe. Bergen released a steady stream of smoke before continuing. "The exiled captain and the Seidkona... What I can't figure out is why they would make their way here without an army."

"Does Kallan know?"

"She does," Bergen said. "She tried to escape with them."

"Of course she did."

Pushing away from the window, Rune grabbed a new bottle of mead. "It took her longer than I expected."

The room filled with the sweet scent of smoke as Rune pulled a chair with him to the fire and sat down beside his brother.

So," Rune said, "where did you find the captain and Seidr User?"

The black embers glowed with streaks of orange as Bergen watched the mouthful of smoke billow into the air.

"The old woman confessed that she released the horses, took Astrid, and started the fire as a diversion, while the captain grabbed Kallan."

Rune furrowed his brow. "Confessed? So easily?"

"Too easily," Bergen said. "She put up no fuss, no resistance when questioned. I almost think she was looking forward to the interrogation. As if she had been looking for us."

Bergen took a slow draw as he rolled the events around before speaking.

"Kallan's captain started in the tower," Bergen said, looking over the pipe and taking another draw. "It took him awhile to figure out you had Kallan in Mother's bower, which bought the Seidr User time to find us in the garden."

Rune nodded and gulped down more mead.

As Bergen released a plume of smoke, he stared at the ceiling. His shoulders were painfully taut against his nerves.

"Rune..." Bergen waited for Rune to swallow his mouthful. "I have to ask. I have to know."

Sweat beaded on Bergen's brow as the fire crackled, filling the silence.

"I find myself searching every shadow," Bergen whispered. "Terrified they followed... Terrified they've found me."

Bergen peered up from the flames. He had no doubt that Rune knew what he was asking. "Did they follow?" he asked, his composure overflowing with fear.

"Do they know?"

Rune handed his flask to his brother, and waited until Bergen threw back a series of gulps before answering.

"They diverted their path before they made it to Alfheim," Rune said then shook his head. "They never saw you."

Nodding in relief, Bergen passed the mead back to Rune.

"Why did you do it?" Bergen asked, forgetting his pipe for a moment. "Why did you go?"

Rune shrugged. "You know the Dvergar better than I," Rune said. "You know they would have killed her."

Bergen forced a smirk, insisting on the lightened joviality to ease his nerves.

"She pulled rank on me," Bergen said.

Rune crunched his brow. "What do you mean?"

"Kallan ordered me not to harm the Dokkalfar." Bergen leaned toward the mantle and emptied the pipe's blackened contents onto the stone as he finished. "She pulled rank on me. Reminded me that she is your vassal."

Rune grinned. "She pulled rank on you."

"How many times have you ordered me to kill that Seidkona yourself? Tonight, I had the chance, but your..." Bergen searched for the word. "...guest... stayed my hand...on your orders."

Rune chuckled.

"Imagine that," Bergen said. "Trying to bring in prisoners and one of them turns the orders on you."

Pocketing the pipe, Bergen shifted himself in the chair and stretched his long legs out in front of him. He fought back the smile as Rune watched with unease.

"She said you talked in the stables," Rune said.

"Daring to breech the subject, are you?" Bergen said, smiling. "We did."

Rune tapped his finger on the flask in his hand.

Bergen glanced at Rune's finger and smirked.

"What did you talk about?" Rune asked.

Bergen stretched and sighed, dropping his arms to the floor and drawing out his answer for as long as he could.

"She wanted to know if I had killed her captain."

"Yeah," Rune said, exhaling as if with relief. "She fretted about him all the way from Jotunheim." He shrugged. "Well, he and the children," Rune added then threw back his head and took a long drink.

"Do you think they're lovers?"

Rune gagged, choked, pulled the bottle away then coughed and wiped his mouth on the back of his hand.

Bergen grinned and waited for Rune to stop hacking.

"There are times when I look at her…" Bergen mused. "I just want to beat every drop of blood out of her that ever stained her father's hands. But she is growing on me," Bergen said. "She doesn't seem too keen on peace, though," he added, taking the mead from Rune.

"My guest is…confused," Rune said.

"Are you sure you want her?" Bergen asked, handing back the flask to Rune.

"I never said I did." Rune gulped down the last of the mead and dropped the empty bottle to the floor.

"You promoted the prisoner to vassal. You took my title and gave it to her." Bergen extended a finger to Kallan's room. "You demoted me for the wench. Can you at least afford me the decency to admit it was for sex?"

Rune smirked. "Always a woman with you, isn't it?"

"Always," Bergen said, sitting back in his chair.

Rune stretched with a groan then pushed himself to his feet.

"What did we ever do before we drank and smoked together?" Rune asked.

"I don't remember back that far. I drank and smoked too much."

Rune grinned and poured over the selection of currant meads and ales.

"What of this thing inside of you?" Bergen asked.

"What of it?"

"You could ask the Seidkona."

"I did. Kallan didn't know."

"I meant the other one," Bergen said.

"The hag?"

"She may know."

"She may." After a moment, Rune settled on an ale. "Kallan must have given you Hel when you escorted her back to her bower."

Bergen shook his head. "I didn't take her back to the bower."

Rune froze. "What?"

"The old Seidkona insisted I lock her in the keep," Bergen provided without regret.

"You— What?" Rune said, suddenly wide awake.

Bergen shrugged. "We had a deal…and Kallan did try to escape. I wasn't about to grant her free run of the castle."

"You *uskit*!" Rune shouted, and sprinted for his boots in the sitting room.

"What?" Bergen called, forcing himself out of his slouch and the chair.

"She'll fry my ass for this!"

"What are you going to tell her?" Bergen asked, suddenly worried.

"Hel if I know."

"Well, you can't tell her the Seidkona ordered it," Bergen clarified. "We have a deal. Play it up like you're there to rescue her. Oh! Tell her you're there to save her from eternal wrath of the Dark One." Bergen crossed his arms over his chest and leaned against the door. "Maybe she'll swoon. Women are fickle for things like that."

"Not likely," Rune said, pulling on the boots he didn't bother lacing.

"Why not?"

"Because," Rune said, "as of right now, Kallan Eyolfdottir, Queen of the Dokkalfar, can't stand the sight of me. If I recall correctly, she had no problems ordering my execution. And sitting in a cell in my keep won't exactly win her over!"

"So you finally admit you want to win her over."

Rune glared.

"What are you going to do?" Bergen asked, still steeped in amusement over Rune's predicament.

"Do my best to convince her that my brother's an *uskit*."

Bergen scoffed. "I mean besides that."

"What I have to do! March up to her accommodations and release her before she gets too upset and tries to kill me again. If I'm lucky, I can walk away with my manhood intact. Is she with her kin?"

"She has her own cell," Bergen said.

"Well, thank you for that. I have some humiliation to endure and it's best if it was done without the audience."

CHAPTER SEVENTEEN

Rune exhaled as he stared at the large oak door within the west tower's topmost room. Between each window, torches encircled the room's circumference, providing light to the circular corridor that wrapped around the handful of cells in the tower's center. On the other side of the oak door, Kallan's temper waged as hot as the fires of Muspellsheim.

Rune's grip tightened around the key ring he had obtained from Ottar. For a moment, he paused at the idea of calling Ottar back and letting him take Kallan back to her chambers. Kallan was less likely to cook Ottar alive despite her loathing for the large brute.

Rune inhaled, sighed, and reached for the door, ignoring the raging knot in his stomach that warned him to run away. The iron key slid into the hole and gently, he turned the key. He held his breath as the lock gave off a soft click that felt more like a war horn.

Cold sweat from his palm smeared the metal knob.

"Kallan?"

A blast of fire assaulted the door, leaving Rune too little time to shift back behind the wood. His pant leg hissed, singed with flame as the door sizzled beneath the heat. Fire rolled from around the edges. The stream of fire abruptly ended, leaving the wood black and charred and allowing Rune a moment to plead.

"My brother is *uskit*!" Rune said from behind the door. Another long stream of flame kept him cowering behind the wooden shield.

"Your brother?" Kallan shrieked from within the dark, hollowed room, affording Rune the nerve to peak around the corner. "It's not your bother whose head I want to roll, now is it?"

"What did I do?" Rune shouted back to Kallan, suddenly too irate to hide from her temper.

"So far? Not much," she said and shoved her way past Rune, leaving him alone in the cell.

His sigh became a growl as he closed the door and stopped short. In the corridor, Kallan waited, arms crossed, head cocked, mouth turned down with her brow. Refusing to placate her temper, Rune shoved past her and made his way around the corridor to a table and a chair where Ottar sat on duty. The spiraling steps carried him down to the landing where a side entrance granted passage to the second floor corridor and a second run of steps that led down to the Great Hall.

Without a glance to see if she followed, Rune sauntered on past Kallan's bower and made his way to his chambers at the end of the hall. There, he swung open the wide, double doors and stopped, stunned, as Kallan swept under his arm and meandered over his threshold. His palms suddenly moist, Rune blew a sharp, brief breath and closed the door behind him.

"Lady Kallan," he greeted casually as he moved across the poorly lit sitting room to the fruits, meats, and meads the servants had replenished.

"Where are they?" Kallan asked, raising her head slightly higher as if to establish her regality in his room.

Patiently, Rune poured himself a goblet of mead, taking much more time than reasonably necessary along with a sip before answering.

"They who?" he finally asked, as if suddenly aware he had a guest.

He watched her nostrils flare as Kallan inhaled furiously.

"Daggon and Gudrun!" she said. "Where are they?"

Rune treated himself to another sip as she brooded. It was good mead, made from a sweet batch of black currants and blackberries. He took another sip, uncertain if Cook had added a touch of cinnamon to the brew.

"Safe," he answered simply enough.

"Release them," she said, still standing in the center of the room.

"Release?" Rune's hand stopped mid-drink, affording her a look of bewilderment.

"They are citizens of Lorlenalin," Kallan said as if this weighed at all in his decision. "Release them."

Rune glanced at the ceiling, posing as one deep in thought, swished the mead about in his mouth and swallowed, then shifted his attention back to her as if deciding.

"No."

Taking another long sip, Rune braced for impact. Slowly, he topped off his drink.

"We are still in a declared state of war, and they are my prisoners." He took another sip from the goblet, relieved to find his backside still intact. "Now if you want to discuss terms of peace..." His voice trailed off, leaving the conversation open for rebuttal.

"Alright," Kallan said. "Release them and we'll talk."

Rune chuckled, took another sip of mead, and shook his head.

"Not a chance," he said, grinning. "How do I know you won't take off the minute I release them?"

"How do I know you have intent on settling for a peace?"

Rune tipped his glass to her.

"How do you have any choice?"

Kallan wrinkled her face.

"You have no intent to reconcile," she said.

"I don't?" he asked innocently, peering over the edge of his goblet. "Why else would I bring you here?"

"To uphold your end of a bargain! Why else indeed," Kallan said sauntering to the platter beside Rune as she glanced over the fruits in front of them.

"Perhaps you want the conflict," she said after deciding on not eating anything from the tray.

"If I desired conflict," Rune said, "I would return you to Lorlenalin. That would guarantee conflict. Or I would kiss you."

He stared into the black liquid in his goblet.

"You think so little of me that you believe I wouldn't reach out on my own for negotiations?" Kallan asked.

"I don't doubt that at all…" Rune lowered the drink. "I do doubt the messenger you have entrusted with said message."

Exhaling, Kallan turned about on her heel and came to stand, gazing out the window. The masts of the longships stretched to the skies in the delta that greeted the lake. There, only hours ago, the Beast inside him fought to suck the Seidr from Kallan's core. He felt it and knew. If given the chance, it would drink every last drop of Seidr inside her, leaving Kallan an empty husk, dead and dried into sand.

Rune exhaled and, gentler, tried again.

"Your Majesty," he said. "Kallan."

Kallan remained unresponsive, keeping her back to him.

"There is only one way to resolve this," he said, "and until he arrives, I have no intention of releasing your Seidkona, your captain, or you, for that matter."

Kallan whipped about, her head poised perfectly on her neck as she glared.

"Once Borg arrives, you can pose any question you may have to him," Rune said. "In the meantime, make yourself at home, get comfortable, and visit the sights, meet the locals. You're not going anywhere."

"I can get out!" she said.

Rune grinned and brought his cup to his mouth.

"I would expect no less of you to try. I'll alert Bergen and Ottar of the challenge and, make note that I can not be held responsible for the whereabouts of Bergen's hands."

"You mock me." In a torrent of gown and hair, Kallan turned for the door.

"Why do you have to be so stubborn?" Rune said, his patience gone.

"Stubborn?" Kallan whirled on him. "You've imprisoned me under false titles and yet you demand my trust. Why should I trust you, Your Majesty, when you've done nothing to have earned it? So long as I am a prisoner here, I will treat you only as you are: my warden."

Kallan turned toward the exit.

"Your arguments have fallen apart, Your Highness," Rune said, his drink still clutched in hand. "You have no need to return to your city to confirm she still stands, Daggon sits alive and well in the tower with the only family you have left…and Eilif and the children are well!"

Her face white and mouth agape, Kallan spun about and stared wide-eyed at

Rune.

"I checked," he said with the hint of a pleased smirk. "Whatever excuses you had for leaving are gone."

Kallan tightened her jaw and resisted the urge to ask more about the children.

"I know you want to go home," he said. "But please heed me. I ask only that you stay here and wait out the week until Borg returns."

"You ask nothing of me," Kallan said. "If I refuse, you will force me."

"Yes!" Rune shouted back, his patience waning again. "Yes, I am! I am forcing a tyrannical, overbearing brat against her will for one week while I sort this out because—despite what you think about me—I am tired of watching my comrades fall on the battlefield. I am tired of telling their wives that they are widows, and I am tired of constantly squabbling with a dry wench when I could be savoring a drink of mead with my pipe beside some well-endowed trollop who has the sense to not test me!"

"That was cruel," Kallan said.

"Yes," Rune said, twisting the knife deeper. "But why was it cruel, Kallan? If you have no resolve but to leave, why do you fret over what bedfellows I keep?"

His words sliced into her and, laden with regret, she met his eyes.

"I guess I don't," Kallan said, "any more than you would fret over my warming Bergen's bed last night."

Rune flinched as he grappled with only a flash of words. Stables. Together. Alone. Very little else suddenly seemed to matter.

"Fine by me!" Rune said, not caring that he was shouting. Kallan turned for the door, but Rune couldn't stifle his rage. "I said I would get you to Alfheim, and to Alfheim I did. You're on your own now, Princess! I am through! By all means, don't let me stop you if you want to leave, but Gudrun and Daggon are my prisoners and they're not leaving my city!"

Rune watched as Kallan threw open his door and slammed it closed behind her, leaving the King of Gunir alone with his anguish.

CHAPTER EIGHTEEN

Torunn had arrived too bright and too early to attend to Kallan's laundering, saying no more than what was necessary as she bustled around the bower. With a mind-numbing pulse that drummed her head, Kallan placated the castle's keeper, who laced Kallan's bodice with a ruthlessness that left her ribs bruised.

Standing in Gunir's deep, vibrant reds, Kallan yielded to the numbness leftover from the night before as she gripped the table for balance.

With a final jerk, Torunn tied off the end of the gown, tucked the laces from view within the folds of the bodice, and whisked herself from the bower, picking up a bundle of laundry on her way out.

Biting back the need to cry, Kallan swallowed her anger and fastened her pouch to her hip. As she lowered her hands to her sides, Kallan stared blankly through the solar at the open sky that greeted her too happily that morning. Long after the cold click of the door faded, a single, empty tear fell down Kallan's face and, at last, she found the will to move. Slowly, she wiped the tear from her cheek and collected her skirts. Her legs moved and Kallan clasped the cold, metal knob of her chambers.

Blind to the bustle of servants, Kallan followed the corridor to the small, lone door at the end of the hall. Without hesitation, she climbed the steps back to the round tower room.

* * *

With her hair tightly woven to the back of her head, Torunn heaved the bundle of clothes down to the Great Hall, stomping every step like a smith's hammer. She snapped a set of orders to a pair of girls, who had stopped to exchange giggles and gossip, and passed them her load with a reprimand and a scowl. After sending them on their way, Torunn headed down to the kitchens, where the scent of venison stew had attracted Geirolf and Bergen.

"Bergen," she asked, bracing her palms with exasperation on the table where both men sat, hunched over matching bowls of stew. "What's going on with my boy?"

"I dunno. Go ask him," Bergen said, taking in a slurp.

Torunn snarled.

"You know as well as I that Rune is too tight-lipped to unload on a woman."

Bergen grinned into his bowl.

"Couldn't get him to talk again, huh?"

"No," Torunn said and stuck out her bottom lip, dropping her shoulders.

"I tried for nearly an hour this morning." She stared at Cook's fire crackling beneath a kettle of stew. "He sent his tray back untouched again."

She paused, giving ample opportunity for either man to speak up voluntarily. Each kept their eyes on their bowl, ignoring her hints and nudges.

"You know he went through five flagons of mead yesterday," she stated as matter-of-factly, and eagerly awaited an explanation.

Geirolf slurped louder than usual.

"You know something's up!" Torunn said, leaning closer from across the table.

Glazed with disinterest, Geirolf and Bergen raised their eyes from their breakfast.

"I know you know!" she said. "What's wrong with him?"

Geirolf and Bergen exchanged a look that confirmed they should start speaking before Torunn personally began removing body parts.

Bergen took another mouthful of stew.

"Kallan."

Torunn shrugged impatiently. "What about her?"

"He fancies the girl," Geirolf said, taking great care to stare into his bowl as he spoke.

"Oh, is that all?" Torunn snapped, releasing the table as she straightened her back. "So why doesn't he have her and be done with this? The man is driving me crazy!"

"Not like that, woman," Geirolf grumbled, looking up from his stew with a cautious eye.

"He likes her," Bergen belted through a mouthful of bread and ripped off another chunk with his fingers.

Torunn's eyes widened.

"He...Sh..." Torunn sputtered. "She's a Dokkalfr!"

"We noticed," Geirolf muttered, clasping his bowl closer.

"But after all she's done...the men she's killed..." Torunn flailed her arms about like a grounded hawk. "After all the widows she's made of our women! She's a callous...a warmonger—"

"Careful, Torunn." Bergen looked her dead in the eye, and Torunn silenced her wagging tongue. "I just sailed for three days with that 'warmonger.' I watched her writhe with more worry for her people than a mother forced to watch her child bleed out." Bergen filled his spoon with stew. "She was twisted into more knots than a fisherman's net."

Torunn dropped her brow, laden with more questions than she had answers.

Geirolf hunched closer to his bowl, leaving Bergen to the wolves of petty gossip.

Bergen said between spoonfuls of stew, "We passed Lorlenalin at sea. Kallan went mad trying to get to it."

Torunn opened her mouth to speak, but words failed her.

"Rune had to hold her back," Geirolf said, standing armed with an empty bowl.

Torunn wobbled her head until she resembled a bird pecking away at tittle-tattle.

"What's wrong with her?"

Bergen looked up from his bowl. "The Dvergar took her, Torunn."

Torunn's mouth fell open.

"She's been usurped," Geirolf said with his back to the kitchens as he ladled a fresh helping into his bowl.

Bergen held Torunn's eye long after he finished, watching her own bewilderment sort itself out.

Regaining her composure, Torunn seemed to retract into her shoulders, suddenly disinterested with any news they may harbor.

"Still…a healthy Ljosalfar would do Rune some good," Torunn mumbled with a twinge of guilt hanging in her voice.

Torunn watched Bergen slurp in some stew as Geirolf pulled the chair back under him.

"Well, Rune will have a time of it finding one that Bergen hasn't wetted himself," Geirolf said into his stew and chuckled.

Bergen flashed a smile to Geirolf and tore off another chunk from his bread.

Torunn shoved out her thin lip and scowled at their snickering.

"I've seen the fight in Kallan first hand," Bergen said. "He deserves someone like her."

Still smiling, Bergen shoved a mouthful of broth-soaked bread into his mouth.

"Bergen!"

A man's voice carried from the Great Hall, forcing an end to their conversation as Geirolf turned to the door behind them.

"In here!" Bergen called back, picking off a crumb from the bread.

The kitchen door struck the wall as a set of heavy stomps clambered down the kitchen steps.

"What is it, Ragnar?" Bergen asked, keeping his interest on his food.

"It's the Dokkalfr!" Ragnar said between breaths. "She's in the tower raising all kinds of Hel."

In an instant, Bergen and Geirolf were on their feet and out the door, their breakfast forgotten on the table with Torunn bringing up the rear.

They rushed to the Great Hall, up the steps, two at a time ahead of Ragnar, and slammed open the single oak door on the second floor. As they followed the spiraling stairwell up to the tower room, Kallan's voice carried down from overhead.

"Let me in!" she shouted.

At the top of the steps, Bergen and Geirolf entered the small room where the table, the chair, and Ottar barricaded Kallan, who stood poised for battle. Ringlets of hair spilled down her front. The red gown she wore made her look as though Seidr flame encased the whole of her body, doubled by the orange flames she held in her hands.

With his own sword out in response, Ottar glowered with an equal amount of loathing as his frame, twice as wide as Kallan's, dwarfed her. His stature did little to deter her.

"Let me in!" she shouted, sending a surge of Seidr to her palms and doubling the flames in size.

"Not a chance, Seidkona!" Ottar tightened his grip on the sword he held over his shoulder.

"Ottar, stand down," Bergen said, keeping his attention on Kallan's hands. Gently, he dared a step toward her. "Kallan."

"Finally!" Kallan sighed and extinguished her Seidr flames as she stood down from her offensive. "I want to see Gudrun!"

Ottar bellowed from behind his scowl. "You come barging in here as if you've the orders—"

"Ottar!" Bergen interjected, keeping his captain in order.

"Your king has given me vassalage!" Kallan said.

Bergen softened his voice, disguising his tension. "He can't, Kallan."

"What?" she asked as if they were old friends.

Her change in disposition astounded him and he struggled to maintain his order.

"Rune passed the word out this morning," Bergen said. "No one is to let you in."

"But I have sovereignty. His order—"

"Still stands on all else," Bergen assured her. "But this…" Bergen shook his head.

Her shock waned almost instantly and Kallan inhaled, crinkling her face in disgust.

"Take me to Rune," she commanded Bergen.

"Very well," Bergen said with a nod.

"No can do, Bergen."

Bergen looked to Ragnar, who stood on the highest step of the stairs.

"What?" Bergen asked.

"Rune refuses to see her," Ragnar said.

"He—" Bergen gulped down a selection of curses he would later share with his brother. "What?"

"I have a right to see my people," Kallan shrieked.

"She has a right to see her people, Ragnar," Bergen echoed, pointing a finger at Kallan.

"I have a right to see my warden!" Kallan said.

"Yes!" Bergen said. "Let her see her warden!"

Kallan looked imploringly to Geirolf, who stood silently beside Bergen.

"Please." Kallan glanced at the cell where she could feel Gudrun's Seidr. "Let me see them."

The fight was gone from her voice, leaving behind the barren worries of a child longing to see her kin. The repressed tremble in her voice caught Torunn's ear, forcing the old woman's jaw taut as she clenched her teeth and pursed her lips.

"I'm sorry, Your Majesty," Geirolf said, slowly shaking his head.

Kallan tried to make an angry scowl, but her quivering lip and slightly raised brow only emphasized a frown. Her chin puckered and the tip of her nose burned. Kallan looked to Bergen, to Geirolf, to Torunn, desperate for a single hand to help her. A knot formed in her throat and, alone, Kallan shoved her way through the Ljosalfar and back down the steps to the second floor.

Gulping down a ball of shame, Torunn watched the fury of red as Kallan's skirts billowed behind her, filling the descending stairs with fading footsteps.

C⤳ ⤳⤵

The great doors of Kallan's sitting room struck the wall as Kallan gasped with anger. With all her might, she slammed the doors, holding herself so tight she bruised her arms. She paced for a moment, bewildered and angry, then stopped. The window drew her eye.

Slowly, Kallan made her way across the sitting room into the bedroom. Leaning into the sill, she gazed through the window. White clouds pushed through the bright, blue sky. Below, the barracks buzzed with life while a blacksmith plinked his hammer somewhere, unseen, in the courtyard.

Kallan couldn't breathe from behind the walls where Rune imprisoned her. She needed to run. She needed to leave. She needed to ride.

At once, her breath slowed and, with a quiet resolve that answered all questions, Kallan slid a shaking hand into the pouch at her waist and pulled out a plain white packet. Staring down at the spell enclosed in leather, she found her breath and her pulse slowed.

Taking in a deep, slow sigh, Kallan returned her attention to the courtyard where she studied the stone steps to the battlement, and the street to the village of Gunir, to the river that curved around the city, and beyond to the forest and Swann Dalr.

CHAPTER NINETEEN

B ergen!"

The shriek shook the calm of the courtyard as Torunn threw back the door to the barracks.

"Bergen!" she said, gasping as she held herself up over the threshold. Among the armaments that dripped from every wall, splayed with the collection of round, wooden shields and arrows that littered the floor, Bergen stood, weighing the balance of a sword among the soldiers.

"She's gone!" Torunn said.

"Who's gone?" Bergen asked, looking up from the sword in his hand.

"Kallan!"

Bergen lowered the sword to his side.

"What do you mean 'gone'?"

"I went to her room and she's gone," Torunn said, rushing into the barracks. She spoke faster than her heart pulsed. "I searched the castle. I asked the servants. I searched the grounds. No one has seen her."

"Did you check the stables?" he asked.

"I did," she said. "Her horse is also gone!"

That confirmation jumped Bergen into action. As he belted his orders over his shoulder, Bergen moved to the door with Torunn, who matched his pace.

"Ottar, check the city stables. Ragnar, run the streets. Joren."

The scout added a skip to his step.

"Sir."

"Take to the docks."

Each man split off to see to their orders.

"Torunn…" Bergen kept his eyes on the keep as he hastened across the courtyard. "When was she last seen?"

"This morning, in the tower with you."

Up the stairs, Bergen ran, sprinting across the Great Hall, past the kitchens, and up the steps to his bower, taking the steps three at a time. As he reached the main landing, he turned to the right, away from his chambers, and threw open the door of the war room.

Peering over a map at a long table, Rune and Geirolf stood upright at the sound of the door banging. The fire behind them roared, adding to the light that poured in from the high rows of windows that stretched the length of the hall.

"Rune!" Bergen bellowed, taking long strides to meet his brother. "She's gone."

Torunn slipped inside behind him.

"What do you mean 'gone'?" Rune asked. "And Astrid?"

"Gone."

Without a word, Rune abandoned the table and sprinted across the room to the door at the end opposite of where Bergen and Torunn had entered.

"Send out riders to the south," Rune said, picking up Geirolf, Bergen, and Torunn along the way. "I want a boat loaded and ready to go up the water ways."

Throwing open the door, Rune crossed a landing and a stairwell that descended to the Great Hall, flinging open the door to his bedchamber. He ignored the lingering scent of pipe, the roaring fire, and the fresh supply of mead. Cutting through his sitting room, he punched open the double doors that led into the corridor.

"She'll most likely head for the bridge," Rune said. "Make your way to Swann Dalr. She knows her way home from there."

Rune strode down the hall, affording a glance to the double doors of Kallan's bower. "Find out from Gunnar when he last saw Astrid," he continued. "It will give us an idea how much of a start she has on us. And have Joren ride out to Lorlenalin," he called over his shoulder. "Have him keep post there for any sign of her return! Go!"

Without objections, Geirolf, Bergen, and Torunn abandoned Rune at the great steps and bounded down to the Great Hall as Rune threw open the lone oak door. There he climbed the stairs to the tower.

The main room at the top was empty save for a lone soldier seated on watch at the ready. At the site of his king, he jumped to his feet and nodded respectfully.

"Your Majesty."

In reply, Rune motioned with two fingers to follow around the small passage, past the cell where Kallan had stayed, to a third door on the right.

"Has Kallan been up here, Torger?"

"Not since this morning," Torger said.

"When was the last time you looked in on the prisoners?" he asked, not bothering to look over his shoulder.

"A couple hours," Torger said, adding a shuffle to his step to keep up.

"Check now," Rune said, coming to stand before the door he wanted open.

The guard scrambled, locating the key without a fumble, and unlocked the door. Backing away, Torger gave Rune allowance to enter.

The door creaked open as Rune pushed the wood, squinting at the cool, blue light that blazed from the center of the room. There, as before, Gudrun sat on a pile of straw, waiting. The silver of her hair flowed down her back as she shifted her gold eyes up from the ball of light that wafted in mid-air before her.

"She's run off again, hasn't she?" Gudrun asked, peering over the orb of light with a calm look in her eye.

"Leave us," Rune whispered to Torger, who had leaned over Rune's shoulder to get a look at where the light was coming from. A moment later, the door clicked behind him.

Rune studied the Seidkona, his guard raised with his suspicions.

"Again?" he asked, keeping his place at the door.

Gudrun smiled.

"I've seen that face too many times to not recognize it for what it is," she said. "I've had that look myself too often to not know what it means."

"You," Rune began. "You asked Bergen to capture you."

Gudrun nodded.

"I did."

"And Kallan...and Daggon."

"I did."

"Why?"

"Why indeed," Gudrun said with a smile.

"Where is she?" Rune asked, frowning with bewilderment at the hag.

"She hasn't gone far," Gudrun said, looking back to the orb before her.

"I know you know the dangers of her actions as well as I," Rune said. "She'll try to get to Lorlenalin."

"Will she?"

"Won't she?"

Gudrun grinned. "I'm happy to see you're up to playing the game with me. Kallan has been running from her station since she could walk," Gudrun said. "She'll be back when she's ready."

Rune furrowed his brow.

"She loves Lorlenalin. Why would she run?"

"She loves her people," Gudrun corrected. "She loves the children. She hates the regulations that come with her station. She hates the restrictions that tie her down. Kallan hates being tied down, just like her mother."

Rune lowered his eyes as he mulled the information around for a bit. He was suddenly reminded of Bergen.

With a sigh, Gudrun waved her hand and split the ball of Seidr into a division of smaller lights that flew to the walls. In that instant, the Beast within Rune roared and lunged at the hovering orbs of Seidr. Its strength brought Rune to his knees. By the time he subdued the Beast, Gudrun's Seidr had changed from a cool blue light to a happy orange that cheerily warmed the room. Only then could Rune see that the barren cell room had since been lavished in every simple accommodation a Seidkona could ask for.

But all this paled in comparison to the fear resonating in Gudrun's golden eyes as Rune watched the color drain from the old Seidkona.

"Where did you get that?" she whispered.

"It was given to me," Rune said quickly, steadying his breath. "I was hoping you could tell me what it is."

"Who gave it to you?"

"A Dokkalfr," Rune said. "The traiter who offered to grant my freedom in exchange for Kallan's death."

"A Dokkalfr, you say?"

Rune nodded.

"But that isn't possible," Gudrun said. "How long ago? When? Where?" Gudrun snapped the questions, one after the other, leaving Rune unsure where to begin.

"Nearly two moons ago, the night Kallan and I left Lorlenalin. A Dokkalfar by name of Borg, and since…" Rune shook his head. "It wants to kill Kallan."

Too quickly, Gudrun recovered herself and waved a thin, aged hand as if wishing away a spent breakfast tray.

"Of course it does," Gudrun said as if this was common knowledge. "It's a Fendinn."

"A Fendinn?" Rune mulled its name over as if knowing what it was could somehow remove it. "Well… Can you take it out?"

"Good gracious, child. What do you think I am?" Gudrun asked. "It shouldn't be too much of a threat. The Ljosalfar hardly have Seidr Users about."

"But Kallan—"

"Is gone, you said, and she isn't anywhere near as strong enough as to attract the attention of a Fendinn. Now then…"

Gudrun shifted her legs out from under her and just like that the conversation was over, leaving Rune reeling with more questions that he could count. "Why are you really here?" Gudrun asked.

"Kallan said you're a Volva."

"So I am," Gudrun said as she set to work brewing herself a cup of tea at the fire pit and cauldron in the room.

"How much can you really see?" Rune asked. "How much do you know?"

Gudrun released a long sigh with a bit of a smile that never waned. She slowly sipped her brew as if savoring the position she held over Rune.

"Only one other has ever asked me that," she said and mused. "Everything that was. Everything that is. Everything that has not yet been."

Rune clung to her every word, examining the wisdom that flowed from the depths of her eyes, her bright golden eyes, just like Freyr's.

Gudrun paused for a moment in idle thought then went on.

"I can see as far ahead as I see back…to the beginning, to the end, from Ginnungagap to Ragnarok."

Rune took a step.

"Tell me," he whispered. "Show me."

Gudrun peered up at the king. Despite her hunched posture, Rune had the distinct feeling she was looking down at him.

"If my daughter's daughter has told you what I am," Gudrun said, "certainly she's told you my price."

"Ask it," Rune bade.

"Oh, I assure you I will…" Gudrun smiled as a slyness that was not there a moment ago gleamed from her eye. "But first, ask your questions."

"And if I your prices exceed my silver?" Rune asked.

"Oh, it isn't silver I'll ask of you," Gudrun said with a grin, "And this…this will be something you can afford."

Rune studied her, weighing in all his options.

"Shall we begin?" she asked, slightly more mischievous than Rune would have liked.

"Where is Kallan?"

Gudrun's stature went rigid. Her eyes became fixed as if she was reading runes through the Seidr several spans away.

"She's in Gunir…under spell.
In the warrens…ever watchful,
Of the children…once forgotten,
Sick and ailing…dead or dying,
Would you know more?"

"What is wrong with that woman?" Rune blurted before he had given much thought to the question.

Gudrun's face split into a delighted grin. "Is that your question?"

"No," Rune grumbled, taking back the question asked.

Does she like… Does she want… Foolish. I can't squander these questions!

"Who is Aaric?" he asked, deciding.

As before when he had asked about the Fendinn, the humor fell from Gudrun's face, leaving behind a darkness Rune couldn't place. Her words were slow as she measured each word before muttering.

"Aaric is the high marshal…and enigmatic friend,
My daughter's bane…My ordained kin,
Bound…by ancient birth."
Coldly, Gudrun peered up at Rune.
"But this is not what you would know."

"Where did he come from?" Rune asked, assessing the shadows that had befallen the room. As if her sight was failing, Gudrun narrowed her eyes and whispered:

"Across the silver sea and void…where the Aesir sing,
The emerald ground…The golden crown,
Lays there…the lost king—"

Coldness blanketed the gleam in Gudrun's eyes. When she continued, her voice had changed—slower, sterner, darker. She shifted her gaze to Rune and spoke as if reading from an ancient severed thread of Seidr.

"Your questions build a road…One I've buried, blocked, and burned."

Rune pushed a knot down his dry throat.

"If you persist…if you pursue …"
The air was thick.
"I will kill you…and your kin."

There was a long moment before Rune found his voice again.

"Who is Borg?"

Gudrun furrowed her brow, perplexed as she searched her sight.

"Borg," she whispered. After some time, she shook her head.

"My eyes are blind," she breathed. "My mind falls black,
That name, no face…nothing, but fear—"

Gudrun shook her head as if trying to clear the air.

"My Seidr is fading. I can not see."

Gudrun bit her bottom lip and tried again.

"Darkness falls on shadowed dreams…like dewdrops shades are shunned from thee,
Where the water falls like rain…when the— Oh."

As if in pain, Gudrun clutched her head.

"I would know more," said Rune, dropping down beside the Volva. "Who killed Kallan's father? Who killed Eyolf?"

Gudrun abandoned the blur of faded images and studied Rune's hardened face.

"I see beyond this world, like dreams,
Where once I looked upon the sea,
There, the dark invades my sight."

She gasped and spoke faster as if trying to race the shadows.

"Cold dreams…cloud sight.
The void, it…devours night."

Gudrun shoved her brittle fingers through her silver hair, desperate for the answers that wouldn't obey her summons.

"I can not see," she said.

"What should I do?" Rune asked, plowing ahead while there was still time.

Gudrun shook her head with an air of sadness.

Rune jumped to the next question, sweat beading upon his brow. "Will Kallan join us?"

The light returned and Gudrun could read the runes again suspended in the distance, hanging on the threads of Seidr.

"Kallan bends with the boughs of the Ash,
The babbling brook that bows the land,
Kira breathes through Kallan's whim,
Riding, whispering, on the wind.
I hear my voice on Kallan's breath,
Vivid and fervent...boisterous."

Gudrun studied the silver of Rune's blue eyes and suppressed a smile.

"Kallan goes where Kallan wills,
Wherever you lead..." She nodded. "Kallan will."

Rune's lips cracked against the dryness. Sweat pooled in his cold hands and he forced the words from his throat.

"Who was the Dokkalfr who killed my sister—?" He lost his voice and gulped. "Who killed Swann?"

Once more, a blackened cloud appeared and blocked all images from Gudrun. She heard the distant scream then silence as a girl took her last breath, and nothing more. Worry crumpled Gudrun's face and she shook her head, failing to clear the fog.

"I can not see, what seeds are sown," she susurrated and Rune's shoulders fell.

"I would know no more."

Slowly, he found his feet and turned to the door.

"It is you," Gudrun said. Rune paused, his hand already on the handle. "You who sent the soldier to ask about Kallan's children."

Rune shuffled around and gazed upon the old woman.

"Why?" Gudrun asked.

There was a long while before Rune answered as he pondered the Volva's reliance.

"I have only…ever…wanted to end this war," Rune said, "and I can't do that without Kallan."

He had barely moved again for the door, when she spoke again.

"There is the matter of my payment," Gudrun said.

A new shadow filled her eyes as if pleading with him to hear.

"Ask it," Rune said.

"Don't let Kallan go back." Her voice wavered with a weakness Rune had thought incapable of her. "Not while Aaric is there." Gudrun shook her head. "Not alone."

With a slight nod, Rune slipped from the cell. Before the door closed behind him, the lights recollected themselves and returned to the ball of Seidr that hovered before Gudrun.

CHAPTER TWENTY

Kallan watched the sun set beyond the river from the outermost ends of Gunir in the farthest backstreets of the warrens. There, looking down from a low hanging rooftop, she found what she had been looking for. Streets of abandoned buildings and dilapidated shacks left to the hungry and homeless.

From a distance, Kallan watched as the starved and lost children tucked themselves into whatever crevices they could find, with whatever garbage they could muster for blankets. Most had settled down for the night. Only a handful of them still cried. The chill in the air bit cold and Kallan hugged herself tighter.

I will wait until the crying stops.

Daylight drained from the earth and another two hours slipped by. Rune's warriors ended their search. The spell would wear off soon and, any minute now, Astrid would re-appear in his stall.

The cries of the children faded in exchange for night's silence and Kallan forced herself to her feet.

I can always come back, she decided. *I have to come back.*

With a long sigh, she brushed the filth from her clothes. Carefully, she climbed down from the roof, securing her grip with her Seidr.

With a breath of relief, Kallan's feet touched the ground and she scanned the warrens. After selecting the quietest road through the thatch and mortar homes, Kallan twisted her way through the village, past the occasional Ljosalfr, up the wide steps to the battlement, and across the courtyard to the keep.

Cold laughter filled the Great Hall, where nearly one hundred of Rune's warriors dined at the tables. The fire pit roared, and they laughed, exchanging drinks for stories as Kallan slipped by them unseen. After making note of Rune's absence among his men, she made her way up the steps to the second floor and sprinted down the hall to her bower. The distant buzz of the rabble below vanished as Kallan pushed the door closed behind her. Falling back against the door, she gasped.

Her chambers glowed with the warmth of lit candles and the roaring hearth. In the bedroom, a warm bath had been drawn and scented with oils of heather, rose, and lavender. A clean set of finely embroidered night garments covered the foot of the bed and trays laden with fresh meats, sugared fruits, and black currant mead buried the tables. A breeze blew in from the solar, taking with it the sweet scent of sage.

Digging the heel of her hand into her eyes, Kallan recovered her senses and immediately began unlacing her bodice and stripping off her clothes. She soaked for as long as it took to absorb the oils into her skin and scrub the filth from her feet.

Afterwards, still damp with oils and bath water, Kallan slipped into the chemise that fell to the floor, and pulled the matching dressing gown on over her shoulders. Leaving her hair free to hang in the breeze, Kallan brushed the short bits from her eyes and hungrily looked over the tray lavished with fruits and salted meats. She had almost started to enjoy herself, when the gentle click of her door interrupted her evening.

With one hand upright and a pear clamped in her teeth, Kallan cradled a ball of orange flame.

"Be still," Torunn said. From the bedroom door, she waited for Kallan to lower her defenses. Despite the uneasiness in her eyes, the old key keeper forced a grin.

Once Kallan realized Torunn wasn't Rune, a slight poke of disappointment stabbed at her chest. With a flick of her wrist and a poorly suppressed eye roll, Kallan extinguished the flame and pulled the fruit from her mouth.

"No one knows you're back yet," Torunn whispered. She dared a few steps forward.

"You were expecting me," Kallan said.

"Of course." Torunn smiled and came to stand before Kallan. "Who do you think prepared your room?"

Kallan stared wide-eyed at the gentle face, unsure what to say as the Ljosalfr intrdocued herself.

"I am Torunn, the castle's keeper," Torunn said, inviting the Dokkalfr to speak.

Kallan gave a single nod, keeping her eyes fastened to the Ljosalfr.

"What do you want?" Kallan asked, hardening her face at the sudden pleasantries.

Torunn folded her hands and dropped them to her front as she peered at Kallan with the same look Kallan had seen from Rune so many times.

"I am here to offer reconciliation." Torunn attempted to soften her voice, avoiding an accusatory lilt in her tone.

Kallan shook her head with a bit of a chuckle.

"Forgive my suspicion," she said, "but I've seen too little from the Ljosalfar that suggests you want to reconcile."

Dropping the pear on the table, Kallan pretended to look through the tray of food.

"Please…" Collecting the folds of her skirts, Torunn followed Kallan along the rows of trays. "I understand your apprehension…your hesitation." Kallan raised her face to the dark outside her window above the tables of food. "I've watched you stand against Bergen and Rune surrounded by a people who despise you."

"For two days you've said nothing to me," Kallan said, staring up at the almost half-moon. "Why the sudden change?"

"For Rune," the woman said. "For Bergen."

Kallan frowned. "Common enemy, common ground?"

Torunn shrugged then smiled kindly despite Kallan's ill temper.

"In a way."

Kallan shook her head.

"You can't help me," she said and, hugging herself, sauntered into the sitting room.

The sweet lake air snapped and whipped the fire's flames. Kallan inhaled deeply, coming to stand in the room's center where a fine, thick fur rug swallowed her toes.

"I know these boys," Torunn said, "every secret, every nuance, every quirk. I know the way they think, the way they hate. The way they love… I know what they drink and whom they fight. I know which bed they sleep in every night. I know what bedfellows they keep."

With one question suddenly at the front of her mind, Kallan turned about, but the twinkle in Torunn's eye stopped her from asking who frequently shared Rune's bed with him.

"You can't tell me none of this information can be of use to you," Torunn asked.

Gentle curiosity narrowed Kallan's eyes.

"Why do you tell me this?"

Torunn smiled.

"I'm too wise to hold my tongue when I shouldn't."

Kallan mulled Torunn's proposition around for a moment.

"Even if you could help," Kallan asked, "why would you?"

With a hearty chuckle that encouraged Kallan to absorb the full humor of the situation, Torunn smiled broadly, multiplying the intricate lines at her eyes.

"In the time I have served this family, those boys have given me an eternity of woes. I am all too eager to pay them back for the years of affliction they have bestowed unto me. Besides…" Smiling, Torunn shrugged. "They deserve it."

Sighing, Kallan shook her head and returned to her bedroom. Exasperated, she settled herself into a chair before the small hearth fire, letting her arms hang off the side of the chair.

"And how could I—"

"Lady Kallan," Torunn said, dropping to her knees beside the Dokkalfr. "Your Majesty."

Kallan gazed at Torunn, shocked at the formal recognition.

"In the short time that you've been here in Gunir, I've seen you rumple Bergen's pride—which, in itself, is a great feat. I've seen Rune run more laps trying to keep up with you and get the runaround he's been needing for a long… *long* time."

Kallan stared at the fire.

"I don't know what transpired since Swann Dalr," Torunn said, "or how the two of you ended up in Midgard gallivanting around with the kings of Men and the Dvergar, but whatever it was—whatever it is—it has worked. Everyone is here at the end of this thing. And we are all very, very tired."

Flames licked the air with a liveliness that seemed to infiltrate Kallan's nerve. She tried to remember the last time she played at a game like this.

It was Daggon, she recalled, thinking back. *He had needed to retaliate against one of Father's jokes that entailed a cauldron of deer blood, the whole of the army, and his horse.*

A small smile tugged at the corner of Kallan's mouth.

"What's the plan?"

CHAPTER TWENTY-ONE

Bergen closed the door of Rune's chambers behind him, not bothering to soften the heavy clump of his boot as he walked.

"Rune," he called through the dark, void of the usual joviality that accompanied him. "Are you still staring at the ceiling?" he asked, coming to stop at the foot of the bed, where Rune had stretched out onto his stomach.

"Hm."

A wad of folded vellum notes rested beside Rune's hand, allowing Bergen to read the scribbled line:

Bound by ancient birth… Silver sea… Aesir sing

The vellum was folded where Bergen couldn't read the next line and then:

…lost…~~crown~~ King. Lost King…Gold crown.

And again…

…void devours night. K…

Bergen relaxed his hand onto his hilt and grinned.

"Oh, you've got it bad if you're writing prose," he mumbled where Rune couldn't hear. "Brother! Rune!"

Bergen added a thump to Rune's foot buried beneath the furs.

"Your lady is back!"

Rune's back stiffened, for barely a moment, then relaxed and Bergen thought he heard a sigh into the pillow.

"Where was she?" Rune said, muffled by the pillow.

"We don't know," Bergen said. "Gunnar was finishing up with the last feeding when Astrid suddenly was there. So we checked the bower and…" Bergen let his voice trail off rather than reiterate the obvious.

He waited a moment for his brother to make a move before pressing the issue further.

"Are you going to go to her?"

"No," Rune said into his pillow.

Bergen flinched, taken aback by his decision.

"No bickering, no barrage, no battle?"

"No, Bergen."

"Well, Hel."

The heavy clump of his boot confirmed Bergen had moved toward the sitting room and Rune lifted his head.

"Bergen." The clump of the boot stopped. "Leave her."

Bergen scowled at the mass on the bed, immobile and unnerved by everything around him.

"Well, one of us should get into it with her and it may as well be me," he said and closed the sitting room door behind him.

It took Bergen a moment to release the door handle, as he fought to convince himself not to go back in and punch Rune in the face.

"Well?" Torunn's hushed exclamation jolted him from his irked state.

"Nothing," he answered, releasing the handle.

"Damn!" Torunn snapped, already thinking hard on the next plan of action.

"Don't worry about it too much tonight, Torunn," Bergen said. "I'm sure your wild head will think up something nasty by dawn. Get some sleep."

He made it as far as Kallan's room when Bergen called down the hall to Torunn, who nervously gnawed at her thumbnail.

"Goodnight, Torunn."

⌒　⌒

Kallan stared at herself in the glass, happy enough with the gown of warm russet she wore. She normally would don a pair of trousers and a tunic for a day like this, but under the circumstances, she felt it would add a sharper sting to her bite.

She ran a flat palm down her stomach then spun on her heel, gently closing the door of her bower behind her, the Seidr pouch of amadou rested idly on her bedside table.

If you want Bergen's respect, challenge him and win fast or lose hard.

She played Torunn's words back as she passed through the corridor, carefully reviewing each word.

Fight them and win. He adores the woman, but respects the blade and nothing throws him into more turmoil than combining the two. He can't pass up a good mead, a good fight, or a good woman.

Kallan swept through the Great Hall, ignoring the occasional pair of eyes that glowered as she entered the courtyard.

Rune is stubborn and speaks little, keeping his head in most cases where Bergen loses it. He observes while he keeps to himself, careful never to leave an opening. His solitude makes up for Bergen's unruliness, but don't underestimate Bergen's unruliness. It's a front he uses to throw off your guard.

Kallan's eyes strayed to the gathering of bare-chested men who planed the logs for the new stable.

If you want Rune's attention, hit him hard. Get in his face where he can't get away. He moves fast and, if you let him, he'll keep ten paces ahead of you. If you're not watching, you will lose him.

And Geirolf? Kallan had asked.

Geirolf goes where I go, every time. Let me handle Geirolf.

Kallan slowed her pace as the clang of sparring grew louder from the courtyard. The door had been propped open, allowing the cool breeze to pass through. Forcing her breath steady, Kallan paused in the threshold and thoroughly examined the situation.

Nearly two dozen men had gathered around the barracks, giving large-shouldered Ottar and Bergen the space required to spar with each other. She watched them quietly as Bergen lunged forward, bringing his sword down onto Ottar, who blocked his attack. Sweeping the blade up, Bergen cut through the air to his left where Ottar barely blocked it and pushed Bergen back.

Regaining his balance, Bergen advanced, bringing his sword to the right toward Ottar's leg. He blocked the sweep as Bergen snapped his elbow with lightning speed into Ottar's face, breaking his nose in the process.

Ottar stumbled, blinded by the taste of his own blood, but Bergen had no pity. He raised his sword and thrust, stopping directly at Ottar's throat, where he held the point of his blade.

At once, the barracks erupted into applause. Onlookers exchanged bets while Bergen gave a congratulatory slap to Ottar, who beamed from beneath the red mass on his face. The rumble granted Kallan the time she needed to glide to a table pushed against the wall, which was adorned with a generous collection of swords, daggers, and shields.

With a curious eye, Joren peered from his place against that wall. He leaned with ankles and arms crossed and studied Kallan, intrigued as she scanned each artifact with a critical eye.

"What are you up to?" Joren asked, keeping his voice below the rabble's expletives. With a hardened cold in her eye, Kallan glanced up at one particular sword that held her attention.

Bergen's voice boomed through the barracks with ease as he spun about, eager for the next victim. "Anyone here dare best me?"

In reply, Kallan took the black hilt in her hand and balanced it easily on two outstretched fingers, her approval won by its craft.

The display caught Bergen's eye and a smug smile stretched his face.

"If it's a long, thick blade the lady wishes, she shouldn't be looking on the table."

Fire flickered to life in Kallan's eyes and she smirked as the barracks burst into uproarious laughter. With a flick of her wrist, she caught the blade and, with a flourish, extended it down to her side as she turned to face him.

"I can best him!" Kallan dared, forcing Joren to squirm uncomfortably in his spot against the wall. Bergen bellowed loudest over the thunder of laughter that filled the barracks.

"Not without that craft of yours, Seidkona," Bergen barked between chuckles.

"Without my craft," Kallan agreed, coolly raising an eyebrow that reinforced her offer.

The barracks grew silent. Bergen glared at the woman, weighing her offer as Ragnar leaned closer from his wall.

"Kallan."

Kallan held her eye on her challenger.

"You might want to rethink this," Joren cautioned.

"You're next," Kallan said, shifting her gaze to Joren. "How 'bout it, Bergen?" Kallan belted, returning her attention to Bergen. "Will it be rumored that you were too afraid of being bested by a woman…" There was an outcry of 'ooh's. "Or will you be humiliated by losing against one?"

Sweat balled in Bergen's palms and he forced his breath steady, suddenly aware of how he ached to go head to head with her. He puffed his chest with a deep inhale that fueled the ferocity she stoked. All jocularity was gone as he stared down at the Seidkona from across the room.

"If it's a lesson you want, Seidkona," Bergen said, "I will be more than happy to instruct."

The game was on as the bets were placed, drawing everyone's attention to the fighting circle. Kallan smiled and glanced at the sword still clasped in hand. With a brandish, she confirmed the balance on her fingers then dropped it to snatch the hilt before it had fallen an inch.

Joren pushed his weight off the wall and came to stand beside Kallan as word passed through the courtyard, gathering onlookers who filled the barracks, muttering excitedly.

"Do you know what you're doing?" Joren asked.

With a smile, Kallan looked up from the blade.

"Where is your king?" she asked, her hardened stare fixed on the scout's face.

"Seidkona!" Bergen spat with impatience.

Turning from Joren, Kallan joined Bergen in the center of the room, balancing her weight on the balls of her feet. Bending her elbows, Kallan raised the sword to block her body and face, and waited.

"No Seidr now, woman!" Bergen barked.

"No Seidr," Kallan said with a grin.

Resuming his stance, Bergen shifted his way to Kallan's right. He lowered his blade and, with patience, tapped Kallan's sword held firm against the taunt. Kallan and Bergen stepped to the side, shifting their balance as they danced, mirroring the other's movement.

With might, Bergen swept his blade to Kallan's right, fully expecting to take her down with his first blow, but Kallan blocked his attack. Again, Bergen brought down his sword, sweeping it toward Kallan's left, and again to her right. Each time, Kallan met his attack with her blade.

CHAPTER TWENTY-TWO

N ot even the slightest scolding?" Geirolf asked from across the war room.

"I've been through this with Bergen," Rune said, not bothering to look up from the maps. "Do I really have to go through this with you?"

"Well, as long as you insist on going through this separately," Geirolf said, "yes."

"Next time I'll send for you."

"I appreciate it."

The room fell silent again as Rune studied the lines and curves that were the lakes, forests, and vast mountains of Midgard, stretching on to the far Northlands, where few had seen and fewer had travelled.

"Oh, come on, Rune!" Geirolf's voice filled the room, but his king only peered over the map. "A quick romp with her ends your misery and makes you tolerable for the rest of us!"

"Leave it alone, Geirolf." Rune said easily, keeping his eyes on the map.

"What harm could possibly come with a quick release?" Geirolf asked. "Bergen will tell ya, i—"

"I've accounted for the loss in the north." Rune tapped the collection of trees to the north of Gunir. "Bergen confirmed the devastation suffered there prior to the Battle of Swann Dalr."

A flash of memory pricked his chest as a sudden flourish of images focused into view of the night before the Battle of Swann Dalr and a certain wandering wench in the wood. Rune closed down the sudden whirl of images and forced his attention to the south.

"The Southern Keep…" Rune pointed to the land between Lake Wanern and the sea. "…has enough men to add to our forces, if it comes to it. Forkbeard hasn't made a move from his seat in a few years. Trade continues without disruption and the alum and tin are still flowing in."

"And the salted fish are swimming out."

Rune peered up from the map. Geirolf grinned and Rune returned his attention to the table.

"The keep should be fine with minimal guard."

Splaying his hands onto the table, Geirolf leaned toward Rune. The wood creaked beneath his weight.

"Your Majesty."

Rune gazed at the mass of river lines mingled with forestry that was Swann Dalr. "Bergen reports his group is on alert and at the ready as soon as we have the word."

"Rune…" Geirolf shifted his face between Rune's head and the map.

Rune turned a warning glare up at Geirolf.

"Would you at least put the girl out of her misery and go talk to her?" Geirolf asked.

Rune inhaled and held his gaze on Geirolf.

"Joren has been instructed to proceed as usual when Borg arrives."

Geirolf exhaled loudly.

"I don't expect Borg to cooperate, so be sure Bergen has his men in position when the Dokkalfr does arrive," Rune said. "I expect they'll need to surround him and be ready to close in."

Geirolf released the table and stood upright as Rune plowed on ahead with the details.

"I want Joren to lead him through their usual proceedings before we make our move. The plan is to take him by force and have him subdued. I expect him to put up a struggle."

"You're as stubborn as your father ever was," Geirolf said, shaking his head.

"Rune!"

Joren's voice carried from the corridor. His boot stomped up the steps two at a time. Panting, he threw open the door and stopped in the threshold, a bright gleam of amusement in his eye.

"Is he here?" Rune asked, standing upright.

"No," Joren gasped." It's Kallan."

"What's wrong?" Geirolf asked.

Grinning from ear to ear, Joren said, "You've got to see this."

☞ ☜

The ring of the blades reached Rune before he could push his way through to the barracks overflowing with people shoving to see. At the head of the line, the secured perimeter of a fighting ring cleared an area for those sparring.

Rune's heart raced with worry as Bergen lunged for Kallan, which she blocked to follow through with a raised blade above Bergen's head. He blocked her blow, but Kallan recovered, swinging her blade toward Bergen's leg. Rune watched him block the advance that sent them into a fury of clashing swords. With each attack, the other met their opponent and blocked the advance head on.

The steel screamed, holding Rune's eye on the sparring circle. Their swords joined at the hilt and they pushed against the other until Bergen smacked Kallan's nose with his elbow, sending blood running down her front. Pain split her face.

Rune's insides thundered with the silent rage that sent his body into a fit of shaking. Too rigid to call out, he stood and watched the blood flow from Kallan's nose. Pain vibrated her skull, pulsing through the mass of blood. Nevertheless, she retained her focus and swung her sword toward Bergen.

Always once more, their blades met, until Kallan pushed Bergen's sword down with her own and, releasing her left hand from the hilt, she slammed the base of her hand into Bergen's cheek, cracking the bone.

He stumbled back, falling to one knee, blinded by the sheer burn that inflamed the whole of his head. His loss of balance allowed Kallan to thrust her blade toward him and stop, holding the point to Bergen's throat.

The barracks fell silent at the sudden end. Kallan's short, deep breaths punched the air as she looked down at Bergen through the mass of blood coagulating on her face. In defeat, Bergen relaxed his sword arm and cued the barracks to explode into wolf whistles and cheers.

The blood covering Kallan's face matched the black from Bergen's broken cheekbone. Blowing a long breath as she came to stand upright, Kallan lowered her weapon and, with the hardened glower still set in her eyes, extended a hand to Bergen, who paused. Scowling, Bergen slapped her hand away and hoisted himself from the floor, coming to stand to his full height. The men in the barracks fell silent again and waited as Bergen stared hatefully down at Kallan.

Rune wrapped his fingers around *Gramm*'s hilt, ready for Bergen to make a move. No one dared breathed as they waited and watched, taking their cues from Bergen. Holding her bloody head high, refusing to cower or back down, Kallan matched Bergen's glower. Tightening her grip on her sword, she prepared herself for another round. And all at once, Bergen smiled, barking a laugh that shook the barracks.

Kallan smiled wide, still panting and released her grip on her sword as Bergen dropped his massive arm onto Kallan's shoulders.

"A woman you may be, Seidkona," he said, laughing and enclosing her in a hug, "but you're a fine swordsman, if I do say so myself."

Unable to stop his hands from shaking, Rune steadied his breath and, without a word of congratulations or acknowledgement, walked back to the keep shaking his head. As he emerged from the back of the crowd, leaving them to their winnings and praise, he made note to kill Bergen later.

Pull string. Inhale. Aim. Breathe.

Rune released the arrow and held his breath as the arrowhead buried itself into a tree. He drew another arrow from his quiver. With the string pulled taut, he held his breath and took aim for an available target somewhere in the bundle of arrows tightly burrowed together in the tree.

After settling his eye on a less than ideal spot barely above the collection, Rune released his breath and then shot as before, his tension still on the rise as he withdrew another arrow.

Rune forced his breathing steady. He had already passed thrice through the reasons why his anger brewed, each time settling on the same answer.

He relaxed his shoulders and breathed before releasing the arrow.

Replaying the blood splattering across Kallan's face, he silenced the nausea that flipped his stomach. Rune took aim. He recalled the amusement on Bergen's face.

Like pitted dogs, he thought.

The arrow gave off a profound *'thwit'* then a *'thunk'* as it struck the wood.

But his anger held, still raging as he remembered the bloody mass he had found curled up, near death, in the cave. Near death and now she goes looking for fights.

Another arrow sank into the tree, and a third, until Rune stared blankly at the mass of shafts protruding from the tree's trunk, his chest rising with every short breath he released. A bead of sweat spilled down his face and he shook, still as frustrated with its source as he had been an hour ago.

Rune tightened his fist around his bow's riser, not seeing the tree, the arrows, or the daylight passing with every hour. He tried to recall the last time such anger was evoked in him. Each time, instead, his thoughts settled on Kallan.

Forcing his worries silent, Rune pulled another arrow from the quiver and took aim, ready to restart another volley.

᧓ ᧓

Darkness blanketed the city. Exhaustion forced Rune calm as he pulled himself away from the range and dragged his aching body to his chambers, where he refreshed his nerves with a basin of cold water and a warm mead.

Torunn bustled in and out, making slight mention of his meal growing cold in the hall. With a silent nod, he shuffled about and redressed himself, while the fatigue pacified his rage and pulled him down into complacent submission.

His shoulder throbbed and he felt each shredded muscle in his back with every movement as he pulled his sleeve over his arm and leaned down to fasten his boots. Slowly, he made his way down to the Great Hall, slipping through the back door in his bedchamber, as far from Kallan's bower as possible.

An unusual buzz filled the Hall downstairs, where the fire roared and the servants shuffled from the kitchen with trays laden with fruits and meats. Warriors entered in handfuls, worn from the day's training as they settled themselves in place around the tables. Kicking the legs of his chair with a pout, Rune took his seat at the head of a table, eager to dine and leave unseen. A servant shoved a large soapstone plate in front of him and, at once, he hunched over his black pudding, set on ignoring the merriment that flowed in from the barracks. An outburst exploded until the laughter and rabble was almost deafening.

With a scowl, Rune shifted an impassive eye up from his pudding to the collection of warriors, who jostled about fresh with the stench of sparring and training. Bergen sauntered to a place at the table, but not before risking a glance at Rune, who chose that moment to shift his attention to Ottar and the dainty brunette tucked under his arm.

The kick to his stomach turned his bottom lip out in a scowl as Rune grimaced like a bitter, poorly aged curmudgeon. Kallan's long hair fell to her waist and swayed with every step synchronized to Ottar's. The laughter in her eyes framed her bright smile as she listened, captivated, by Ottar's every word.

"I followed that bird call for two hours," Ottar said above the uproarious merriment, "running around in circles and doubling back, only to find Bergen here had been the damn bird I'd been chasing!"

"I was just as surprised to find your ugly face on the other end, answering my calls!" Bergen said.

Kallan laughed, filling the hall with a warmth that left Rune holding his tankard in a death grip. Ottar found his seat across from Bergen and quickly, eagerly—

Too eagerly, Rune thought, curling the corner of his lip into his nose.

—guided Kallan onto the bench beside him. Together, the warriors dove into the smorgasbord of breads, stews, sugared fruits, sausages, puddings, and salted wild game splayed out in front of them.

Famished from the day's training, they swapped mead and meat for anecdote, paying no mind to their grimacing king at the table's head. Within minutes, as mouths filled with food, the initial thunder of laughter settled into a continuous flow of boisterous sound that mingled with the sweet scent of the seared meats and brewed drink.

The hearth fire battled with the torch light, adding to the glow of the room, and easing Kallan into a drugged state of euphoria that had little to do with the mead. Dropping her guard, she listened to the jovial nature of the men around her.

By mid-bowl, Ottar shifted his weight to face her more comfortably, his body lax from the mead.

"Tell me, lass…" He slurred his baritone. "…where did a woman such as yourself ever learn to fight?"

The question stopped her hand and she lowered the bread soaked with broth to her bowl. Catching the deep scar buried in Bergen's brow, she shifted her attention to Ottar.

"During the Dvergar Wars, we had little choice but to recruit any and all who could fight." She answered with as little detail as possible. "Since then, it's an assumed requirement that has become a tradition carried over from our days in Svartálfaheim. Everyone learns to fight."

Ottar's question had pulled every ear to her answer and her audience hungrily waited for more.

"What he meant," Bergen said with a gentle smile, "is where did a Seidkona find the time to learn swordplay in between your additional studies?"

Kallan's cheeks flushed red as she lowered her eyes to her soapstone bowl. A knot caught in her throat as she recalled the endless sessions alongside her father and Daggon.

"My father ensured my training was thorough," she said. The tone in her voice discouraged further inquiries.

The fire popped and the men eased back in their seats. At once, the table shook beneath Ottar's palm.

"Well!" he said gruffly. "I'm off for the night."

Several others were standing and stretching while a few remained in their seats, immersed in their own conversation.

"M'lady," Ottar bid and, taking up Kallan's hand, brushed a kiss across the back of it. "Bergen," he nodded to Bergen, who offered Ottar the back of his hand.

Still clutching Kallan's hand, Ottar landed a slap on the back of Bergen's.

"Don't keep her up too late," Ottar said. "I plan to go a round with her tomorrow."

Kallan's face burned red as she took back her hand, paying no mind as Ottar slogged from the table back to the doors, leaving Kallan to Bergen's company. A few more men dispersed, leaving the room unusually quiet.

Kallan shifted a hopeful eye to the head of the table and Bergen grinned. He watched, wallowing in the comfort of a full belly and full-bodied mead, as Kallan's hope sank to dejection at the sight of Rune's empty seat.

"He left us a while ago," Bergen said, crossing his arms onto the table and leaning closer, still grinning. His confidence gleamed with mischief in his black eyes.

Kallan lifted her attention from her empty bowl.

"I don't care," she said, irate that Bergen knew too much.

"You don't?" he asked, knowing too well the lies she told that masked her thoughts. "It's funny," he said, stretching his arms up over his head and arching his back. With a smirk and the slyness of a wolf, he re-folded his arms on the table. "He said the same thing about you."

Kallan snapped her head to the side with a huff.

"*Uskit*," she grumbled, staring down the table still loaded with a grand portion of uneaten food. The servants had not yet begun to clean up. At once, Kallan's thoughts wandered to that of the children and the warrens. If she were home, she and Eilif would have loaded their arms with all the food and drink left untouched.

The Hall was nearly empty now, save for two men at the end of the table still engrossed in their conversation. Unfolding his arms, Bergen stood from the bench and extended a hand in invitation.

"Come," he bade with a smile. "I have something to show you."

Kallan burned three shades of red and failed to gulp down the ball in her throat as she scrambled for a reply. Refusing to wait, Bergen took up her hand, oblivious to the stale terror still frozen on her face, and pulled her away from the table toward the door leading up to his chambers.

CHAPTER TWENTY-THREE

Bergen led Kallan through the Hall to the far corner where the stairs descended into the kitchens. Just as she hoped he would pull her down the steps to the butlery, he led her straight around the screens passage that concealed a single oak door. Without a word, Bergen opened the door and meandered up the steps.

The castle hummed with a rare quiet as Kallan followed Bergen up a narrow stairwell with a single window. The steps spiraled to a landing where she shadowed him to one of the only two doors that flanked the stairs.

"That's the war room."

Bergen nodded to a door on the right as he unlocked the door on the left.

"This…" He was certain to look her dead in the eye as he pushed the door open. "…is my room."

Her neck burned and Kallan forced the words past the lump.

"B-B-Bergen, I…"

His mouth split into a wide grin, knowing that his reputation preceded him, and swung wide his chamber door. He stepped into the dark, cavernous sitting room and gave a look that urged her to follow.

The hearth and the candles were cold. The only light came from the moonlight that poured in from the double set of windows where Kallan glanced at the astounding view. Rivers riddled the moors of Alfheim. Fields of thick, tall grasses, the sporadic tree, and a small lake extended past the city below.

Bergen gave a guttural groan, pulling Kallan's wide-eyed worries back from the window to the berserker, who was mid-stretch. Kallan felt the moisture pooling in her hands and she did her best to concern herself with the décor instead of the man in front of her. The same lavish furs and richly carved woods found in Rune's chambers decorated Bergen's. Aside from the collection of empty flagons dumped in a corner, and the generous number of swords and daggeres strewn about, their bowers were nearly identical.

Across the fur-laden stone floor, a sliver of firelight slipped out from beneath a second door. From behind, she watched Bergen strip off his tunic and drop it to the floor as his hair fell down his bare back seconds before Kallan caught the faintest of scarring in a slit of moonlight. He paused long enough to kick off his boots and dump them to the side as he sauntered, too lax, to the bedroom. He stretched his neck and pulled on a shoulder, purposefully flexing his back with each move.

Kallan wrung her hands as Bergen neared the closed door.

"B-Bergen."

Half-stripped, Bergen dropped his hand to the door's handle and paused long enough to flash a smile, obtusely aware of where her eyes lingered. He casually hooked his thumb on his pants, purposefully drawing her eyes.

"It shouldn't take long," Bergen said and watched the formidable force of the Seidkona, crumble.

Obediently, Kallan followed.

Bergen candidly lowered his eyes down her front with a delighted smile filled with wonder. "You object and yet you follow."

His grin widened, adding another shade of red to Kallan's complexion. The door creaked as Bergen pushed against the oak. Light from the bedchamber poured into the sitting room. She debated returning to her room or running straight to the stables for Astrid, riding out, and putting as much distance as she could between her and Rune's brother.

Stepping aside, Bergen extended an arm and invited her inside. The light spilled over the tips of her boots, beckoning her. With a furrowed brow, she peered in, catching the moving shadows. She took a step and found Geirolf's face first. He grinned happily, multiplying her confusion as she stepped into Bergen's bedchamber. The round room of the west tower glowed with the warmth of the hearth fire.

With her heart pounding, Kallan shifted a suspicious brow and rounded the corner of the door. In that instant, she gasped.

"Gudrun?"

The old woman smiled, her eyes brimming with tears.

Forgetting to breathe, Kallan sprinted across Bergen's bower to his bed, where she fell into Gudrun's arms. She shook as she sobbed, clutching so desperately to her mother's mother, who returned her embrace.

Daggon's giant hand cradled Kallan's face like an affectionate father suddenly holding a daughter he once believed dead, planting a kiss on the top of her head.

With shaking hands, Gudrun lifted Kallan from her lap and cupped her slender face, lifting her eyes to her own. Tears streamed down the old woman's pale cheeks and she grinned widely at the girl.

Daggon slid his palm down from the top of Kallan's head to her cheek, coaxing her eyes to him.

"My lady," he breathed. Kallan fell into him and he held his king's daughter. "My dearest lady," he muttered and kissed the top of her head again.

Looking at Daggon, Kallan choked on a gasp at the collection of gashes that gouged the right side of his face. Raising her hand to his face, Kallan gently traced the largest of his scars from his temple to the prominence of his jaw. His warm, amber eyes glowed with the smile buried within the tumult of his beard and he pressed her hand to his scarred face.

"I dreamed…" Kallan tried to explain the barrage of dreams that had filled her sleep for nearly two moons. "What happened?" Kallan asked in a breath.

"I'm fine," Daggon said. "Everyone is just fine."

His words were all she needed.

Overcome with relief, Kallan fell into his arms and sobbed, shaking as she clung to his neck, unconvinced he was real enough to be there should she wake.

Gudrun's gaze shifted to Bergen through the flood of tears as she softly rubbed Kallan's back.

"Thank you," she whispered.

Bergen returned a single nod from the threshold, where he leaned with his arms crossed, unable to take his eyes from Kallan. She held onto Gudrun until her tears subsided and she was composed enough to lift herself from his embrace.

Brushing away the tears, Kallan immediately faced Bergen, each hand still clutching Gudrun and Daggon.

"Why?" Kallan asked.

"Torunn's idea," Bergen said, pointing to the castle's keeper beside Geirolf. Both stood, hidden in the shadows against the wall.

Kallan turned to Torunn, dressed in her nightgown and dressing gown with her hair tied back in a tight braid down her back. She sported a grin to match Bergen's. The dried salt lines that trailed each cheek matched her reddened eyes.

"You mean to ask why," Torunn said and Kallan nodded.

The key keeper sighed.

"Rune has a stubbornness that was only outmatched by his father. When he thinks he is right, there is no changing his mind. I watched you long enough to know he was wrong about this."

Kallan looked from the key keeper to the old man and the berserker. The berserker. The legendary Dark One who wore the scar she had given him like a badge. She needed to talk to Rune. She needed to sort this out no matter who this Borg was.

"Help me again," Kallan pleaded, her eyes suddenly infused with a strength the Ljosalfar hadn't seen before. The corner of Torunn's mouth tightened with a suppressed smile and she matched Kallan's determination.

"What do you need?" Torunn's eyes gleamed with mischief, sending chills down Geirolf and Bergen's backs. Both released a breath of relief once they realized it was meant for Rune.

With a calculated precision, Kallan grinned, drawing everyone's attention to her.

"Rune refuses to speak to me. He insists on waiting for a traitor to show himself in a week's time."

"Traitor?" Daggon said, suddenly alert.

"Later," Kallan said as Torunn interjected her piece. "But there's no guarantee—"

"With me here, he may not show at all," Kallan said. "We can't wait."

"What did you have in mind?" Bergen asked.

"Tell Rune I've ordered you to release Gudrun and Daggon."

Torunn gasped as Geirolf guffawed at the proposal. Daggon sat, delightfully amused at Kallan's ambitions while Gudrun proudly beamed.

"You want us to do what?" Torunn asked.

"They are here now," Kallan said, cool headed. "House them wherever you need, if you must, so long as Rune believes I've released them."

"Now, one moment, lass," Geirolf said. "It's us who takes the heat if this goes awry."

"Tell him I overpowered you."

"Bergen…" Geirolf studied the lax form still leaning in the doorway. "What do you think of this?"

The fire crackled patiently as Bergen kept his thoughts his own for a while longer, pondering the proposal thoroughly while everyone awaited his word.

"Rune is convinced the answer to his problem is to ignore Kallan." Bergen shifted his gaze from Geirolf to Kallan, awaiting a protest that didn't come. "He intends on sending her back to Lorlenalin when the city is safe for its queen's return."

The color drained from Kallan's cheeks.

"He plans to commence diplomacy through a series of letter heads and ambassadors," Bergen continued. "The problem is, once he thinks he's right, there's no bending him. But I've watched him." Bergen shifted his attention to Geirolf. "I've watched them." Bergen nodded, indicating Kallan and Rune. "There's a reason why he refuses to see her. She gets to him. She can break him. If he wants peace so badly, he's going to have to do this with her, or not at all."

"Surely he doesn't believe settling this matter can be done without a meeting of those involved," Daggon interjected, while Geirolf mulled over Bergen's proposal.

"He does," Bergen said, still holding his arms across his bare chest, "and he's convinced he can do it by shoving Kallan out of the way."

Daggon barked an open laugh, shaking his head in hopelessness.

"Good luck with that," Gudrun bid.

Kallan flashed a scowl to Gudrun.

"I say we do it," Bergen declared, studying each face, giving each a chance to voice their objections. "We've all talked to him," he said. "None of us have the weight to go against him with the same level of effectiveness as Kallan. I say we use that to our advantage."

"And if he doesn't budge," Geirolf asked, peering from his corner at Bergen. "What then?"

Bergen grinned widely, hoping the opportunity would present itself.

"We try harder."

CHAPTER TWENTY-FOUR

Rune stared at the ceiling for as long as he could postpone the day. The first of morning's light flooded his room. Sighing, he rolled onto his stomach and buried his face in his pillow along with his discouragements.

"Rune?"

The click of his sitting room door accompanied Geirolf's voice. Rune gave a grunt that confirmed he heard.

"Rune," Geirolf called from the doorway.

"What did she do now, Geirolf?" Rune spoke into his pillow, muffling the words.

The question stopped Geirolf in his place, leaving him stunned at the random question.

"I just thought you'd like to know," Geirolf said upon entering the room, "she's released the prisoners."

Rune turned his body around, throwing the pillow to the floor as he sat up, his mouth agape.

"She what?"

"She gave the order first thing this morning," Geirolf said. "Bergen complied and granted her request after she made mention of frying his balls off with that lightning of hers."

"Son of a—"

Rune threw the furs off his bed and scoured the floor for his trousers all the while unleashing a slew of curses.

"She's in her sitting room enjoying her breakfast if you're looking to have a word," Geirolf offered as he watched Rune force a boot on the wrong foot followed by the other, not bothering with the laces.

"She?" Rune seethed as his second boot forced him to take a seat. "Oh no," he said. "I'll not play steward to that...that... Where's Bergen?"

Geirolf repressed a smile, but held a gleam in his eye.

"With the lady."

Rune's foot hit the floor with a thud and Rune sat, staring at Geirolf.

"Should I have Torunn make up a place setting for you?" Geirolf asked, mustering his most innocent sounding tone. "They're dining in Kallan's solar."

Rune sat for a long moment, contemplating his next move. After that moment, he laced his boots.

"Take word to Bergen. Have him meet me in the war room immediately."

On the landing between his bower and the war room, Bergen forced the grin from his face. He didn't doubt that Geirolf had not failed to mention Kallan's additional company at breakfast and wallowed gleefully at the range of assumptions Rune would have made in the last hour. Preparing for an ambush, Bergen blew a sigh and pushed the door of the war room open.

With a strut that defied Rune's station, Bergen sauntered across the stone floor to the center tables were Rune poured at maps and letters. Bergen hated this room. The high ceilings entombed the room in a ceremonial glow that permanently harbored the oppressive arrogance of the elite authority belonging to the crown and his brother. *Thank Freyr for that*, Bergen thought. The hearth crackled behind the table, adding to the room's stuffiness.

"Where are they?"

The room carried Rune's voice with a cold that made Bergen ache for the warmth of his bed and the nearest wench.

"Who?" Bergen asked naivly, putting as much discomfort on Rune as the room bestowed onto him.

Rune peered up from the table with the same fitful eyes from their childhood, rather than the pompous glare of a king.

"Don't play this game with me, Bergen. I know too well you had something to do with this. The whole thing reeks of conspiracy."

"Conspiracy?"

Rune straightened his back, preparing for battle.

"Perhaps you've made more enemies than you've realized," Bergen suggested.

"Bergen—"

"Why don't you ask her?" he asked, his irritation diminishing his better intentions. Rune slammed his fist to the table.

"Damn it, Bergen! Why couldn't you leave this alone?"

Sincerity blanketed Bergen's face, forcing the cold of his black eyes still as they burrowed into Rune.

"You didn't have to see her writhing with agony when I told her she wasn't allowed to speak to her kin…or you."

Rune huffed.

"Clearly you have no idea what horrors that girl harbors," Bergen said, forcing back a smirk.

"I don't—"

Bergen watched the fire burn in Rune's eyes as he scrambled to keep his composure.

"I watched it burrow its ugly head into her for nearly an entire moon!" Rune said.

"Clearly, the message was lost on you."

A cool annoyance settled over Rune as he glared at Bergen from across the room.

"Since when do you care for the Seidkona who bestowed that mark upon your brow?"

"Since you forced her under my guard, where I've watched the Seidkona break from the torment of her own benevolence!" Bergen said, eternally amused by the rage he evoked in Rune.

They both huffed and spent their best glowers for the occasion.

"And what of you?" Bergen asked, easing back on his own temper. "When did you come to care for the queen who slaughtered our people?"

Refusing to answer the question posed, Rune stomped to one of the windows. The sky stretched beyond the forests in the north. He listened to Bergen's footfall as he came to stand at his side, where he always seemed to be.

"I understand why you refused her council," Bergen said. "But to ban her from seeing her own kin… That extends to a branch of cruelty—"

"Until I can determine which of her kin has lent aid to Borg's cause, I suspect all of them," Rune said, refusing to let Bergen finish that accusation.

"And now?"

Rune met Bergen's eye.

"The old woman is innocent," Rune grumbled, displeased.

"Gudrun?" Bergen asked.

"We call her by name now?"

With a furrowed brow and their game forgotten, Bergen and Rune exchanged frowns and returned to the view.

"Gudrun is a seer," Rune said suddenly. Bergen snapped his gaze from the window.

"Did—"

"I already asked," Rune answered before Bergen could get the question out.

Sadly, Rune shook his head and gazed at Bergen.

"She couldn't See," he said.

Bergen furrowed his brow and returned his attention to the view.

The sky was clear and free of both fog and cloud that morning.

"What would cause a seer to not See?" Bergen thought aloud.

◦⤺ ⤻◦

Kallan moved her arms with the trained efficiency of a swordsman as she wielded her Seidr in and up and around, surrounding herself in strings of gold while taking great care to thread the strands of Seidr in between the fronds and plants in the solar. While Daggon studied the progress of Kallan's position and her improved form, Gudrun scrutinized the blue flames Kallan coddled in her palms that fed the golden threads.

As Kallan finished gliding through the kata, she extinguished her flame, released her Seidr, which settled around her, and straightened her posture beside the table laden with breakfast trays.

"And you say the Naejttie had found it?" Gudrun asked gravely.

Kallan was quick to nod.

"Halda said they found the Seidi years ago."

"And when she spoke," Gudrun asked, "whatever she said doubled the Seidr in size?"

Kallan nodded.

"Never mind the Seidr," Daggon interjected. "You said the animals were twice their usual size?"

"Thrice," Kallan corrected.

Daggon blew a breath of incredulity.

"Could you make out what she said?" Gudrun asked. Kallan shook her head and Gudrun gave a displeased hum, pulling her thoughts inward.

As they ate their breakfast around the table, Geirolf and Torunn listened quietly to Kallan's tale of the Seidi filled with giant plants and animals. Kalla recalled how she and Rune had met a Naejttie who led them to a Seidi, and how her words procured a fountain of Seidr and bilrost formed.

"What is it, Gudrun?" Daggon asked, eager to hear the silent dealings Gudrun amassed in her head.

After a while, she sighed.

"A Seidi is an area of sacred ground," Gudrun explained. "To find one is…" She ran through a collection of choice words and debated saying 'impossible.' "… rare," she finished.

Slowly, Gudrun began as if systematically selecting each word.

"Centuries ago, there were more Seidi before the Vanir went through and destroyed them all. Fearing the Aesir would gain further access to the Seidr, they buried them. I haven't seen one myself in nearly a thousand years."

"Where do they come from?" Torunn asked.

Gudrun sighed again, her mind still preoccupied with something she didn't dare give voice to.

"Kallan was right to call it a spring," Gudrun said. "Like new mead bursting old water skins, the Seidr builds until it bursts from the thread lines beneath."

Daggon thought for a long moment, watching carefully as Gudrun pursed her dry lips. She was holding back and skirting around too much to be honest.

There was something she was intentionally not saying.

Gudrun tried a different approach when four blank stares looked back at her.

"When the snows thaw and the ground can't hold the excess supply, springs emerge, seeping from the main water source. Travelling clans in the Southern Deserts dig wells down to that water supply. The Seidr is the same."

"So there was a surplus of Seidr," Kallan concluded, "causing it to overflow and spill out into the Seidi." Kallan furrowed her brow. "But where would the excess Seidr come from to cause a spring to emerge?"

Before Gudrun could scrounge up an answer, the door of Kallan's sitting room whined open, drawing their attention to Bergen, who slogged across the sitting room toward the solar.

"Well?" Torunn asked, too eager for Bergen to reach them.

He shrugged, pursing his lips.

"He refuses to see her," he said.

The room filled with simultaneous sighs.

"Alright," Kallan said, puffing up her chest with a bout of readiness. Gudrun and Daggon exchanged a pair of grins. "Dismiss the castle's staff."

"What?" Geirolf barked as Torunn spat, "Are you mad?"

"Just for a day," Kallan said. "Leave Rune to his keep…alone."

"The castle gets mighty cold this time of year, Kallan," Geirolf said.

Kallan grinned with a slyness worthy of Bergen.

"That's the idea."

"Kallan, you don't know what you ask," Torunn said.

"Don't I?" Kallan asked, maintaining her grin. "Have I not my own keep to run?"

Gudrun returned to her meal. Daggon stretched his arms up over his head as he leaned back in his chair.

"Hold off," Bergen cut in as Geirolf and Torunn moved to rebut.

All attention turned to Bergen. Everyone was silent for the moment as he mulled over Kallan's proposition. After a moment, he met Torunn's eyes and nodded.

"Do it."

"Bergen—" Geirolf said.

"The entire staff?" Torunn interjected.

"The moment he goes to sleep tonight, let the fires burn out," Bergen said without a glimpse of humor.

Silence permeated the room as they looked from one to the other.

"Well..." Torunn broke the indecision with a heavy sigh as she pushed herself up from the chair. "I have a lot of work to do, if tomorrow we're doing nothing."

With a prolonged groan, Geirolf followed Torunn's lead and forced himself to his feet. "I'll pass the word among the barracks."

With matching grins, Kallan and Bergen watched as they took their leave.

"What will you have us do, Bergen?" Daggon asked when the door latched behind them.

With a grin that seemed to widen by the minute, Bergen looked to Daggon.

"Go pick some fights in the barracks. That'll keep Rune running all day."

CHAPTER TWENTY-FIVE

A chill gnawed Rune's bare shoulders. Half-asleep and disgruntled, he pulled at the furs, slapping the edge of the blankets as he yanked them higher. Buried deep within the pocket of warmth, Rune groaned with a stubborn irritation that wouldn't ebb. The unmistakable snap of cold bit the top of his head left exposed to the open air.

He tried to remember if he had been hunting with Bergen, and tossed the idea from his head before foraging for a more reasonable explanation. Wallowing in his bad temperament, he recalled the evening prior and, in a torrent of temper, Rune whipped off the pile of furs and stomped to his feet, clenching his teeth against the cold that pierced his flesh.

Eager to purge his miserable mood at the first passerby, Rune looked about and grew more irate at the abnormal lack of people present. His eyes shifted to the cold hearth and its pile of white ash void of flame and heat.

Too cold to emerge from the blankets without a shirt, Rune grabbed a fistful of furs from his bed and yanked them violently over his shoulders, grumbling a slew of curses under his breath as he stomped to his sitting room.

The second hearth, as cold as the first, stoked his rage all the more.

"Torunn!" he bellowed, then listened.

The corridor was unusually quiet.

Ready to fire off at the first person he saw, Rune stomped to the door and ripped it open then stopped. The hall was empty.

The usual warmth and laughter that always seemed to ascend from the Great Hall with the myriad of scents from the kitchens was oddly absent. Hunger clamped his stomach and Rune realized the lack of smells from the Great Hall probably meant a lack of breakfast.

"Torunn!" he roared again and waited.

Echoes reverberated down the hall past Kallan's room.

Kallan.

Rune narrowed his eyes into threatening slits he wished her to see and, crinkling his nose, slammed his door. He wasn't sure how she had done it, but he had a suspicion forming in the depths of his gut. Aside from Lorlenalin's palace brat, he was the only one left in the keep. Deciding he would deny her the glory she sought, he tightened his grip on the furs and stomped back to his bedchamber.

With more fuss than he would have cared for, Rune started a fire and found some clothes. With a fresh slew of curses, he grumbled loudly down to the kitchens, where he confirmed the absolute vacancy of the keep. He rummaged through a collection of bags, located a handful of apples and some dried meats, and returned to the Great Hall after grabbing an extra two helpings of mead.

Back in his room, the fire crackled, fighting back the chill. Rune dumped the armload of food and drinks onto his bed and passed through the back door of his bedchamber, across the landing to the war room. Within five minutes, he had found the wax, the charts, the maps, and a collection of sealed letters containing the most recent reports of Gunir's imports and exports.

"Joren!"

Nothing but echoes answered.

He began filling his arms with sheets of blank vellum and a bifolium.

"Geirolf!"

Silence.

With a huff, he collected the last of his supplies and stomped back to his room. Beside his food, Rune dumped his maps and sealing wax, and reviewed his progress. Then he stomped to his window and stared out over the barren courtyard.

The battlement doors were closed. The barracks, too quiet. Even the workers constructing the stables had abandoned their work.

"Bergen!" Rune projected over the deadened courtyard.

His echo was the only reply.

Pulling his head back inside, Rune scowled at the pile on his bed. The fire had died down some and he scowled at the thought that he would have to haul armloads of firewood up from the cellars.

Rune gazed again out the window and furrowed his brow. A lone speck, cloaked and suspicious, glided across the stone yard.

Quietly shuffling to the window, Rune took great care to stay hidden in the shadows of his room. At once, he recognized Kallan's dainty step. Fruits and meats from the kitchens filled a large basket she clutched protectively. A few vegetables confirmed she had also raided the castle gardens. Snarling, Rune made note to scold her later for her thievery as he watched her slip through the battlement doors.

Disgruntled, he abandoned the window and set to work, sorting through his provisions and the day's work.

Silence and solitude made up Rune's day. The only disturbance was that of a random though frequent skirmish below between Ottar and Daggon. Pleased to have found somebody, Rune made haste to the courtyard only to find Daggon standing alone in a mass of disgruntled upheaval that Rune had to contain.

He walked the keep once, searched the barracks and the stables where the horses were his only company and promptly gave up, all the while knowing Kallan was somehow behind this. More than once, Rune stood from his table and headed for Kallan's chambers, each time forcing himself back to his work with a bottle of mead. Too often, he found himself glaring at the window.

Pulling the furs closer, he gulped down an exuberant helping of mead and slammed the bottle back to the table as he pretended to look over the maps.

He ignored the passing afternoon that darkened too slowly into the evening, and often pulled at the furs around his shoulder, throwing his head back for another bout with the drink. By mid-day, he had eaten through the fruit and the meat. By the final hour of the day and the seventh mead, long after the sun settled behind the horizon, hunger forced Rune's head up from his work.

He pushed aside the map and leaned back in his chair with a tip of the inebriate. The waxing half-moon was bright this night. Forcing himself to his feet, Rune made his way across the room and quietly closed the door behind him. At the double doors of Kallan's sitting room, Rune stopped. Light emerged from the crack and he entertained the thought of breaking down her chamber door and unleashing his pent-up irritation on her.

"Should have let the damn thing kill her," Rune grumbled.

Balling his fists, he forced himself down to the kitchens for more meat and mead.

Rune descended into the dark kitchens, blackened by the late hour. Fumbling to the storeroom, he scuffed about with the slight tip of a drunk and dragged his hand along the table for direction and balance. With the bang of the door, he punched the wall, released a series of choice words he reserved for the occasion as he limped into the buttery. Upon finding the mead, he threw back his head and drowned his curses in one long sequence of gulps.

Plopping down onto a stool, Rune sighed and dropped his head back onto the wall. The kitchens were black save for the single strip of moonlight that poured in from the gardens. He stared at the rafters hidden in the dark and threw back another gulp.

"Bad day?"

The sweet affection of Torunn's voice jolted Rune from the stool.

"You!" Rune growled, wincing through the dark and still clutching the bottle. "Where is everyone? I've spent my day getting nothing done! The only one who've I've been able to find is that giant brute of a captain, who insists on picking fights with Ottar, who won't sit still long enough to ask where everyone is! Where is Bergen? Where is Geirolf?" Rune slurred loudly, granting Torunn no time to answer. "Where's my food?"

He could hear Torunn's unimpressed sigh through the dark and he squinted to see better, impatient for his eyes to adjust to the darkness, and cursed himself for not bringing a light.

"Bergen and Geirolf are hunting," Torunn said patiently. "Your food…" She looked at the shelves of the buttery and turned to the larder abundant with food. "…is beside you."

"Where're the cooks?" he slurred, already unsatisfied with whatever excuse she would give.

"Home," Torunn said.

"I am your king!" Rune barked. "What is the meaning—?"

"We were given orders by another, who was granted the power by you." Torunn's eyes sharpened as if daring Rune to challenge her and Rune secretly wished his eyes hadn't adjusted to the darkness after all.

"And so, in following her orders, we followed yours," Torunn said.

Rune grimaced as he threw back his head to take another mouthful of mead. His unyielding frown remained on Torunn as he drank.

"I want to speak to them now," Rune said. "Now!"

"No one is here to accept your summons," Torunn said. "Except Kallan."

"I rescind my order!" Rune said, thinking ahead.

Torunn's eyes narrowed into slits.

"Kallan has already given us instruction to ignore that order were you to give it." Her nostrils flared with her breath. "And we wouldn't want to disobey our king, now would we?"

Rune threw the flagon across the room. Mead splattered on the walls. Torunn held her eye unwaveringly on Rune.

"Mind your temper with me, Son of Tryggve," she said. "I maintained your father's tantrums centuries before you were born."

"I'll not have her," Rune said. "I will starve before I accept her summons."

"You just might," Torunn said.

With a whirlwind of temper, she spun on her heel and ascended the steps to the Great Hall, leaving Rune alone in the kitchens to brood.

CHAPTER TWENTY-SIX

The air was stiff and filled with a stagnant chill. Pulling at his tunic, Bergen stepped into the cold, dark corridor and closed the door to his brother's bower behind him. Immediately, he stopped dead at the old woman, who seemed to appear from the air. Dressed in a chemise and dressing gown, Gudrun held two fingers upright, the tips of which fed a single orange Seidr-flame that flickered and danced with a personality all its own. Orange and black streaks decorated the wall, submerging her ancient face in a dangerous glare and catching a bit of the gold in her eye as she spoke.

"What's the report?" she asked, keeping her voice low.

"He's asleep," Bergen said.

Gudrun nodded, keeping her thoughts private.

"Geirolf came back with you, I presume?" Gudrun asked.

"He's in the larder now hanging the hares," Bergen said.

"I'll let Torunn know to send the servants," she said after a moment and quietly, swiftly shuffled down the hall. A cold lingered behind her and her Seidr flame flickered. The light shuddered.

"Gudrun."

Gudrun paused and gazed at the berserker.

"I spoke to Rune," Bergen said.

A soft smirk pulled at the corner of Gudrun's mouth.

"You did."

"He said you're a Volva." Bergen's throat was dry. "That you have the Sight. You can See."

The Seidr flame flickered and Bergen studied her eyes, expecting a denial. Instead, Gudrun's smirk grew into a small grin.

"I am," Gudrun said. "I do. I can."

Bergen clenched his fist.

"How much can you see?" he asked. "What do you know?"

Amused, the old woman retained her smile and narrowed her steady glare.

"You brothers… You share a lot." The gold in her eye glistened. "He asked the same of me."

"Did you lie?" Bergen asked and exhaled sharply through his nose. "Can you really See…or is it a guise for money?" Bergen's breath was increasing. "Some Seidkona do that. They lie and cheat and take your money, leaving you with false premonitions."

Gudrun kindly peered through the slits in her eyes.

"You doubt my skill?"

The chill in the air thickened.

"I see you," Gudrun said. "Is that enough?" Bergen inhaled deeply. His large chest expanded as he stared down the short woman. "No?"

Darkness blanketed her face.

"Your eyes are different," she said. "Like the Dvergar. I know you weren't born that way. I know they once matched the silver-blue eyes of your brother."

Bergen widened the black of his eyes and Gudrun entered his mind as she peered through the dark and the flickering light.

"I see the Dvergar prisons and the cage that held you," Gudrun whispered. "I see the darkness that kept you, and the girl."

Bergen's palms shook as they beaded with sweat.

"And a Dvergr dying on the floor beneath your blood-soaked hands clutching the elding blade you plunged into her heart… That blade, in fact."

Paying no mind to his white fists, Gudrun glanced at the elding handle of a dagger sheathed at his waist.

"I know, you loved her once," she said, "I know that she—"

"Enough!" Bergen barked and, clawing at his back, he tore his shirt over his head as if the tunic itself suffocated him, as the black of those walls closed in, as the stench of those halls ate his skin. And a perfect, pale face turned up at him and her eyes implored in that moment as he watched the life drain from them.

Panting, Bergen fell to the floor on his knees. His bare shoulders shook in Gudrun's light and he dug his fingers into his eyes. He wiped the sweat from his brow and checked his hands twice for blood. Her blood. Running his shaking hand through his hair, he regained control of his breath.

"Very well," Gudrun obliged, saying no more on the matter. "Is there something else you'd like to know?"

Pinching the bridge of his nose, Bergen closed his eyes.

"Swann," he said and raised his gaze to Gudrun.

"Swann," Gudrun repeated, shaking her head as Bergen picked himself up off the floor.

"My sister," he said and waited for the Volva to speak.

"If your brother told you that he spoke with me," Gudrun said, "surely he told you my answer." Sadly, she shook her head. "I can not see your sister's killer. I'm sorry."

Turning to leave, Gudrun hung her head low. The orange of the light moved with her.

"Please," Bergen said.

Cold streams of sweat streaked his face as Gudrun looked back to see.

"What he did to her..." He shook his head. "How we found her... What it did to us... Please."

"I can not See," she said and took another step.

"How?" Bergen called after her. "How can a Seer not See?"

Gudrun sighed and stopped in the hall.

"Do you know how a Volva's Sight works?" she asked.

Gazing up at the berserker, she ensured she had his attention. Bergen shook his head.

"I can look through your eyes," Gudrun said. "Past the mask you wear, and see your memories there." Bergen held his breath as she continued. "I can follow the memories buried in the Seidr."

"The Seidr?" he repeated, furrowing his brow. "It has memories?"

"It lives," Gudrun whispered. "It remembers."

"And with it, you can See," he asked, doing his best to forget his own ancient memories.

Gudrun smiled gently.

"But what would cause a Seer to not See?" he asked.

Gudrun shook her head.

"I don't know," she replied. "It requires a great amount of Seidr and strength to block a Seer's ability and more so to block only certain visions of the Seidr while keeping other aspects and visions functioning. No one—"

At once, her eyes fogged over mid-thought as if coming to an understanding. And just as quickly, an empty blankness passed over her face, and the Seidr flame on her fingers was lost, plunging them in the darkness and the moonlit corridor.

"Gudrun?" Bergen asked. "Gudrun, are you alright?"

He clutched her arms, giving her a shake. The fog in her eyes cleared and Gudrun gasped.

"Yes." She sighed as if she had just awakened from a deep, dream-filled sleep. "I'm sorry, dear boy, I forgot what I was saying."

Bergen furrowed his brow.

"Can all Seidkona See?"

"Only some," she said as if there had been no interruption at all. "Very few. Almost none."

Gudrun shuffled to leave.

"Can Kallan?"

Gudrun shook her head.

"She has never... No..." Gudrun sighed. "There was a time, when she was much younger, that her mother and I believed her Sight would surpass mine."

Bergen cocked his head, assessing Gudrun's words with more caution than she was aware.

"What happened?" he asked.

"It started small," Gudrun explained. "She couldn't See one particular thing, then another. After a while, it faded until it stopped and then she could See no more."

Content with her answer, Bergen gave a nod, concluding his questions as he mulled over each word. Sleep replaced the massive weight that seemed to drift and he felt himself wishing for his bed.

"Goodnight, Bergen." Gudrun grinned and shuffled herself toward Kallan's bower.

"Gudrun."

The old woman paused, knowing the request before he spoke it.

"Please," he bade. "About the girl… Please. Tell no one."

A gentle grin stretched the ancient wrinkles on Gudrun's face and she smiled kindly.

"I keep many secrets for many people," she assured. "Yours are no different."

Bergen tried to nod his appreciation, but failed as the click of Kallan's door filled the hallway.

CHAPTER TWENTY-SEVEN

H e said what?"

Kallan slammed her palms onto the breakfast table as she stood amid the outbursts of Geirolf, Gudrun, Daggon, and Bergen. At the door of Kallan's solar, Torunn nodded regretfully as she relayed her conversation with Rune from the night before.

"Where is he now, Torunn?" Geirolf asked as he raced for the next plan of combat.

"In the war room with his breakfast," Torunn said.

"Another day." Bergen rose to his feet, rearing to execute. "Indefinitely... until he breaks."

As if in response, Kallan stood suddenly and snatched up an assortment of fruits, breads, and berries. After piling the food onto her tray, Kallan took up the platter and breezed her way to the door. Her skirts billowed in a flourish of green.

Wide-eyed, Kallan's troupe watched her attempt to turn the door handle while balancing her breakfast tray.

"Kallan?" Daggon called.

"Where are you going, lass?" Geirolf asked as Kallan's littlest finger caught the handle just right.

Kallan pulled the door open.

"To Rune's room."

In a great wave, Daggon, Geirolf, and Bergen were up as Gudrun, smiling with delight, poured herself a cup of tea.

"Oh, you've got to let me in on this one," Bergen said, beaming with amusement.

"He wants to ignore me," Kallan said, "then I'll go where he can't avoid me."

With the hem of her skirts vanishing into the corridor, Kallan swept down the hall toward Rune's bower. Geirolf and Bergen exchanged glances with Daggon then looked to Torunn, who looked as surprised by Kallan's directness as they did.

With a smirk, Gudrun blew on her steaming cup of herbs.

"This reminds me of the time I courted a Seidr Wielder back when I was foolish enough to do such things," she said. "Stubborn old thing he was. Smart too. He could run Seidr spells around me that left me dumbfounded out of my wits. Could brew a spell better than any Seidr User I had seen in my days too. But stupid where interests of the heart were concerned. Couldn't take a hint if you tied it to an angry crab and shoved it down his pants."

Gudrun took a loud, slow sip from her tea, indifferent to the four sets of eyes fixed on her.

"Should we tell him?" Geirolf proposed.

A four-part chorus of harmonized pshaws filled the room.

"No," Daggon exclaimed as Bergen said, "I'm not."

"Don't," Torunn added. "He wants to be so stubborn... It serves him right."

⊱ ⊰

Rune stared from the war room window, his mind too cluttered to appreciate the evening's clear sky. Moonlight blanketed the greens of the forests in a silver blue, but his thoughts were too distracted to see. The door creaked open and Rune turned from the window to Joren.

"You wanted to see me," Joren said from across the room.

"Yes. Come." Rune motioned to Joren, inviting him to stand at the table. "How long have you been in my services, Joren?"

"A long time, sire. I entered your army shortly after..."

Joren's voice trailed off.

"Speak plainly, Joren," Rune said.

"After the Massacre of Austramonath, sire."

"Seven hundred years," Rune muttered. If he was disturbed at the mention of the massacre, he didn't show it.

"Nearly," Joren said.

Rune exhaled and leaned over the map splayed out before him.

"I've reviewed the troops a hundred times over," Rune said as he studied the span of land southwest of Lake Wanern. He tapped a finger to the north of Gunir where it rested on the name 'West Man Land.'

"Before the war with the Dokkalfar, our numbers exceeded thousands," Rune said. "Hundreds of thousands. Those numbers were all that allowed us to stand a chance against the Dokkalfar's advances in blacksmithing and metallurgy. Now, with Roald's men at the Southern Keep, Thorold's army vanquished in the north, and what little remains of Bergen's army here in Gunir, we barely have fifteen thousand."

Rune let out a long sigh with all the years and all the weariness of those years.

Joren remained silent, taking in the information his king provided.

"It is with great fortune that the Dokkalfar lost their queen when they did. We don't have the numbers left to stand against them."

Rune stared at the peninsula that was Dan's Mork on the other side of the Kattegat.

"Forkbeard," he whispered and dropped a finger to the peninsula. "That Dani has hardly sat quiet in his halls since he snagged the rule from his father ten years ago. Since then, we've been forced to triple our defenses southwest of the Wanern. I sit back anxiously anticipating his next move while that Dani sits ever vigilant, marinating in his insatiable greed, waiting for the chance to extend his powers to Alfheim. If only I could be certain…"

Rune dropped his arms and stood as he returned to the window were he stared up at the night sky.

"If Forkbeard remains unmoved until things settle with the Dokkalfar, then I could pull in the troops without fear of where the Dani may move. If we ally ourselves with Lorlenalin's queen—" He couldn't bring himself to say Kallan's name. "—we would benefit so much from that alliance."

"What will you have me do?" Joren asked, ready to follow where his king may lead.

Rune returned to the table and looked over the map from Gunir to Lorlenalin to Dan's Mork across the Kattegat.

"Centuries ago," Rune said, "you came to me with news of a spy." Rune raised his eyes to Joren. "Borg," Rune said, pondering the name with a certain distaste that wrinkled his nose. "He stayed to himself, kept in the shadows, and provided intelligence in exchange for his privacy. Until now, I have never questioned his terms. Until now, I have never had the need to do so."

"What does my king wish of me?" Joren asked.

"Tell me everything," Rune said. "Where you meet him, when you meet him, who he is, and how. Everything."

Joren furrowed his brow and nodded slowly.

"If he finds out," Joren gently reminded the king. "If he knows—"

"I'm aware of the risks," Rune assured him. "And in a fortnight, none of that will matter."

Joren inhaled deeply and thought for a moment as he collected his centuries of data while Rune granted him the silence and waited. Several minutes had passed before Joren spoke.

"Borg comes here once every fortnight," he said. "Every full and new moon, he finds me."

Rune cocked a curious brow.

"He finds you."

"I never know exactly when," Joren said. "No meeting is ever prearranged. That was one of the stipulations. He's cautious, and this sort of…arrangement has always ensured his privacy."

"And you are his only contact," Rune said. "No one else has ever seen him? No one else knows?"

"Well…" Joren chewed the inside of his cheek. "That's not entirely true."

A wide-eyed fury flickered in Rune's eye.

"Bergen knows."

"Bergen," Rune sighed. "Why am I not surprised?"

"Quite by accident, I assure you," Joren said.

Rune waited fixedly for Joren to embellish.

"We've always complied with Borg's conditions per your instructions…" Joren hastened through a flourish of words.

"How does Bergen know?" Rune asked, deepening his frown.

Joren returned to chewing the inside of his cheek, doing his best to sort out the occurrence. He rushed through the explanation, eager to catch Rune up on the details.

"It was shortly after Bergen's return…shortly after you decided to end the conflict. King Eyolf had already declined peace and Borg had just established contact. I was on the East Road from Swann Dalr. It couldn't have been our third meeting. We were still precarious with the details delivered from our last meeting and were waiting for Borg's initial bit of news to check out. That day on the East Road, he provided King Eyolf's position and strategy…that Eyolf would be declaring war."

"And it checked out," Rune confirmed as he remembered it.

"Of course," Joren said. "We were suspicious at first and unsure if it was a trap, but Borg came through. A few weeks later, Borg showed up again with another lead."

"Then another," Rune added, coming to understand fully how the situation developed.

"He gained our confidence in no time," Joren said, "And he's been finding me ever since."

Rune crinkled his brow in thought, ensuring he missed nothing.

"And each meeting was unplanned," Rune surmised, looking to Joren to confirm.

"Every time," Joren said. "Unplanned and unscheduled, but predictable. Once every fortnight around every new and full moon, Borg showed himself."

"And Bergen…" Rune asked, pushing the topic back to the question. The scout looked as if he would throw up, but continued nonetheless.

"Right, Bergen. Well, you know how Bergen is…" Joren paused to allow Rune to comment.

He didn't.

"There was an afternoon when I was out on the road and Borg approached me. We spoke and exchanged the newest information and he left. The conversation went as well as it could, but when I started on down the road, once I was sure Borg was out of sight, Bergen appeared."

Rune arched a pensive brow.

"He was…" Joren rolled his eyes in search of the words. "Entertaining someone."

"Of course he was," Rune said.

"Bergen was heading back to Gunir himself, when he chanced upon our meeting," Joren said.

"How did Borg take the news when he found out?"

"Oh, he never did," Joren said quickly. "Don't get me wrong. Bergen and I fretted for a good long season before we realized Borg had come, been seen, and departed without being the wiser."

Rune stared at him unimpressed, bored, angry beyond expression... Joren couldn't tell,

"Afterwards, Bergen and I agreed to say nothing," Joren said. "The fewer who knew, the less likely it would get out…and Bergen feared losing a powerful asset over such a stupid mistake."

Rune gazed out the window to the night sky.

"The moon will be full in three days' time."

Joren nodded.

"Yes."

"I don't expect him to stay long or come quietly," Rune said. "Part of me expects him to not come at all, with Kallan's absence."

Joren waited in silence as Rune slowly walked back to the window.

"Is he ever late?" Rune asked.

"He is always punctual."

Rune nodded, at last pleased with something Joren said.

"I'll have a small guard of my best men following you that day," Rune said. "You will not be alone…not for a moment."

Joren nodded.

"A handful of men will be entrusted to you. You are to describe his appearance. Teach them to recognize him. Too many questions hang in the balance whose answers could resolve many issues."

Joren exhaled as he recalled the voice always buried at a distance in the shadows. Rune returned to the table and peered over the map. His eyes rested on the peninsula of Dan's Mork where Forkbeard occupied his throne.

"Whatever agreement we may have had with Borg is at an end," Rune said.

"This war will not continue, which makes Borg an expired asset. I need him in our custody before he realizes his time is up. He has answers I need."

A stronger tone surfaced as Rune dropped a finger to Alfheim, his eyes ever fixed on Dan's Mork.

"Forkbeard is the new threat. A foothold here in Alfheim would ensure a clear, unforeseen passage into Midgard that no other position could grant. I can't pull Roald's men from the south and leave ourselves open to an attack from Forkbeard, but I fear I have no choice. It's a risk we'll have to take."

"What will you have me do?" Joren asked.

"I hope, with our combined forces, we have a chance to stand against Forkbeard. But, sadly, this means we will have to weaken our front lines in the process."

"Why not just wait until after the alliance is secure?"

"Because I fear the Dokkalfar will make their move sooner than the alliance, and if they do, we don't stand a chance. There will be nothing left in Gunir to negotiate. No..." Rune shook his head. "We must be ready to stand together against the Dokkalfar if the need arises. Be prepared to ride out the moment Borg is in our custody. I'd have you leave now if I could afford you. Once the queen addresses Borg, it should clear up a few misunderstandings that will allow us to unite our forces against Forkbeard. We just might have the alliance my father sought to form centuries ago. With the might of Roald's army, Gunir's army, and the Dokkalfar, we might just survive this."

"As you wish," Joren said.

"Good night, Joren," Rune bid and leaned over the table once more.

"Good night."

Rune listened to the door close behind Joren and he stood a while longer over the map. With a wide yawn, he straightened his back and stretched.

Pained with exhaustion that made him long for his bed, Rune trudged out of the war room. A mild ruckus in the Hall rolled up the stairs and Rune grunted with exhaustion. Too tired to entertain but stomach twisting with hunger, he made a mental note to have Torunn bring something up from the kitchens.

Pushing open the door to his chamber, Rune glanced about the lit room and stopped dead. Splayed out on his bed, staring at the ceiling in a daze, Kallan laid waiting. Quickly, Rune took a sharp step back into the hall and quietly closed the door.

His hunger forgotten, Rune stood wide awake while subtle tufts of soft perfume wafted with him into the hall. For a moment, he forgot to be angry and argued with himself to go back in. Shaking his head, Rune battled to keep his sense about him, despite the blood draining from his brain. With clenched fists, he followed the narrow, spiraling stairs down to the Great Hall.

Rune peered around the screens passage. Relieved to find Geirolf sitting alone while taking his evening meal of boiled pork, he crossed the Hall, half-crouched to hide himself from Ottar and the barracks men. The result was an abysmally botched slink.

"Geirolf," Rune whispered as if Kallan could hear from his chambers.

With an angled brow, Geirolf turned from his stew. "Your Majesty?"

"Why is Kallan in my room?" Rune asked.

"Uh…" Geirolf shifted his eyes. "Perhaps you should ask Bergen why a girl would be in your room."

"No." Rune snapped his head to the screens passage and the side door. "How long has she been there?"

Geirolf restored his attention to his pork.

"All day from what I know."

Rune jerked his head back to Geirolf in disbelief and waited for Geirolf to move.

"Well…" Rune paused, ready for Geirolf to take action. "Get her out!"

"Rune." Geirolf dropped a hunk of meat to his plate and shifted his weight to his elbow on the table. "There are two things I've learned about women. One: You accept their illogical idiosyncrasies."

Geirolf paused to think about this for a moment.

"They're women. It can't be helped. And two…" He waited until Rune poked his head closer. "If there's one you want and she's willingly waiting in your room…" Geirolf's bottom lip quivered with annoyance. "You don't send her out!"

Rune huffed with impatience.

"I don't…" Rune lost his voice and moved on, deciding Geirolf wouldn't help him. "Where's Bergen?"

Geirolf peered over his old nose.

"Do you really want to send Bergen in there?"

Rune shifted his eye to the table in reflection. "Never mind," he added with a pat to Geirolf's back.

With a hidden smirk, Geirolf watched as Rune crept his way to the grand steps leading up to the second floor and the bedchambers.

As the heel of Rune's boot vanished up the steps, Geirolf leaped from the table and dashed down to the kitchens to Bergen, Gudrun, Daggon, and Torunn.

Rune pushed open the door to Kallan's empty bower. Her scent slammed his nose and twisted his nerves into knots. After running his hands over his face and through his hair repeatedly, he nearly ripped the belt from his waist. Dropping himself into a chair, Rune carefully leaned *Gramm* against the armrest and then unlaced his boots before tossing them to the floor.

Obtusely aware of Kallan's intent, Rune pulled off his shirt and fisted his knuckles into the cloth as he rested his arms on his knees and leaned forward in the chair. Wondering for the moment why he wasn't in his own chambers with her, he exhaled and leaned back in the chair.

At once, deciding he was too unnerved to eat, he threw his shirt to the floor and made his way to her bedroom. A wave of her scent engulfed him at the threshold and Rune released a loud, exasperated growl. Fighting back the urge to peel off his skin, he fell onto the furs of her bed, not daring to crawl beneath her blankets.

It was a long, wearisome wait before his body finally allowed him to sleep.

CHAPTER TWENTY-EIGHT

Kallan pressed her fingers against the stone of Rune's window. Her body shook as she stared at the moon, pooling all her anger into her hands. Torunn, Geirolf, Daggon, Bergen, and Gudrun watched in silent worry. Her breathing was erratic.

"How far do I have to push?" Kallan's growl trembled with anger.

"You could wait here," Torunn said.

"Or the war room," Geirolf suggested, knowing Rune's contempt for changed habitat.

Bergen crossed his arms over his bare chest and leaned in the doorway. "You know him as well as I. Regardless of where she goes, he'll only skirt around her."

"He pushes her away with as much resolve as you couple with one," Geirolf grumbled.

Anger glowed in Kallan's eye as she turned from the window and settled her attention on Rune's brother as if to rebut. But she stopped, suddenly becoming conscious of Bergen's wide, bare shoulders and muscular frame. The room grew quiet as one by one they noticed Kallan's enlightened interests. Kallan dragged her gaze from Bergen's waist to his torso, to his face where Bergen met her eyes.

With a revived enthusiasm in her step, Kallan held his eye and moved toward Bergen, sweeping right by him as she made her way to the back door of Rune's bower. Eagerly, she yanked open the door. Kallan was across the hall and throwing open the door to the war room by the time the others jumped in step behind her.

Wide-eyed comprehension obscured Bergen's face and he doubled his pace.

"Kallan!" Bergen beckoned as she marched herself across the room, past the table strewn with maps and to the door on the other side.

"Kallan!" Bergen called again, desperate to keep up.

Surprised to find it unlocked, Kallan threw open the door to Bergen's chambers and slipped inside his sitting room.

"Kallan!" Bergen kept on her heel.

With jaunty amusement, she spun at the center of his sitting room, forcing Bergen to balance himself unnaturally to prevent falling into her. He shook his head in protest. "It's my hide on the line. He won't come after you. He'll hunt me down and peg my ass to his target!"

"Not if you're with me, he won't." Kallan grinned slyly. "Besides," she said, looking him over once more. "You're not actually bedding me."

She spun on her heel, sauntered through his sitting room with a skip to her step, and happily swung open the door to Bergen's bedroom.

"He won't stop long enough to hear that part!" Bergen cried as she disappeared into his room.

Kallan's troupe followed behind Bergen as she playfully dropped herself onto the foot of Bergen's bed. Her face split wide with a grin, convinced this idea would work.

"He didn't seem to mind when he offered you to double up with me that night," she argued, looking up from her boots as she freed the laces.

"He made that threat knowing you wouldn't follow through!"

Bergen watched her drop a slender boot to the floor. Her petite toes wiggled delightfully in the air. He clenched and unclenched his fist, fighting back the wave of images bombarding his imagination.

"Kallan, don't you think you're going a bit too far with this one?" Geirolf chimed in as she unlaced her second boot.

In answer, she dropped it to the floor beside the other.

"What about you?" Bergen barked, looking to Daggon and Gudrun, who stood in the doorway, content to watch the events unfold. "What say you?"

With a set of matching grins, Daggon and Gudrun exchanged looks.

"This is a woman whose stallion is named 'Astrid'," Daggon said.

Kallan threw herself back onto Bergen's bed.

"Who learned the spells I taught her with the sole purpose of slipping past the guards," Gudrun said with a hint of admiration.

"She mastered the swords long before she bothered with diplomacy," Daggon noted, peering down at Gudrun in fond recollection.

"And learned the Seidr only to best her father in battle..." Gudrun placed an affectionate hand on Daggon's arm as a reminder.

With a gentle nod, Daggon looked back to Bergen.

"We learned a long time ago to let Kallan go where Kallan goes," Gudrun said. "Our only purpose in teaching her was to ensure she could survive her own whims."

They all gazed at Kallan sprawled happily on Bergen's bed, her hair splayed in a mass of disorder over the pillows and furs as she stretched her arms to the sides as far as they could go.

Bergen noted the space left from the tips of her fingers to the edge of his bed and followed her hands down to her body.

"I'll get you some extra blankets, Bergen," Torunn said, taking her leave.

"Kallan," Bergen growled miserably at the contented lump on his bed. "Are you sure this isn't some ploy to finish me?"

He clenched his fists again somewhat peeved at the sight of an un-rumpled woman on his bed.

Without lifting her head from the furs, she studied the stone overhead, remembering what Rune's looked like. With a satisfied smile, she answered plainly, "Perhaps."

CHAPTER TWENTY-NINE

Outside beneath the pale moon, night blanketed Gunir. Borg stood cloaked by the Seidr and shadows. He would direct the conversation where it needed to go and had made up his mind hours ago where this day would end. He watched the Ljosalfr rise before the sun in his usual fashion. As the first of morning light crept over the trees, the Ljosalfr stepped into the morning and fed his horse then bid farewell to his sister who then lingered down the road toward the village. With hungry eyes, Borg watched the young woman and allowed his thoughts to stay with her a bit longer.

She was far from view before Borg lifted the cloaking spell and stepped into the pale, morning light. The Ljosalfr lifted his axe.

In mid-swing, Joren looked up from the freshly split wood, his face too placated to read. The axe head split through the wood, leaving its victim to fall to the ground with a series of hallowed thuds.

"You're early," Joren greeted. His heart beat so loudly, he was certain Borg could hear it.

Borg lowered his hood to reveal his dark face and one good eye. He kept his deep voice hushed with urgency. Joren forced his composure to be indifferent as he memorized the black hair, the sleek cheekbones, and pointed nose that matched the chin.

"Rumor of a capture has reached me," Borg said. "Two Dokkalfar."

Joren gulped uncomfortably, willing his temperament to relax. They hadn't expected him so soon. They weren't ready.

"The rumors are true," Joren said.

"Have you been able to identify them?" Borg wasted no time arriving to the point of his visit.

"They refuse to give us their names," Joren said, scrambling to postpone Borg's unexpected arrival.

The disappointment was apparent in Borg's eyes and Joren clambered for an idea that could prolong Borg's stay long enough to lure him to the keep.

"Refuse," Borg repeated. "So they live?"

"For now." Joren scrunched his face with an impassive show and lavished his tale up a bit. "If they are who we think they are, the king will want to trade with Lorlenalin and gain the upper hand we've been looking for."

Darkness passed over Borg's eyes.

"To make such a trade one would need to be sure," Borg said.

"One would," Joren said, keeping his composure indifferent to Borg's proposal. The Dokkalfr allowed the air to thicken between them before speaking again, forcing the words forth with natural ease.

"I know the faces of those who escaped," Borg said. "If I were to see them, I could identify them."

Exultation burst within Joren's chest as Borg's words granted him the pass he needed.

"I could make the arrangements," Joren said evenly, holding his breath with every second. His mouth was painfully dry. "When would you—"

"No," Borg said. "Now."

With a stiff nod, Joren forced a smile and handed Borg all of his cards.

"Very well."

CHAPTER THIRTY

The clatter and rumble of a fire poker stirred Rune from his disquieted sleep. He pushed the noise aside, failed, then woke with a grunt, forcing his eyes to focus in the dark.

"Torunn?" he asked through clouded sleep. "What are you doing?"

"Rune!" Torunn exclaimed with forced surprise. She rose beside the grand hearth of Kallan's bedchamber. "What are you doing in here?"

He dug the heels of his hands into his eyes, forcing the last of the sleep from them. "I needed a place to sleep," he said.

As if she didn't know, he thought.

"What was wrong with your bower?" Torunn asked stupidly.

With a sigh, Rune fell onto his back, too tired to keep himself upright, and spoke to the ceiling. "Kallan was there. I didn't feel like dealing with the fuss so I came in here seeing as how she took my room for the night."

"Begging your pardon," she interjected.

Rune stopped rubbing his face long enough to look at the key keeper.

"Kallan didn't spend the night in your bower."

Rune furrowed his brow and dropped his hand.

"Course she did. I saw her," Rune insisted. "Geirolf told me she'd been there all day."

"Well, for a couple hours, yes," Torunn said. "But she and Bergen took dinner together and…" Her voice trailed off. "She didn't stay there."

Wide-eyed, Rune leapt from the bed, with no sign that he had been asleep only moments ago.

"Where did she stay, Torunn?"

"I thought you knew," Torunn said, suddenly looking very mousy. "Kallan wanted to speak to you, and when she left, I thought—"

"Where is she, Torunn?" With every word his shoulders expanded, doubling in size as the black of his eyes swelled like Bergen's.

"Where she's been all night," Torunn said. "In Bergen's room."

With a berserker's precision, Rune flew through the room, taking up *Gramm* as he threw open the door of Kallan's bower. Still dressed in just his trousers, Rune vaulted down the hall and descended the stairs to the Great Hall.

From behind the screens passage, Geirolf spun to Kallan and Bergen. "Here he comes."

Displaying no fear, Kallan swept past Bergen, who had moved to grasp his sword, then cursed himself for not bringing one, and stepped out from the staircase with gallant posture that displayed no fear. As if simply descending her chambers for breakfast, Kallan led Bergen into the Great Hall and stopped at the sight of Rune coming toward them.

"Don't let me die, Princess," Bergen muttered into Kallan's ear.

She flaunted a smirk, catching the light in her eye as she beamed affectionately up to Bergen, instigating a red of Rune's glower that flared with renewed rage.

With a jolt, Rune pulled *Gramm* from its sheath and cast the casing aside. It slid across the floor with a shriek as the blade rang out and gave song to Rune's roar.

"Bergen!" Rune raised his sword.

The metal struck metal, jarring Rune from his trance as he looked past *Gramm*'s spine to the hilt of Kallan's dagger.

His gaze rested on her sharpened eyes, hardened on the other side of their blades.

"Get out of my way, Seidkona," Rune growled with the fire alive in his voice. "I'll deal with you after."

"You'll deal with me now," Kallan said from behind her dagger.

"I will listen after his head is mounted at the gates of my keep, now move before I add yours alongside him!"

Kallan pushed against their blades. Rune stumbled back before regaining his balance. With a flick of a wrist, Kallan collected a ball of flame in her palm and repositioned herself to fight.

"If it's my head you want, then you can have it if you can take it," Kallan said.

Her fire shimmered blue as it grew in Kallan's hand.

"Rune..." Geirolf said. "Please...heed the lady."

But the black of Bergen's eyes caught Rune's sight. Images, countless images, flashed through his head. Rune shook with a rage that fueled his temper.

"Of all the requests," Rune shouted. "Of all my orders I've given you, you had to break this one!"

Kallan added more flame to the ball of Seidr.

"Rune." Torunn's gentle voice called from somewhere behind them. Rune didn't hear as his gaze fell back to Kallan.

"Out of my way, Dokkalfr!" he barked.

"Not until you've heard me," Kallan spat.

Rune sneered.

"I have never spoken to one of Bergen's trollops! I'm not about to start now!"

Kallan extinguished her Seidr flame at once, sending a silence through the Hall. With a cool hand, Kallan sheathed her dagger. Calmly, quietly, Kallan strode across the Hall, her head held high, and slammed her hand into Rune's face.

Rune stumbled against the force. Fire impaled his cheek, leaving him blank for a moment. Before he could recover his balance, Kallan dropped her empty palm to his shoulder and pulled the Seidr from him. The Beast within Rune roared, but Kallan paid its temper no mind.

In an instant, Rune felt his own Seidr drain, and his grip on *Gramm* weakened. Rune lowered the blade. His eyelids ached to close. Heavy with sleep, he struggled to fight. He fell to one knee, too drained of strength to stand.

Kallan leaned down to him until her breath grazed his ear. He could smell the untouched perfumes of soft rose that blinded his senses.

"He did not have me," she whispered.

Rune forced his eyes to hers despite his apparent exhaustion, desperate for a sign she spoke the truth. Pushing past the pain from where she had slapped him, Rune studied her face.

"I'm to believe that he didn't touch you although you slept in his bed?"

She tilted her head down with a smirk perched on her lips.

"How else could I get your attention?"

"You seek to gain my affection by warming his bed?" he asked, unamused.

"Affection?" Kallan furrowed her brow. "You think I summoned you to sleep with you?"

Her voice reverberated off the high, stone walls around them.

"Why else?" he asked.

Rune watched her rage implode as the last of her rational composure receded.

"Of all the—"

Kallan released his shoulder and his strength returned as she released his Seidr threads and the Beast settled, pacing angrily on the leash it bore. At once, Kallan's palms filled with a pair of blue flames that roared.

Rune staggered to his feet, *Gramm* still clutched tightly in his hand. Both monarchs were oblivious to the growing audience as Daggon and Gudrun entered the Hall via the kitchens.

"You can hardly blame me," Rune bellowed back, taunting Kallan's riled temper as he caught his breath. "With the number of passes you made—"

"I made!" Kallan barked. "You kissed me!"

Her voice thundered through the keep, adding a sudden jolt of interest to everyone's attention as they all watched the spectacle before them.

"An act I spend every moment regretting and, I assure you, it won't happen again!"

Brandishing the depths of her Seidr, unmasked a look that cut through him. Kallan inhaled and screamed, sending a pair of pillared flames that flanked Rune's sides.

Undaunted, he stood between her columns of Seidr, panting to catch his breath, too exhausted to dodge her onslaught and too lethargic to battle her any longer.

All at once, Kallan ceased her offense and dropped her arms to her side. In that instant, the color drained from her face, widening her eyes like round jewels. Her mouth opened as if to speak, but no sound came.

Rune risked a glance to Bergen, who stood as afflicted with dread as Kallan. Realizing they looked at something behind him, Rune turned to the double doors of the Great Hall where the first light of morning spilled into the hall. There, two black silhouettes framed in the sun's light stood: Joren, the loyal scout, and Borg—the man who bestowed the Fendinn inside him—looking as horror-stricken as the rest of them.

None dared breathe as all eyes met Borg and he, in turn, learned each face: the Dark One, the captain, the Volva, the king, and the queen—

The queen. An invisible hand twisted Borg's insides.

—who Aaric had proclaimed dead, standing alive and well and as spirited as ever.

On the ball of his foot, Borg spun through the door and left Joren alone in the light.

As one, they moved, forgetting the quarrel as Rune, Bergen, Joren, and Geirolf sprinted for the door.

"Joren! To the gates!" Rune barked. "Seal the doors! Bergen! Flank the north!"

Enveloped by the morning light that blanketed the open courtyard, the three men stopped and stared, stunned at Ottar, who gripped the back of Borg's neck and twisted his arm around with ease.

"Is this what you're after?" Ottar called, giving an sharp yank of Borg's arm up and around his back as the Dokkalfr attempted to wriggle himself free. His wiry frame buckled beneath Ottar's firm grip as his hair fell over his face that contorted into a snarl. He peered at Rune with a large, blue eye and one blind eye.

"I see you are not good on your word, Ljosalfr," Borg said with a profound hate as he stared up at Rune. "You owe me a murder."

Rune stared down at the sniveling Dokkalfr in Ottar's grip.

"You should have killed her when you had the chance," Borg spat, earning himself a pop of his arm as Ottar pulled his shoulder out of place.

Borg screamed sharply, but it quickly became a whimper. Beads of sweat formed on his brow, adding to his overly greasy look.

Disgusted, Rune stared down, remembering too well the deal offered almost two moons ago.

"Take him to the keep," Rune said.

Ottar obliged with an overexerted shove up the stairs to the keep.

Still battling against Ottar's large frame, Borg stumbled over his own feet as he fumbled his way ahead of Ottar, through the wide doors to the Great Hall. There, he dug his feet into the floor and for a moment, he hung, unmoving, as he glared across the room at Kallan. Vile contempt twisted his face as Kallan met the familiar eyes too large for his head. Her face white, Kallan stared, unable to move as Ottar gave a hard shove and pushed Borg along.

Outside on the steps of the keep, Rune unclenched his fists and gazed darkly at the scout.

"Joren," Rune said.

"Borg has never been early before," Joren said. "There was no time. I didn't—"

Rune raised a hand, forcing Joren to swallow his words. Joren's face fell white.

"What did he say?" Rune asked.

"He came to identify the prisoners. He heard they were captured and—"

"I know what he wants," Rune breathed as enlightenment cleared his face.

"Joren," Rune said with exercised precision. "You know what I need you to do."

Joren nodded and started down the steps toward the stables.

"Bergen," Rune said.

"Yes."

The berserker stepped in at attention and met Rune's fist. Bergen stumbled and, clutching his jaw, turned back to Rune. Opening his mouth, Bergen cocked his jaw back into place with a pop. Bergen was still rubbing the point of impact when Rune clamly straightened himself up and rattled off the orders as if Rune hadn't just punched Bergen in the face.

"I need you to ride north—"

"But there's no one left."

"We have to try!" Rune shouted, sounding more strained than he had meant to.

"Aye." Still stretching his jaw, Bergen started toward the barracks for his horse.

With a heavy sigh, Rune looked back to the keep's door, dreading the next order of business.

"Hey, Rune!" Bergen called from across the courtyard.

Rune peered over his shoulder at his brother.

"I didn't touch her!" Bergen shouted and, giving a tip of his hand in farewell, he darted the rest of the way to the barracks.

Unable to ease the sneer that twisted his face, Rune trudged up the steps to the Great Hall. A heavy hand fell affectionately to Rune's shoulder, lifting his attention from his encumbrance.

"What can I do to help, lad?" Geirolf asked.

Ignoring Geirolf's offer, Rune turned his attention to Kallan, who stared fixated on a single, distant stone in the wall, idle and blanketed in impassive awareness. Hovering around her with spreading concern, Daggon, Gudrun, and Torunn attempted and failed to reach Kallan's consciousness.

The soft echo of Rune's footfall struck the stone like cold droplets of water as he came to stand before Kallan.

"Kallan?" He forced his voice gentle.

The fight in her was gone.

"Kallan," he said, softer. "Princess."

With a deadened gaze glassed over with a wall of unbroken tears, Kallan looked from the stone to Rune as if seeing him for the first time.

"Kallan," he tried again.

Stiffly, Kallan looked from Rune to Gudrun to Daggon. She had no need for their words. Numbed to the shock, she gazed at Rune and forced her legs to move. Wordlessly, she pushed past Rune and trudged up the steps to her bower where she locked the door between them.

CHAPTER THIRTY-ONE

Who sent you?" Ottar barked, slamming his fist into Borg's face. "Who?"

His knuckles struck Borg a fourth time, then a fifth as the Dokkalfr gazed through the blood and sweat. With his arms extended, pulled taut by the chains that secured him to the stone wall, his body hung limp on a dislocated shoulder.

"Speak, boy, and I'll let him stop," Rune said, leaning against the wall of the dark cell as if bored.

"Who sent you?" Ottar bellowed again and landed another punch in Borg's side.

A definitive crack confirmed the snapping of at least two ribs and Borg gasped to catch his breath.

"Did Kallan's marshal put you up to this?" Rune asked.

A cold, dark laugh cut through the cell like sky wyrm scales on stone and Borg smiled.

"What makes you think I wouldn't be willing to do this myself?" Borg spat through a mouthful of blood and a swollen lip.

"I am no fool to think a *Nidingr* is the mastermind behind all this," Rune said.

Borg peered at Rune with a blood shot, blackened eye.

"You don't have the intelligence to compose something this large on your own," Rune added and Borg spat a mouthful of blood on the floor.

"No…" Borg gasped. "Just the nerve."

Ottar pounded his fist into Borg's stomach, leaving the Dokkalfr unable to gasp for air. At last, Borg breathed, long and deep, as he took in air again. His broken ribs flexed against his lungs, causing him to gasp deeper and harder. He managed to lift his bloodied face in time to see the sleek, slender curve of a short blade as Ottar turned to face him from a small table laden with refined metals glistening in the light of a lone torch.

"This is a Khukuri." Ottar's eyes glistened with malice. "The Dark One brought this back from Khwopring during his travels in the eastern mountains."

Ottar turned the blade over so that the black and silver metal caught the light.

"This is wook steel—Urukku steel, they call it. The metal is not just hammered, but folded so that I can do this…" Ottar bent the blade one direction then the next and the metal obeyed with ease. "The blade was designed to move without breaking or flaking."

A bead of sweat mingled with Borg's blood at his temple and streamed down the side of his face.

Ottar smiled. "I can stab, cut, slice, and skin anything with this blade."

Ottar stroked the flat of the blade as he walked toward Borg strung to the wall. He slid the flat of the blade down Borg's bloodied cheek.

"I can start at the ankles and shave the skin off," Ottar said. "Or start at the neck and move up the face then down the back."

Borg gritted his teeth. Blood pooled in his mouth.

The door whined open, spilling a fresh streak of orange light into the dimly lit room. The ivory and ebony handle in Ottar's grip glistened. Like rivers, black coal streaked the steel of the blade that curved elegantly toward its tip.

"Rune," Daggon said.

Neither Ottar nor Borg afforded a glance to Daggon, who stood on the threshold.

"Let me," Daggon bade, drawing Rune's attention from Borg for the first time since his arrival. "He's Dokkalfr. He was our traitor before he was your spy."

An unusual darkness permeated Daggon's gaze—as dark as the day Rune had believed Kallan dead on the battlefield in Swann Dalr.

"I wish Bergen were here," Ottar said, staring down at Borg. "They don't call him the 'Dark One' for nothing." Ottar peered closer and lowered his voice for only Borg to hear. "Bergen loves taking spikes used for the horse's crescents and hammering them down through the tips of your fingers right at the nail. It's a pity Bergen isn't here."

Borg shook. With either hate or fear, Ottar couldn't decide.

"Let me," Daggon said, meeting Rune's impassiveness.

With a simple nod, Rune pushed himself off the wall.

"Ottar," Rune said.

With a snarl, Ottar turned slowly from Borg and, passing the Khukuri to Daggon, he followed his king through the door. Before the metal click sounded behind him, Ottar was certain it was fear that filled Borg's eyes.

⁂

Rune lay on the stone floor of the war room ignoring the ever-growing debate between Ottar and Geirolf as his thoughts wandered across the keep to Kallan's chambers. There he knew she was already throwing up her walls while she descended deeper into the chasm buried in her mind.

"We can't just sit here," Ottar said. "Waiting for the next move to come from Lorlenalin… The Dokkalfar could be moving right now!"

"Borg hasn't spoken yet," Geirolf cried, leaning across the table. "You have no idea what the Dokkalfar are up to or if Borg is even linked to them. What you propose is a full scale attack on Lorlenalin without reason."

"Exactly!" Ottar slammed his hand on the table.

The vehemence in each rebuttal grew as Rune quietly lay pondering on the floor.

"They won't see it coming!" Ottar said. "We'll have the upper hand!"

"They are Kallan's people!" Geirolf bellowed. "This isn't just Borg anymore! It's the whole of Lorlenalin's army! We don't have the manpower! What people would die, would die for nothing!"

"We will have the upper hand as soon as they see Kallan alive and well, blasting her way back to her throne!" Ottar insisted.

Rune smirked at the vision supplied by Ottar.

"Besides…" Ottar waved his hand. "We also have Gudrun."

"Two Seidkona are hardly an army," Geirolf growled.

"One Seidkona is all we'll need," Ottar dismissed confidently. "The second is for insurance."

"Insurance." Geirolf snorted. "What you propose is murder! Kallan doesn't have the mind in her to fight!"

"Exactly!" Ottar growled. "A good fight can cleanse the most profound troubles!"

"Or blow up in our faces when she runs off wreaking all sorts of havoc!" Geirolf said. "Kallan won't sit still—"

"Enough!" Rune shouted from the floor. "You're wasting your heads on talk. We're not moving anywhere until Joren and Bergen get back."

Rune's outcry left Geirolf and Ottar silent as he resumed his thoughts on Kallan.

"What we need now is numbers."

The door clicked then creaked as Gudrun and Torunn entered into the room.

"Any word?" Geirolf asked eagerly.

Rune cocked his head at a peculiar angle to better see their faces from the floor. Gudrun remorsefully shook her head.

"She refuses to open the door or take in her meals," she said.

The whole of the room seemed to sag at Gudrun's answer.

Heavy with guilt, Ottar mumbled aloud, "Well, she is in no state of mind to face him, let alone fight. The poor's girl's been through enough."

Geirolf glared at Ottar, who suddenly avoided eye contact.

"Rune." Torunn's voice cut through the room. "I've held my tongue too long."

Her tiny footsteps drummed the opening notes of his dirge.

"When do you plan to speak to her?" she asked.

The creak of the door nearest Bergen's chambers added a sudden stuffy chill to the room as all eyes turned to Daggon.

While wiping thick blood from his hands with a rag, Daggon slowly, sadly, shook his head.

"I'll end up killing him before that one talks."

With a sigh, Rune slapped his palms to the stone and jerked himself off the floor. With a quick shuffle, he rested his back against the wall to face his group of assorted players and sighed again.

"I need a drink," Rune grumbled.

"There's plenty of time for that after we hear your answer," Geirolf said, demanding an answer to Torunn's question.

The five companions leaned closer, eager for the word that would send them or keep them. Rune looked from face to face then sighed long and deep.

"I suppose it's time we share our side of things," Rune mumbled, more to himself than his company.

Daggon finished wiping his hands and joined Gudrun's side.

"Torunn has been keeping you updated on Borg's position, I presume," Rune asked, meeting Gudrun and Daggon.

"She has," Gudrun confirmed, and the women and Daggon moved closer.

"Borg came to us years ago with enough military information to keep one step ahead of Eyolf. On occasion we sent him with request for negotiations or proposals for a truce, but we were told that every offer, every message, was rejected then met with more hostilities. Now Kallan says she never received a single summons and that, if she had, her marshal would have delivered such summons."

Daggon and Gudrun both looked as if Rune had slammed their heads together.

"Hm," Daggon grunted. "Aaric."

"Aaric," Rune repeated. "Tell me about Aaric."

Daggon and Gudrun exchanged glances: consulting, arguing, and deciding all within that look. Daggon nodded and Gudrun sighed, reluctant to proceed.

"Aaric is Kallan's high marshal," Gudrun said.

Rune thought long for a moment.

"It is he who banished you?"

"He is," Daggon said. "He—"

"Aaric never wanted war," Gudrun interjected. "If Aaric launches a battle because he believes Kallan is dead, then he truly believes that Kallan is dead. He does what he must for Lorlenalin."

"Can we trust him?" Rune asked pointedly.

Gudrun pursed her lips, stopped herself, and thought for a long while.

"He wouldn't ever harm Kallan," Gudrun finally spoke.

Rune brooded as he walked to the window and stared out over the city to the river where vast longships pulled into the harbor.

"For seven hundred years, I've sent summons after summons to Eyolf," Rune said. "For seven hundred years, I have fought a vengeful foe. Within two moons, I have narrowed our position down to this: Either Borg altered the messages delivered to Aaric, or Aaric never delivered our summons to Kallan."

Rune stared at the table, too deep in thought for a moment to continue.

"Kallan claims she sent Aaric with similar declarations for me." Rune raised his eyes to the Dokkalfar. "We have never received any such declaration. Ever. And, until my stay in Lorlenalin, I had never seen your Aaric. It is possible he hired someone to carry Kallan's message to Gunir…even Borg perhaps. It is also possible he was passing information to Borg down from Kallan's court.

"Aside from Bergen accidentally stumbling onto a chance meeting centuries back," Rune continued, "Joren was the only one allowed to work with Borg per his conditions. Needless to say, when Borg came to me and offered me my freedom in exchange for Kallan's life, I didn't recognize him as anything more than a rogue Dokkalfr who had it out for his monarch. But there was too much in question to just lend my aid blindly and kill his queen without, at least, understanding his intent in this. And that is where Borg's plan backfired…when I kept Kallan alive."

"You wanted to be sure you weren't doing him a favor at your expense," Daggon said.

"Exactly," Rune said. "What Borg didn't count on—what none of us saw coming—was the Dvergar's involvement in this."

"The Dvergar?" Daggon furrowed his brow. "What do they have to do with this?"

Rune released a long, audible sigh as he walked to the window and rested his arms in the frame. It was a long while before he answered.

"The Dvergar have been following Kallan since the summer thaw. They took her almost as soon as she and I rode from Lorlenalin. I found her nearly a fortnight later half-dead in a cave less than a day's walk from the gates of Svartálfaheim. My guess is, the Dvergar were after her pouch."

Gudrun and Daggon exchanged a silent glance.

"Before I had a full day to withdraw the details from Kallan, a usurper of Midgard calling himself king began hunting us for that same pouch. Now I don't know if the Dvergar and a deranged king are related to a rogue mercenary. But too soon, there were too many players. Too much was not adding up and I couldn't blindly abandon Kallan to the Dvergar. And I knew if I sent her back to Lorlenalin, I'd be handing her over to Borg who had already expressed a keen interest in her death. So, I brought her here until I could sort this out."

With every word, Daggon amassed a scowl as if he had swallowed a rotten fish. "What happens now?" he growled.

Rune exhaled patiently.

"We determine who is behind this."

"The players may be linked, or they may stand alone, each working to their own goal. Borg could be working for someone else. He could be workingfor himself."

"He sure wants us to think he's working for himself," Ottar said.

"Which only convinces me more that he is working for someone else," Rune said, peering down at the table. "Borg's plan required Kallan's death. And, until this morning, he believed his plan had worked."

"And his plan only works if Kallan is dead," Daggon said.

Rune continued.

"Now if Aaric is working with Borg—if Borg did in fact pass my summons on to Aaric—then Kallan's death would ensure Aaric keeps the throne so long as the Dokkalfar people believe Kallan is dead."

Rune gazed at Gudrun and Daggon. "But you suspected Kallan lived. Aaric couldn't afford you finding Kallan and bringing her back, which may be why he exiled you."

"Assuming Aaric is behind this," Daggon said.

"Borg is here," Rune said. "He is harmless."

"But Aaric," Gudrun said.

"We need to know what side he's on," Rune said. "If Aaric is behind this and he learns that Kallan lives, he will seek to protect his holding with the desperation of a drowning rat."

"And if he isn't?" Daggon asked.

"Then he will welcome you back with open arms," Rune concluded his summary.

Daggon sighed as Gudrun inhaled with the staleness of one who hadn't moved for a long while.

"All we need to do is get to his troops," Daggon said, staring at a table knot.

"But as long as you are branded a traitor, there's no one there who will grant you an audience with the high marshal," Torunn said.

Geirolf stifled a chuckle that emerged as a snort.

"They'll hardly deny their own eyes if they see Kallan frying up Aaric with that Seidr of he—"

"She will not go," Rune said.

All looked at Rune, who took the time to meet each of their astounded gazes.

"I will not send her to her death," he said. "I've invested too much of my time to ensure she lives and will not risk her life for a chance this will work."

No one argued.

"Besides," he continued with a lightened air, "I've been singed one too many times to just hand her over to Aaric. No. If I have my say, she'll stay locked out of harm's way until I can personally parade Aaric's head on *Gramm*'s point, or guarantee he'll step down to welcome her back."

Together, they nodded, keeping their silence.

"More than ever, I need to know Aaric's motives," Rune said.

"Motive?" Daggon asked, crinkling his scarred face.

"If I was Aaric and sent a spy to check on the status of two traitors, and that spy never returned, I'd launch the largest attack I could at the one thing that threatens my throne," Rune said.

Geirolf guffawed.

"You think he seeks to attack Gunir?" Torunn belted.

"Are you mad?" Daggon's voice rumbled the room.

"What other choice does he have?" Rune's voice rose above the chorus of objections. "You said yourself he blames Gunir for the death of your queen. What other choice does he have? To sit by while Kallan slips a message to Lorlenalin that she lives? He won't run. He's invested too much in this to run. Now either he moves as we speak to avenge his dead queen, or he moves as we speak to destroy the one thing that could expose him. His only option is to advance before he loses the troops that support him."

"If Aaric is behind this," Daggon amended.

"But supposing Aaric's innocent?" Geirolf interjected. "We'll be launching a war against a high marshal who believes we killed their queen."

"All the more reason to be the first to march," Rune said. "Either Aaric is innocent and seeks vengeance for Kallan's spilled blood, or Aaric is vulnerable and can't afford to have Kallan seen by his troops. Either way, Aaric's next move is to attack."

"But Gunir has lost too much," Torunn pleaded as if Rune's hypothesis was the backing of Aaric's plan. "We don't have the manpower to stave off an attack."

"That's why I've sent for Roald and Thorold," Rune said.

"You're pulling back our defenses?" Geirolf said, suddenly at attention. "When Forkbeard sits as a vulture on his throne waiting for our borders to diminish strength?"

"His scouts are ever vigilant," Torunn said. "He waits for the moment you pull back!"

"I have no choice!"

The room fell silent once more, forced to accept the situation for what it was.

"My hands are bound," Rune said. "And the only chance we have to ensure our existence is to reinforce the weakened fountainhead here at home. For if Gunir were to fall, the forts would have nothing left to defend!"

"And if Forkbeard moves?" Geirolf asked, giving voice to the one thing that plagued every Ljosalfar's mind. "What then?"

Rune's shoulders slumped in defeat as he exhaled, unable to answer for that possibility.

"There is a way," Gudrun said, speaking up from Daggon's side.

The Ljosalfar gazed at the Volva.

"Surely there must be someone who believes Kallan lives as we did. There must be some who want to believe that Kallan lives. If we could get to one of them, just one to speak for us…"

"Eilif," Daggon said, earning a warm smile from Gudrun.

"Eilif," she confirmed.

"He's unprotected. Easy to get to," Daggon said.

"Always in the warrens with the children," Gudrun said.

"Unguarded and away from the palace courts."

"Who is Eilif?" Torunn asked.

"Eilif," Daggon said, smiling, "is Kallan's nursery friend and personal scribe."

"They grew up playing together," Gudrun explained.

"And collecting orphans they dressed in my tunics…" Daggon said. "If anyone waits with bated breath for Kallan's return, it's Eilif."

"If you're caught, what you suggest is a death sentence," Rune said, knowing Gudrun knew this.

"What we suggest is to save our queen," Daggon said.

"You are not under my commission," Rune reminded them. "I do not order you to go."

"Your Majesty," Daggon said, "we share a common enemy. Whatever aid we can lend is ours to give."

Rune lowered his head in thought as Daggon continued.

"You lost a spy when you lost Borg. We no longer have a high marshal we can trust. Aaric proclaimed Kallan's death and took her throne then exiled us."

Rune peered up at him.

"What do you propose?" he asked.

Daggon slowly exhaled and straightened his back.

"I will ride to Lorlenalin and find Eilif. With his power in the courts, Eilif can get me in. I will face Aaric and declare that Kallan lives. I will make him hear that Gunir seeks peace. I will force him to know that Kallan breathes."

"Aaric has ordered your execution." Rune stared him hard in the eye. "You know what you do."

"I have always, ever only served my queen to preserve her life and ensure her continued existence," Daggon said. "And I will ride for that cause once more."

With a nod, Rune lowered his eyes, releasing Daggon from his gaze.

"And what of you, Gudrun?"

The old Volva inhaled deeply as she cocked her head higher with her own agenda.

"She is my daughter's daughter," she said. "My blood flows through her. I will ride to Lorlenalin and rip Aaric's heart through his nose should he deny my kin the throne that is hers."

Rune pursed his lips, nodding in acknowledgement as he entertained the image she provided.

"See the horse master for mounts," Rune said. "Gunnar will have your horses saddled and ready to ride within the hour."

The Dokkalfr and the Seidkona glowed with renewed energy as they turned and bounded out the door. He waited for them to pull the door closed between them before releasing a sigh and whispered aloud his hope.

"May Odinn keep you."

ᥴᥱ ᥒᦾ

The midday sun blazed over Lorlenalin, which glistened like a white opal in the light. The day went on as much it had for several weeks now. The Dokkalfar went about with their lives as undisturbed as they had been restless.

Within the palace, Aaric pushed open the doors of the war room, paying no mind to the young scribe scribbling fiercely onto a scroll he dearly cradled. The vast hearth fire roared behind the table littered with maps, letters, and seals. The iron wheel suspended from the ceiling illuminated the room, providing an unwanted cheery mood to the room.

"Eilif," Aaric said, addressing the scribe who hadn't looked up from his writings.

"Marshal," Eilif said as Aaric approached the table. "I have here the final numbers as you requested, which should be ready…almost."

"I've ordered the men ready," Aaric said.

"The men?" The scribe stopped writing and turned to Aaric, whose wide shoulders dwarfed Eilif's wiry frame.

"We're going to battle," Aaric said and searched the table for parchment and pen.

"Battle?" Eilif asked.

"Kallan is dead," Aaric said. "We are without monarch, and I'll not sit here waiting for Gunir to move first. Once you have the final numbers, I'll have you draw up the order for me to sign and seal."

Eilif stared blankly at Aaric, unmoving.

"Well, get on with it," Aaric said, shuffling papers about on the desk.

"Who is Kallan?"

Aaric snapped to attention and searched Eilif's empty eyes.

Kallan was barely older than Eilif, who was slow to mature and had always been too small for his age. He ate less than the orphans he and Kallan cared for. Eilif, who grew alongside Kallan. Eilif, who collected Lorlenalin's orphans and loved them as their own. Eilif, who forever walked a step behind their queen… All of that seemed to hold no shadow in Eilif's eyes as if all he was, all he knew, had been forgotten.

"Don't you remember your lady, Eilif?" Aaric muttered, but the scribe only looked on appearing more confused than ever.

Fand.

Aaric curled his hands into fists.

But why? he pondered. *Why would Fand wipe his memory?*

"Please finish things up in your chambers, Eilif," Aaric said.

Nodding, Eilif clutched the scroll to his chest and shuffled out the door, which he closed with a soft click.

Aaric sank into the chair with his back to the fire, and dropped his face into his hands.

His anger was waning and with it, his strength. There, alone beneath his grief, the high marshal broke. Tears streaked his faced lined with the ancient runes few could read. His wide shoulders shook, and the marshal cried silently.

After all this time…

Aaric dug at the heat in his eyes, putting an end to his tears.

After all this time… Think, Aaric willed, pinching the bridge of his nose as he recalled the last moment he had seen King Rune and Kallan.

"Take her," Aaric had said to the Ljosalfr King within the stables. *"She lives. She's fine. But you must get her out of here."*

"Why—" King Rune had asked.

"There is no time. Take her horse," Aaric had said. *"The brown destrier. He rides faster than the others."*

"B—"

"I'm giving her to you now go or you'll both be dead!" Aaric had said, knowing Fand was near.

"She's Seidkona," Rune had argued. *"When she wakes, I won't be able to hold her."*

Aaric opened his eyes wide and released his nose.

Rune has the Fendinn.

With a flicker of hope, Aaric ceased his grieving.

The Shadow within Rune will have blocked Kallan's Seidr, even from my view. Rune may have kept her alive after all.

The more Aaric thought, the more he was certain. Kallan was alive.

That Shadow, not even Danann knows, Aaric mused. *Only the Drui knew about the Shadow…and Fand. But Gudrun and Fand believe it destroyed. And Volundr…*

Aaric shook his head.

Volundr doesn't care for anything anymore, not since Kira's death.

"There is still a chance…"

Aaric walked to the window and gazed out at the waters of the Kattegat. Within a few hours, the sun would be setting beyond the waters.

With Fand believing Kallan dead, it will buy me time enough to act. Under the guise of vengeance, the Dokkalfar could move on Gunir. If Kallan is alive, I will find her and get us out, all before Fand learns that Kallan lives. A simple spell can make it look like I died in battle, and Fand will end her search for Danann's Drui. If Kallan lives, we will leave Alfheim. We'll go into hiding. No one, not even Gudrun—

Aaric's face paled with a new fear.

Gudrun.

If Daggon and Gudrun find her, if they bring back news of Kallan's survival, the hunt would resume and this time, Danann or no, Fand would kill Kallan herself.

CHAPTER THIRTY-TWO

Rune peered down from his window into the black of night. Gunir slept soundly, leaving behind the light breeze and whistling winds. For hours he stood, staring at the night clearly ornamented with the cold light of the stars bristling around the last slice of moon that seemed to cling to the sky with all its hope.

He pushed a deep sigh through him and allowed his thoughts to wander to Kallan in her bower. He looked out over the rooftops that filled the bailey and stopped, tightening his brow. A lone, cloaked figure slipped through the courtyard. From this window, he identified Kallan's dainty swagger and, a moment later, was out the door, flying down the back steps to the Grand Hall.

Rune arrived in the courtyard just as the hem of Kallan's cloak vanished through the battlement. In silence, he slipped behind her, taking great care to keep his distance while keeping her in sight from where he followed in the shadows. Kallan entered the main road of the city and walked for a ways, before turning down a shallow street. With the stealth of a mercenary, Rune slipped in and out of the darkness, always several steps behind in time to see Kallan take the next turn or alley.

The streets were growing narrower and the buildings more dilapidated with every rounded corner Kallan made. She stopped frequently to cast a precarious gaze over her shoulder before proceeding deeper into the darkness until Rune was certain they had entered the poorest district of the city. There, weathered doors had all but fallen apart and rodents frequently crossed his path.

It was then, once Rune was certain the condition of the streets were as bad as they could get, that Kallan stopped abruptly. She didn't move or turn or lower her hood, but remained in an open street where barrels and wooden crates had been dumped along with unwanted rags, piles of rotting fish heads, and heaps of mildewing hay from the stables. Bits of leather too worn for reuse or mending had been abandoned among the collection of garbage.

Rune crouched behind the side of a building, eagerly watching. The night was quiet and the stones of the street glistened in the vanishing moonlight. Rune stretched his neck out from behind the building, anticipating Kallan's next direction, when she spun and fired a blast of blue.

As Rune flattened his back against the stone, her Seidr flame struck the corner of the wall where Rune's hand had been moments ago.

"It's me!" Rune cried from the darkness, hoping it would deter her attack.

Silence.

Slowly, Rune peered around the corner. Kallan was gone.

He dragged his eyes over barrels, hay, and rusted scaffolding and almost pulled his head back around when the tip of a dagger pinched his neck. Rune gulped.

Guided by the blade of the dagger and the will of its wielder, Rune ever so carefully turned back around until he pressed his back flat against the wall and gazed at Kallan. The lapis blue of her eyes held the moon's light. With a stern stare, she assessed him quietly then smirked.

"Following me again?" she asked, with a snip of a playful tone on the edge of her voice.

"Oh, come off it," Rune said, carefully pushing the blade from his throat.

With a muted chuckle, Kallan sheathed her blade.

"There was a time when I could put a blade to your throat and you would actually respect its wielder. I miss those times," Kallan mused.

"What are you doing out here?" Rune asked, but Kallan had fixed her attention to a single rooftop directly behind Rune.

Creasing his brow, Rune looked in time to catch the faintest glimpse of a small hand, long, black hair caked with filth, and a dirtier face cast in shadow with his back to the moonlight.

"Come on down then," Kallan invited warmly. "I have food."

The boy didn't have to be told twice. He scaled down from the rooftop, through the scaffolding and dilapidated ruins of the house so quickly that, had Rune blinked, he would have lost sight of the lad completely.

Crouched over so far that he could have run on all fours, the boy slithered along the edge of the street and was at Kallan's heels before she had lowered the basket she had hidden quite nicely under her cloak. Another five waifs appeared and joined the one buried in Kallan's basket.

Granting them the space to forage, Rune and Kallan backed away and allowed the children full access as they rummaged through the fruits and breads. They wasted no time devouring the pastries Kallan had swiped from the kitchens.

Stunned, Rune looked to Kallan, who stood grinning down at the children as they ate.

"How did you find them?" Rune asked by the time another two had joined the group.

"It isn't hard," Kallan said, delighted at the growing crowd plowing through the perishables. "Once they get wind of food, word spreads. Kaj," Kallan called and the first lad with matted black hair poked his head up from the basket, a loaf clutched in each hand with his cheeks bursting with bread.

Crouched to the ground, Kallan pulled an apple from her pouch and began slicing it into pieces. His eyes widened in wonder as he gazed upon the Seidr that spilled like juice over Kallan's hands.

"Let me have a look at you," she said.

Eyeing the apple, Kaj obeyed. He swallowed the mouthful, probably too soon, and stuffed one of the breads into his mouth, freeing a hand for the apple. As he harbored his treasures, eating quickly to keep them, Kallan took a closer look at the lacerations and bruises that composed his body.

"How did you know they were here?" Rune asked as Kallan placed a hand atop Kaj's head. Without objection, the boy began on the apple and Kallan went to work.

"They had to be," she said. "I know how many of your men I've killed. I know how many of them must have had children."

Beneath the street dirt, the purple of Kaj's bruises faded yellow then vanished. Within his body, what old fractures and breaks he had mended as the life in his eyes filled in.

"How did you know they wouldn't run from you?" Rune asked as Kaj finished the last of his apple and returned to the bread.

"Some did," Kallan said then smiled back at the boy. "Go. Eat." Still clutching his bread, Kaj ran back to the basket.

"Vibeke," Kallan called and held out another apple.

The dulled, hazel eyes of a girl barely six winters old peered over the heads that still rummaged through the basket.

With a gleam in her eye, Kallan smiled and wiggled her finger encouraging Vibeke to approach. At the sight of the apple, Vibeke's eyes glowed and, forgetting the basket, she charged Kallan, who surrendered the apple and scooped up the tot in a series of fluid movements.

By the time Kallan turned to answer Rune, the child had eagerly sunk her teeth into the apple with a crisp crunch that snapped the air.

"But... Why are you here?" Rune asked as Kallan bounced Vibeke on her hip. "Why would y—"

"Well, it isn't there fault their king is an obstinate war-monger," Kallan said and spotted a fresh cut, red and inflamed with infection, on an older boy who had pulled his head up from the basket.

"Here," Kallan said, dropping Vibeke into Rune's arms. "Make yourself useful."

Within the hour, Kallan had nearly finished sorting through the children, administering spells and herbs to each where needed and mending scrapes, lacerations, and broken bones before sending each off clutching an apple.

"Sit still, Haas," Kallan scolded gently as an eight year old squirmed in her hands.

"It hurts," he whined and Kallan narrowed her eyes to better see the depth of the cut behind his ear. Rune leaned closer over her shoulder, eager to get a better look at Kallan's work.

"How did you get this?" Kallan asked and wiped the wound clean with a bit of dry cloth.

"I fell," Haas answered, bored.

Kallan released his ear and wetted the cloth with the juice of her apple then returned to the sight of the injury.

"From where?" she asked.

"From the roof of Thor's Shadow," he answered. As he spoke, Kallan siphoned a thread of Seidr into him.

"What were you doing at the tavern?" she asked and Haas shrugged.

"Looking for food."

"Well," Kallan answered with worry, "don't. I'll be back tomorrow with more food."

She scrutinized her work and lowered him back to the ground. As soon as he snatched his apple from Kallan, he was off and made a comfortable seat out of a pile of soiled hay nearby.

"Where did you learn to heal?" Rune asked as Haas began his apple.

"Gudrun," Kallan said. "Mandatory Seidr skills. Just the basics in the event you ever improve your aim."

Kallan flashed Rune a quick smile and picked up the basket before he could protest.

"She wanted to be sure I would live," Kallan said and watched as, one by one, the children returned to their homes in the shadow.

"You underestimate my skills," Rune said and a little hand pulled at his pant leg.

Large, round eyes buried in a dirty face stared up at him. One of the orphans, no more than five, donned a glower she had learned from Kallan.

"Are you Rune?" the child asked.

"I am," Rune said. And as swift as the whooper flies, she pulled back her leg and landed a kick in the middle of his shin.

The child was off before Rune could howl.

"What th—?" Rune said, holding his leg with a slew of curses at the ready, but Kallan had gone on ahead without him, leaving him alone in the street with his wound. Forced to use his freshly bruised shin to catch up, Rune limped after her.

"What was that for?" he asked.

"I don't know," Kallan said, gazing up at the sky and delighted for no apparent reason. "Maybe she doesn't care for your politics."

With a glower, Rune shook off the piercing pain in his shin and hobbled alongside Kallan as they made their way back through the streets.

The night was clear, permitting a full view of the moon. A cold wind rushed through the stone streets and Kallan pulled her cloak tighter.

"Winter is on the horizon," Rune said, staring into the distance. "You can smell the frost in the air."

"Hm." Kallan grinned, breathing in the crisp scent of ice in the wind. "I love the winter. It's like curling inside a wonderful warm blanket against the cold."

"And spring?" Rune asked, looking upon Kallan as they rounded another corner.

Kallan inhaled deeply the night chill and grinned.

"Spring feels like I've been wearing the same old blanket for six months and I finally get to throw it back and enjoy the fresh air."

The streets widened.

"Why didn't you give them your cloak?" Rune asked as Kallan pulled the wool closer.

"Something like a cloak would launch a small war in a place like the warrens," she explained as darkness descended upon her jolly mood. "The children would go as far as to kill for it." Her voice fell barely above a whisper. "Eilif and I learned that the hard way."

They said nothing for several more alleys.

"How did you find them?" Rune asked.

"It isn't hard," she said. "Once they find food, blankets, and medicine, the information spreads like wild fire. You only need to find one really. The rest will find you."

"Have you always been welcomed in the warrens?" Rune asked, eager to keep her talking.

Kallan shook her head.

"Not at first." They turned another corner. "When my father led us to Lorlenalin, there was little for me to do. The settlement was barely a fortress then. I would slip out with Eilif and we would run the streets while my father carved the city into the mountain. We found the children quite by accident, I assure you."

Rune's sudden bought of laughter filled the sleeping alley, pulling Kallan's eyes from the night moon.

"What's so funny?" she asked defensively.

"You," Rune answered, wiping the tears from his eyes. "Just imagining you as a child, running about."

Kallan crunched up her face.

"Well, I was probably a fright better than you!"

"Bergen and I both, mind you," Rune corrected. "He took to the women right away...always the women with him."

"Your poor mother," Kallan chuckled aloud, but her gentle amusement ended abruptly. "I lost my mother in the Dvergar Wars."

They walked side by side and Rune watched the hard realization sink in as Kallan said it.

"I'm just like them," she said. "Orphaned by war."

Ever vigilant, Rune prepared for Kallan's tantrum, anger, and flames. But a compliant pensiveness came in its stead.

"Only, I have Gudrun and Daggon and Aaric and Eilif."

The silence swelled comfortably between them as they walked, each submerged in their own thoughts as they nestled into the other's company.

"I suppose you were the same," Kallan said after a moment. "Like Bergen. Always after the women."

"No," Rune said. "Couldn't be bothered. I was more interested in my studies."

"Ugh," Kallan groaned, "Studies. Odinn! There were times I drove Gudrun batty with my lack of enthusiasm." She proudly grinned. "I escaped every chance I could. I spent more time just trying to find a place where no one could find me when I was called for lessons. When I did, I could be guaranteed a full afternoon of peace and solitude. My favorite place was at the top of Livsvann overlooking the sea. No one ever found me there."

She lost herself in memories as Rune smiled fondly at his own.

"There was a cave that had eroded back into itself," Kallan continued. "Oh, but I haven't been there in years. It was so high that I believed I could touch the moon if only I dared reach for it. I never did."

She stared at the sky, lost in thoughts.

"I used to go there every night to wave at Hjuki and Bil. What about you?" she asked.

"Me?"

"Surely you must have gone somewhere to escape your nagging tutors and droning lessons."

"I didn't." Rune spoke profoundly as if setting an example. "I loved my schooling, my tutors, and my lessons. When Geirolf called, I gleefully abandoned my bow for a chance at more politics."

"You lie."

"I do," Rune declared, holding his eye on the end of the street with his chest puffed out.

Together they broke into a quiet chuckle before Rune finally answered.

"Swann Dalr."

Kallan cocked her head grinning.

"Swann Dalr? The valley?"

"That's where I would go. A long time ago, anyway."

A quiet dark drowned out Rune's lightheartedness. The battlement came in sight as they neared the end of the bailey.

"There were places there where the foliage just flowed from the ground and formed a massive rug of greens and grass," he said. "Trees as tall as your moon… I used to race Bergen to see who could reach the top first. And the view…" Rune blew an impressed breath. "There were these gorges that plummeted down as deep as your Livsvann was high, carved in the earth by a single trickle of water that had worn through it for centuries. There were places where Bergen and I would mark the level of erosion to see how much further the water carved out every fifty years or so. And, if you found just the right overhang, you could see right down the gorge to the lake."

Rune gave a bemused scoff at his childhood folly.

"I was convinced that if I jumped, I could fly." Sadly, he shook his head. "I haven't been there in years."

"Why don't you go back?"

"Time." He shrugged and pulled his eyes from the main steps to gaze upon the slender curve of her jaw. "Kallan. Speak to Borg."

Her foot froze on the first step. She stopped and turned her face down.

"I have nothing to say to Borg," she said, her voice suddenly dry.

Rune shook his head. "You can't ignore him forever."

"Why do you do this?" she breathed, hurt filling her eyes.

"Do what?" he asked.

"Ruin this," Kallan chirped. "Why must you always ruin this?"

Unsure of what she meant, Rune urged the matter on ahead.

"He has most of the answers we need," he said. "He can help us, but he won't talk. Everyone has had a go with him, but he's sealed up tighter than a mute Rus. Perhaps if his queen were to confront him abou—"

"There is nothing I have to say to a…a…traitor!" Kallan flushed red. "A *Nidingr!*"

"He may know who killed your father."

"Enough!"

And before Rune could rebut, Kallan collected her skirts and fled up the steps to the keep.

CHAPTER THIRTY-THREE

Kallan stared at the imperfect sliver of moon with her burning eyes swollen red. She tucked her legs tighter to her chest as she sat, curled up in her chair and wrapped in the blanket, too stiff to look down, and too far to see Joren at the Southern Keep where he waited atop his steed, peering toward Gunir.

The gates of the Southern Keep flew open as a ruckus ensued, giving heart to the thousands of troops who rode out from the stables. At Joren's side, Roald—a wide-shouldered Ljosalfr, as boisterous as Bergen was sly—joined him. His wild black hair flowed down his shoulders. His grand voice released the order, calling his men to order and Joren watched as they fell into line, riding out behind Roald. Buried in the shadows and unseen by all, a Dani crouched in the dark with his orders from Dan's Mork.

Bolting from the tree where he cowered, the Dani mounted his horse. He was off through the woods to the south, heading back toward the ship that waited there without care for the fort in the north where Bergen slid from his horse.

With his long stride, Bergen made his way to the base of the keep and called over the parapet with a booming voice. The gate was unbarred and the oaken doors opened to grant the king's brother entrance. Soldiers greeted and welcomed the berserker, each eager to bestow a hardy slap to his shoulder, each unaware of the message Forkbeard received that same hour as the Dani, ragged and worn from the road, rushed to his king in Dan's Mork.

The scout's words jolted Forkbeard to his feet as Sigrid, Forkbeard's wife, stiffened at attention, her eyes wide with blood lust. Forkbeard gave his orders and the scout scurried from his King's Great Hall in, feeling high on the approval given by his king. Within minutes, the courts and keep at the center of Danelaw buzzed with talk of war, unbeknownst to the pensive thoughts that brewed from Gudrun, who rode with a fury alongside Daggon, desperate in the cause that drove them.

Rune studied the imperfect sliver of moon. Sighing, he moved away from the window and passed a rough hand over his face while digging the sleep from his eyes. A tap on the door jerked his attention.

"Come," he invited, and the door flew open with Roald's grand bellow, which warmed Rune's blood with a hope he hadn't felt in days.

"Joren sends your summons and I answer!" Roald greeted. "How now, dear cousin?"

The heavy clomp of Roald's boot seemed to shake the floor as he crossed the sitting room to Rune.

"What wench and mead do you have waiting for me?" Roald greeted with a jovial smile.

"Roald!"

Unable to hold back a wide grin, Rune embraced the son of his father's brother. "Still as bad as Bergen, I see?"

"Worse! You must be confident to pull my men from the south," Roald said.

"Desperate, Cousin," he corrected. "Not confident. I am left with little choice so long as a rogue is about. Come."

Rune directed Roald to the corridor.

"I'll explain all with food and drink—"

"And women, Cousin. Don't be holding out on me."

Laughing to himself, Rune called down the corridor as he closed the door behind him. "Torunn!"

Her arms loaded with a bundle of blankets, the key keeper paused at the top of the steps to the Great Hall.

"Serve the meat!" Rune bade. "Bring the drink!"

She gave an obedient nod and descended the steps, still clutching her load.

With an uncomfortable jerk, Rune shuddered as he paused unexpectedly at Kallan's closed doors. Three days ago she locked herself in. Three days ago Rune began circling his bower, unable to sit, unable to reach in and pull her from the chasm that engulfed her.

"Come," Rune said, not bothering this time to try the handle on Kallan's door. Instead, he led his guest down to the Great Hall, all the while hating himself for not breaking down Kallan's door three days ago.

With lingering curiosity, Roald eyed the double doors and followed Rune silently down the steps, his own set of questions suddenly brewing.

ᑕᔆ ᔆᑐ

The smoke in the Great Hall billowed, adding another layer of warmth around the table strewn with bare bones and crumbs. After emptying their flagons, Rune and Roald lounged at the table with their pipes. The fire crackled beside them.

"By the gods," Roald answered, lowering his pipe in awe.

Rune peered up at Roald.

"You see why I had no choice," Rune said.

"Oh, I see," Roald said, lowering his pipe to the table. "So what then? We wait for Bergen and Thorold before we march?"

Rune took a long, pensive draw from his pipe and looked past the smoke that rolled between them. "We wait. Daggon and Gudrun are out there. I coddle what little hope I have for their return."

"You're certain the side they're on?" Roald leaned closer, eager for Rune's answer.

"They defected when Aaric banished them. He's lost them to their loyalty for Kallan. They won't go back."

Roald arched a brow. A bemused grin tugged at the corner of his mouth.

"Kallan," he said, taking a final draw from his pipe. "Of her, you've said so little," Roald chided, resting the pipe on the table.

Rune eyed him suspiciously as he took a long, silent draw from his pipe. As he leaned back on the bench, Roald stretched then slumped back, crossing his arms out on the table.

"You never did answer me, Cousin."

Rune smothered his pipe embers as he slowly exhaled the last of the smoke.

"You've arrived a day or so ahead of Bergen," Rune said, still fixed on the black of the pipe bowl. "I'm afraid you'll have to see him about a wench dur—"

Rune lost his words and his hands froze. His throat clamped shut as Kallan descended the stairs. The deep blues and silver of her gown glistened as she moved, adding a touch of welcomed cool against the suddenly stuffy warmth of the Hall. He balled his fists, cursing the sweat that accumulated down his spine as curiosity whipped Roald's head around.

With enthusiasm, Roald beamed wide and he leapt from the table, smashing his knee in the process. As Rune silently willed Roald's leg broken, he watched Kallan with a mix of anger, glee, and relief while Roald scampered toward the Dokkalfr. He had barely shifted his gaze when Kallan settled herself onto the bench beside Roald. She shifted a softened glance to Rune.

"I'm ashamed of you, Rune!" Roald said, settling himself down beside the lady. "Keeping this treasure all to yourself!"

Rune held his grimace on Kallan, desperate to learn her new game and quick.

"Have you eaten?" Roald asked, nearly snapping his neck to better face Kallan, who poured her attention over Roald.

"Just," Kallan answered with a polite grin, and Rune entertained thoughts of breaking Roald's neck himself.

Roald beamed like an idiot and rambled, desperate to strike a topic of conversation that Kallan would respond to.

Nauseated at Roald's mating rituals, Rune rolled his eyes and reached for the flagon in front of him.

"I've known Rune and Bergen since they were wee lads, romping about the rivers and dalrs with naught but an arrow shared between them…causing more trouble than their beautiful mum could handle."

A spark of interest awakened her glazed eye and a subtle jerk lit Kallan's face. For the first time since meeting Roald, she was genuinely interested in something he had to say.

For the sake of his own preservation, Rune downed half the bottle, knowing Roald had her. The ball in his gut twisted, knowing the interest was somehow at his expense. Rune tipped the bottom up for another mouthful and tuned out Roald's droll. He was nearly through the bottle when two distinct words made it through his sobriety.

"—somewhere alone."

Rune's flagon struck the table with a grand bang, causing Kallan and Roald to

jump and forcing a sneer from them both.

With Kallan's trite 'yes,' they rose from the table together.

From the corner of his eye, Rune glared at Roald's large hand cradling the small of Kallan's back as he escorted her to the back of the Hall toward the screens passage. As the door leading up to Bergen's chambers closed behind them, Rune gulped down the last of the mead and slammed the flagon to the table.

"Torunn!"

His fist struck the table.

It wasn't long before the woman scurried from the kitchens.

With misery about him, Rune threw a crumpled glance at Torunn and grumbled a single word.

"Mead."

CHAPTER THIRTY-FOUR

The grains of the planks bore into Rune's forehead as he rocked his head back and forth on the table. He tightly clutched the near empty flagon as his insides writhed with loathing for his cousin. A hard thump announced the arrival of his next drink, and a chair scraped the stone as Geirolf settled himself beside Rune.

"I hate that room," Rune grumbled into the wood. "I'll have it burned before Bergen gets back, I think."

He listened to Geirolf's gruff sigh.

"Rune," Geirolf said. "Might I interrupt your self-brooding and speak plainly?"

With his brow still mashed into the table, Rune rolled his head to the side to better look at Geirolf. The wood grains left their mark imprinted into his face. His hand still clutched the flagon.

"With the men from the south arriving, and thousands from the north on their way with Bergen... How do I put it..."

Geirolf rubbed his heavily stubbled chin as Rune stared blankly at him.

"Kallan glistens like a new, foreign sword..." Geirolf bobbed his head to his own story. "Refined, unseen, and honed to perfection with a fuller that just…shines in the sun. They're all gonna want their turn to hold it," Geirolf said. "They'll fight and bicker and pass it around, each wanting it for his own as they admire its hilt and test its balance. They'll give it a few practice swings and they'll turn it about to read the inscription in the ricasso… Hel, a few may even name it."

Geirolf exhaled, shaking his head in admiration as Rune still lay with his head on the table, staring.

"Get your ass down to the blacksmith and close the deal or you had better get mighty used to your sword seeing some action before you have your turn to hold it."

Geirolf's chair scraped the stone as he pulled himself up from the table.

"And Odinn only knows what condition the sword will be in by the time you get your turn," he added and shuffled himself off to Torunn and the kitchens.

Rune heaved a long sigh and pulled his head up from the table. He glanced about the empty Hall and slowly decided to agree with Geirolf. Leaving the flagon at the table, Rune trudged to the door beside the kitchens and glanced down the three steps past the larder.

In the kitchens, servants buzzed with a healthy excitement as they whisked food off to the barracks where Roald's men had settled in. Among the bustle, Geirolf sat at a table nursing a mead beside an empty chair usually reserved for Bergen. Rune pulled open the door leading to his brother's chambers. A conspicuous twinkle from the old man's eye almost went unnoticed as Rune closed the door behind him.

Despite his sour mood, Rune couldn't help but admire Bergen's insistence that his chambers be next to the kitchens.

"For the sake of the food and the wenches," Bergen had added while groping the cook and a mead.

Slowly, Rune started up the steps, not bothering to compose an excuse for the rude interruption he was rearing to give.

The stairwell curved with the wall as Rune passed the lone window and glanced out across the gardens. Paying no mind to the waning moon or Kallan's subtle grunt outside, his foot touched down on the next step. He looked to the platform at the top of the stairs and stopped.

Another grunt from the window forced him to lower his foot back down to the step. He waited and listened.

A third unquestionable grunt confirmed he had heard right. Holding his breath, Rune poked his head out the window and looked down to the vacant gardens. A fourth grunt directed his attention up.

For a long while, he stared up at Kallan, who hung fastened to the wall of his keep. Her fingers and toes were poised with slivers of Seidr secured from each digit that, he could only guess, she used to secure her grip. Curious, the Shadow Beast lifted its head within Rune.

Rune waited to be flummoxed, then wondered why he wasn't, and watched for a moment longer as she shifted herself to the next run of stones. It was with a furrowed brow and a head full of questions that Rune inhaled slowly.

"Kallan."

Kallan gave a jump that lost her footing and stopped Rune's heart all before pulling herself flat against the stone. Panting from the adrenaline rush, Kallan snapped her head to the window where Rune's head protruded.

"*Uskit!*" Kallan exclaimed and proceeded to scale the wall.

Rune forced the calm in his voice steady. "What…are you doing?"

"I'm…" Kallan guided her foot to the next stone and grunted. "…escaping."

Rune cocked his head at the obvious and tried again.

"Yes. I can see that."

The moonlight caught the silver of her gown. He glanced down to the gardens and up again to Bergen's window.

"But why are you escaping?" he asked. "I mean…" Rune blew a 'pshaw' and rolled his eyes. "I figured it would come to this, but…Why aren't you taking the stairs?"

Exasperated, Kallan growled and gave a subtle nod to the wall, accompanied with an eye roll.

"If I could…" Kallan lowered her hand, directing the Seidr between the next run of stones. "I'd burn you."

"Yes." Rune nodded in agreement, unable to suppress the grin that tugged at his mouth. "I'm sure you would."

He assessed the sixty pace fall she would suffer if she slipped and twisted his neck uncomfortably back to Kallan.

"This wouldn't have anything to do with my cousin now, would it?"

"Roald?" Kallan grunted against the stone. "Oh, no. He's lovely."

She lowered her foot to the next run.

"Just a bit too forward," she said, bringing her hand down.

Rune nodded, the smirk pulled tight on his face.

"He kissed you, huh?"

"He tried."

"Where'd you leave him?"

"In Bergen's sitting room," Kallan grunted. "I slipped into Bergen's bedchambers…and took the only path of escape."

"The window?"

"Obviously."

"You couldn't just blast your Seidr at him?" Rune asked, amused at the conversation.

"An attempted mating ritual hardly warrants a death sentence."

"You could've just declined his advance."

"He didn't seem the type to slow down long enough to hear it," Kallan said, and Rune nodded. Kallan gasped then held her breath.

"You don't seem surprised by any of this," she said once she found her footing again.

"This isn't the first time a woman has scaled the walls to get away from Roald."

She paused for a moment as she studied the wall for her next foothold.

"Besides," Rune said with a shrug Kallan couldn't see. "I figured he'd try."

Kallan gave a grunt as she lowered herself to the next run.

"You were so sure?" she asked, watching her grip.

Rune nodded, rethinking his answer.

"Well… You're alive." Rune glanced up at Kallan, allowing himself the rare opportunity to relish a glimpse of what little flesh the wind permitted among her many skirts. "And you are a woman."

Kallan stiffened against the wall, suddenly aware of Rune's perspective. She tried to look down to confirm her suspicions. Failing miserably, she flattened her stomach against the wall, inhaled, and released an irate sigh, then returned to her climb.

"There really is little else that Roald needs to think he has a shot with you," Rune said, not bothering to take his eye from the view.

"So…arrogance runs in your family," she said, descending the last two runs. Extending his arms, Rune welcomed her waist into his hands and guided her safely through the window.

Kallan threw her head back. Heaving, she sighed and extinguished her Seidr. She paused to regain her breath. "And I can safely assume that any sons of yours will be as arrogant and as conceited as you are."

Rune eyed the lock of hair that fell to her waist.

"As much as any daughter of yours will be as stubborn, temperamental, stubborn, difficult, and as stubborn as you," Rune added a grin.

Kallan took a step closer as if sparring.

"Well, if she's your daughter, she'll most assuredly be bossy, irrational, and rude!"

"Are we discussing our children?"

Shock jolted Kallan into check, and Rune delighted in watching her skin flush red.

She shoved past Rune, purposely slamming her shoulder into his, and started down the stairs. Instantly, Rune lunged and, pulling her back, closed his mouth onto hers, no longer preserving the sense to let go. He held her in place while he had his fill, bearing down deeper, his mind and body aching with want of more. He felt her respond as she pushed into him.

For a brief moment, both abandoned their senses, twisting their arms around the other and not bothering to care about the repercussions or the impossibilities that plagued them as they clawed tighter, needing to be closer.

Rune wrapped his arms around Kallan's waist and pulled her up from the step below him. Together, they fell back onto the steps still having their fill. In as much time as it took Kallan to claw her way down Rune's body and succumb to undaunted recklessness, Rune flinched with an unease that shook the appetite right out of him.

His grip relaxed and he clutched her arms, prying her away with trembling hands as the reality of their situation sank in. With her face fallen and betwixt with horror, Kallan shook her head.

"Why?"

Rune shoved his hands through his hair.

"Is it the war?" she guessed. "My people? Me?" she whispered this last word.

Stupefied, Rune stopped and stared wide-eyed at the hurt already building in Kallan's eyes.

"You think I stopped because of you?" he asked.

"Why else?"

Her voice quivered. For the first time since he had known her, she appeared helpless and frail, as if she would break from a strong, passing wind.

Engulfed with sudden understanding, Rune shoved his fingers through her hair and rested his forehead against hers as if willing the tension from his mind.

"Kallan… Get to your room."

She didn't move, and her disobedience taunted him.

"If you don't leave right now, I will deduce that you want me to continue, and I won't stop. The stairwell isn't exactly comfortable."

Her cheeks renewed with the red Rune was quickly growing fond of and, obediently, she forced herself out of his embrace and off of him. Holding herself upright against the wall, Kallan proceed down the steps.

"And Kallan…" Rune recovered the control in his voice.

She looked back.

"Next time Roald pursues you, take the stairs."

Wordlessly, Kallan left Rune still sitting on the steps, shifting uncomfortably in his own body as he forced himself not to follow.

CHAPTER THIRTY-FIVE

Clenching her skirts in her hands, Kallan stiffly walked up the steps from the Great Hall, all the while cursing Rune for pulling her through the window. In the corridor, she dropped her skirts and shuffled to her chambers as she pushed open the door of her sitting room.

Torunn had the fires crackling against the late summer chill that had settled in. The first of the snows were drawing near. At once, Kallan busied her fingers with the unlacing of her bodice as she moved to the bedroom chamber and froze at Roald standing against her door frame.

"Good evening, Your Majesty."

The heat on her neck returned.

"Evening," she replied, wishing more than ever for a cloaking spell on hand.

With a long sigh, Roald sauntered across the sitting room and came to stand before her.

"I get the impression," Roald said with a sly grin, "that you had an entirely different motive for agreeing to see me alone tonight."

Kallan stood, forgetting that her hands still clung to the lacings of her bodice.

Roald stared sternly down at her. "When you didn't answer the door from

Bergen's bechambers, I took the liberty to enter. I never would have believed a woman would climb out of a window to escape me."

Kallan lowered her hands from her gown. Her chest expanded, forcing her head high as she inhaled.

"Perhaps I've done you some good." Kallan smiled.

"Perhaps," Roald said, taking a few steps closer.

Kallan cocked her head, unsure if he would shout, rage, laugh, or coninute where things left off.

"I'll tell you what I'm going to do, Your Highness. I am going to leave you now and report to the barracks," Roald said. "I suggest you hunt down my cousin. I think we both know to which one I am referring."

The tension melted from Kallan.

"Thank you, Roald," she said. "But your cousin—and we both know to which one I am referring—found me in the stairs."

Roald nodded. "Good. And now, my sweet lady."

He planted an innocent kiss in the open palm of Kallan's hand and escorted himself to the door as fast as Kallan could say, "One moment."

Curious, Roald turned back to Kallan.

"Your Majesty," he said.

"There is something I'd like to ask you."

"Ah." Roald nodded. "This must have been your true intentions then?"

"What happened to Bergen?" There was no smile on Kallan's face.

The words wiped all joviality from Roald's face and he came to stand at full attention, studying her hardened face for a hint of amusement.

He spoke only after her cold eyes convinced him she was serious.

"You bring up a dark topic, Kallan Eyolfdottir."

She reserved her focus, refusing to back down without an answer.

"It's his eyes, then?" Roald asked. "You noticed the unchanging black of his eyes."

"Among other things," Kallan said, remembering the scarring that spanned his bare back and his unusual loathing for tunics.

Roald sighed and glanced about for a flagon of mead.

Empty-handed, he sighed again and composed the words to move on. He ran his hand over his mouth several times, as he collected his thoughts on where to begin.

"Where I begin depends a lot on how much you know."

Roald paused, giving Kallan the chance to back out.

"Have you stumbled yet upon the maids ranting about Swann?"

"Swann?" Kallan asked, thought for a moment, and then shook her head. "No."

"No, I didn't' think you would," Roald said. "Mention of her name is almost banned within the keep. Well, then… I guess I should start at the beginning before Bergen's eyes changed."

"He wasn't born like that?" Kallan asked.

"Oh, dear lady, no," Roald said. "Bergen was made like that. Let's see. You've met the twins, Rune and Bergen. I doubt very much you were ever acquainted with their father before the war began. Your father would have known him, but neither you nor your kin would have laid eyes on the queen mother, Caoilinn."

"K-Kw-Kway Linn?" Kallan practiced the foreign sounds for herself.

"Aye. Caoilinn," Roald said and gazed out the window at the moon as if pulling the stories from ancient thoughts nearly forgotten.

"Have you ever heard the stories of the maidens who hide deep in the forests across the sea, cursed with incomparable beauty and blessed with the freedom to change forms?"

"You speak of the Swann Maidens of Eire's Land," Kallan said, remembering the tale told to her so many times by Gudrun. "Born with a beauty so rare that any man who lay eyes upon them would be driven to madness. In most cases, any man who saw them would instantly become so smitten that he would not eat or sleep until he had her. He would spend every waking moment looking to keep her for himself."

"In some cases," Roald said. "In the weak-hearted, a man's desire for the Swan Maidens would outgrow his senses, and he would attack them. Until one maiden, desperate to end the rapes of her sisters, begged for mercy from the gods. And Kara reached down from Odinn's halls and granted them the ability to change form and fly."

"So they might escape their assailants and fly to where none could find them," Kallan said.

"Yes." Roald sighed. "Having heard of these women, Tryggve set out to find one for himself. He had just reached his elding and was as restless as Bergen. He believed none but a Swann Maiden was suited to wife the son of the great Lodewuk."

Too easily Kallan could see Bergen making the same declaration for himself.

"Tryggve arrived upon the shores of Eire's Land and scoured the forests until he found himself a bevy of Maidens," Roald said. "He had sailed from Alfheim equipped with a plan to capture one, but made no preparations for what happened next."

"What did happen?" Kallan asked.

"He was so smitten by the beauty of one so fair that he came to love her in that instant. So much so that he couldn't bring himself to force himself upon her. Instead, he sat and watched from a distance lest he approach and frighten her. Unable to sleep, unable to eat, unable to leave her side, Tryggve sat and watched and waited, all for the sole chance to gaze upon her beauty."

Roald paused to smirk, amused at the irony before he continued.

"He had been so intent on capturing a lady of Eire's Land that he failed to foresee his own captivity. He sat and watched so often and for so long that the Maidens grew curious of their sentinel. Most grew accustomed, until they unlearned their fear, forgot their hate, learned to trust Man."

Roald grinned.

"I embellish of course. It always sounds better this way. One evening, long after the Maidens had grown used to Tryggve's vigilance, there was an ambush. A faction of men had come to claim their brides. There was a brawl. Tryggve jumped in to save the women, but although he proved victorious, a sword had pierced the heart of the one who had enthralled him, his Caoilinn. Mortally wounded and lacking the skill to save her, Tryggve carried her from the wood and sought out a village for a healer. He was successful in this endeavor and stood by her night and day, ensuring her heart was mended.

"Several weeks passed before Caoilinn was well enough to travel and return to her sisters. But upon their return, they discovered Caoilinn's bevy had gone."

"Where did they go?" Kallan asked.

"From the devastation Tryggve described, another faction had come in his absence."

Kallan's face fell and Roald continued.

"Lost to her sisters, Caoilinn implored Tryggve to keep her. So it was, after five years, Tryggve, son of Lodewuk, returned to Gunir with his beloved Swann

Maiden. By then, her adoration for him had grown and that midsummer, they wed. In less than a year, Rune and Bergen were born. Roughly seven winters after that, sweet Swann followed."

"Swann?"

Roald nodded.

"Named for her mother's gift and blessed with a beauty that paled Caoilinn's. She was a precious, little thing," Roald recalled with a weighted grief in his eyes. "The family's jewel."

"What happened to her?" Kallan asked.

"That year our war began, the year of the massacre. While gathering the willow branches for the Feast of Austramonath, Swann was slain. The boys found her in the dalr." His voice cracked.

"Dalr." Kallan spoke the word in comprehension. "Swann's Dalr."

"Swann's Dalr." Roald nodded. "We heard the boys howling and we came running. Bergen was kneeling on the ground cradling what little was left of Swann's little, perfect body. She was stripped down to her bare bones and drained of her blood—" Roald swallowed a tight knot in his throat. "After being broken, stripped, and raped, she was gutted and left to die in a pool of her own blood."

Roald tightened his jaw as he blinked at the burning in his eyes.

"Swann's death shattered the family. Caoilinn was devastated. Right there on the steps of the keep, she pulled every bit of her powers to save her daughter. But she gave too much. She drained the power of her own life source and it still wasn't enough. Instead of saving her daughter, Caoilinn killed herelf. Her death marked the end for Tryggve. His grief consumed him. The man was too far gone. His heart, too broken. With madness, Tryggve rose up from Caoilinn's death and, with sword in hand, vowed revenge against the Dokkalfr who killed his Swann and destroyed his Caoilinn.

"He was gone so quickly... There was no time. We tracked him, too late, to the main road that leads to Lorlenalin. All we found when we got there was the massacre left in Tryggve's wake: the mothers hewn as they clasped what little was left of their children's bodies.

"We returned to Gunir to find Tryggve still drenched in the blood of the Dokkalfar babes, weeping at Caoilinn's side and begging her lifeless corpse to forgive him...and when she didn't answer, he shoved his own blade through his heart."

For some time now, Roald stared beyond Kallan, who silently wept, unable to meet her eyes.

"The tragedy struck Bergen hard. After taking up his father's vow, Bergen fled to Svartálfaheim to rally the Dvergar against Eyolf and finish what his father had started. We would not see Bergen again for one hundred years."

"A hundred—" Kallan gasped.

"Rune," Roald whispered. "He ascended the throne without father, mother, sister, or brother. Suddenly orphaned and alone, the King of Gunir stood against Eyolf's wrath knowing someone had to answer for the Massacre of Austramonath. Rune had no criminal to hand to Eyolf and no Dokkalfr to name for Swann's slaying. Desperate to survive, Rune matched Eyolf's rage as his own grief formed a hole that began with the image of Swann's gutted body. The grief-stricken mother so absorbed by sorrow that it killed her... Caoilinn's death taking the heart of Tryggve until a shell of a man rose against the Dokkalfar in a berserker state...and Bergen, his only brother, lost to an unknown fate."

Roald's voice had started to shake, forcing him to pause to recollect his nerve.

"The one hundred years," Kallan whispered. "Where did he go? What happened?"

Roald met Kallan's eyes.

"We've been trying to figure that out for centuries. Bergen's story came in pieces after years of silence. What little we know, we managed to piece together in between the tales he spins. Instead of hearing him out, the Dvergar captured Bergen and imprisoned him in the bowels of Svartálfaheim for nearly one hundred years. Enslaved and forced to work in their mines, he endured the Dvergar's prisons until even the shirt on his back reminded him of the hole in the ground where he lived all those years."

Kallan closed her eyes, remembering her own imprisonment. Those two weeks shackled in the Dvergar caves had felt like a lifetime. She couldn't begin to imagine one hundred years of that Hel. She returned her gaze to Roald.

"Long after his silver-blue eyes formed to the sunless caves," Roald said. "Long after the thick walls of his cell closed in on him, Bergen escaped. When he returned...darkness pervaded his core. The black of his eyes would no longer adjust to the day's light, clothes proved a constant reminder of the cell that suffocated him, and the cold...the intolerable cold of our winters no longer fazed him.

Roald shook his head. "But something else...something else happened within those caves. Something changed him. He will speak of it to no one."

Roald hung his head, recalling a grief he had fought so long to forget. He gulped several times, forcing his eyes dry as Kallan rolled his story over until she remembered every word.

Catching a single phrase, she found her voice several minutes later.

"Why..." she asked, forcing Roald's face to hers. "Why did Tryggve believe Swann's death was carried out by a Dokkalfr?"

"An arm ring bearing your mark..." Roald pointed indifferently to the signet ring upon Kallan's finger. "Rune found one near the body."

"I see," Kallan said, lowering her eyes to the floor. "And Tryggve was grief-stricken."

Roald nodded.

"Rune reached out to Eyolf, desperate to be heard... But—"

"There is no honor in this... No excuse that will ever justify the slaughtering of those children," Kallan said, quoting her father. She had heard him say those words so many times before.

Roald pulled in a long, deep sigh.

"By summer's end, the war was in full scale and alone, Rune stood his ground against Eyolf's army."

Kallan nodded, unable to look Roald in the eye as the final word closed his tale. His feet shuffled against the stone, forcing a desperate cry from her lips.

"Roald."

The large, burdened man looked back and waited.

"I'm sorry," she found the breath to say.

With a heavy eye, he gently smiled.

"We all are, lass. Every last one of us."

He trudged away, and the door clicked close. A breeze cut through the thick air of her sitting room, drawing Kallan's attention to the moon.

"Swann," Kallan whispered, aligning the pieces Roald left to her. "Bergen and Rune."

Questions still unanswered pulled her darkened eye toward the keep.

"Borg."

CHAPTER THIRTY-SIX

R une stared at the fire through the plume of pipe smoke. The door of his sitting room opened and clicked close. Rune took another draw as Roald came to stop at the door.

"Be gone, Roald," he grumbled as the smoke billowed with his breath then lofted as the next stream pushed into it like rolling clouds.

He took another, longer draw from his pipe. Without a word, Roald sat in the vacant chair beside Rune, who stared through the smoke. Resting his elbows on the armrests, Roald emitted a long, loud sigh and stared into the fire, ignoring Rune's persistent scowl.

"She knows," Roald said.

The words stopped Rune's hand and he glared, awaiting an explanation.

"You told her?"

Roald nodded then tipped his head back at an angle.

"She had no idea," Roald said.

Rune released another puff of smoke in thought.

"I suspected she didn't."

The flames licked the stone as they flickered wildly in the hearth.

Indifferent to his guest, Rune silently picked at the embers in his pipe.

"Any news from Gudrun or Daggon?" Roald asked, easing closer to the subject at the front of his mind.

"No," Rune said curtly and took another mouthful. "I sent Joren out to keep an eye on Aaric's movements. I've asked that he also keep a look out for Gudrun and Daggon while he's there."

A chill pushed in through the window, bombarding the bubble of heat that the fire and pipe created. The smoke plumes spun about in silent disarray then found their way again as the breeze subsided.

"Rune?"

Rune peered up from his pipe, the bit resting casually between his lips.

"When all this comes together and Kallan is forced to fight—"

"Kallan will not fight." Rune said.

"She won't sit still," Roald warned.

"I'll lock her up in her room." Rune shifted his eyes to the flames. "I will post guards at the door. I will bind her with rope, if I have to. I will not see her forced to choose between siding against me and killing her own."

"Choose?"

Roald furrowed his brow as Rune drew from the pipe, determined to ignore him. He leaned closer to better force his ear. "She has her city, her people, and full intent to return to them. I have no doubt the girl would provide an entertaining romp, but what makes you think she would ever choose the life of a Ljosalfar over a Dokkalfar?"

"Kallan believes she can stop it," Rune said. "She is convinced that once her people see her, they'll know she lives and will follow as they once did."

"You seem doubtful."

"Wary." A plume of smoke wafted from Rune's mouth and he lowered his hands to his lap. "Her plan is…simple." Rune brought the pipe to his mouth once more. "Too simple. Kallan isn't stupid. Her training was thorough. Rigid, even. I have no doubt she can hold her own in battle against any of us, but against her own?" Rune shook his head. "I don't see her capable of looking her own men in the eye and running them through with her blade. And now that she knows the lives and faces of the men here…" Rune shook his head.

"Will you go to her?" Roald cut in, too impatient to wait for Rune to sidestep the subject further.

"What?" Rune said, looking over from his pipe. "Tonight?"

Roald leaned forward, resting his arms on his knees.

"She's willing, cousin."

"I don't have the luxury to cloud my judgment with her bed."

The words affected Rune more than he wanted to admit. Slouching ever so slightly, he stared back at the fire and released a rather large plume while feigning contentment with his decision.

"Oh, come off it, Rune!" Roald's voice stabbed the lethargic warmth of the bedchamber and forced Rune to jerk himself awake. "You kicked her out of my bed to keep that precious treasure all to yourself, and now you're planning on leaving her un-rumpled?"

"Your bed?" Rune said from between the bit. "I found her clinging to the side of my keep."

"The intent was there. The metaphor stands," Roald insisted. "You sought to trash my night with the lady. At least have the decency to bed her in my stead... Odinn knows, one of us should."

Roald fell back into his chair, an arm draped over the back, plagued with his pondering.

"Has Bergen had her yet?"

Rune's grip visibly tightened on the bowl of his pipe, oblivious to the heat.

"Ah..." Roald grinned. "He has—"

"I will not bed down with something I can't keep," Rune said stiffly.

"How is this any different than any other wench you've had?" Roald asked.

"She isn't any 'wench' I've had, Roald. She isn't anything I've had."

Rune sighed, releasing the edge off his temper.

"She is different," Rune agreed.

At once, enlightenment swept Roald's face and he straightened his back to peer closer.

"Oh... You want her to wife."

Rune scoffed.

"Because I won't bed her?"

"*Because* you won't bed her," Roald reiterated, ignoring Rune's brooding.

Making a loud click, Rune bit down hard on the mouthpiece and grumped.

"I can't risk angering a monarch we're at war with over a single night of indulgence."

"Hm. How convenient for you," Roald said and waved his hand, indifferent to Rune's argument. "Arrangements are made all the time to unite fylker and clans."

"Yes, fylker," Rune agreed, lowering his pipe. "Allied fylker. Not two peoples on opposing sides of an ancient war. And not when one of them can throw fire!"

Roald shook his head smirking at Rune's stubbornness.

"Besides," Rune dismissed. "She won't abandon her post, my people won't accept her as queen, and Bergen refuses responsibility."

"And yet, you still want her to wife," Roald said.

Rune rolled his eyes.

"Good night, Roald."

With a heavy sigh, Roald lifted himself from the chair.

"I never said I didn't approve," Roald added before closing the door behind him and leaving Rune alone with the only fire to warm him.

CHAPTER THIRTY-SEVEN

Kallan pushed open the thick oak door of Borg's cell, spilling light across the stone that struck the bloodied mass hanging on the wall like a tattered tapestry. With a flick of her wrist, a single ball of light rushed to the ceiling where it hovered, casting a tinge of blue around the room as she closed the door behind her.

The door's thud jarred the room and encouraged Borg to raise his head. Streaks of black flowed free from the nape of his neck and painted the back of his shoulders. Kallan clenched her teeth against the rising need to vomit.

"So," Borg grunted. "Ever victorious, the Queen of the White Opal appears."

His black hair dripped with blood too thick and too fresh to dry. Something white, which Kallan guessed was a bit of his tooth, rested on the floor beside him. His hands were mangled balls that churned her stomach. Only one of his eyes seemed to function, despite being bloodshot and blackened from his crushed nose.

"Who are you?" she asked, ensuring she kept her distance.

A low, throaty chuckle filled the cell.

"I'd expect no less from the likes of you, Your Highness…" he sneered.

Kallan dared a step closer, desperate to recall the outline of his face through the mass of blood.

"Who sent you?"

Borg released another low chuckle and coughed.

"So that's it now?" He relaxed back onto his chains, allowing the shackle to tug at his limp arm pulled from its socket. "I didn't break under the grunt Helbent on watching others writhe so that he has something to jack off to tonight… or the noble captain who justifies his own sickness in the name of his queen."

Borg spat on the floor. Blood splattered the stone and sprayed the hem of her skirts.

"Such heinous acts, too many, are already justified in the name of a queen, their gods, and their country," Borg said. "No… Now they're sending the dogs, the Seidkona herself, to bend and break me."

He managed to curve his swollen face into a malformed smile, confirming that more than just one tooth was missing.

"Who are you?" Kallan whispered, fighting the rising wave of nausea. "What dishonor did I do that you would turn your venom on me?"

Borg dropped his smile and peered with his one eye at his queen.

"I hate you more for failing to even remember." He inhaled against the sharp pain of his crushed ribs.

"Can't I undo this?" she asked.

"So quick to walk…to stomp on those beneath you, all so you can stand tall," Borg rambled aloud, paying no mind to Kallan's question. "You don't bother to see who it is you're standing on while you reach for your stars, princess."

"I have done nothing to you," Kallan said.

Borg gazed at Kallan as if seeing her there for the first time.

"You, Your Majesty, have done the most to me." He spat his bloodied saliva as he spoke.

"Did I know you once?" Kallan asked.

"So prestigious in your own that you can't even remember the lives of those you've crushed beneath you."

"Then help me remember so that I may right my wrong," Kallan pleaded.

"If this was a wrong that could be fixed, I wouldn't hate so much!"

Sweat pooled in Kallan's hands as she clenched her fists and took a step closer.

"There is a chance to end this," she offered. "King Rune desires peace for our people. There coul—"

"You think I want peace?" Borg bellowed.

"Don't you?"

"Never...would I want peace... You and your peace," Borg scoffed. His face twisted as he spat. "Your dance never changes. The song you play is always the same. All you ever spoke of in the warrens was your peace...you and your peace!" Borg met Kallan's eye through the pale, blue light. "I will see no peace for any Ljosalfar, and will not rest until each of them is dead!"

His chains rattled as he shook with rage, but Kallan, disconnected, drifted into the back of an old memory.

"The warrens," she whispered. "Borg... No." Slowly, Kallan shook her head. "Borg was your brother's name..."

Comprehension blanketed Kallan's eyes.

"The day was cold and gray. A fog had fallen over the massacre that was Austramonath... Austramonath," Kallan gasped. "Kovit," she said and remembered, lifting her eyes to the bloody mass supported by chains on the wall.

Kovit sneered at the sound of his name and made a derisive sound.

"The ravens were feasting upon the dead when a small boy—you emerged from the fog carrying a corpse. You were the first," Kallan said. "Eilif and I began collecting the orphans that day. Oh, Kovit. Little Kovit." Her face fell with grief as she played through the dark memory. "Is this what you have become?" she asked, but he didn't answer. "You left us with no notice.

"You came to us through the massacre carrying your brother, speaking through sobs and half-crazed," Kallan said. "Not even three moons later, you were gone."

"You refused!" he spat, drawing Kallan's eye from the memory as if seeing Kovit for the first time. "You didn't bring him back." Kovit crinkled his nose in disgust.

"He was missing an arm and his spine had been cleaved in two," she said. "His guts had spilled out his back."

"He lived!" Kovit cried. Tears burned his face.

"He was already dead, Kovit."

"You didn't even try," he growled, heaving a breath through his mouth that shook him with rage.

"Not even Gudrun could bring him back," Kallan argued.

"He was alive!"

Kallan stared, cold and calculative, and waited.

"You never understood!" Kovit heaved. "He must live! He must— Mother said he must, that we both must live! Just live. But you let my brother die…then spoke of your peace. Your peace… Always your damnable peace! Did Tryggve desire peace when he killed my mother? I was there!" Borg bellowed. "No excuse can justify that massacre! No excuse can justify the lives slain there, your father always said! He saw! He understood!"

"I underst—"

"She threw herself onto me as the berserker went for my brother! He turned on my mother and slaughtered her! And you speak of peace, your peace!" Kovit stared at Kallan like she was a slug that had oozed from the bottom of the sea. "I only lived because he never thought to look for me. He never finished me! The massacre…" Kovit gasped. "I live and am left with these images! There are things I can not unsee!"

His sobs filled the cell as Kallan looked on, wordless and numb.

"He left me alone with my hate," he said, "Always my hate! Always…always."

His whimper quieted.

"And the hate goes on… And the grief passes on and another child vows their vengeance," Kallan muttered and raised her eyes to Kovit. "How many more must die before you have your fill? How many more like you must enter the warrens? How many more until none are left, Kovit? How many more must die?"

"You know nothing of grief," he growled. "You wouldn't understand. Of my—"

"Don't I?" Kallan spat, tightening her balled fists. "I took to the warrens because of my mother, because there were others like me on the streets."

"On the streets," Kovit scoffed. "Others like you, princess? Oh yes, you in your palace. You understand the hunger, the filth, the desecration of the warrens from inside your precious, perfect, palace walls."

"I gave everything I could to you. I lost my mother and then my father," Kallan said. "You dare speak to me of not knowing, not understanding the hole, the grief, the emptiness that burrows its way through? Carving out your heart until nothing is left. Not even the strength to die!"

Her shoulders shook with a rage she fought to keep in check.

"Did you punish him too, Kovit? Was it you who took my father from me?"

Calmly, quietly, Kovit met her eyes.

"No."

"Who sent you?" Kallan shrieked. "Who wants me dead? Who crossed your palm with silver?"

Kovit grinned.

"You think none desire your death?" he asked. "That no one could hate Lorlenalin's princess? I did," he volunteered. "I did and she found me. I, who would be willing to do it for free."

"But she paid you." Kallan cocked her head in question and Kovit chuckled.

"She didn't pay me to kill you." Kovit shook his head and dropped his dark smile. "She paid me to stay quiet."

"Who, Kovit?" Kallan repeated.

"I just can't say," Kovit said.

"And the Dvergar?" Kallan asked. "Did you pay them as well?"

"They found me," he answered, too tired to fight anymore. "They paid me."

"They found you?" Kallan whispered. "How did they find you?"

"I didn't care who killed you or how or when," Kovit droned, not hearing a word Kallan said. "I only cared that you suffered as much as I."

"You didn't summon the Dvergar, then," Kallan said.

"No, but they wanted you." Kovit hung his head. Sleep was taking him.

"But they couldn't get to me," Kallan said.

"So I found someone who could," Kovit said.

"Who, Kovit?"

"Gunir's king."

Kallan's face fell white.

"Rune?" Kallan's thoughts fell into disorder. "B-But Rune didn't... Rune wouldn't."

Kovit peered up from the floor.

"Rune was a disappointment."

Kallan's fists twitched with the temptation to fire her Seidr at him, but Kovit didn't seem to notice.

"The deal was…the king would kill you the moment he was alone." Kovit had dropped his head again. "They were to find your body near Lorlenalin and assume you died in battle. And until recently, I had believed the job was done."

"But the Dvergar… They had paid you…" Kallan said.

"I sent them after you when the king left Lorlenalin. I figured the two adversaries could work it out. Either way, you had been taken care of and my employer would be content and I could wash my hands of both the Dvergar and the king."

"Who sent you?" Kallan snapped, irate with his indifference.

Kovit raised his head to show her his wide grin.

"I have no idea."

"Who sent you?"

Kovit attempted to shrug.

"Can't say."

"What do they plan?"

"Ah…" A light in his eyes seemed to glisten. "That is what I've been waiting for. Now that, I can answer," he whispered.

Kallan didn't dare move from her place as Kovit widened his grin. Blood seeped from his split lip.

"They're coming for you, Kallan," Kovit breathed. "They'll find you and they'll take you back. It's only a matter of time before you go home. You belong to them."

"Who?" she asked.

Kovit shrugged again and closed his grin, hiding his teeth.

"Can't say," he smiled. "But they're coming."

Glaring down at the remnants of Kovit and Borg, Kallan spun on her heel and snapped her wrist just as she threw open the door and slammed it again, leaving Kovit alone in the dark.

CHAPTER THIRTY-EIGHT

Kallan marched down the corridor, past her rooms to Rune's bower. Undaunted, she flung wide the doors of Rune's sitting room then swept through the rich décor. A moment later, she yanked open the door of Rune's bed chamber.

Dressed in just his trousers, Rune turned to catch the firelight shimmering on the silver strands that laced her bodice. Too late, he gazed at the fire in her eye as she slipped her hand around *Gramm*'s hilt where it rested against the door.

Rune dove for the sword. Kallan stepped in and landed her fist in his eye, sending the king flying back onto the trunk at the foot of his bed. Before Rune could check for blood, Kallan released a blast of pure Seidr. A gush of wind caught his chest and flung Rune back and over the bed.

"Had to stop a war?" Kallan shrieked, and Rune leapt as Kallan swung the blade and missed.

"Had to declare peace?"

Rune hopped back, and *Gramm*'s tip grazed his belly, leaving behind a thin line of red.

"You lied to me!"

"I never said—"

"You kissed me!" Kallan said and fired another blast of wind. The shot grazed his pelvis and slammed him back into the wall and his supply of mead.

"You let me believe you actually did this for me!"

"Kallan, wait! I can explain!"

Rune scrambled onto his bed as Kallan circled around the farthest side to corner him.

From the sitting room, Geirolf and Torunn peered in, followed quickly by Roald, a wench, and a menagerie just as Kallan swung *Gramm* again. Rune moved, but had run out of bed and fell to the floor.

"Day after day trudging through Midgard…"

Kallan sent another blast of Seidr just as Rune dove for the door leading to the war room.

"Starved and wet and cold…"

Rune flattened his back to the wall, nearly smashing the looking glass in the process, and did his bravest to confront the Seidkona.

"Eating nothing but your damn fish while you insisted one of my own had betrayed me!"

"But Borg did—"

Kallan lunged and swung the blade down, leaving Rune barely enough time to snag up his bow and block the blade, deeply gouging the riser.

"You took me from Lorlenalin to kill me!" Kallan shouted and swung. The blade struck the upper limb of the bow severing it.

"You were one of them!"

She swung again and caught the grip.

"And I believed you! I actually started to believe you! And I let you put your hands on me!"

"You spoke to Borg," Rune said, beneath his bow.

"Yes, I spoke to Borg!" Kallan shrieked, lowering *Gramm* to her side. "And I know everything! How you lied to me! How you and he had a deal! How you agreed to kill me!"

"I never killed you," Rune said.

"Is that why you came for me?" Kallan asked as he cowered beneath his bow. "Why you rescued me from the Dvergar? Because you had to make good on your deal?"

"I didn't kill you!" Rune said. "See? You're standing there trying to kill me!"

Kallan released a high-pitched growl and lunged, forcing Rune to take up his bow and block, locking *Gramm* at the hilt.

Glancing at the damage done to the bow, Rune let slip a smile and Kallan slipped a fist through their weapons to punch him in the mouth. Rune fell back into the wall as Kallan stood screaming over him.

"You scolded me for my lies and half-truths! You were right there alongside me with your own fair share of lies! You were working with the very spy you planted to betray me!"

"But I never did—"

"Enough!" Kallan turned the blade down, driving it into the end table beside him.

Unarmed, she stood heaving over him.

"Negotiations are over!" she said. "If you insist I am free, then I go! I leave first thing in the morning with my kin! And if you have any objections, Your Highness…" she said this with a derisive tone. "Then I suggest you imprison me to keep me here!"

In a rage, Kallan marched to the door, ready to burst through the crowd of onlookers that had gathered to watch from the sitting room.

Rune called from the floor, "But Aaric—"

"Aaric isn't working with Borg, Rune!" Kallan turned on her heel.

"Borg told you," Rune said.

"Borg told me!"

"But Aaric," Rune said, trying to push himself up from the floor. "You can—"

"A woman hired Borg, Rune!"

Rune's shoulders dropped.

"First thing in the morning, Your Majesty!"

"But, Kallan—"

"Your services are no longer required!"

And as sharply as she was cold, Kallan swept from Rune's bedroom, leaving him alone with their audience.

CHAPTER THIRTY-NINE

Gudrun and Daggon rode through the night, stopping only to rest the horses. Too exhausted and worn to speak, they made their way slowly along the Alfheim Wood. Another day's ride and the tops of Lorlenalin's white towers would greet them.

"Hold up," Gudrun said, pulling back on the reins.

"What is it?" Daggon asked.

The air settled and Gudrun reached beyond this earth, into the fibers where the Seidr flowed. There she felt it, like a lone ripple along a perfectly still surface. Strong, powerful, and too close to ignore.

"It's too late," Gudrun whispered. "She's here."

In an instant, Gudrun slid from the saddle and threw open a saddle bag.

Daggon slid off his horse. "Gudrun?"

"Here," the old woman said, handing Daggon her pouch. "Inside you'll find my strongest cloaking spell."

"You know I don't do your Seidr spells, woman—"

"There isn't time," Gudrun said.

"Then let us be off an—"

"Daggon! Please!"

Daggon studied Gudrun's golden eyes.

"If I've ever learned anything, it's when not to argue with you, Seidkona." Daggon accepted the packet from Gudrun. "Very well, woman."

Daggon swiftly pulled himself back on his horse.

"Ride ahead," Gudrun said. "Don't look back. Don't stop. You must get to the city. In my chambers, beneath a floor board under my chest."

"What am I looking for?"

"You'll know it when you see it. Whatever you do, no matter what happens, get it and my pouch to Kallan. She'll know what to do."

"What of you then, lass?"

The winds picked up, whipping Gudrun's long silver hair about.

"Go!" Gudrun called.

"Gudrun."

"There isn't time!"

The raven called and Gudrun shrieked. "For once, Daggon! Do as you're told!"

"Alright."

Daggon nodded and whipped the reins, sending the horse into an instant gallop.

"Ride fast," Gudrun called. "Ride hard. Don't look back!"

The wind continued to whip about as Gudrun looked on.

"No matter what happens," she whispered.

The winds settled, and Gudrun turned to her horse.

"Drui," Fand breathed. Delight rose in her chest at the sight of the Seidkona. Pulling the threads of Seidr through the air, Fand stirred the winds back up and forced Gudrun to spin about in search of her assailant.

"Drui," Fand repeated in sing-song then watched in amusement as Gudrun withdrew her Seidr staff.

A raven fluttered and a moment later, the bird stretched her neck as if sliding off the feathers. As the raven shifted its form, Fand uncurled and grew until the Fae stood, her long black hair falling to her waist and spilling over the white gowns that shimmered gold with Seidr dust over the flawless skin of Under Earth.

"Yours is the Seidr I sensed!" Fand exclaimed. "Oh, this is a delight!" Rolling her shoulders back in display like a bird preening, Fand rolled her neck and deeply inhaled.

"Fand," Gudrun gasped as if finding her voice. "I might have known this was you. Everything reeked of a spoiled palace brat."

"Oh, such hate." Fand feigned hurt. "When I picked up your trail, I was certain the child was still alive."

"Kallan…" Gudrun muttered.

Fand inhaled again, smelling deeply the scents on Gudrun's clothes.

"You smell like cursed berserker," Fand said, groaning in delight and smiled. "How is Bergen?"

"Friend of yours?" Gudrun asked.

"Not quite."

"You found my trail," Gudrun said. "Now why couldn't I sense yours?"

Smiling, Fand shrugged.

"Search me," she said and lunged, throwing a thick line of white Seidr straight for Gudrun, who met Fand's attack with the Seidr staff and directed the stream of Seidr into the ground.

Fand fired with her other hand, forcing Gudrun to greet Fand's Seidr, direct and lead it into the ground. Again, Fand fired and Gudrun met Fand's attack.

"So what do you plan to do with yourself once you've killed me?" Gudrun asked.

"Oh, don't take it personally," Fand said. "I'm just wrapping up loose ends."

"Killing ten thousand wasn't enough?" Gudrun snapped.

"Ten thousand is nothing if not you three. Tell me." Fand narrowed her gold eyes into slits with a sly grin. "Where is Volundr?"

"Never found him, did you?"

Gudrun dropped to the ground. With palms flat against the earth, she summoned and pulled the charges Fand had fired at her only moments ago. The Seidr erupted and, leading the Earth's Seidr on the strands of Fand's Seidr, she launched Fand's attack back at her.

Fand opened her palms to the Seidr and invited the energy back in, but Gudrun had summoned too much from the Earth, and the force blasted Fand through the air. Several feet away, she struck the ground, giving Gudrun enough time to counter.

"And after you kill me, what then?" Gudrun said, already accumulating a condensed quantity of Seidr in her palm. "You'll kill Aaric, I presume?"

Fand was on her knees.

"Only a little," she said. "He and I have a deal that is keeping him alive a little longer."

Fand lifted her hands, throwing back the Seidr from one palm, and another, and a third as Gudrun directed the shot with her Seidr staff, dodged the second, and consumed the third into her palm as she pocketed the staff. Gudrun raised both palms, firing off a continuous stream of light and Fand charged, dodging Gudrun's attack.

Fand fired a single shot at Gudrun's head. Gudrun dodged and directed the continuous stream, forcing Fand to leap out of the way while releasing another shot.

Gudrun dropped to dodge Fand's shot and fired a round of light, once, twice, thrice, The fourth sliced Fand's cheek.

Her perfect, pale cheek.

Fand stopped dead in her tracks and touched the bit of blood etched on her face. Fand gazed at the bright red on her finger as if seeing mortality for the first time in her ancient existence.

"The first flaw in an otherwise perfect complexion," Gudrun said. "Did the palace brat get a booboo?"

Screaming, Fand fired and fired.

"You have no idea the delight I had in killing Kira!" Fand shrieked as she fired round after round of white at Gudrun, who dodged and danced in desperation to avoid Fand's Seidr.

Again and again, Fand fired as she walked closer, closing the range between her and Gudrun.

"I'll drain the life from the last of you!" Fand screamed, still firing and not giving Gudrun a chance to do anything more than move.

"I'll destroy your secrets!"

A single strand struck Gudrun's shoulder.

"The lies!"

The next strand struck Gudrun's thigh and she dropped to a knee.

"The key!" Fand shrieked.

Fand clamped her fingers down on Gudrun's brow, positioned so the thumb and middle finger encased Gudrun's temples.

"I'll send them all to Hel with you," Fand said. "Where is Volundr?"

"Don't know," Gudrun said. "Haven't seen him."

Without pause, Fand thrust her lines of Seidr through Gudrun's temples and shoved her Sight through Gudrun.

Gudrun buckled under Fand's Will as the Fae goddess sorted through the lifetime of memories locked in Gudrun's mind.

"I'll take what you won't give," Fand mused. "Back," she muttered as she ripped through the memories.

Kira's smile. Kallan's birth. Ori and Kallan playing in the Dvergar mines. Kira's death. Bergen's screams.

"Further," Fand muttered through gritted teeth.

A tree. An ancient tome. An underground library.

"I know this place," Fand said and then drove her Seidr deeper, ignoring Gudrun's body jerking under her hand.

Danann and Dag standing so ancient, so regal over the thousands of dead Drui in Eire's Land. Gudrun and Aaric and Volundr. A much younger Gudrun writhing with pleasure under Volundr. A shadow, and—

Fand gasped and pulled her hand free. At once, the seizing stopped and Gudrun fell limp to the ground.

"What have you done?" Fand asked, ignoring the lines of blood seeping from Gudrun's temples. Almost kindly, Fand kneeled beside Gudrun's crumpled body and gently touched her hand. "All these years without your love…"

Gudrun heaved in reply, unable to move, to speak. The damage was already done. Fand was certain Gudrun wasn't Gudrun anymore.

"Pity."

Securing her life lines to Gudrun's Seidr, Fand, within a few short breaths, pulled all the Seidr from her. The gold from Gudrun's eyes drained, leaving behind a set of lapis blue irises that matched Kallan's. Her skin, preserved by the Seidr, shriveled and dried, and all the years of the Eldin and life of the Alfar vanished in those few moments, leaving the Drui a withered husk void of Seidr.

Fand released Gudrun's corpse, already cold to the touch. Almost bored, she sauntered to Gudrun's horse and unsheathed a sword secured in one of the saddle bags.

Humming a little ditty, Fand wandered back, as if taking a simple stroll through the wood.

"Sing and skip o'er Faerie mounds,
O'er the river and through the dalr."

Raising the sword, Fand heaved, and in a single swipe, dropped the blade through Gudrun's neck.

"And then there were two."

CHAPTER FORTY

Kallan woke the next morning to the steady patter of rain that added a cold, gray drizzle to the keep. The scent of hot fire and damp earth mingled in the air as if cooking out the wet rains from the lingering stale chill. From the warm furs and wools of her bed, she watched the rains welcome the reds and dying greens of autumn that punctured the fading life of Alfheim. The sun had barely risen behind the clouds, encouraging her to linger with the morning drizzle before forcing herself to move.

The keep stirred with the same hesitation. As if the chill outside had slowed their feet, servants took longer serving breakfast, Fires took longer to stoke to life as if the humidity had dampened the fire wood. The scent of porridge and blood sausage lingered from the kitchens through the Great Hall to the bowers.

Torunn dragged herself about the chambers and dully laced Kallan's deep scarlet gown. Within the Great Hall, Geirolf quietly ate his bowl of hot mushy grains, slurping to the sounds of the hot fire. Beside him, Roald hunched over the table cradling an almost empty mead he had nursed all morning. Geirolf was mid-bite when the doors of the Hall swung open, sending a deafening boom through the keep and jolting everyone from their dreary sleep.

With a wide, mischievous grin soaked through with rain, Bergen dropped his hand from the door, flanked by Thorold, who stood as soaked as Bergen. With wide shoulders, towering height, and a fine, single scar that trailed the left side of his face, Thorold assessed the Great Hall through his mass of black hair and braided beard.

~ ~

"Up, Brother!" Bergen shouted, giving a wet slap to Rune's bare foot. He rounded the side of Rune's bed and stopped to observe the lack of a female form.

"Where's Kallan?" Bergen asked, entirely too perky for so early in the morning.

Rune released a groan and rolled with the pillow clamped to his face. Bergen struck Rune's leg with the arm of the drenched overcoat.

Rune grunted.

Leaning down to the pillow, Bergen allowed the cold rain to drip onto Rune as he bellowed.

"Where's Kallan?"

Rune slapped the pillow to Bergen's face and forced himself upright, emphasizing the morning's grogginess.

"Have you checked your bower?" Rune said, swinging his legs over the side of his bed and digging the sleep from his eyes.

"Why isn't she here with you?" Bergen asked, refusing to give Rune space free of the dripping overcoat.

Miserably, Rune dropped his heavy hand to his lap and forced his eyes to focus on Bergen, Thorold, and Geirolf standing around his bed.

"What the Hel happened to you?" Bergen asked of Rune's black eye and swollen, split lip.

"Bergen…" Rune tried then gave up, deciding he was too tired to argue.

"What happened to my bow?" Bergen shrieked, taking up the mangled bow that had been tossed aside in the corner.

"Kallan and I…we…she…"

Bergen grinned, forgetting his bow.

"That good, huh?"

"Kallan's still in her room," Roald said, coming to stand in the doorway.

"Oh." Rune grimaced. "You're still here?" he asked of Roald.

Digging his fists again into his eyes, Rune winced at the sharp shots of pain sent burning through his face. He stretched and yawned as a series of cold, wet drops fell onto Rune's comfortably warm legs and feet.

"Gi'off," Rune grumbled, pushing back on Bergen, who still wore his saturated travelling clothes.

"Come on! Awake!" Bergen declared, giving a sloppy, wet slap to Rune's bare shoulder. "We have news! We need mead! Geirolf, fetch your wench! Get the mead and have her bring salted meats…enough for five and yourself if you want. And bring Kallan!"

"Told you countless times, not my wench…" Geirolf grumbled as he trudged out the door to find his wench.

Displeased with his wet shoulder, Rune scowled and forced himself up from the bed.

"Thorold." Rune nodded to the tall captain standing behind Bergen.

As he shuffled his way to the chest at the foot of his bed, his company cleared a path. With a sharp headache that drummed his head, Rune pulled on some pants and a tunic.

After stripping the cloak from his shoulders and peeling the shirt from his back, Bergen dumped the clothes over the back of a chair to dry. With a great amount of banging and clutter, he pulled up a chair to the fire and dropped himself down, stripping the saturated boots and wraps from his raw feet.

With a lot less clumping and shuffle, Thorold followed suit and dropped himself into a chair in Rune's chamber. Within minutes, Geirolf was back with Torunn, an armful of mead, and a tray full of candied fruits and salted meats. As soon as Torunn placed the tray on a table, the men happily gorged themselves. She quietly took her leave as the men relieved Geirolf of the mead.

Ignoring the tray of provisions, Rune snatched a bottle and slumped back into his chair from the night before. A flash of red caught his eye and Rune lifted his face to Kallan standing quietly in the doorway. She had already donned the leather overcoat gifted to her by Ori, and, for a moment, Rune pondered what had become of their brief companion.

"My lady," Rune greeted Kallan too formally.

"Your Majesty," Kallan coldly rebutted.

After a moment, the shuffle and scrape of chairs pulled their attention back to the room and Kallan shifted her attention to each face, taking in all who had joined them. She sharply inhaled and stiffened her back as Thorold gave a slight nod, acknowledging Kallan.

"Lady Kallan," his bear-like voice flowed like smooth mead.

"Captain," Kallan nodded.

Bewildered, Rune looked about as if an explanation would suddenly erupt from the floor.

"You know each other?" Rune asked, so perplexed as to question the amount of mead he had already consumed.

"They do, Rune," Bergen said as he chomped down on a large strip of salted venison. "It's why we're here."

Rune looked from Bergen to Kallan to Thorold to Kallan and waited.

"You remember the Battle of Swann Dalr," Bergen said, refreshing Rune's memory through a mouthful of meats, and Rune rolled his eyes.

"Yes," Rune said, vividly recalling the blow he sent to Kallan's head, and her pale face as he recognized her from the wood. He almost vomited as he recalled Borg's offer to exchange Kallan's life for his freedom. His black eye suddenly hurt tenfold.

"I remember," Rune said. *Ages ago, it seemed.*

"Do you remember why we lost that fight?" Bergen asked, chomping down another strip of meat and filling his mouth with warm, thick mead.

Rune thought back from Aaric's offer, Kallan dying on the forest floor, the Seidkona, and the wandering wench... Rune clenched his jaw as he shifted a swollen eye to Kallan and recalled the boar and her stance to spear the boar with her Seidr.

Bergen gulped twice, oblivious to his brother's absent-mindedness, and pulled the bottle from his mouth.

"Kallan sent troops to the north, forcing me to ride to Thorold's aid," Bergen said, pulling Rune back to the conversation.

Silently, Rune nodded, suddenly aware of his sweating palm clenched to the neck of the bottle.

"You had just returned from the assault in the south," Bergen continued.

The memory flared to life as Rune remembered.

"Yes," Rune brooded. "Daggon had the advantage when his queen ordered him to pull back and abandoned his victory."

He shot a scowl toward Kallan, who smiled with delight.

"The queen," Bergen repeated. "Really, what happened between you two last night?"

"Only after we regrouped in Swann Dalr did we realize the extent of our losses," Rune said. "Daggon's troops had meant to weaken us, not annihilate us."

Bergen popped a small bit of meat into his mouth. "And I, having received word of an attack in the north, rode to Thorold's aid and left Swann Dalr vulnerable to an attack. When I arrived at Thorold's Keep, it was as I feared. Thousands lay dead. I hadn't been there half a day when Joren arrived to tell me about the attack in Swann Dalr." Bergen shook his head. "I had to leave Thorold to his slaughter for a chance to preserve the king."

"We delayed burning the corpses," Thorold said, filling the chamber with his rich baritone. "We waited for three days...but Odinn never came. The Valkyrjur never rode to clear the battle field. Just as we were ready to give up and begin burning bodies, my troops rose again."

"Well after I had seen the number of warriors dead at the Northern Keep," Bergen said.

A proud grin twinkled in Thorold's eye, as his gaze came to rest on Kallan still standing in the door.

"Rose up?" Rune asked.

"Awakened," Kallan corrected.

All eyes met hers for an explanation, and Kallan inhaled. From her pouch, she withdrew an apple and tossed it across the room to Rune, who caught it one-handed.

Still clutching the bottle of mead in one hand, Rune bit into the apple and at once felt the clotted blood in his eye thin and break up as the purples, blacks, and blues faded from his face. All eyes watched enthralled as his lip mended itself and the sharp bruises and pains he woke with that morning vanished.

"It was a sleeping spell," Kallan said. "A spell that Gudrun concocted on a grand scale to put any within a certain range to sleep for a period of time."

The hushed room stared in disbelief at the Dokkalfr as Kallan passed a glance around the room.

"We didn't desire devastation," she said. "With what we had planned in Swann Dalr, we knew we would succeed with or without slaughtering thousands in the north." She shrugged. "We didn't need you dead. We needed you distracted. It would have been wasteful to kill so many without cause."

"Why, with such a power, didn't you simply end this sooner?" Rune asked.

"It was a new spell," Kallan said. "Gudrun only recently obtained the ingredients, a very rare...rare ingredient. We used the last of it on the batch we mixed for that advance. It took as long as it did to perfect the results. Otherwise, paralysis sets in and you won't wake."

"How many?" Rune asked, at once realizing the grandeur of the news Bergen harbored.

"Four thousand," Thorold supplied, barely able to contain the glint in his eye.

"Why was no word sent with this information?" Rune asked with his eyes fixed on Thorold.

"It was," Bergen said.

"Several times," Thorold said. "Until Bergen arrived, we thought you knew."

"How—"

"Someone somewhere intercepted the scout," Bergen said.

"Borg," Rune said.

"Possibly," Bergen said. "Four thousand, Rune."

"But how do you know the queen?" Rune asked. "At what point did you…"

The words were lost in Rune's throat.

"I made an appearance a day before the attack," Kallan said, filling in the blanks. "I summoned his counsel to offer a chance to surrender and appeared as the Seidkona. I had no intent to reconcile, and I knew Thorold wouldn't make a move without your consent. I also knew that you were in the south with Daggon. That was our plan, after all. I wanted Thorold to see the Seidkona in the North and report her position—my position—in hopes you would send for Bergen and alter your defenses at Swann Dalr. And you did."

"With the four thousand from the north," Rune asked, "and another five thousand from the south, we are left with ten thousand here in Gunir. Kallan, where do your numbers stand?"

"We last counted our own at seventeen thousand, nine hundred. You can count my own and Gudrun's Seidr enough to even out those numbers if it comes to a fight."

Rune gave a subtle twitch at the mention of Gudrun's name. Bergen bowed his head into the strips of meat. Geirolf shuffled uncomfortably in his chair.

"What?" she asked. "What's wrong?"

The air stiffened as everyone waited for Rune to answer.

"Gudrun isn't here," Rune muttered and braced for what was to come next.

"What do you mean?" Kallan asked. "Of course she is. I just sent Torunn to—"

"You didn't tell her?" Bergen asked. His disbelief blanketed his face.

"Tell me what?" Kallan asked.

Rune exhaled then paused a moment before answering.

"Gudrun and Daggon left."

Rune's confession left Kallan white.

"When?"

"Four days ago."

"Where, Rune?" The edge in her voice was shaking.

"Lorlenalin…to rally support and confront Aaric," Rune said.

"You let them go?" Kallan's pitch scraped the ceiling.

"I advised against it."

"You sent them to their deaths!" Kallan said.

"It was their idea," Rune said.

Bergen released a long, regrettable groan.

"Gudrun insisted she go," Rune said.

"And you didn't stop her!"

The fire crackled as all eyes silently shifted between Rune and Kallan. The rains had begun to fall hard, adding a metallic drum to the fire's chorus.

"Well then?" Kallan belted.

"Well, what?" Rune asked, waiting, watching her from across the circle of the bodies.

"Go get them!" she said with a wave of her arm toward the door.

"Kallan…" Rune sighed. "We're on the brink of battle. I can't leave now."

"Never mind!" Kallan threw her arms to the air. "I'm leaving today anyway!" she announced and spun on her heel.

"No, you don't!" Rune said.

"I don't see how you have a say in this!" Kallan said.

"You're alive today because of my invested interest! Between the two of us, I have worked harder to keep you alive! At this point, I have more of a say regarding your livelihood!"

"Then lock me up!"

"You stay!"

Bergen released a second long groan on behalf of his brother.

Kallan snapped around, furious with his order. She glared back as each waited for the other to break. With a flourish of skirts that followed her like whipping flames, she stomped from the room

Bergen leaned forward in his chair toward Rune.

"You still haven't stoked her yet?" he asked.

"You didn't exactly leave us in the best of all moods," Rune said.

"She was plenty in the mood last night before you went and ruined things," Roald said. "What was your excuse then?"

Bergen peered down disappointedly at his brother.

"So, where are we now?" Thorold asked, pulling the topic back to the war.

Rune stared blankly into the hearth, his thoughts toggling between two brewing matters.

"I will not bring war to Kallan's city," he said. "An offensive move will guarantee Kallan's loss of cooperation. We wait for Aaric to move. For now, we wait."

"And if he doesn't?" Bergen asked.

Shuffling away from the platter of meads, Rune slouched into his chair and tossed the stripped apple core into the flames.

"Bergen." Thorold's gruff tone forced Bergen's attention from his brother as Rune threw back his head for a drink. "You've been inside Lorlenalin's walls. How did you get in?"

"Borg led us in through the stables," Bergen said. "The entrance is tucked behind Livsvann Falls."

"We'll only need to draw him out," Thorold said. "All we need to do is get in, make our presence known, and get out before he can assemble the troops. He'll advance if he sees us accumulating forces in Swann Dalr. From there we can make our move."

"What you're talking about is hitting him hard and unseen from the direction he won't be looking," Rune said, looking up from the fire.

Thorold opened his mouth to confirm as the door banged open. The men snapped their attention to Joren who stood, saturated down to the bones and panting from a hard run. The heavy crackle of falling rain filled the room.

"The Dokkalfar—" Joren gasped, battling to speak between breaths. "They come, not three days off."

The men rose as one, pushing back the chairs as they stood.

"How many?" Rune asked.

"Twenty thousand," Joren said.

"By Odinn," Roald muttered.

"It's begun then," Rune said with a slight nod. "And we will rise up and meet them. Bergen. Roald. Thorold."

Each man waited at attention, eager for his orders.

"What will you have us do, Rune?" Thorold asked.

"Do we ride out?" Roald grinned.

"No." Rune shook his head. "We'll need our strength against those numbers. What we need is a fortress. We'll let him come to us."

"But the children! Our women!"

"Empty Gunir," Rune said. "Send our people to the north. And be quick about this. We must be ready to meet the Dokkalfar outside the city at the plains of the Klarelfr in two days."

With a brief scuffle, each man took their leave as Rune dropped the bottle on the platter and dumped himself onto his trunk for his boots.

"Rune," Geirolf said, cradling a pair of meads. "You have me as a healer, you know that. I'll march with you into battle as always and once more. In the meantime…" He turned for the door. "I'll be helping with the evacuations if you need me."

"Any sign of Gudrun or Daggon?" Rune asked, glancing up from his laces at Joren.

The scout shook his head, sending droplets of water flying. "I didn't see anyone on the road."

Rune returned to his boots.

"Rune."

The scout waited for his king to look back up.

With apprehension, he lowered his voice, ensuring a certain Dokkalfr couldn't hear should she be near.

"I was able to get close enough to hear," Joren said. "No one remembers Kallan."

Rune slowly lowered his foot back to the floor.

"No one recalls," Joren said, shaking his head. "Their memory is gone… Taken from them. As if she never existed. If Kallan were to stand before them this day, they wouldn't know her from a Ljosalfar. They will kill her."

"By the gods," Rune muttered. Doubling his pace, he returned to lacing his boots. "Joren, I need you to do something for me. Fetch two of the guards and have them posted outside Kallan's door."

Torunn quietly closed the sitting room door behind her as Rune paused to rethink his orders.

"And station two more at the base of the keep in the courtyard beneath her window."

"Rune," Torunn said.

"And have Gunnar hide Astrid," Rune said. "I can't risk her following us and, believe me, she will try."

"Rune," Torunn tried again.

"I'll go to her myself and tell her the news. I expect her full temper on this one."

"Rune." Torunn's voice was louder.

"Find Bergen," Rune said. "Speak to him. Update him on the situation. He'll need to inform Roald and Thorold of this as well."

"Rune!"

"What, Torunn?"

"She's gone."

The blood drained from Rune's face as he met the fear-stricken hollowness in Torunn's wide, round eyes. Remembering Kallan's last words, Rune stood sharply from the trunk. Without a word, he marched through the door of his bower and descended the stairs to the Great Hall.

His shoulder nearly smacked into Bergen, who barely had time enough to flatten his back against the wall at the base of the steps.

"Bergen. You're in charge," Rune called, not bothering to look over his shoulder as he swept by.

"What?"

"I'll be back in two days," Rune added.

"Where are you going?"

Rune threw wide the double doors.

"What if you're not?" Bergen asked.

Rune looked back to Bergen.

"Don't wait for me."

The grand doors slammed with a hollow boom that left Bergen alone in silence flanked by the throne beside him.

Rune dumped Astrid's saddle over the horse's back, giving Kallan cause to jump.

"What are you doing?" she asked, attempting to pull the blanket flat beneath the saddle he buckled into place. Rune raised an eye to Kallan and ignored her question.

"Don't try to stop me," she said with a brittle bite in her voice.

"Who said I'm here to stop you?" Rune asked, adding a tight snap to the buckle. "I'm going with you."

Kallan's eyes widened.

"This is my kin," she said. "My family. I'll not go anywhere with you and hand you the opportunity to stab me in the back!"

Rune kept his hands busy, but peered through the strands of his hair that had fallen loose from the tie-back.

"Funny, I thought you'd want to keep me where you could watch me."

"You lied to me!"

"You don't know what you're up against, princess," he said.

"Don't—" Kallan ground her teeth. "Don't I?"

With a final snap of the buckle, Rune rested his arms across the saddle. Holding Kallan's tongue with his glare, he spoke with a hushed flourish of words.

"Aaric moves with twenty thousand."

"Twenty—" The blood drained from Kallan's face. "It doesn't matter!" she said, recovering her temper. "They'll hear me! All I have to do is—"

"No one there will know you as Queen of the White Opal." Rune dropped his eyes back to the saddle. His fingers moved quicker than ever as he moved on to the bridle. "You can leave that title behind you."

He turned from Astrid to ready one of the fjord horses for himself as Kallan ducked around Astrid's neck and followed.

"What is that supposed to mean? My people—"

"Have been cursed!" Rune said, leaving the job to lock eyes with Kallan. "Someone has taken their memory from them! They won't know you. They don't remember you! If they see you, they'll kill you without question."

Kallan furrowed her brow in an attempt to hide the wall of tears.

"This fight is my own," she said, returning to fasten Astrid's saddle. "I must do this alone."

"You're so certain Gudrun won't be opposed to your intrusion?" Rune asked.

"I spoke to Borg."

"So you've said."

"He said they're coming for me."

Rune pulled Kallan's hands from the buckles..

"Did he say who?"

With fallen shoulders, Kallan shook her head, realizing that in the end, Kovit had said very little.

"Well, I've had enough of this," Rune grumbled with a hastened pace to his horse.

"What are you doing?" Kallan asked.

"With your legions marching here, I have no time to waste roaming about the forests looking for Gudrun," Rune said. "I need answers and Aaric has them. Besides, if Gudrun has made it to Aaric, we'll have the best odds of finding her there." Rune snatched up his horse's bridle from its hook. "And I have a few words I'd like to share with Aaric."

The color returned to Kallan's face and she leaned closer with a new sparkle in her eye.

"What do you propose?" she asked, bouncing on her heel as she gleamed with anticipation.

"Do you have your pouch with you?" Rune asked. "We're going to need it."

CHAPTER FORTY-ONE

Through the rains, Kallan and Rune rode across the river-streaked plains of Alfheim. Their faces burned from the battalion of water drops that bombarded them as they rode. They stopped multiple times to give each horse one of Kallan's apples, and were on the road again shortly thereafter, refreshed for the hard ride south.

The rains had barely let up by the time the early afternoon sun settled behind the mountains, leaving behind clear skies and the blanket of early evening that granted them unseen passage to the edge of the Dokkalfar camp.

Soaked beneath the stars, Rune and Kallan quietly dismounted and fastened their horses to a withering tree almost bare of its crimson leaves. As Rune unsheathed *Gramm*, Kallan withdrew and dispensed a spell, taking care to grasp Rune's hand as the last of their corporeal selves faded before their eyes.

"This is so weird," Rune whispered, raising *Gramm* to his face. Turning the blade over, he saw nothing.

"Sh," Kallan shushed and pulled Rune through the forest toward the Dokkalfar camp buried deep in the Alfheim wood.

"Do you know where it is?" he asked, keeping his voice below a whisper.

The sweet snap of fresh rain and heavily churned earth invaded their senses as they slunk through the damp leaves and the soaked foliage.

"We had several camps stationed in the wood for transport." Kallan peered over her shoulder at invisible Rune to ensure he heard. "Aaric should be here."

Moments later, they were near enough to hear the familiar jargon and trills of Kallan's native tongue. The scent of warm spices brewing within the stews of the Dokkalfar fires stirred Kallan's appetite. Longing stayed her feet as the urge to lunge into the camp and join her brethren overcame her.

Rune gave her hand a gentle squeeze.

"Soon," he whispered from close behind.

With a nod he couldn't see, Kallan blew a quiet sigh and reasserted her focus. Recalling the initial goal, unwilling to let go, she tugged Rune's hand and continued through the forest's edge.

As they drew nearer, they stopped long enough to peer from behind the foliage. Several steps away, out from the cover of trees, was Aaric's tent. Around the tent, Dokkalfar bustled, sharpening their weapons or eating. Most had turned in for the night. Rune tugged Kallan's hand, drawing her attention toward him.

"There," she heard Rune say and could only assume he pointed toward the largest of tents.

"Come," Rune bade and pulled Kallan to her feet as he took the lead and tugged her toward the tent.

Warm light spilled from beneath the hides, where they came to an abrupt stop. With great care, Rune listened at the door, confirming the silence inside before pushing aside a small bit of the hide to study the layout.

A fire burned in the center of the vast room, while an array of furs and weapons dripped about the living quarters. A full set of pristine armor waited on display in the corner of the room. Against the farthest end of the tent, a table had been brought in and was strewn with maps. To the one side of the tent, a large, fur bed and a chest lay idle while, on the other, a table lavished with fruits, mead, and meats drew their attention. There, Aaric stood pouring a drink.

He had sleeked back his hair framed with the war braids that flanked the side of his face, allowing Rune to scrutinize some of the many etchings inked into his shoulders and up his neck.

"Ready?" he whispered.

Kallan nodded then gave Rune's hand a squeeze when she remembered he couldn't see her. Tightening his grip on Kallan, Rune slipped into the tent and pulled her in behind him.

As Aaric turned to examine the sudden chill from the tent's flap, Rune released

Kallan's hand, and Kallan released the spell.

"Aaric?" she said.

With a flagon of mead half raised to his mouth, Aaric fumbled and dropped it, spilling it all over the floor.

"I told you not to bring her back," Aaric said to Rune, keeping his voice low.

Rune shook his head, confused.

"You never spoke to me before this night."

"No, you wouldn't recognize me," Aaric said.

A sudden outburst outside jerked Aaric to attention.

He briskly moved to the tent flap and peered outside.

"Just the soldiers," he muttered once the raucous died down. Aaric dropped the flap.

"You must leave," he said. "Quick. Before she gets back."

"She?" Kallan asked.

"Go! Now!" Aaric said and, taking Kallan's arm, did his best to shove her toward the door.

"Aaric, please!" Kallan said, yanking her arm free.

"Kallan, please," Aaric said. "You can't be here."

"But—"

"Gudrun can explain," Aaric said, taking up Kallan's arm again. "Ask her about the Drui. She'll know what that means. Now go!"

"Gudrun is coming here," Rune explained.

"What?" Aaric asked allowing Kallan to take back her arm again.

"She left to plead our case to you," Rune said.

Aaric shook his head.

"She can't... Please! Just go! There isn't time!"

"Aaric?" Kallan said.

"Don't come back. I'll find you," he said to Kallan.

"Aaric!" Kallan said.

"Please get her out!" Aaric said to Rune.

Shoving them toward the door, Aaric guided Kallan only a foot when the flap reopened and a tall woman with golden eyes, long black hair, and a single scratch of blood on her right cheek entered with something clutched in her right hand.

The woman looked stunned as she stared at Kallan. Kallan studied the woman's golden eyes so like Gudrun's, and her flawless skin so unlike anything seen in Alfheim or Midgard.

Quite suddenly, Aaric grabbed Kallan's wrist. She felt the flow of her Seidr shift as if the motion unlocked a door that released a lifetime of memory.

In that instant, a whirlwind of images bombarded her mind, flooding her head with pictures, too many to sort and too blurred to see, each accompanied with a chorus of sound all played at once.

Aaric's grip tightened painfully on Kallan's arm as Rune watched the woman stiffen then flush white with sick.

Time suspended them there as Kallan's eyes flickered as if trying to keep up with the onslaught of images, countless images that flashed with sound and color and all at once.

"No!" the woman screamed and threw the thing she clutched at Kallan.

It hit Kallan, who stumbled back, breaking Aaric's grip on her as a pair of empty, ancient eyes stared at her.

"No! It's not done!" Aaric shouted as Kallan unleashed a shrill cry from the depths of her core. Gudrun's sickly gray head lay on the floor at Kallan's feet, ending a trail of long, silver strands dyed red with blood as anguish cleaved Kallan's heart in two. All strength left her as she sank to the floor with Rune, who pulled her back up, desperate to keep their guard raised.

The woman stood, heaving with rage. The Beast within Rune awakened and roared as Kallan snapped her hands alive with flame.

The woman matched Kallan's offense as Kallan's cries became a run of insufferable screams and both women charged. Rune's Fendinn jumped, and Rune lunged, dropping his hold over Kallan as Aaric threw himself in between the women, his own line of white Seidr secured to the end of the Seidr the woman had thrust at Kallan.

"*Nidingr! Uksit!*" Kallan shrieked in between a long slew of indecipherable curses and incomprehensible sobs as she threw herself at her assailant, held back only by Rune's arms.

"Get her out of here!" Aaric bellowed over Kallan's shrill.

"Kallan!" Rune shouted. "You can't take her!"

Not caring that Rune couldn't hold back the Fendinn, not caring that Aaric had added a tether of Seidr to Rune's Fendinn or that he had a mass of such power, Kallan fought Rune's grip, desperate to get to the woman who had Gudrun's head.

"Stand down!" Aaric shouted to the army that arrived at Kallan's cry. "Back to your posts! Let them pass!" Aaric shouted over Kallan's intermittent sobs.

Rune glared over the heap that was Kallan as he yanked her toward the door.

"I'll say again, Ljosalfr," Aaric said, still holding the woman's rage at bay. "Do not bring her back here!"

Nodding, Rune clamped down and pulled Kallan out of the tent where the sudden cold stabbed at the whole of her body and reminded Kallan that she lived—that she breathed—and forcing her to accept what she saw. Around the camp, the army surrounded them, ready and eagerly waiting, wanting Kallan to advance and leaving barely enough room for them to back into the forest from whence they came.

A trail of screams followed as Rune dragged Kallan into the wood when the last of her strength gave out and Kallan crumbled into a pile of sobs. Scooping the broken girl from the floor, Rune carried her into the dark and ignored the countless eyes on his back.

"Stand down, Fand," Aaric ordered, still holding Fand's Seidr to his own.

"Out of my way, Drui!"

"When I am dead," he said. "Only then will you touch that child!"

"So be it."

Fand sent another surge of Seidr, which Aaric matched, accepted, and took.

"I've killed one of your kind already this night, Aaric! Two Drui is quite a feat to boast! Don't force me to make that mark, Drui!"

"You will not touch her," Aaric repeated.

"I will…and you will live long enough to watch her die," Fand seethed.

Emitting another surge, Fand sent Aaric flying back. Before he could stand, she fired a blast of wind into his gut that left him airless and gasping on the floor.

"I can't kill you," Fand said as Aaric writhed on the floor, desperate to breathe. "Not yet."

As Fand heaved with rage, her appearance changed. Black images and runes surfaced on her flawless skin that darkened and shifted until it mimicked the scarring of Aaric's skin. Her nose grew long and a beard grew in as Fand's hair shortened and braided itself to match Aaric's. She gained two inches in height while her feminine form melted into a wide straight back, and tight chest that filled with muscle to match the centuries of sword fighting Aaric had mastered.

"I doubt any of this can be hidden from Danann any longer," Fand mused as she stared down at Aaric with his eyes. "And may I speak plainly," she said. The last of her seductive voice was fading.

"I'm sick of trying," she said in Aaric's voice. "Guards!" Fand called and two men nearly fell into the tent. Fand pointed at Aaric. "This Seidr User is an imposter! Bind him!" she growled. "Chain him up. But keep him alive. I want him near me at all times."

⁊⁊ ⁊

The light from the campfires faded, leaving Rune stumbling in the dark as Kallan whimpered and sobbed.

"Almost there," he said, but Kallan heard nothing.

He tossed her into Astrid's saddle, and taking up the reins of his mare, pulled himself onto Astrid. After pulling Kallan into him, Rune sent Astrid into a light canter, back through the wood with his horse in tow.

A darkened hour passed before he dared to rest. Kallan's sobs had weakened to subtle whimpers by the time Rune stopped to rest the horses. Together, they slid from the saddles, onto their knees on the ground.

Hushing her, Rune pulled Kallan into his lap and rocked her, allowing her to cry against him.

"I'm sorry," Rune breathed as he swayed. "I'm so…so sorry," he muttered between her sobs.

Several hours were lost before Kallan finally succumbed to sleep, lulled by the relentless rocking as Rune muttered his constant apologies beneath his breath.

CHAPTER FORTY-TWO

*S*ongs and screams filled the silence until Kallan was certain the voices she heard were no longer echoes. She screamed long. Kallan waited for her to stop, to breathe, to give voice to her plea, but all she did was scream a single, unending breath.

Kallan tried to see past the shadows, to see where the screams and music were coming from. She narrowed her eyes, unable to see beyond the tall, black figure among the darkness. She waited, hoping the swirling clouds would soon dissipate. She could barely make out the tall, wide back of a man. Sudden sticky warmth forced her to look down at the blood that dripped from her arms, and she was suddenly aware of the dagger in her hand.

She tried to move, but the blood pooled at her feet from a stream of red, holding her to the ground. The urge to throw up was strong as she followed the stream to her side, only a few arm lengths beside her. The screaming grew louder and the song grew clearer until she could make out the words.

"Sing and skip o'er Faerie mounds,
O'er the hill and through the dalr,
Where the Fae King's halls are gold,
Where they sing their songs of old."

Snapping her head away from the blood, Kallan opened her mouth, peering through the shadow to call to the man for help. She knew she had said something, but the shrill sound and the song drowned out her voice.

Kallan tried to raise her arm, but failed to move, weighed down by the dagger she clasped. The black cloud wafted and ebbed like fog rolling in. She looked back to the trail of blood and tried to see through the darkness where the trail would end. She willed her leg to move, but her foot would not obey. She squinted in hopes of sharpening her sight.

There was something there in the dark at the end of the blood trail.

The darkness swirled and Kallan dared a glance to the man standing in the shadow. He refused to turn, to see what she now saw too clearly from behind. She opened her mouth to call out, to warn him, but no sound came. She wondered why she had to warn him.

Helplessly, Kallan watched as the new shadow raised its sword and thrust the blade through the man, into his back, and out again. Then the shadow was gone, leaving behind a stream of black blood that flowed. Red streaked the black floor and ran, like a stream, toward her and Kallan opened her mouth to join the screaming, but a song came instead.

"Through the wind the spriggans play,
O'er the sea where they stay,
The queen of Fae, she sits there still,
Tending the earth beneath her hill."

Kallan's empty arm was suddenly heavy. Shaking, she looked down to a bloodied silver sword in her hand. She jerked to drop the sword and failed. The screaming and song were growing louder. The sword and dagger pulled her down, and now she fought to stay up as the screaming persisted…as she lost herself in the music.

"Sing and skip o'er Faerie mounds,
O'er the hill and through the dalr,
Where the mystical Fae King's throng,
Fills the earth with ancient song."

Kallan tried to thrash, to free herself from the blood that thickened around her boots. Black blood mingled with red. She couldn't stop trembling there in the dark and the sword and the dagger pulled painfully on her arms.

"Through the wind the spriggans play,
O'er the sea where they stay."

Kallan watched helplessly, peering up as the man fell onto his back and his dead, hollow eyes stared up at her. Dread pierced her chest like a sickle of ice and she forced her face from the lifeless gaze of her father, back to the blood that trailed off into the fog

"The Faerie queen, she sits there still,
Tending the earth beneath her hill."

And all at once the song and the screaming stopped. The black cloud cleared and, at last, Kallan saw the naked body dumped in a heap on the ground as her long, golden hair flowed with the river of blood and her perfect, pale skin smeared with red.

Her lifeless, silver eyes stared out between the fingers of a perfect, red handprint, the scream and the song still frozen on her face, and a single slit from her breasts to her navel stretched the length of her belly, where the blood flowed from her and across the floor to the tip of Kallan's dagger.

The screaming started again and Kallan snapped open her eyes to the black of night and the chill that came with the breeze. Strands of her hair were glued to her brow with beads of sweat.

Rolling onto her side, Kallan vomited and, almost immediately, realized the last scream had been her own.

Within minutes, her body settled and the hollow, massive chasm flooded back and she remembered. The bottomless empty eyes, the silver hair streaked with blood. Kallan sobbed. She closed her eyes for only a moment, but the images flooded back, too vividly to keep her eyes shut. She threw them open again, gasping and desperate for the dizziness to pass with the nausea.

"Easy," Rune shushed, pulling her onto her back.

Kallan stared wide-eyed at the small fire he had going. Her hands violently shook as she willed her nausea to settle.

"It's just a dream," Rune said gently, still holding her.

Streams of hot tears fell from her eyes as she searched the open night sky. Kallan clasped her head, desperate for the images to stop.

"I dreamed—" Kallan gulped down a sudden rise of bile. Her lip trembled. "So much, I don't want to remember," she whispered. The hole inside of her only seemed to expand. "I saw my father in the dark among the shadows…and a girl… bleeding out from the knife in my hand…the knife."

Kallan gave a sudden jerk of her palms as she remembered the weight of the weapons. Desperate to ensure they were gone, she pulled madly at her fingers. Memories of the black pools of blood surrounding her feet flooded back, and she curled herself up and rolled to her side. Tucking her knees against the bottomless chasm inside, Kallan hugged herself against the empty cold that penetrated her. She clutched her arms so tightly she bruised them.

"Kallan." Rune pulled at her to sit up.

"Please," Kallan begged, aching to stop moving and die. "Let me be."

Forcing her up from the ground, Rune pulled her into him as he rested his chin onto the top of her head and sighed.

An unnatural cold permeated her core, leaving her unusually colder than the first of the winter winds should have allowed. Silently, Kallan shuddered beneath her sobs.

"Never, never," Rune whispered as he rocked.

"The pictures don't stop," she said. "They invade my mind. Too many pictures…" She pressed her brow. "I can't see them all."

She was silent for a moment as she remembered the dream all over again.

"She screamed in the dark," Kallan whispered, terrified to close her eyes. "And I killed her… Long, golden hair…white, white skin…and there was blood—so much blood."

Rune rocked.

"She looked at me, but saw nothing with her silver eyes…through the palm printed in blood on her face."

Rune instantly stilled mid-rock.

"So many faces," Kallan breathed. "So many voices…and a song. There are too many…and they are screaming…and I can't hear the words."

Rune became rigid as he stared out into the darkness, his mind whirling faster than the deluge of pictures in Kallan's head. Then he continued rocking, saying nothing.

"I can't hear the words," Kallan muttered.

CHAPTER FORTY-THREE

Thick clouds covered the skies that muted the first of the sunlight and promised more rain by the day's end. It was barely after sunrise when a light sprinkle began. Kallan and Rune emerged from Swann Dalr and rode through the maze of rivers and trees, into the plains that preceded the Klarelfr.

The plains stretched on to the river. Over the stone bridge, they rode through the vacant streets of Gunir and on to the empty courtyard. There, Rune called out into the silence.

"Brother!"

Inside the barracks, still clutching his flagon and fatigued by the two-day evacuation, Bergen lifted his head from the table.

"Bergen! Brother!"

Despite his stiff back, sore from sleeping hunched over the table, Bergen leapt from his chair with renewed vigor, banging his knee on the table. He winced then bellowed.

"Roald!" Bergen rubbed his leg and shuffled away from the table.

"Geirolf! Thorold! They're here!"

Before Roald could awaken, Bergen had taken up his sword, abandoned his flagon, and limped into the courtyard to greet them along with the wave of warriors Rune's voice had alerted.

"Any news!" Bergen barked, pushing his way through the sudden crowd that seemed to be growing. "What's the word?"

Gently, Rune pulled Kallan from Astrid and lowered her to the ground beside him as Bergen added a slap to Rune's back in time to catch a glimpse of Kallan's face. Weakened to the brink of tears, Kallan quickly lowered her gaze to the courtyard stone and collected Astrid's reins, but not before Bergen caught a glimpse of gold in Kallan's eye.

Instantly stifling his merriment, Bergen watched as Kallan quietly slunk off to the nearly restored stables with Astrid in tow.

"Torunn!" Rune called out after searching the faces for the key-keeper.

With her hair pinned tightly to the back of her head, Torunn scurried from the keep in a flourish of skirts and tightly-bound nerves. She stopped dead in her tracks at Rune's voice just as he shifted an eye to Kallan. Her stiff nod confirmed her understanding and she accepted her orders and turned, making her way toward the Dokkalfr.

Rune had barely passed his reins to a nearby stable hand when Bergen managed the question.

"What happened?"

❧ ❧

"How did the evacuations go?" Rune asked with a sigh as he pulled off his tunic and threw it to the floor of his chambers.

"The women boarded the ships with the children and set sail up the Klarelfr to the Northern Keep only yesterday," Bergen answered, stopping in the middle of the room. "They should be well out of harm's way."

"What's left?" Rune asked, pulling on a fresh tunic.

"We've moved everyone else into the keep and have nearly finished emptying the storage houses. Provisions have been counted."

Rune idly nodded and poured himself a drink, taking a long, leisurely sip until Bergen gave an impatient grumble.

"Well?" Bergen growled. "Is there news?"

Rune lowered the drink from his lips and stared through the window at the gray sky. The rains had started to pick up again.

"Gudrun's dead."

Bergen dropped his jaw and jerked as if Rune had poured ice down his back.

"How?" Bergen mumbled once he found his voice.

Rune stared into his drink. After a long silence, he just shook his head, unable to explain who he saw or what he saw.

A fresh breeze blew through the window.

"Be ready to leave by morning," Rune said and threw back his head, polishing off the mead before pouring himself another.

He gave a sigh after gulping down half the flagon.

"We will ride out to meet the Dokkalfar across the Klarelfr where the plains meet," Rune said, still lost in idle thought.

"Where's Daggon?"

The question dropped Rune's shoulders and left him brooding as he emptied another flagon. This time, he took the flagon and didn't answer as he trudged into the sitting room where Torunn had the fire roaring and a platter of food waiting.

Rune dropped himself into a chair across from the fire and threw back his head for another round.

"Where is Daggon, Rune?" Bergen asked, coming to stand beside his brother. His brow darkened with worry.

Rune pulled the flagon from his lips and heavily shook his head.

"We don't know."

Bergen pulled up a chair beside him.

"What happened?" Bergen asked.

Rune shook his head, unable to explain about the Fendinn or the woman or Aaric. He knew no words to explain how much Seidr had filled that tent.

"There was a woman," Rune began. "She and Kallan tried to kill each other. Aaric touched Kallan," he said, trying to fit words to what he saw. "I don't know how to explain it." Rune thought for a moment. "Kallan changed."

"What woman?" Bergen said.

"I don't... I don't know her. I've never seen her before in my life. She had more Seidr than Gudrun, though."

Bergen's face fell white, then green with sick as Rune continued.

"Kallan looked as if..." Rune balanced the bottle on his knee, ignoring

Bergen. "She saw something...and Aaric..." Rune shook his head. "He looked like he had seen the dead rise up from Valhalla."

"Where is Aaric now?"

"The other side of Swann Dalr," Rune said, returning the flagon to his mouth. "He was holding back that woman when he let us go."

Bergen jerked his head.

"He let you go?"

Rune stared at Bergen over the flagon as he threw back his head for another drink.

"If Aaric wants her dead so badly, then why would he let her go?" Bergen asked. "Especially when he had someone right there who would do the job for him?"

"I don't know," Rune replied, shrugging as he stared into the flames.

The fire crackled as another breeze, stronger this time, passed through the window.

"The woman threw Gudrun's head at her," Rune said, keeping his eyes on the flames.

"Who is this woman, Rune?"

Rune shook his head.

"I don't know. Aaric could have killed us at any time," Rune said.

"But he didn't," Bergen said.

"No." Rune shook his head. "He didn't. He seemed more interested with keeping Kallan away from that woman than anything else."

Bergen paused still reviewing the information.

"This woman, Rune," Bergen said. "What did she look like?"

"Really, Bergen? Now?" Rune sighed and Bergen stood, pushing his hand through his hair.

"That's not all," Rune said. "After Aaric touched her, Kallan's been seeing things...things she shouldn't know."

Bergen furrowed his brow.

"Bergen," Rune said. "Kallan saw Swann."

The blood drained from Bergen's face, leaving his face stark white at the memory.

"Did she see—"

"I didn't ask," Rune said before Bergen could finish the question. "Kallan described her to me, exactly as we found her centuries ago. She was singing that damn song of yours in her sleep. Kallan woke up screaming. She doesn't know what she saw, but the description she gave…" Rune shook his head. "The print of blood on her face…"

Rune lost his voice, unable to continue.

Bergen gulped down a helping of vomit as they mulled over what little information Rune had.

"She's in no state to fight," Rune said. "She was having issues just recognizing her men there. Joren's report was right. They didn't recognize her. Bergen."

Bergen looked from the fire.

"They didn't *know* her. They looked at her like she was a stranger."

Rune brought the flagon to his mouth, sighed, and shoved himself out of the chair.

"Tomorrow we rise to battle. Tomorrow we meet him. Have the men ready by dawn."

"What of Kallan?" Bergen asked.

As Rune pulled open the corridor door, he called back over his shoulder.

"Kallan stays."

❧ ❧

"What did you do to her?" Torunn snapped at Rune moments later as she closed Kallan's chamber door behind her.

"How is she?" Rune asked.

Torunn's shoulders dropped.

"She's hungry, but won't eat. She's exhausted, but won't sleep. She cries, but won't speak. She just stares out the window in her bower. Occasionally, sleep forces her to nod off, but then she shivers awake and digs at her eyes. She seems afraid to close them."

Rune exhaled and nodded.

"What is wrong, Rune?" Torunn asked.

Rune raised his eyes to meet hers and forced the words out for a second time. This time it was slightly easier, but sharper.

"Gudrun is dead."

"Oh…" Torunn's hand flew to her quivering mouth and tears glossed the old woman's eyes. Rune watched helpless as the center of his castle's strength crippled beneath the news. Devoid of words to comfort Torunn, he gently patted her back and relieved her of her duties.

He didn't look back as she hurried down the steps like her feet couldn't beat the flood of tears that would come.

Rune drew in a deep breath and slowly exhaled.

"There's going to be a lot of crying around here the next few days," he muttered and pushed open the doors of Kallan's quarters.

The sitting room was empty. Rune gazed at the rain that streaked the blues and greens of the solar glass windows and shuffled his way to the bedroom door Torunn had left open. Staring blankly out the window with tear-glazed eyes, Kallan sat with her arms tightly wrapped around herself.

Torunn had bathed and dressed her, and had the sense to slip her into a plain chemise and dressing gown. A single bare toe peeked out from beneath the hem. An untouched cup of steamed herbs waited on the small table beside her.

Rune's chair scraped the stone as he pulled it around and seated himself across from Kallan. Casually, Kallan tilted her head to better see him and caught a line of gold encircling the vibrant blue of each eye. In a constant stream of falling tears, Kallan sat rigid and silent.

"Kallan."

The rain splattered the keep, the courtyard, the stone window frame and Kallan stared and watched the rains as if the skies cried with her.

"I saw the water falling high from the face of the mountain. But Lorlenalin was gone. The mountainside was bare." Her voice was hoarse from screaming. "I saw my father, but I didn't know him…and I didn't care."

Rune sat quietly as he watched a fresh tear slip down Kallan's face and she lowered her eyes to her fingers.

"What's happening to me, Rune?"

Rune shook his head and gently replied, "I don't know."

"Where is Daggon?" She raised her face to Rune's as another tear spilled down her cheek.

"I don't know."

Without an answer, Kallan looked back to the window and sighed as her tears continued to fall.

"Kallan."

The courtyard seemed quieter. A dog barked.

"I can't save them," she whispered. "Not father, not Daggon... Not the children. Or Kovit."

Kallan's voiced cracked and she studied her hands again.

Rune resisted the urge to ask who Kovit was.

"Not Gudrun," Kallan muttered.

"Your people need you, Kallan."

"I've lost my people," she said, raising her eyes to Rune's. "My city..."

She heaved a deep sigh that left her exhaustion visible.

"Kallan, you must sleep."

She shook her head and looked back to the window.

"I can't," she said. "The images...too many pictures... It won't stop. When I close my eyes, I see the girl, the blood... So much blood. I couldn't save her either."

Slipping his hand into Kallan's, Rune pulled Kallan to her feet with him. He could feel the burden bearing down on her.

"Come," he said.

Too weary to battle Rune any longer, Kallan followed him to the bed. There, he passed her the cup of steamed herbs Torunn had left out for her. He distinctly smelled valerian root and something strangely aromatic rise out of the cup.

He waited, ensuring she took every drop, then guided her down to the bed, surprised that she obeyed. Holding tightly to her hand, he worked to pull the furs over her with his free hand.

"Rune?"

"Yes, Kallan?"

"Please stay with me."

Still clutching his hand, Kallan released a long sigh and closed her eyes. At the side of her bed, Rune stayed, watching until at last sleep took her.

CHAPTER FORTY-FOUR

Silence permeated the keep. From across her chamber, the fire crackled and Kallan rolled onto her back, absorbing the ache from her neck, through her spine, down to her legs.

She listened to the soft patter of rain steadily falling through the black sky outside as she laid there, devoid of thought. The hole in her chest was raw from the pain, but, for the first time since leaving Gunir, she could breathe with ease again.

She dared turn her thoughts toward Gudrun and winced against the chasm throbbing inside her chest. The unbearable stab had finally dulled to a muted ache she could live with and Kallan released a loud, long sigh as she cocked her head to the window.

The images were still constant, though less intrusive now. She tried again to sort through the pictures, to find an individual face or pull out a single, comprehensible word from the millions. The cluttered jargon was still indecisive and Kallan shoved the attempt aside. The images were tolerable now that they seemed subdued, and she wondered if she was simply getting used to them.

Forcing herself to her feet, Kallan swung her legs over the side of the bed and welcomed the pain of moving. She paused as a wave of sorrow encompassed her and left her obtusely aware of how deep the emptiness penetrated. At once, she longed to fill it.

Without apprehension, her thoughts shifted to Rune and decided, despite the late hour, to find him. Leaving her shoes, Kallan closed the door of her bower behind her.

Only the light of the waning moon lit the hall as she walked to Rune's chambers. With a natural ease, she slid into his room and softly pulled the door behind her. Her back stiffened, alert at the sudden scent of wood and earth engulfing her. For a moment, she forgot what she was doing and gave a slight shake of her head, willing her legs to move across the empty sitting room toward the bedchamber.

The crackling fire was the only life in his room. She paused as she looked at his boots left carelessly on the floor, his shirt thrown over the back of a chair, and an empty flagon of mead left on the side table next to his pipe.

Her chest burned and the urge to find him pulled her toward the back of the room to the door. In an instant, she knew where he was and proceeded to the war room on the other side of the landing separating the war room from his bower. The warm light poured from beneath the door, giving little light to the passage between his chambers.

Without hesitation, she opened the door and, in spite of her grief, a minute grin tugged at the corner of her mouth. Alone, Rune sat slumped in his chair. Still clutching a mead in one hand, he had rested his head onto his arms on the table. The hearth fire spit and popped behind him, casting an orange glow about the room. He had left the single candle to burn low and pool wax into the cracks of the grain. Thunder gently rolled a great distance off and joined the metallic spatter of the rains.

Gathering her skirts, Kallan quietly glided across the floor. The soft pat of her bare feet grazed each cold step.

"Rune," she said quietly.

Her voice was enough to stir him, and only then did she realize he hadn't been sleeping at all.

"You're awake," he said, sitting upright and releasing his mead.

She watched as he leaned back in his chair, stretching his spine before exhaling and looking at her to assess her overall composure.

"How are you?" he asked after taking the time to follow her hair down to her waist and back again to her feet.

"Better," she said. Her heart pounded hard in her chest. "The tea…" she tried to ask casually, uncertain of what to say.

"Valerian mixed with something Bergen brought back from Râ-Kedet. Not sure what it is, but it does it well."

"Where is everyone?"

"Asleep."

Kallan nodded, biting the bottom corner of her lip.

"Are the images still there?"

Kallan listened to the drumming of the rain and countless more pictures flashed by with incoherent jargon.

"Always," she said, wishing them gone once more.

The sharp smell of the fire's smoke mingled with the sweet scent of the rain as it wafted in, carried on the wind, then dissipated once more and left the rains to gently patter in tune to the crackling hearth.

"We ride at dawn," Rune reminded her suddenly, uncertain if she even knew the plans. "I can have Torunn brew you more tea if you'd like and—"

"Rune?"

She spoke his name with a prick of fear and, at once, he realized how soft and clear her voice had always been.

"If you win this, where am I to go?"

Her question filled the high ceiling, leaving behind a worry that weighted down the air and filled Rune with the same dread he had meant to avoid indefinitely.

"I imagine you'll go back to Lorlenalin," he said.

Kallan flicked her eyes down for a second while composing her follow up question.

"And if I win?"

Rune's insides wrenched at the unknown.

"I always assumed you'd just kill me when the opportunity presented itself." Rune shrugged. Her hair fell like ringlets down her front, where his eyes lingered on the collar of her dressing gown. "I guess you could put me back in your cell. Every now and then, you can come down and use me for target practice or fire up your Seidr a—"

"I don't want to go."

Rune stared into the ring of gold that strangely encircled the blue in her eyes. An arm's length away, Kallan stood as he waited for her to falter, to weaken. Instead, she stood plainly before him, finally strong enough to stand, stripped of her inhibitions as she stared hard into him.

The look in her eyes was enough to encourage him.

Rune flew from his chair and was on her. Desperate to lose himself in her, he took her face into his hands and kissed her hard. Inhaling sharply, he breathed deep her perfumes then stopped as the Shadow Beast awakened and rose its curious head.

Slowly, Rune pulled back, leaving Kallan unsated, unkissed, unrumpled in his arms as he rested his hands on her shoulders.

"This thing," Rune said, unsure of what it would do.

Kallan shook her head. "I don't care."

She curled her fingers into his back as if refusing to let go. Her encouragement was all he needed.

"*Faen it!*" Rune said, and again, he dove back on her, this time without worry or concern for the forethought that had haunted him since Jotunheim. Sliding his hand through her hair, he held her in place as he drank his fill. She returned with matching eagerness and shoved him hard into the table, which only riled him further. Holding her waist, Rune was on her and guiding her toward the door back to his chambers, his mouth never leaving hers as she dug and pulled at him.

They hit the door hard as Kallan sank into his mouth. At every move, she welcomed his advances. When he dared pull back, Kallan tightened her grip, denying him the chance to release her. At the door, Rune fumbled with the handle. A slight nip on her neck gave him the chance to open the door before she retaliated with a set of nails digging into his back.

The door swung open and, reclaiming his mouth, Kallan pulled Rune across the landing. A moment later, he slammed his hands into the wall, bracing himself up over Kallan as he let her fumble with the handle this time. The door swung open and, still pawing at each other, they eagerly pushed into Rune's bower. Determined to see the night through, Rune kicked the door closed behind them.

CHAPTER FORTY-FIVE

Rune stretched the length of his bed and opened his eyes to the dark of his room. Outside, the sun had not yet risen, but the first of the birds had started to sing. He rolled onto his side and glanced down at Kallan. She snoozed quite peaceably on her belly. An arm hung relaxed over the side of his bed and her hair pooled down her back, over his pillows, and down the side of his bed.

Taking care not to wake her, Rune lightly brushed Kallan's cheek with his lips. He quietly slipped from the bed and began shuffling through their clothes scattered about the room. As he found his, he threw what else he found on the trunk at the foot of his bed where he quietly set his boots.

"Do you really think you'd sneak off without my knowing?"

Her eyes still closed, Kallan lay. Rune pulled up his trousers and fastened them.

"I figured it was worth a shot," he said, casting a satisfied grin over his shoulder at the disarray that was Kallan. Taking a seat on the trunk, he pulled on his boots.

A moment later, he returned to the bed and Kallan. Brushing her arm, he added a soft kiss to her brow and brushed back one of her long locks from her eyes.

"It's nearly dawn," he muttered. "Battle will soon be upon us."

Without a word, Kallan rolled to her back and gazed up at him while he took up the charm around her neck and turned it over once, then he gently returned it to the crook of her neck and stared, in awe of the golden rims that encircled the blue around her pupils. The rings glowed, undeniably visible in the early morning blues, and had grown noticeably wider overnight.

"My senses haven't deceived me," Rune whispered, studying the intricate rings of each eye. "The color is changing."

Kallan furrowed her brow and, inhaling, looked to the first rays of sun. Like a silent eruption, the sun struck the sky, pouring its lights over the endless stretch of rolling black clouds streaked with shadow and filling the heavens with a sea of red as if the sun itself ignited it with flowing lava.

"Rune?"

Caught up in the sunrise, Rune gazed down at Kallan, who slipped her fingers into Rune's just as the door of his chamber flew open and Kallan vanished beneath the blankets and furs with a squeak.

"Rune!" Bergen bellowed with his hand still on the door's handle. "We're ready!"

He stopped long enough to spot the lump in Rune's bed and grinned widely as only Bergen could.

"Finally!" Bergen exploded with a magnificent gruffness through his grin. "Was it worth the wait?"

"Status!" Rune barked, pulling a tunic on over his head.

"Roald and Thorold wait with their men," Bergen said. "Nineteen thousand wait ready to ride."

"I'm on my way," Rune replied, fastening his belt.

Bergen gave a nod and grinned once more at the lump.

"Hey, Kallan," he greeted.

A tiny hand poked from beneath the furs and waved 'hello' in response.

"We'll ride in ten," Rune said as he unsheathed a dagger and inspected the blade.

The furs of the bed flew down and revealed Kallan's disheveled head.

"I'll be ready in five."

Scrambling, she tugged the furs around her.

"We'll be gone by then," Rune said.

"Bergen," Kallan pleaded, snapping her head to Bergen for aid.

"I'm gone," he said, cutting her off while he still could and added, "See you down there, Rune," before closing door behind him.

Rune shoved the dagger into its sheath on his belt and took up his bow and quiver beside the bedside table.

"You can't fight your own kin," Rune said sternly. "And I'm not about to let you fight mine."

Rune secured the quiver to his belt with his dagger. Taking up his bow, he came to stand beside the trunk at the foot of his bed and collected the pile of clothes resting there.

"We have no use for someone who stands neutral," he concluded.

"There is still a chance I can stop this," Kallan said, kneeling on the bed.

Rune shook his head. Expecting this tirade from her, he had prepared for it.

"You saw where this could end," Rune argued and admired the inflection her nostrils gave when they flared. "Aaric's unpredictable and, at the moment, he holds your throne."

"I'll take it back from him," Kallan said.

"Will you? Because it may come down to that."

"Those are my people, Rune. I'll not leave them to be slaughtered."

Rune turned for the door.

"I'm going with you," she said.

"Well, unfortunately..." Rune glanced over his shoulder as he took the handle. "...I've got your clothes."

Holding up a fist full of Kallan's chemise and dressing gown, Rune dashed out the room, slammed the door behind him before Kallan could summon her Seidr.

"Ruuuune!"

In an instant, Bergen was there to meet him with a chair they propped up against the door to secure the handle in place.

Kallan's screech carried through the chamber to the hall as the door rattled against a solid boom, a kick, and a shriek.

Side by side, Bergen and Rune stood, stupidly impressed by their own ingenuity.

"To think," Bergen boasted, grinning, "we could have ended the war centuries ago if we had just applied this trapping technique."

"Ruuuune!"

"Rune." Bergen threw out his chest and beamed. "We just caught a Seidkona."

The knob remained fixed in position despite the aggressive jerking Kallan exercised on the other side. The door rattled beneath another boom and a shrill cry.

"Are you sure this will hold her?" Bergen asked as an afterthought.

"It held you for hours during your tantrums," Rune reminded Bergen, who nodded at the old memory.

The door trembled beneath what, they could only imagine, was Kallan's Seidr as she released another screech.

"She's going to break my stuff," Rune deduced. "You remembered to lock the other side?" he asked with a slight twinge of worry hanging at the end of each word.

Bergen thought for a moment as he listened to the wood sizzle and crackle beneath the Seidr flame.

"I did," he answered and resumed his head bobbing.

Kallan had just started another wave of Seidr flame on the door.

"You know, we're going to die the moment she gets out."

"Yes," Bergen said. "But for now we are victorious! Let's go!"

And, eager to get the distance between them and the Seidkona, the brothers bolted for the corridor.

"Aaric's troops will be nearing the plains by midday," Rune said as they rushed down the stairs. "Any word from Joren?"

"So far, nothing, but the day is early," Bergen said as he gleefully hopped down the stairs behind Rune, snaring a handful of dried meats from the dining tables before heading on to the stables for Zabbai.

* * *

"Of all the stubborn... *Uskit!*" Kallan muttered as she ransacked Rune's room and rummaged for anything that could aid in her escape. She pulled out drawers and blankets, combed through the wardrobe, and shuffled eagerly through the chest at the foot of his bed, adding her own colorful entourage as she grumbled beneath her breath.

After pulling one of his tunics on over her head and snapping her hair free from his shirt, she fell to her knees and shuffled through the contents he had stored safely within the chest. She pushed aside a blanket, an embroidered tapestry, and what she could only guess was his first hunting bow.

Resisting the urge to snap them in two, she gently laid aside a pair of weathered arrows carefully wrapped within an old satchel. With care, she lifted the satchel and found a dagger encrusted with black, polished stones. Favoring the dagger, she placed it into her lap.

Entertaining her curiosity, Kallan permitted her temper to ebb and settled down with the satchel and dagger. The bag was heavy. Inquisitively, she tugged at the drawstring and dumped its contents into her open palm.

She barely caught a glimpse of her own intricate crest bearing the House of Eyolf forged into an arm ring, before an onslaught of images burst to life inside of her and just like that she remembered.

Gasping, Kallan lost her breath from the impact as a vivid, perfect picture came to life of Motsognir standing before the forge in Nidavellir, bending the metal into the arm ring she held in her hand.

She saw, too clearly, the grand forge of the Dvergar as it faded into another image and looked upon the face of her father. With a smile, he accepted the arm ring from Motsognir as it passed from its smith to its owner, an agreeable exchange between old friends.

The image changed again as Kallan watched her father proudly present the arm ring to Aaric, who smiled as a brother upon her father. Behind him, she saw the vibrant golden eyes of her mother standing beside Gudrun with the same ancient eyes.

A moment later, they presented themselves to Eyolf's court in Svartálfaheim.

Aaric stood beside his king, the arm ring secured over the black sketches stained into his bicep as he gazed adoringly—too adoringly—upon her mother.

The image changed again as Kallan strained to keep the vision on her mother, but the picture had faded into the great mountains of Lorlenalin where Livsvann flowed. There was no city or grand palace. Only untouched stone not yet honed into the citadel that would become the White Opal. Alone, Aaric stared from the mountain to the sea. She watched him order his soldier to lay the first stones of Lorlenalin's keep.

She saw the citadel rise, and the first of Lorlenalin's forts form. She saw herself, barely seven winters old, as Eyolf stood at Lorlenalin's keep and told

Aaric of Kira's death.

She shook, crazed with loathing, as Aaric smashed the soapstone basins and shredded the blankets in his chamber. She buckled under the rage that rippled through her as they stared down at the arm ring resting on the table before him. She saw his eyes glisten with the same gold as Gudrun and her mother.

One scene blurred as another cleared and Aaric stood before her, his palm firmly placed on her brow as he muttered indecipherably, taking her memories from her. Kallan saw her ten-year-old self, staring blankly back into nothing as Aaric sealed her gift of Sight.

A scream disrupted the image, and Kallan gulped. A tear slid down her face. Too well, she knew that scream.

The fog cleared and, once more, she looked down at the pale, perfect body of a young girl. But this time, she knew her. Swann writhed beneath Aaric, filling the forest with her desperate shrill cries. Helpless, she watched Aaric silence her screams as he snapped her neck.

Coldly, as if focused only on a job at hand, Kallan watched Aaric turn to the Seidr light that poured from a pile of leaves and grass. A freshly born Seidr spring, a *Seidi*, not yet old enough to alter the life around it, flowed from the ground.

She watched Aaric's hands scramble as they shuffled the leaves about, but he needed to close it. He needed to close the spring. Kallan gawped as Aaric muttered a charm and sealed the *Seidi*. Slowly, the Seidr faded and Aaric ceased his incantation. He did his best to bury the mound in leaf litter. Only then did Kallan notice his missing arm ring.

She quietly watched Aaric stand and, as if he had been reviewing trade imports in the war room, he walked off and left Swann dead on the forest floor. Kallan was certain the scene was done, but the image didn't change. As Aaric left, a young Kovit slipped in.

The scene changed again, but not before Kallan caught a glimpse of Borg stripping Swann's body. When he was done, Kallan stared, pale with horror, as Borg pulled himself from Swann. A moment later, he plunged a dagger encrusted with black polished stone between the woman-child's breasts and cut down the entire length of her belly. Within seconds, her body was drained of its blood.

As if to finish the job and leave his mark, Kovit placed his bloodstained hand on her face. A woman screamed from somewhere off in the distance, and suddenly alert, Borg sat up. Hurriedly, Kovit pulled a Dokkalfr arm ring—Aaric's arm ring—from his pocket and tossed it on the ground beside the dagger. He fled and a moment later Bergen and Rune arrived.

Trembling, Kallan made to reach for the girl as she faded into the shadows.

Too late, the scene had changed.

In the shadows of an ill-lit room, in the canyons of an unknown land, water ran gold and magnificent night birds, black and lean with tail feathers that reached an arm's span, flew low to the running waters. Aaric stared at a woman with long black hair, pale perfect skin not of Alfheim or Midgard, and eyes that glistened gold like Gudrun's. At once Kallan knew her. With her back to Aaric, the woman gazed into the night from a ledge Kallan knew not where.

"We need Kira's daughter," the woman said and Aaric shook his head skeptically.

"There is no way Eyolf will let Kallan go. He will throw all of his army into finding her and rally his allies to join him. He won't simply let the last of Kira be taken from him."

The woman seemed not to hear him. For a long while, she watched the strange birds skim the waters with the tips of their tail feathers and a stream of rippled water followed their flight.

"A king's head is worth its weight in gold," she said. "Eyolf needs to go."

She spoke with a sultry, soft tone and the vision changed again.

Too well, Kallan knew this image.

Once again, she stood outside the Dokkalfar Keep where she last saw her father alive. This time, he stood subdued, masked by a spell and with a blade pressed to his throat outside the keep. Eyolf was watching her past self, crying out his name, while listening to Aaric whisper threats into his ear.

"If you answer her, I will kill her."

Kallan watched her past self call again then vanish into the keep. But her father was there outside, arched against the blade poised at his throat. The door of the keep swayed back and the last of Kallan's skirts vanished into the keep. Knowing too well what events would come, Kallan opened her mouth to call out, but no sound came.

This time, she watched helpless as Aaric thrust the length of his sword up into her father's back. Aaric released her father, muttered a charm that lifted the spell on Eyolf, and fled, still cloaked by the spell that hid him.

Kallan gasped as she tried to scream, her body rent by the memory as she watched her father die. Any second now, her past self would stumble out of the keep and find him. Eyolf had managed to drag himself to the door and pull himself up against the frame. Kallan called out, screaming, helpless all over again as she watched her father die in her arms a second time.

Kallan was still sobbing when the scene faded one last time.

The day's light shone on the horizon. Too clearly, Kallan could see the lines of pikemen ready on foot before the rally of equestrians who waited for the command from their king, perched high at the ready upon his horse. His forked beard trailed down the length of his chest and he held his arm for the cue.

Kallan followed the path of his eyes across the Klarelfr River to Gunir, where she looked upon Rune. And there at his side, her own eyes looked back encased with rings of gold. The images diminished until they vanished, releasing Kallan and leaving her once more in Rune's bower.

Inhaling, Kallan dropped the arm ring and fell forward violently onto her palms as she gasped uncontrollably, deafened to the clink of the dagger as it hit the floor.

Her throat burned as she swallowed wave upon wave of vomit. She realized she had been screaming at one point, leaving her throat shredded and raw. Drips of sweat fell, and Kallan held herself there, shaking as she stared at the floor and replayed the images over once more.

Still shaking, she understood and raised her eyes from the floor, feeling the Seidr flow freely as if the arm ring had razed a barrier. The onslaught of images focused into view and, with relief, she could clearly hear each voice separate from all others.

Her fingers clawed the wood floor as she met her own eyes in the looking glass and saw that the last of the blue was gone. The same golden glow that had once shone bright in Gudrun's eyes now encased her pupils.

Kallan stood, fueled with an urgency that knew no bounds and charged with a new hate that consumed her. Free to pool her Seidr at will, free from the seal that Aaric had caged her in centuries ago, Kallan raised her palms to the door and blasted it, the chair, and parts of the stone out of her way.

She scooped up the dagger and arm ring, and marched from the room. After snatching a pair of Rune's trousers from the back of a chair, she made her way to her own chambers.

Within moments, she was dressed, armed, and fuming as she stomped her way down to the stables, not bothering to acknowledge the many questions that flowed from Torunn as Kallan rode Astrid hard out of Gunir and across the river.

CHAPTER FORTY-SIX

The waters of the Klarelfr blazoned red in the sun when Rune and Bergen dismounted from the west side of the Klarelfr and passed their reins to a soldier who greeted them. Moments later, Rune and Bergen threw back the flap of the tent pitched alongside the river.

"Thorold, news," Rune called to Thorold, hunched over the map table as Roald stood passing orders to his captain.

"Still no word," Thorold said. "Of the scouts we sent, only two have returned with updates on Aaric's progress."

"What of Forkbeard?" Rune asked. "How is the scout from Dan's Mork doing?"

Thorold shook his head.

"Still no word," Roald said. "Forkbeard hasn't learned that we've stripped our borders."

Rune blew a short breath and nodded.

"We can assume," Rune muttered. "Any word from the Northern Keep?"

"The children and Elders have arrived and settled," Bergen said. "I received confirmation only this morning."

Rune nodded again.

"I expect Aaric here by midday," Rune said. "And if he doesn't, then tomorrow, we make our move."

Bergen's eyes went wide at the thought of holding the raging Seidkona another day. The door wouldn't hold out until then.

"But Kallan—"

"We can't wait for Aaric," Rune said. "We're ready and hopes are high."

Bergen leaned against the table with his arms crossed, impatiently waiting for the sound of the battle horns as Thorold began pacing the room.

"We have the advantage here at our borders," Rune said, dragging his finger across the map as he spoke. "Our archers will be stationed with me here on the highest ground to the west. Bergen, have your men ready to the east. Be ready to flank the Dokkalfar once Thorold lures them here, to the center."

Each man nodded in turn, comprehending his position.

"Roald will come in from behind, closing the ranks. With luck, we can lure them to the plains and hold them. For now, we have the advantage as Aar—"

A sudden chill engulfed the room, forcing the fire to flicker violently. All eyes turned to the door, alert with the readiness of battle. Eager to see Joren, the room drooped with disappointment at the arrival of Kallan, holding back the pelt from the door.

"She escaped," Bergen said as Rune flushed red.

Donned in a plain blue dress, Kallan stood ready for battle with her pouch fastened at her waist next to her own dagger. In her hand, she clutched a blade with black stones that drew Rune and Bergen's eye and turned their faces white.

"Leave here, Kallan," Rune said, and returned his attention to the table.

A flash of rage crunched Kallan's face as she dropped the pelt behind her.

"Rune," Kallan said.

"I expect movement from the west," Rune continued to Bergen, Thorold, and Roald, who all tried to ignore the fuming Seidkona.

"Rune, hear me!" she pleaded. "You can't do this!"

Sighing, Rune dropped his shoulders and pulled himself from the map.

"Kallan. Your head isn't right in this. You're dealing with too much to be a part of this." Her eyes flared with the insult and he knew he'd pay for that later. "You're too close to make the calls that need to be made," Rune said, turning back to the map.

"There are things here you don't know about," Kallan said, taking a step forward.

Rune returned to the table and continued. "I've already received word from the scouts that Aaric is on the move—"

"It isn't Aaric, Rune!" Kallan shouted. "The Da—"

"Bergen, get her out of here," Rune said.

Bergen stepped and Kallan moved.

Igniting her Seidr, Kallan sent a blast of wind that threw Bergen to the floor. Before Bergen could stand, before Roald or Thorold could advance, Kallan lunged, pushing Rune back against the table and raised the black jeweled dagger to Rune's throat.

"Look at me, Rune!" Kallan barked. "Look at my eyes!"

The lapis blue was gone, replaced by the Seidr that encircled the black of her pupils. Rune stared into the rings of gold—Seidr gold—and his own eyes widened in awe.

"I can See," Kallan breathed. "I can See everything... And we don't have much time."

"By the gods," Thorold breathed, stepping closer.

The urgency she delivered demanded their attention and the three men listened as Kallan released Rune.

"Aaric marches now," she concurred as she turned the blade around and handed the hilt to Rune.

"He's on the horizon, and he isn't alone. Forkbeard comes. They seek to take all of Alfheim for the Dani."

"But the scouts—"

"Are dead," Kallan cut Roald off. "Forkbeard has been watching. The whole time. Too much of our focus has been on Aaric and Borg to have noticed."

"Are you certain?" Rune asked with unease.

"Certain," Kallan said. "I can See everything as far back as the Dvergar-Svartálfar Wars and further still."

Bergen slowly stood, absorbing the shock Kallan brought with her words, one question at the forefront of his mind.

"What do you See?" Thorold jumped in, cutting Bergen off before he could ask the only question on his mind.

"Forkbeard is on his way," Kallan said. "They sail up the river now."

"How many?" Bergen asked.

"Fifteen thousand," she answered.

"Fiftee..." Roald's voice trailed off.

"With Aaric's twenty," Thorold mumbled, stricken with sick.

"Against nineteen thousand," Rune said.

Kallan eased her shoulders, conceding to Rune's deduction to take over for her.

"They stand against us with two armies," Roald said, looking to each face for an answer.

"Rune," Thorold said, "If we take down the Dokkalfar, if we secure victory before Forkbeard's troops arrive—"

"It's only a matter of time," Kallan interjected. "Forkbeard doesn't come with ships and men. He brings the support of the Empire."

"All of the Mainland," Roald gasped.

"We can not simply defeat him." Rune peered at the map beside him. "We must abolish them."

The rains began to fall and pattered on the side of the tent.

"We have one day to turn the tides," Rune said. "One day to be the victor. If we don't stand in a better position by tomorrow's eve, we don't stand a chance against Forkbeard."

"Against nearly twice our numbers in two days," Bergen said.

"Aaric seeks to use Forkbeard as a second wave," Kallan said. "He'll take down whatever is left of you."

"Joren." Rune turned to Kallan. "Can you see Joren or Daggon?"

Kallan's shoulders visibly fell and she shook her head.

Backs slumped with worry as they all scrambled for a plan. Shouting outside and panic disrupted their silence and the first of the war horns sounded. In an instant, Rune took up his bow as Rune's commanders fled the tent alongside he and Kallan just as the second horn was blown. A third horn then another filled the whole of the camp until the call of the war horns encompassed the valley, alerting the troops to battle.

As one, Bergen, Roald, and Thorold scattered to prepare their men, leaving Kallan to Rune.

"The Dokkalfar are on the horizon!" Bergen called and vanished into the troops.

"Ready the arms!" Rune shouted back over the chorus of horns. "Kallan!"

Rune grabbed her arms.

"Get back to the keep n—"

The horns drowned out his voice, followed by the uproar of his battalions.

"My fight is here!" she argued.

The horns sounded again, this time from the horizon as archers formed their lines.

"There is no side for you to fight on!" Rune roared.

Ljosalfar archers fell into line, readying their bows as Rune bolted from the camp to join them.

"I have no where else to go!" Kallan called after him, but he didn't hear.

The horns sounded a final time, calling the last of the men to arms.

Alone, at the river's edge, Kallan stood looking upon the lines of archers who drew their bows at the ready.

'Go' she saw Rune say, unable to hear his voice over the thunder of troops to the south.

Slowly, Kallan turned.

With mouth agape, she stared into the mass of her people, all looking down at her with the same vile hatred she once held for the Ljosalfar. Now, amid the Ljosalfar, Kallan stood, helpless to stop either side.

CHAPTER FORTY-SEVEN

Across the plains at the base of the hills across the Klarelfr, Fand glared down at the masses before her with Aaric's face. A weak grin stretched her mouth.

"Ready the arms," she bellowed with Aaric's voice. The Dokkalfar obeyed as Fand kept her gaze fixed on the lone Seidkona staring up at her from the Klarelfr.

Bound and dumped on the ground, Aaric stood, his own face masked from the soldiers who saw only an unknown face.

"Don't do this," Aaric said.

"Do what?" Fand smiled and raised an arm. "You're doing it."

Fand dropped her arm.

Releasing a cry, the Dokkalfar snapped their arms with a militia's precision and charged full speed into the plains where Thorold's warriors waited.

The ground thundered beneath Kallan's feet as she stared wide-eyed at the Dokkalfar clasping axe and spear. Together, they cried out for their victory, blind to their queen among their enemy. Unable to take up arms against them, Kallan held her breath, uncertain how to stop the charging mass.

The white of their eyes grew visible.

The first of the soldiers drew nearer, until Kallan could make out the madness in a scarred, young face as it closed in. Kallan remained paralyzed and the first soldier raised an axe, eager to cleave her head.

His scream rent the air and he fell to the ground. A Ljosalfr arrow protruded from the center of his back.

Kallan looked to the west, and there she caught Rune's eyes as he lowered his bow. His shot was the cue his archers had waited for and instantly, a volley of arrows filled the sky like black rain.

"To arms!" Thorold bellowed as his men tightened the shield wall across the defense lines. "Ready!"

His voice carried over the cries of the Dokkalfar as Kallan watched her brethren fall beneath the shower of Ljosalfar arrows.

"Kallan!" Thorold called, alerting her to her open position.

The Dokkalfar charged with the madness of the berserk and Kallan, collecting her nerve, joined Thorold's side behind the shield wall.

Another volley from the Ljosalfar showered the Dokkalfar and many fell, but not enough before meeting the shield wall. Dokkalfar jostled the Ljosalfar that stood against the impact and brought down sword as they came.

Rune released a final volley onto the Dokkalfar aimed at the back of the advance. He raised *Gramm* to the sky and released his battle cry. From across the valley, Bergen joined his brother's cry and he too raised his sword.

Together, they charged the Dokkalfar, each leading their own army to the front. As Thorold held them off at the shield wall, the Ljosalfar assailed the flanks of the Dokkalfar.

"And another," Fand calmly ordered. "Ready the next wave," she called out over the clashing metal below.

Sword rose up with axe, and five thousand Dokkalfar poured down the hillside, flooding the base of the valley and joining their comrades as they ripped into the Ljosalfar.

They cleaved their way to the heart of the valley as they rent the shield wall in two.

"Hold your ground!" Thorold bellowed over the clang of sword against shield as the front broke against the first wave.

With her Seidr, Kallan blocked blow after blow against the deluge of attacks that came from all sides. Refusing to rise offensively, she buckled beneath the weight of a Dokkalfr's axe just as she threw up her Seidr shield. Her head snapped back from the impact as he forced Kallan to her knees while maintaining her shield. From the corner of her eye, Bergen battled with an unequalled ferocity as he cleaved the men of her army with his sword, making his way toward Kallan.

With ease, Bergen thrust and drew up his blade, cutting through the Dokkalfr that had Kallan pinned beneath his axe. Bergen pivoted, spilling the Dokkalfr's insides as Bergen swung his blade down.

A berserker, blinded with rage, closed in. As Bergen impaled a soldier, the berserker raised his sword and unleashed his cry. Without thought, Kallan released her Seidr and sent a blast of flame that missed Bergen's back. The flame struck the berserker's face and Bergen turned to plunge the sword through his chest.

As Bergen kicked off the body and grabbed the sword from the corpse, Kallan rose to her feet, shaking as she stared wide-eyed at the Dokkalfr she had killed.

"Kallan!" Bergen cried. "Sword!" He shoved the blade into her cold hands.

Without thought, Kallan took the hilt and thrust the blade, catching an assailant, who fell, impaled by her blade.

The horror glazed her face. As Kallan looked down into the eyes of her kin, his face met hers, and, moments before the life left his eyes, for a fleeting second, he knew his queen and the breath left him.

Kallan's arms weakened beneath the weight of the sword, deafened by Rune, who called to her as he brought down his opponent.

"Kallan!"

She heard nothing as the hilt of her sword slipped from her hands and the blade fell to the ground.

"Kallan!" Rune cried.

Shoving a Dokkalfar to the ground, Rune drew back his bow and fired, then swung the bow into the face of a Dokkalfr. Taking up his dagger, Rune thrust the blade into the heart of a soldier. The body slumped to the ground and Rune fought his way to Kallan.

"Kallan," Rune called as another soldier lunged for Kallan in time for Rune to jerk the dagger up and into him. To the ground he fell beside Kallan, who knelt, stupefied.

"Kallan!"

Slowly, Kallan raised her face.

"You shouldn't be here!" Rune shouted then turned, impaling a Dokkalfr.

At the top of the hill, Fand held back a wide grin.

"Ready the archers for their second wave," Fand said from high upon Aaric's stead.

The words slammed into Aaric, leaving him sick on the ground.

"Fand—"

"Aim," Fand barked and, forced to take her eyes from the battle, glared at Aaric.

Aaric's bottom lip quivered, forcing him to clench his jaw.

"Fire."

The volley came with the command, drawing Bergen's attention to the trees where Fand sat hidden behind Aaric's face. He plunged his blade into a soldier and turned to impale another before the first had touched the ground.

Kallan and Rune looked to the sky as arrows flew overhead. Alert once more with the need, Kallan slammed her hands to the sky, drawing her Seidr from her core. Silver blue flowed across the sky like water as Kallan encompassed the whole of the armies beneath her Seidr shield.

The sharp clang of *Gramm* confirmed Rune had resumed fighting, leaving Kallan to support the ward.

"Again," Fand ordered beneath her breath.

Like black rain, another volley fell, and another, striking Kallan's shield then dropping harmlessly to the ground, over and again. Kallan shook beneath the weight of the ward, but held her Seidr until the last of her strength gave out. Exhausted, she collapsed, breaking her ward as she fell.

"Roald!" Rune cried, knowing his words were lost to the battle.

With the speed of a vintage archer, Rune took up his bow and fired a shot to the far distance in the southwest where he knew Roald waited for the signal.

Gasping, Kallan dug her fingers into the blood-soaked soil as she held her face up from the ground on her knees. Desperate to stand once more, she glanced to Rune for aid as she watched him bring down another Dokkalfar.

Within the forest, Roald received Rune's signal and delivered the command to his troops. With spears raised at the ready, he gave the order and charged Fand from behind, seeing only the high marshal seated upon his horse.

Leading his five hundred with his battle cry, Roald tightened his grip on his spear and charged just as Fand turned. The madness took Roald, and hungry for victory, he sprinted with all of his strength. He had barely seen the Dokkalfr's face and the etchings of black scribed on an arm before a sudden flash of red and a wall of flame burst to life between Roald and his target.

Roald was moving too fast to stop and collided with the wall, face first. Within heartbeats, he was on the ground, clutching his face and screaming as the Seidr flame melted the flesh from his cheek.

Deep within Rune's core, hardly asleep, the Fendinn awakened and rose. This Seidr it knew. This Seidr it wanted. Throwing back its head, the Beast roared and erupted, breaking the leash that Rune had formed.

Screaming, Rune fell to his knees as a shadow emerged. Like a cloak of black Seidr, the Shadow encompassed his skin like a fine fitted glove that hugged his flesh. The shadow released a shrill cry, drowning out Roald's screams as it lunged for Fand's Seidr.

"No!" Rune barked and forced to the ground, he poured all his strength into the Fendinn, holding it back as he unleashed a long scream.

To the southwest, Seidr flame poured from Fand's hand. Her flame grew as it climbed to the sky. In an instant, Kallan saw the wall change its course and, forgetting her exhaustion, leapt to her feet before she could scream the warning.

Her hands were up once more, and Kallan dispensed the last of her energy, shielding against the massive amount of Seidr flame Fand poured onto the plains. Kallan buckled beneath the weight, screaming with the fire's roar as she fought against Fand's Seidr.

As Kallan's shield spanned the skies, the Fendinn drew back enough for Rune to pull it in and hold it under control. Exhausted, Rune looked to the source of the fire and followed the Seidr to Kallan, who buckled beneath the weight of the firewall. Her legs were failing. Her core was visibly drained of its energy. It was only a matter of time before her endurance would give out and she would fall completely, leaving them all, Dokkalfar and Ljosalfar, exposed to the mercy of Fand's Seidr. Again the Fendinn, reawakened and roared, but this time, Rune was ready and locked it in place.

"Fall back!" Rune cried. Standing, he shoved a Dokkalfr to the ground. "Retreat!" he called and looked to Bergen, who nodded and called to Thorold.

"Fall back!"

Rune wielded *Gramm* until the last of Kallan's strength left her, and, pushing back, she fell to the ground nearly unconscious.

The field was beginning to clear of the Ljosalfar, who had already begun to flee from Fand's flame. Still, wave upon wave of fire and arrows showered down over the plains.

Sheathing *Gramm*, Rune fell to a knee beside Kallan and raised her up from the ground. Behind them, the fire roared relentlessly as Rune mustered the strength to stand and run. Around them, soldiers fell, speared by arrows that flooded the sky or singed beyond recognition as their flesh peeled away. Twice Rune stumbled, slipping on pools of blood and flesh.

With a sudden jerk, Kallan cried out, forcing Rune to glance over his shoulder to an arrow protruding from the back of her thigh. He cursed himself and hastened his pace, securing his grip on her.

Countless bodies lay immobile, still fueling Fand's flames as it consumed them and black smoke rose to the sky. Only when the Seidr flame ceased did the shower of arrows end, leaving Rune to stomp over corpses and blood as he made his way to the edge of the Klarelfr where Bergen met him with a mount.

"She's been wounded!" Rune shouted, hoisting Kallan onto the stead. Beads of sweat poured down his face as he pulled himself up behind Kallan, who had fallen unconscious.

"Bergen, get Roald!" he ordered, taking up the reins.

Blood flowed down Kallan's leg.

With a nod, Bergen released the bridle, and Rune sent the horse into a sprint for Gunir.

"Go after them," Aaric shouted, watching the masses abandon the dead and wounded left to die on the plains.

Aaric watched Fand's sickly grin tug at his cheek.

"I'll let them live to meet the Dani," Fand decided, taking a final moment to look about the field before turning the horse around.

"Will you not look for the wounded?" Aaric asked.

Fand paused, looking back at Aaric as the guards collected him from the ground.

A tinge of annoyance glistened in her eye. Glaring with loathing at Aaric, Fand flicked her wrist and unleashed her Seidr-flame into the wounded, Ljosalfar and Dokkalfar alike.

CHAPTER FORTY-EIGHT

"Geirolf!" Rune cried across the courtyard, desperate to find the healer among the chaos.

The stench of the wounded filled the air as Rune joined with the screams of mourners. Wave upon wave of Alfar poured into the courtyard, too wounded to drag their broken bodies further while others collapsed with the last of their strength.

"The wounded!" Rune cried as Torunn came running. "Get them inside! And find me Geirolf!"

Pandemonium filled the square as a handful of healers directed women to collect those in dire need of immediate care.

"We have the Hall ready!" Torunn said, flying from one soldier to the next, assessing lacerations, burns, and missing limbs. Soldiers clambered up the stone steps into the Hall, combining their strength with that of a comrade so they could walk at all.

"Geirolf!" Rune called, pulling back on the reins as Geirolf rushed from the keep. "Kallan is wounded!"

Rune guided Kallan's limp body down to Geirolf.

"Bergen!" Rune bellowed, looking about madly for his brother as Geirolf carefully lowered Kallan to the ground to better examine her wound.

"Here!" Bergen called from the steps of the keep, supporting Roald on a shoulder.

"How is he?" Rune asked as he slid from his mount.

"He's burned bad," Bergen called back as he walked Roald to the Hall. "He's lost half his face and he'll lose the arm...but he'll not be dining in Odinn's halls tonight."

Rune's stomach eased.

"Once you have him in Torunn's care, find Thorold!" Rune said over his shoulder, and turned his full attention to Geirolf, who had pushed Kallan's skirts out of the way to better inspect the wound.

"Odinn's Valkyrja have taken him," Bergen said with a strain in his voice.

Rune bowed his head and closed his eyes against the sudden gust of wind that left him as he bit back the urge to scream.

Drowning his grief, Rune gulped back a helping of defeat and barked his orders.

"Regroup all who can stand! Get back to me with numbers!"

Rune looked at Geirolf, not seeing that Bergen nodded.

"How bad is it?"

"It's struck the bone." Geirolf raised his eyes to Rune's. "We can't push it through."

Rune nodded, knowing the diagnosis before Geirolf spoke the words.

"I'll have to cut it out," Geirolf said.

Rune nodded, desperate for the numbness to settle in.

"Get her upstairs."

ᓚ ᓚ

The arrow snapped, jerking Rune alert to the quiet of Kallan's bower. Water spilled down his hand as he wrung the water from the cloth, following Geirolf's instructions. Holding his breath, Rune forced his mind blank as he watched Geirolf's aged hands whisk themselves over Kallan's leg. On her stomach, Kallan lay on the bed in front of him as Geirolf worked with a steady hand.

He sliced her skin and, with a set of pincers, pried the piece of iron from her leg. Blood flowed freely as Geirolf wiped the sweat from his brow.

"Should I summon a tailor?" Rune asked, uncertain of Geirolf's decision.

The old man shook his head.

"The smith. We'll need him to burn the wound closed," he said, pressing his hand tightly down around the wound. "Are you done with that fire?" Geirolf barked, not bothering to glance at the maids beside him.

"Nearly," one meekly answered.

"I need coals!" Geirolf shouted. "Make them red!"

Rune had hardly reached the sitting room when Kallan's breath filled the room.

"Rune," she called, certain she heard them right. "My pouch."

With her eyes still closed and sprawled out on her belly, Rune fumbled through the pile of possessions dumped into a chair until he found the pouch lying with a dagger and Kallan's dagger. A moment later, with shaking hands, he handed it to her.

"Get out," Rune said to the maids, who scurried without question from the room, closing the bedroom door behind them.

Blood flowed as Kallan propped herself up on her elbows.

"Kallan, don't move! Get yourself back down," Geirolf grumbled.

Digging through her pouch, Kallan soon found Idunn's apple and bit a chunk from the flesh. Kallan pulled the piece from her mouth and handed it to Rune.

"Place this over the wound and squeeze the juices into it," she directed. Geirolf furrowed his face with disapproval.

"The wound isn't primed for apple juice, Kallan! The wound will go bad if—"

"Do it!" Kallan said and took a second bite from the apple.

With a grimace, Geirolf glowered at Rune, who grabbed his dagger from the chair and quickly followed Kallan's direction without question.

Golden Seidr flowed with the apple's sweet juices as Geirolf stared wide-eyed with disbelief at the fibers closing her flesh. The more Kallan consumed of the apple, the more the wound healed until all of the cut vanished, leaving behind no scarring.

With a sigh, she pulled herself upright and rolled onto her back.

"How many?" she asked, disinterested with healing her body further.

"Bergen is still getting me numbers," Rune said as Geirolf stared in awe at the restored color in Kallan's face.

"How bad was it?" she asked again, knowing he knew more about the devastation than he let on.

Abandoning Rune to the wit of the woman, Geirolf collected the pincers and supplies from the bed as Rune cast a warning to Geirolf to not answer.

A sudden clamor of voices rose from the courtyard.

Exchanging glances, Kallan flew from the bed and raced Rune to the window in time to see Bergen drawing arms against two Dokkalfar.

Before Kallan could object, Rune fled the room, leaving her to scramble for a skirt to cover her legs.

"Stand down!" Bergen ordered, his sword raised to the Dokkalfar.

"We aren't here for a fight!" one of them said, despite the hole dripping blood where his eye had been.

"Back off!" Bergen howled.

Behind him, barely a handful of his own men perched, ready for the word to attack. Desperation hung on the Ljosalfar with a madness that taunted their tempers to the edge.

"We look for aid!" the Dokkalfr cried, burdened beneath the weight of his comrade, who leaned on him nearly unconscious.

"There is no medicine here that can be spared for Dokkalfar blood!" Bergen said.

"Bergen, hold!" Rune called as he ran from the keep. "Stand down!"

Bergen tightened his grip on his sword.

"Brother, look at them," Rune bade, placing a hand on Bergen's shoulder. "They can barely stand."

"Wielders of craft...armed with lies and deceit," Bergen grumbled. "These are the sons fashioned from the grounds of Svartálfaheim!"

"Ragnar?"

Kallan's voice cut through the tension, easing Bergen back as she stepped to the front.

Despite the socket of his eye still flowing with blood, Ragnar smiled.

"My lady," he gasped and nearly broke into a sob. "My eyes didn't deceive me. I knew I had seen— I've come to do your bidding."

The formality required the last of his strength and Ragnar dropped to the steps, taking his comrade with him. To her knees, Kallan fell, pulling her Seidr and administering her skills.

"These men need aid!" Kallan said.

"They're Dokkalfar," Bergen reminded her, not so eager to invite them in.

"So am I!" Kallan bit back.

"We hold no oath to their kin," Bergen said, pointing at them with the tip of his blade.

"I do!" Kallan glared as Seidr poured from her hands into her kin.

"Enough," Rune said, putting an end to their squabble. "Bring them in."

With a scowl, Bergen gripped Rune's arm.

"We have no room for our own." Bergen held his voice low enough for only Rune to hear. "The Hall is full. Torunn is forcing us to set up wounded here in the yard."

"We'll make do," Rune said as his men lifted the dying Dokkalfar from the steps. "We'll have to. Against Forkbeard, we'll need all the help we can get."

Bergen released Rune's arm and the Ljosalfar carried the Dokkalfar inside.

With great agility, Kallan rose to her feet, fastening her hair behind her shoulders. Her golden eyes sharpened with a determination that bombarded Rune with worry.

"What are you doing?" he asked.

Kallan exhaled with a huff of impatience.

"This battle is not yet over," she said, rolling up her sleeves. "I have work to do."

Stomping off after Bergen, Kallan pushed her way into the Hall before Rune had a chance to argue.

Kallan scanned the length of the room. From the double oak doors to the steps of the kitchen, past the throne to the screens passage and up the stairs, Kallan assessed the numbers that filled the Great Hall with blankets, furs, and bandages. Bergen's men found a vacant corner for the Dokkalfar near the kitchens and settled them in as Rune joined Kallan at her side.

"Are you certain you can handle this?" Rune asked, earning a sharp glare from Kallan.

Within moments and without a word, she found a place to begin and settled herself down on the floor beside the first of thousands to be treated.

The scent of boiling leek and onion filled the Hall as Torunn ordered the onion soup be served to every soldier. Where the scent of herb rose from gapping stomach wounds, they moved on, leaving the soldier to die clutching fast to their sword in hand.

The fires roared and the smith and tailors were constantly at hand to assist with stitching or the searing of wounds as needed. Screams filled the Hall late into the night as the keep became a second battlefield, where mutilated limbs were sawn off and cauterized. Other wounded lay awake, writhing in pain as they slowly bled out through their bowels.

Soon, the stench of blood and death mingled with that of burned flesh and seeping bowels that filled the keep, adding a level of nausea that placated their nerves with numbness. From soldier to soldier, Kallan passed, administering Idunn's apple and submitting the spell where it could help. But there were too many to be seen by one as she did what she could to pull from her core and keep them alive long enough to be seen by Torunn or Geirolf.

The lanterns devoured most of their oils by the time the last soldier had been healed. Exhaustion emanated from those left standing as the last of the screams died down to subtle groans.

"You should sleep," Geirolf said, not bothering to wipe the blood from his hands. "I don't trust those Seidr apples of yours to do what the body should."

Kallan glanced with deadened eyes. Silently she nodded, until her head wobbled into a shake as she dug the sleep from her eyes.

Exhausted, she turned to the great doors of the Hall and, without a word, walked into the cool night air. Stiffening her back against the sudden cold, Kallan blankly turned for the stables and Astrid.

CHAPTER FORTY-NINE

The stench of corpses hit Kallan's nose the moment she opened the doors of the keep and descended the steps to the courtyard. The rains had come and gone sometime during the night while Kallan worked on the wounded, leaving the dampened stench of the smoldering battlefield. The cold of night had settled in, adding a chill to the air and a silence that encumbered the forest. Animals had not yet returned to their burrows, bringing an unnatural hush to the silent wood.

On the other side of the Klarelfr, the desolation spanned the plains to the trees that began where the land rose up. Only the fog obstructed her view as she scanned the endless carnage that was Gunir's plains. The bodies had long grown cold.

Releasing Astrid's reins, Kallan slid off the horse and made her way through the dead. The ground squelched beneath her feet, emitting a pocket of odor with every step that reeked of feces and burnt flesh.

They had been quick to flee and left with no time to go back and collect the wounded. Now she stood among them, hopelessly examining the field, desperate for any sign of life. The mangled bodies of Dokkalfar rested where they fell alongside the desecrated Ljosalfar. Abandoned weapons lay in the waste. Several swords had been broken. A few had their blades bent back to prevent their use in Odinn's Hall, lest their owner consider vengeance.

Huffing, Kallan stopped and studied the wide field of corpses. Her breath rolled into tiny puffs of fog as it punched the air. Tears, too dry to fall, burned her eyes.

The heavy crunch of a boot jerked her attention around, and she met Rune standing at a distance behind her. His hair hung with the same somber tone as the battlefield. He said nothing as he stood. His exhausted death-like stupor mirrored her own.

"My father—" Kallan gasped, gazing upon the dead. "He sent Aaric to Alfheim."

Rune took a step closer.

"He loved my mother once…in Svartálfaheim." Kallan tried to remember all the memories, all the pictures, and there they were before her again. She saw each one as clearly as she saw her bloodstained hands. "A woman… She needed me. The woman who killed Gudrun…but Father was in the way." Kallan gazed at Rune. The tears glistened in her golden eyes.

"Swann found a *Seidi*… Aaric killed Swann to hide it," Kallan said. "And Borg…" She couldn't begin to explain what she had watched him do to the body.

Rune went white as a quiet rage filled his eye and he clenched his teeth.

A lone tear spilled down Kallan's cheek. "Aaric killed my father."

Kallan shuddered. Looking back to the dead, she hugged her arms tight.

"This… I never wanted this," she gasped and shook her head, viewing the carnage.

"Never wanted this," she whispered.

Rune stepped through the corpses.

"You shouldn't be here," he gently spoke, coming to stand beside her.

"I couldn't leave them," she said, looking to each corpse. The tears flowed free. "They knew me once. I couldn't leave them."

The wind rustled, upsetting the silence. A cold wind blew and bit her face.

"I can see everything now…yet almost nothing. Images that come and go. They cloud my mind. And this, none of this…" Kallan shook her head. "This is never what I wanted."

"My lady?"

The ailing voice cracked as it reached them.

Together, Kallan and Rune turned to the shaking hand of a bloodied warrior, too mutilated to identify his race. Ignoring the blood and waste, Kallan fell to her knees beside him, and ever so gently, raised him from the ground.

Empty eyes that couldn't see searched the sky as Kallan grasped his black hand already chilled by death. The stench of bowel pierced the air as Kallan leaned closer. She barely made out the unmarked side of his face left untouched by Fand's Seidr flame.

"The voice of my lady reaches me in my final hour," he spoke.

"Eilif," Kallan gasped, recognizing what little remained of his face in the darkness. The Dokkalfr turned to Kallan's voice.

"I see you," he muttered blindly, unaware that his remaining eye no longer worked. "You've come for me. My dearest friend."

He tried to smile, revealing his blackened teeth through a distorted face.

"You have come to guide me then to Odinn's halls," he sputtered, gasping through the pain he no longer felt.

Kallan opened her mouth to speak, ready to correct him and tell him she still lived, but stopped herself. Clamping her jaw, she nodded, tightening her grip on his cold palm as she willed her sobbing silent.

"Yes," she finally forced from lips. "I am here."

"My dear, sweet lady." Eilif relaxed into Kallan's arms, suddenly calm. "My queen." Kallan pursed her lips against the tears that fell.

"I am sorry." Eilif gasped. "I —"

"Sh…" Kallan hushed, grateful for his blindness." Sleep now, dear friend. Sleep."

Slowly, she wrapped her fingers around the hilt of her dagger sheathed at her waist.

"Kallan," Eilif began. "Will you feed the children?"

Tears flowed as Kallan nodded.

"I promise," she whispered.

"You must feed the children," Eilif said then deeply gasped as his body stiffened against the blade of Kallan's dagger.

"Kallan… K… Kallan."

Eilif whispered her name until, with his final breath, he entered Odinn's halls.

Sobbing, Kallan closed his eyes and then mustered the strength to ever so gently lower the body back to the ground as she withdrew her dagger from his heart.

No longer holding back the flood of tears, Kallan wiped Eilif's blood on her skirts and forcefully sheathed the dagger. Lifting her face to the sky, Kallan stood several arm lengths away from Rune, who watched quietly, unable to speak the words to ease her heartache.

Kallan shuddered against the cold as the wind rushed over the dead. Rune dared a step toward her.

"Kallan," he spoke.

"He was a scribe in my father's court." Kallan balled her hands into fists. "We would run the streets... He climbed the Livsvann with me once." Kallan smiled through her tears as she remembered. "He couldn't even lift a sword."

Rune kept his distance.

"He was a scholar!"

The words shook the silence as her voice reverberated through the night.

"He didn't belong in battle! He couldn't even fight!" Kallan turned to Rune. "How can I win this? Whatever men may fall, I lose. If I fight with you, my own kin dies by my hand! I can't possibly stand against my enemy knowing you oppose—"

Kallan lost the words and searched the night for the answers.

"I don't belong anywhere," she muttered.

"Kallan."

Closing the last of the space between them, Rune pulled her into him, and Kallan, wrapping her arms around him, welcomed his warmth. Dropping her head onto his chest, she buckled beneath her grief. There in Rune's arms, Kallan cried until the last of her tears were spent.

The fog rolled peacefully over the sleeping dead and Kallan turned her head against Rune's chest.

A dark figure moved in the darkness. Kallan raised her head and focused her eyes to see. The figure grew larger as it stumbled carelessly over the bodies. A moment later, the fog rolled with the wind and the figure emerged. Kallan gasped.

Standing in the dark, she and Rune stared at the hunched forms of Joren and Daggon. They leaned against the other with the last of their strength. With whitened knuckles, they peered across the dead at Kallan and Rune. In the hand at his side, Daggon clutched Gudrun's pouch.

CHAPTER FIFTY

A stream of smoke rose from Rune's pipe as Rune gazed out his chamber window. Across the Klarelfr, a handful of men collected the dead onto pyres. Rows of smoke pillars rolled to the sky. He had listened with Joren, Torunn, Geirolf, Bergen, and Kallan as Daggon quoted Gudrun's words back perfectly.

"She said nothing more?" Rune asked, lowering the bit from his lips.

Daggon shook his large, red head. His scars flickered like shadows across the firelight.

"I did as she instructed." Regret filled his words.

"A sleeping spell." Rune stared with disbelief, mulling over the success rate in his head. "You want to put the entire army to sleep?"

"We've done it before," Kallan assured him, remembering Thorold's army.

"Will it cover Forkbeard's forces as well?" Bergen asked, less concerned with the impossibility of their proposal.

"There is only enough left for one spell," Kallan said, knowing the bundle in Daggon's hand was all that had been left of Gudrun's furtive supply. "If we wait for Forkbeard's troops to arrive, it won't cover everyone, and I can't differentiate Ljosalfar from Dokkalfar from Dani. When I administer it, we will lose some of our own for a period."

"Everyone will sleep," Bergen said.

"We will still have to fight Forkbeard's forces," Rune said, deciding. "But there is enough to maintain Aaric's army?" he asked, peering across his room at Kallan.

She nodded.

"How does it work?" Bergen asked, eager to hear all the details.

Kallan was quick to oblige.

"Once I release the spell, it spreads," she began. "I have some control over where it goes, but whoever comes in contact with it—whoever breathes it in—will sleep. There is no selecting one man from the next, but with the right runes, I can protect a handful of us."

"Will it put Aaric to sleep?" Bergen asked.

"If Aaric is as skilled in the Seidr as we think he is," Kallan said, "he'll be able to avoid its affects, but he'll be alone."

"Alone should give us the advantage to take him down," Rune said.

"That might be all the time we need to do this," Bergen said.

"How long will they sleep?" Rune asked from his window.

Kallan sighed as she ran the calculations over.

"A lot of this depends on the dosage, and how thin it's spread," she answered. "If a full batch is used for one man, he will sleep for a week. If a fraction of the usual dosage is used for a whole army, they may sleep for only moments. In one test Gudrun and I did, they only experienced a substantial case of drowsiness."

"How much can you produce with this?" Rune asked.

"This is the last of Gudrun's supply," Kallan said, "It may yield half a batch for what you're suggesting. I can guarantee the armies will sleep, but only for minutes."

"That isn't much," Bergen grumbled.

"That wasn't Gudrun's goal." Kallan quelled a smirk.

"What do you mean?" Rune asked, withdrawing from the window.

A gleam hardened Kallan's eyes.

"Based on the advancement of Aaric's abilities and the state we found Eilif in, they were under the influence of another spell…one that blinded them to me." Kallan relaxed her shoulders. "This sleeping spell will break it."

"How soon will it work?" Bergen asked, cutting Rune off.

"The spell immediately passes through them," Kallan continued. "Within moments, everyone will be unconscious. It will take maybe twice that long for the affects to subside and their bodies to clear it…maybe longer, but not by much."

"What kind of state can we expect them to be in when they wake?" Geirolf asked.

Kallan gazed at the old healer.

"Disoriented. Confused. Many may experience severe headaches. Possible nausea. One or two may not wake up," she warned.

Releasing a plume of smoke, Rune looked to his scout. "Joren. Where are Aaric's troops now?"

"They're regrouping," Joren said. "We expect them to be ready to advance at daybreak."

"And Forkbeard?" Rune asked.

"They'll be here by midday," Joren said.

The coals cooled and the embers died in Rune's pipe as he submerged himself in thought. "Only fourteen thousand stand against Forkbeard's forces."

"What will you have us do, Rune?" Bergen asked, desperate for any plan better than the one Daggon had.

Rune relit the coals and drew long and deep from his pipe. He blew the smoke as everyone in the room waited for an answer. Unseen, he shifted an eye to Kallan, who stood charged at the ready to fight.

"We're waiting for your orders, sire," Geirolf said.

Rune sighed, and fought down a smirk.

"Fall back," Rune said. "We'll give them Gunir."

"—Are you mad?" Geirolf barked.

"—We're a handful against thousands!" Bergen quipped.

"—What of the wounded?" Geirolf asked.

"—We can't just leave them!" Torunn cried.

"We have no choice!" Rune barked through the chaos, instilling order once more. "The city has been taken! We have no alliance to fall back on! All who we have are here!"

Silence filled the room.

The fire popped as the truth of their demise settled in, weighing them down to despair.

"What if you had allies?" Kallan's voice cut through the silence. "Would you stay to fight?"

Rune looked at her hard through the smoke, knowing the thoughts that brewed in her fickle mind. He had to force his eyes darker to keep from smiling.

Rune glowered across the room. "If we had allies, Gunir would stay to fight."

"And win," Kallan amended, her golden eyes brimming with determination.

"You've lost your power, Kallan Eyolfdottir," Rune coldly reminded her through the smoke. "And with it your people."

"I can reunite them," Kallan assured him and narrowed her hardened gaze onto his. "With Aaric out of the way…"

"She's right, Rune," Daggon said, speaking up at last in his queen's defense." Her people are still loyal to her. They just can't remember her."

Rune matched Kallan's scowl as he lowered his pipe.

"If Aaric should fall, and you lift this spell, can you guarantee your people will know you?"

"I will make them know me," Kallan said, refusing to let him doubt her, "I will make them hear me."

"And if they know you, what assurance can you give me that you will fight alongside Gunir?"

"Don't be foolish to think this only affects you," Kallan said. "If Forkbeard were to take you, and the walls of Gunir should fall, what assurance can you give *me* that he won't look to Lorlenalin next?"

Rune sighed, milking his role for all he was worth. He stared into the fire for added effect.

"A gamble on an ancient enemy that rests on a single promise following years of deceit…" Rune raised his eyes to Kallan. "What will you have me do?"

"Join me."

Rune rested the bit of his pipe on his lip as everyone looked to Kallan, waiting with sustained breath for a reply from their king. With a huff, Kallan suddenly stood, head erect and shoulders back as she took a step closer, presenting all she had to Gunir's king.

"Son of Tryggve!" Kallan addressed Rune as if she stood before the king in his court for the first time wearing gowns of gold instead of bloodied rags—as if there never had been the Dvergar or Aaric or the centuries of bloodshed.

"Lord of Gunir! I am Kallan, daughter of Eyolf, Queen of Lorlenalin and Lady of the White Opal! I come before you on behalf of my people. We look to you now for an alliance. I implore you, please…forge this alliance with me. Help me win back my army so that we may stand together against our foes who look to annihilate us."

Rune lowered his pipe. Holding Kallan's gaze, he came to stand at full height before her.

A suspended pause gripped the air as they waited and Kallan stood her ground, matching the hardened glare in Rune's eyes as he assessed her.

Without a word, Rune extended his hand. With regal composure, Kallan took his hand and sealed their alliance.

"Do it," Rune decreed. "It's the only shot we've got and I'm not about to squander it on naysaying."

He released Kallan's hand.

Without a thought, Kallan left for her bower, snatching Gudrun's bag from Daggon and rolling up her sleeves as she dragged Torunn along beside her.

"Well…" Geirolf stood from his seat. "I'll make my rounds. If you need me, Rune, I'll be with the wounded."

Rune nodded as Geirolf departed.

"Why do we have to put our troops to sleep, Rune?" Bergen asked. "Why can't we keep them back and wait for the spell to pass?"

"Because, Bergen," Rune said, "if something goes wrong with the spell, we'll have the whole of the Dokkalfar army charging at Kallan and I. As much as I'd love the advantage, the risk is too great. Joren." Rune looked to the scout.

"My king."

"Ready every man who can raise a sword. Spread the word. Let them know of the plan. We can't afford to have them caught off guard. That may help to decrease the confusion when they wake."

"Yes, my lord." Joren nodded, accepting his orders, and swept out of the room, leaving Daggon with Bergen and Rune.

The final click of the door cued Bergen to stand with a groan.

"I need a drink," he said and trudged to the tray picked over of meats and mead.

"Can she do it?" Rune asked Daggon, cutting Bergen's celebrations short.

With the flagon in hand, Bergen gazed at Daggon, eager for the answer as much as Rune.

"Kallan has always been sharper than the blade she wields," Daggon said with a sigh, settling himself into a chair. He rested his large arms on his knee in thought. "She took her studies as serious as her instructors…when she bothered to show up. But she seemed to harbor a natural gift for the spells."

Daggon stared into the flames, lost in thought and unwilling to give voice to the countless memories that gave him hope.

"Yes." He nodded with a gentle grin as he meandered through ancient memories. "Kallan can do it."

A bit more relaxed than he had been moments before, Bergen picked over the tray of food while Rune relit his pipe. Neither caught the smile on Daggon's mouth.

"There are things Kallan can do that not even she knows she can do," Daggon added.

Torunn stood over Kallan's shoulders, entranced by the speed of Kallan's hands. The fire crackled behind them, mingling its light with the candles she had lit and casting as much light as possible onto Kallan's makeshift worktable in her sitting room.

"What is a spell?" Torunn finally asked as Kallan finished crushing the foreign, white root within the grindstone. Fine powder now settled into the base of the stone.

"A spell is one of the three uses of Seidr that can be mastered," Kallan said as the water she heated over the single flame beside her began to boil. "A Seidkona can wield the Seidr, using it as it passes through the earth, the air, or the waters. Sight is the gift and art of Vision one can hone with the use of the Seidr. A Voluspa is a Seer's Vision."

"The Seidr doesn't pass through fire?" Torunn asked in hopes to better understand the concoction Kallan brewed.

"Fire is energy. Enery is Seidr. A compacted form of Seidr…and is only one of Seidr's many forms."

Kallan didn't look up as she dropped a handful of leaves into the water to better extract the oils. "Spells are powders, gases, or liquids infused with the Seidr to attain a desired effect. With further study, runes can be used to siphon the Seidr, direct it, or enclose it within an object." Kallan glanced up from her work for a moment. "That's how my pouch works."

Torunn watched, still engrossed with Kallan's hands as she began tracing a set of runes into the fine powdered root with her finger.

"One must be sensitive to the Seidr to pull it from its natural source and wield it at will," she continued. "More study is required to mold it into a substance, but the Sight…" Kallan shook her head. "That is only passed on through blood. Either you have it or you don't. And you don't stand a chance of having it unless you are of the bloodline."

"Bloodline?" Torunn asked. "Have you always had it then?"

"Her mother did," Daggon said as Bergen and Rune bombarded him with questions. "It was strange that Kallan never developed the Sight."

"How will Aaric's hindrances affect her?" Rune asked, recalling Kallan's explanation of Aaric siphoning her Seidr to block her memory when she was just a child.

"It may return over time to its full power," Daggon said. "On the other hand, she may, forever, be hindered in that sense." Daggon shook his head. "We won't know until time has healed her of the damage done. On the other hand, we may never know. I know very little of this matter really. Who we need is Gudrun. She coul—"

His stomach clamped as Daggon suddenly lost his voice. Clamping his jaw, he looked to the fire, allowing the heat of the flames to dry the tears from his eyes.

"What of Lorlenalin?" Rune asked, changing the subject to ease his grief. "What condition did you find her in?"

Daggon sighed deeply as dark images rolled through his mind.

"There was almost no guard," he said. "If the women and children of Lorlenalin were there, we didn't see. Aaric used every abled and non-abled body for his army. Stripped the city of its citizens. Cooks. Key holders…" Daggon shook his head. "Everyone was gone. It was upon a happy chance that Joren found me there."

Torunn watched the Seidr flow from Kallan's palm into the runes.

"I thought Seidkonas always carried a Seidr staff."

"You're confusing me with the Iss Land Seidr Wielders," Kallan said, too focused to smile at the mistake. "I never had a use for such hindrance."

"And the runes?" Torunn asked as she peered down at the white powder.

The sharp stench of boiled herbs rose from the bowl of water above the flame.

"The runes only guide the Seidr." Kallan snapped her wrist, disrupting the Seidr flow, and took up the Seidr-infused powder, pouring it into a bowl. "The words alone do nothing. The runes themselves are just runes. But both can be used together as a tool just like this grindstone. Together, we can reach a desired effect. A Seidr staff is usually etched with runes to allow better control over the Seidr." Kallan averted her attention to Torunn. "I can use the runes to form a shield of Seidr that prevents the sleeping spell from reaching Rune and Bergen."

"Couldn't you use the runes to shield all of them?" Torunn asked.

"I could," Kallan said as she gently punctured a single, small hole into the thick stem of red flower. "But the efforts would require so much of my concentration, I wouldn't be free to fight. And with a Seidr User on the battlefield, I need to fight."

Without further question, Torunn watched as Kallan collected the milky white substance that seeped from the stem. She soon extinguished the flame that heated the water and waited only a few more minutes before dropping a dried mushroom into the brew.

With practiced craft, Kallan worked through the early morning hours until she emerged from her sitting room clutching a small bag and smelling of herbs that lingered with a stale bite.

Kallan pushed open the door to Rune's bower. She wasn't surprised to see him without his tunic, clutching a pipe as he stared out across the river to the empty plains. Still clasping the bag of herbs, she came to stand beside him.

"You can almost hear it." Rune spoke over the pipe.

Kallan looked out into the forests beyond the river where pillars of smoldering bodies lay. In the distance, she could hear it: the sound of the march. The subtle thunder of thousands shook the ground as the Dokkalfar marched to Gunir's walls.

"They come," Rune said.

CHAPTER FIFTY-ONE

Dump him there," Fand growled with Aaric's voice to the guards hauling Aaric behind her at the edge of the Alfheim Wood. Aaric hit the ground a few feet from Fand, giving him sufficient view of the plains ahead as his guard remained vigilant.

Fand smiled over the painted mimic of Aaric's shoulder as she gazed at him.

"No protest? Not even an attempt to escape?" she played.

Aaric started back at his face worn too well by Fand. "I won't give you the pleasure."

Fand frowned.

"You will watch, Drui, as I rip the heart from your precious princess," she spat before turning to the battlefield, eager to begin the end as the Ljosalfar marched to join them.

Across the river Klarelfr, Bergen's men marched with rekindled hope to the open plains of Alfheim that wrapped around Gunir's bailey. The gray and white of the clouds loomed overhead, mingling with the vast blacks of the brewing storm. The ominous veil forced a heaviness in the air that added to the tension and enveloped the whole of the army.

Armor and sword clanked in time with the monotonous thunder of the warriors' march across the scorched plains, past the piles of smoldering bodies. Rune waited with his men across the river to the barren fighting grounds north of Gunir. Upon arrival, Bergen broke from his battalion and rode on ahead to the circle of runes and Kallan kneeling on the ground in her red skirts.

With two fingers poised, she etched the final figure into the soil and completed the circle. She scrutinized each rune then stood, brushing the dirt from her skirts.

"How exactly does this work?" Bergen asked, expecting a lot more than a few squiggles drawn in the dirt. He studied the runes that formed a circle around a patch of earth. There was just room enough for three men to stand beside each other comfortably without feeling awkward.

"The runes are infused with Seidr," Kallan said. "They'll recognize the spell and guide it around you so it won't touch you."

Bergen raised a doubtful brow, antagonizing Kallan's mood.

"Don't stand within the circle and sleep the battle away, for all I care," she grumped and spun on her heel before climbing onto Astrid. A moment later, she rode down the line of the archers.

"I think I liked her better when she feared me," Bergen muttered as Rune joined Bergen beside the ring. "Too much of that sounded like Gudrun."

"What did you do?" Rune asked.

Dismissing Rune's questions, Bergen entered the circle and silently debated the merit of Kallan's Seidr as Rune too stepped into the circle. Bergen looked his brother up then down, assessing the mere inches of space between them.

"This is uncomfortably close," Bergen said. "Are you sure two men will be enough?"

When Rune didn't answer, he looked to Kallan, who returned from her assessment.

"Hey!" Bergen called. "Are you sure this is enough?"

"A small group, or any group, segregated from the army will tip Aaric off. Your instructions are clear," she said firmly. "If you leave the circle before I finish administering the spell, you will pass into sleep with your men. Stay within the circle and you can fight."

She pulled back on the reins, bringing Astrid to a halt as she flicked back a strand of hair over her shoulder. Kallan flashed Bergen a smirk.

"Of course, if you feel you can't handle it, by all means, choose a handful of men to stand with you."

Bergen and Rune exchanged glances.

"We can take him," Bergen said, confidently.

Within view of the front, Aaric's battalion lingered over the hillside with what little morning sun could break through the pending storm.

Outside the circle, at the back of the infantry, Roald threw back his head and downed the last of a mead he had brought with him.

"You're a fool for standing here," Rune said, catching a glimpse of the bandaged stub of his right shoulder.

Roald fired back a grin.

"I would shame my fathers if I didn't fight while I still had a strong arm and two legs. Besides…" Roald widened his grin. "…your Dokkalfr insisted I take her damn apple with me."

With vigor, Roald tucked his flagon under his stub, took up Kallan's apple from a pocket, and bit into the fruit, nearly cleaving it in two.

"I feel great!" he proclaimed through a wet mouthful of Seidr.

"Everything is set," Kallan said, looking down from her seat on Astrid. "We'll wait for the advance to distract them then I will release the spell."

Rune nodded once as the thunder of feet swept the plains from the far edge of the wood. He tightened his grip on his bow and released a short breath.

"I still say we should have the archers ready," Bergen grumbled.

In the distance, the Dokkalfar ranks aligned, following the first of Aaric's orders. The rows of Dokkalfar raised their bows.

"If Kallan's spell goes well, those archers will join us," Rune said.

Roald threw a grimace over his armless shoulder.

"Why am I not in the circle?"

Engaging his archers, Rune mirrored the command and cued the Ljosalfar to ready their spears. The air was thick and eerily still.

"Because," Bergen said, keeping his eyes on Aaric seated upon his horse, "you're too weak to keep up!"

The Ljosalfar's battle cry filled the plains, drowning out Roald's vulgarity as the Dokkalfar released their arrows from the forest's edge, signaling Rune's army to unleash their volley.

Raising her arms to the sky, Kallan muttered a charm and raised a canopy of Seidr. A blanket of opaque blue poured from Kallan's hand as the Dokkalfar arrows plinked off Kallan's ward that spilled down the whole of Rune's army.

Rune waited between volleys and gave the command.

"Fly!" Rune cried and launched his spearmen out from under the protection of Kallan's ward.

Their feet pounded the ground like thunder. With spears raised, they advanced, seeded with bloodlust to avenge their kin.

"Now!" Fand screamed in Aaric's voice, sending the Dokkalfar charging into the plains to meet the Ljosalfar.

The air echoed with cries as Kallan withdrew the ward and took up handfuls of fine powder from her pouch. Bits of Seidr from the shield rained down in a show of gold and light.

"Now!" Rune shouted to Kallan and, at once, she released the Seidr.

Below her breath, she muttered, pulling on the threads of Seidr from the winds. Gently, a controlled breeze blew up into the mixture and released the tiny, white specs into the air. Her words carried the wind through the field, taking her spell with it as the clang of spears collided.

In a gradual wave that moved unnoticed, the warriors bore against their armaments as the weight of their weapons increased. Sluggishly, the Alfar wielded their swords and spears, burdened with an unnatural mass that slowed their movements until, too weak to stand, they began to collapse beneath their armor. A few surrendered their weapons as their bodies fell. Others dropped to a knee. Their eyes, too heavy to keep open, closed.

From atop Aaric's horse, Fand stared, crunching Aaric's brow into a wrinkled mass.

"The child has learned well," Fand muttered, knowing too well the cause for her faltering army. "Let's give it back, shall we?" Fand said, smirking at Aaric, who maintained his scowl. Snapping her hand high, Fand threw back the wind with Kallan's spell and sent it soaring to a corner of the field where it dispersed, dropping everyone within its path. A gust of wind picked up and carried a piece of it toward Rune, Bergen, and Roald where it encompassed Kallan's circle, but never entered it.

"What are you doing in here?" Bergen asked of Roald, who had subtly stepped behind the runes as the cloud of spell engulfed them.

Roald only grinned as realization blanketed Kallan's face.

"He knows," Kallan muttered.

Without warning, she sent Astrid into a full gallop behind the few Ljosalfar left standing to battle her brethren.

"Kallan!" Rune called, taking a step to follow, but Bergen dropped a heavy hand to Rune's shoulder, holding back him within the circle. The spell had barely begun to disperse.

Forced to concede, Rune watched as Kallan exchanged a new flourish of words.

Pulling out a second handful of powder, the winds rose up and with it, her craft. At the end of the line, she pulled from the Seidr, forcing it through her and doubling it up. Willing the wind back, she gave a thrust, sending the spell back against Aaric.

Fand braced against the impact as heat flooded her chest. Extending an arm, she threw up a ward, shielding herself, Aaric, and his guard from Kallan's spell. Fand's glare hardened as she fixed her eyes on the queen. The spell dispersed and last of the warriors dropped, engulfing the plains in silence.

Turning Astrid about, Kallan scanned the battlefield strewn with sleeping warriors. The cold winds burned her face with its chill as she panted deeply. She embraced the cold that churned her blood and balled her abhorrence into the mass of her Seidr. With the ring of her sword, Kallan extended her blade to the sky, let free her battle cry, and charged, inspiring Bergen, Rune, and Roald to abandon their circle and join in the hunt for Aaric's demise.

Down against their spears, Rune swung *Gramm*, too angered to buckle against the weight of the spear. Beside him, Bergen allowed the fury he often buried beneath his black eyes to erupt, cutting all who dared stand in the path of the Dark One as he swung his blade with mastered precision. He gutted one and cleaved another, fueled only with his will and his rage as Kallan rode hard toward Fand.

Cold sweat spilled down Fand's back as Bergen took his first swing. Frozen, she watched the rains beat down on the blade that pulsed with Seidr.

"Go," Fand said, sending out Aaric's guard to the field. Obediently, they charged the Dark One.

"Something wrong?" Aaric asked with a twinge of delight in his tone. In horror, Fand stared at the blade in Bergen's hands, paying no mind as Kallan formed a ball of blue flame in her palm.

"Not at all," Fand said, and turned her gaze to Aaric. Astrid's hooves pounded the earth as Kallan drew near, and Fand jerked her arm, sending a stream of Seidr that arched through the air and collided with Astrid's chest, throwing Kallan from her mount. Releasing a scream, Aaric burned the bonds from his wrists and stood just as quickly, charging Fand with a lance of Seidr. His Seidr met Fand's palm as she clamped her hand down around Aaric's and pulled his Seidr lance into her.

"Damn you Drui," Fand muttered. "Kallan can take the life from you."

Releasing Aaric's hand, Fand turned the horse about and rode hard into the plains toward Kallan.

The battlefield vanished and the flash of light blinded Kallan and robbed her of sound. The ground struck her, breaking her body and leaving her breathless. Enclosed in silence, she battled to breathe, but no air came. Kallan punched the ground and clawed her throat, flailing about as she fought to gasp. But a nameless pain crept in, shutting her down as her lungs failed to expand. Despite all efforts, the air wouldn't come and the void closed in.

Seconds lasted like days as Kallan's consciousness faded between empty black and thoughts of death until, at last, the shadows faded. Sound returned, and Kallan gasped long and deep. Her stomach stopped convulsing and Kallan breathed.

Inhaling deeply, air filled her lungs. Kallan cleared the darkness that had nearly taken her. Panting, she pulled herself onto her knees and dug the tips of her fingers into the soft, cold earth. The soil was damp from the rain that had started to fall, slowly at first, then hard in a heavy shower.

Around her, the Alfar slept. The sharp clang of sword and spear mingled with Rune shouting indecipherably as sound flooded back. Her vision focused and she lifted her face from the ground. She was certain she heard Bergen's boisterous laugh in the distance as he speared an opponent.

Kallan searched for her bearings, looking through the dismal gray that cloaked the battlefield. Unable to breathe, she stifled a sob as she rested her eyes on the heap that was Astrid's body.

"Oh, no."

Kallan faltered as she fumbled and clambered to the stallion's side. With trembling hands, she touched the velvet of his chestnut nose. His lifeless, brown eyes stared into nothing as his mouth hung unnaturally agape, frozen in the exact position as when the life had left him.

The shaking that started in her hands travelled like tremors into her body. Someone screamed, but she didn't hear.

"Astrid." Kallan's voice cracked.

Again, she failed to hear Rune call her name. Her grief drowned out all sound. Unaware of the thunder of hooves striking the ground from the edge of the battle where Aaric emerged from the forest, Kallan kneeled and passed a gentle hand over Astrid's face.

"Kallan!" Rune called, running hard toward her, over the bodies and the battlefield. "Kallan!"

Madness settled where comprehension failed Kallan and with a wild eye, she glanced up just in time to see Rune racing toward her, reaching out for her as he cried her name—as Fand slid off her horse and released a stream of Seidr from Aaric's hands.

The Seidr arched and the Beast within Rune rose up to meet it, but this Seidr consumed the Beast. The Beast screamed as Fand's Seidr impaled Rune, twisting his body and launching him into the air. Horror obscured Kallan's face as she watched his broken body slam the ground with a definitive thud, taking the last of her sense with it.

Lost to the sound of the battle, lost to the dismay that consumed her, Kallan scrambled to Rune's side, oblivious to the winds and rains—oblivious to the Fae goddess who took the form of a raven and flew from the plains.

Kallan's head quaked with incomprehensible disorder. No longer able to steady the shaking that passed through her, Kallan brushed her fingers across Rune's face and succumbed to the confusion that clouded her senses. Droplets of rain streaked his lifeless brow. The last of her reason tipped into darkness.

From the Alfheim Wood, Aaric ran through the battlefield to meet her. Overhead, the raven cawed.

"Coward!" he shouted at the bird. It replied with a gleam in its golden eyes, and Aaric turned his attention back to Kallan.

The trembling in her body had stopped. Calm took her and the sounds of the battle died away with the last of his men, leaving only the hard patter of rain and the snort from his horse.

Bergen and Roald lowered their arms and assessed their surroundings. Gray and dead encompassed them in the rain as Bergen, with a smile on his face, found Aaric running full speed at Kallan. Panting, Bergen trailed the Dokkalfr's gaze to a heap dumped on the ground before Kallan.

The jovial gleam in Bergen's eye vanished. All color drained from his face as his body fell numb to the world, and Bergen knew his brother. Terror sent a cry from Bergen's throat as he sprinted across the plains and fell to his knees beside his brother.

As if all life had drained from her eyes until only hate remained, Kallan raised her gold, arctic eyes to Aaric. Through the rain-soaked strands of hair, Kallan stared. Coldly, she clamped her fingers around *Gramm*'s hilt and took the sword from Rune's dead hand.

Aaric slowed to a stop several feet from Kallan.

"Kallan," Aaric called over the rain. "Don't do this."

Numbed by the pain, deadened by hate, Kallan rose to her feet. And the rains fell. A callous calculation erased all feeling, save for the mass of rage that filled her. From the air, she drew on the threads of Seidr, undeterred by the skill of her foe, consuming her sword-less arm with an energy she compacted with her own.

The winds snapped about, biting the skin as the rains bombarded the battlefield. Aaric hardened his stance, refusing to back down from the Seidkona's wrath. With a step, Kallan brought her arm around and sent a single stream of white toward Aaric's head.

The sudden attack left him stunned, but only for a moment. He re-directed her attack, forcing her Seidr to the ground, exactly as Kallan had seen with Gudrun.

"Kallan! Please!" Aaric cried.

Undaunted by his defense, Kallan sent a second blast, which Aaric re-directed as he had before.

"You must hear me!" he said, taking up a blade from the ground.

Another surge of white Seidr flew from Kallan's hand and, slowly, she made her way toward Aaric. Each time, he seized it and guided it into the earth beside him until his tactic became predictable.

"Please don't make me fight you," Aaric said.

Kallan fired the Seidr she pulled through the wind until she closed the last of the space between them. Scrambling, Aaric stumbled back then fired off a stream of his energy as she hoped he would.

Impervious to the amount of Seidr Aaric wielded, Kallan raised Rune's sword, blocked the attack, and siphoned the energy into the blade until *Gramm* sparked angrily. Beads of sweat rolled down Aaric's temple as Kallan sent another surge of white that Aaric fed into the ground. He retaliated and streamed more Seidr and Kallan blocked, diverted, and pulled Aaric's attacks into the sword.

"Kallan," Aaric said. Heaving, he managed a step back. "There's workings here you don't—"

Kallan snapped her wrist, releasing a white stream of lightning that cut Aaric short.

Gazing past Kallan's glowing white blade, Aaric found the golden eyes through the rain. With a jerk of his arm, he took up his sword and swung to block.

The cold clang of his blade resonated through his arms and he glanced down at a dagger with black, polished stones caught at the hilt. He pushed off the blade

Aaric swung his sword, and caught *Gramm*. The Seidr-charged sword sparked as they wielded their blades down and around. Aaric lunged and Kallan blocked. Aaric thrust and Kallan sidestepped as *Gramm* sparked in Kallan's grip.

Flicking the dagger, Kallan sliced Aaric's face and he fell back, tapping the strip of blood on his cheek. In the time it took Aaric to take a hand from his sword, Kallan sheathed the dagger and snapped her hand up as Aaric fired a stream of Seidr that Kallan caught with her bare palm.

Siphoning the Seidr into her own, Kallan welcomed and pulled Aaric's Seidr into her, charging her own strength. The gold of her eyes gleamed bright white as she fed Aaric's Seidr down into the earth.

Breaking off his Seidr, Aaric reached for his sword, but before he could raise his blade, Kallan fired a blast of wind that struck his chest and sent him barreling through the air. He landed with his sword and a crunch. Groaning, Aaric clambered to his knees and Kallan brought down her sword. A deafening clash caught Aaric's blade and Kallan landed a punch between their blades, crunching Aaric's front teeth.

Aaric fell back, holding his mouth, and scrambled to his feet, the front of him painted red.

Scowling, he lunged and Kallan let him come down against *Gramm*. There, Aaric bore his weight over her. And once he believed he had her, when he believed her strength would falter, Kallan plunged the stone-encrusted dagger up, beneath his sternum, and ripped open the core of his Seidr.

Immobilized by the gash to his stomach, Aaric fell to his knees as Kallan brought Rune's sword to rest on his shoulder. Aaric opened his mouth to speak, desperate to utter any word to stop her, as Kallan positioned the blades onto his shoulders.

She panted. Her unyielding rage seethed. And Kallan saw nothing, not the wide eyes of Aaric's voiceless plea, or the gurgle he emitted with his last breath as she released the Seidr from *Gramm* seconds before crossing the blades through his neck.

Kallan pushed off the body, raised the dagger, and plunged the blade into Aaric's body over and over.

For Swann. For her father. For Rune, she stabbed the corpse again and again.

For Astrid, for Gudrun, for Eilif, until the pain she was starting to feel again dissolved.

For Kovit.

But the pain didn't wane.

A strong, hand firmly caught her wrist and Kallan spun about to meet Bergen's wide, black eyes through the downpour. Through the rain, she saw his tears.

"Kallan."

He spoke with a grief as grand as her own.

Huffing, she studied his face blanketed by raw hate that wouldn't let her go. The rain pattered quietly and mingled with their tears.

"I've been where you're going, lass," he whispered. Bergen sadly shook his head. "Don't go there."

Jerking her wrist free, Kallan lowered the blood-soaked blade and glared at Aaric's headless body. Without a word, she turned to the lifeless heap of Rune.

CHAPTER FIFTY-TWO

Soaked through with blood and rain, Kallan heaved deeply with rage. Numbed to the weight of the sword in her hand, she stood in the rain as hate surged through her. Ignoring Bergen and Roald, she stumbled over the sleeping and the dead to Rune's side. To her knees, she fell, deadened to the pain pulsing through her.

Each movement sent a voiceless scream tearing through her as Kallan examined Rune. His body had already begun to grow cold. The Seidr had long left him. A spell could not bring him back any more than a Seidr-infused apple from the gods could.

Desperate to deny what she already knew, Kallan looked wildly about from Rune's feet to his face. Desperate for a solution to jump up and save him, but nothing came. The rains only fell.

Hot tears streaked her face as she fell deeper into the truth that demanded she accept what she knew. Madness started to take her and she let it. Buckling beneath the loss, her hands flew to her face and Kallan broke. Behind her, Bergen stood beside Aaric's corpse, taking in the scream that rent the air as Kallan's grief filled the chasm Rune's death left in them both. She shook as she sobbed, frail and weak as if she would crumble beneath the gentle patter of the rain.

Her mind succumbed to the darkness that would become her insanity, willingly falling into that void, but something darker stirred from within, pulling on her desperation to live.

"No!" Kallan screamed and she punched the earth.

Determination ignited her strength and, snapping her head up, the gold of her eyes glistened. She knew, too well, the threads Gudrun taught her and she, at last, could reach them.

"If I have to pull all the Seidr from all the earth, I will bring it back for you," Kallan muttered.

Crazed with the refusal to fail, Kallan placed her hands upon Rune's chest and willed herself to reach into the far depths of the Seidr, down past her core, into the deepest chasms of the earth.

Into the ground, Kallan pushed her consciousness, following the threads of Seidr. They mingled with earth and air through the waters, and on to the ends of the world. It was there she followed the threads, and siphoned the energy, pulling on all strands like a weaver, who would pull from a tapestry. And together, at once, the Seidr slowly started to obey and shift.

Kallan pulled the energy out from its hub and directed it along every strand. Deeper she dove into the black stretches of the unknown where the Seidr first dwelled beyond the Gap. Kallan merged with the lines that flowed to the seas, plunged to its depths, and farther still until she lost herself in the Seidr.

It carried her down to its chasms where it grew, secreted far beneath the earth and the sea, where it lay forgotten in the golden palaces of the Aes Sidhe.

The Fae palaces of Under Earth glistened. Beside a golden river of Seidr that encircled a city, Danann raised her perfect, pale face from the waters and turned her ageless, golden eyes to the East.

Dag's soft footfall grew louder as he entered the white courtyard and came to stop beside her. He too, with his golden eyes and tapered ears, had felt the tremor and stared. Both seemed to drip in threads of Seidr, as if their clothing itself was woven with its strands.

"What is it, Danann?" he asked, as intrigued by the disruption as she.

Danann's long, golden hair fell past her finely tapered ears to the river's edge where it swayed in the gentle winds.

"Something stirs in the Northern Way," she breathed and sharpened her senses.

Dipping her delicate hand into the Seidr river, she waited and reached out along the threads with her own Seidr as she followed the path to the disturbance.

A delicate smile pulled her mouth into a fine curve and Danann lifted her eyes to Dag.

"The Drui breathes," she whispered and Dag sharply inhaled.

Stiffening his back, he looked to the east.

"Nine hundred years," Dag breathed and shifted his gaze to Danann, who had withdrawn her hand from the river.

"There was a child," Danann gasped. "And the Seidr of the Drui flows right to her," she said with an ever-widening grin.

"I'll summon the guards," Dag said, but Danann placed a hand on him.

"No," she said. "We wait. She will come to us."

Into the sea, back through the air, the Seidr raced like water along the threads. Back through the earth, it flowed up into Kallan, who pulled the energy into her and down her arms into Rune.

With a sudden gasp, Rune arched his back against the surge and breathed free of the Fendinn's hunger.

Kallan pulled back her hands as if his life had burned her. Breaking the flow, she released the Seidr. Gasping, Rune lay with his heart beating hard against the massive flow of energy Kallan had poured into him. As if trying to regain his whereabouts, Rune looked wildly about. The clouds had diminished overhead and left a bright, clearing sky as he regained control of his breath again.

"You… *Uskit!*" Bergen barked over Kallan's shoulder.

With astounding relief, Kallan gasped and, free to feel once again, she fell onto Rune, shaking beneath her tears. Around them, the spell dispersed and the Alfar stirred.

With Bergen's help, Kallan and Rune rose to their feet.

Ever smiling, Kallan clasped tightly to Rune's hand, paying mind to little else.

"We have a problem," Roald said, drawing Rune and Kallan's attention to the battlefield.

The spell had worn off and the first wave of confusion had lifted. The second wave was settling in as Dokkalfar recognized Ljosalfar.

"We don't have much time," Rune said. "Re-form the ranks," he ordered and joined Bergen to restore order.

They scrambled, reforming the Ljosalfar, but the Dokkalfar, abandoned and leaderless, took up sword against the only known enemy surrounding them.

"Reform the ranks!" Bergen bellowed, urging the Ljosalfar to find order among the chaos and abandoning all worry with the Dokkalfar.

Pockets of skirmishes grew, disrupting the ranks as confusion settled in where the Dokkalfar stood.

"Enough!" Kallan bellowed, forcing her voice out over her people.

A wave briefly calmed the skirmishes, but once they failed to see Aaric mounted, ready to lead them, they rose up again.

Siphoning her Seidr, Kallan inhaled again and located each life source. If she failed to unite them now, she would have failed completely.

"Enough!" she screamed again, this time adding a harmless pulse of Seidr through the wind.

Dokkalfar and Ljosalfar alike faltered against the force and the call of a Dani horn sounded, forcing all eyes to the east.

"He's here," Rune muttered, looking out among the fifteen thousand that stood on the horizon, ready with armed archers and spearmen.

൮ ൲ഽ

The Midgard king of Dan's Mork gazed to the west. The numbers before him were staggering, but unorganized as small skirmishes continued to break out. Forkbeard's blood chilled as he gazed upon the Alfar. He furrowed his brow, knowing instantly that something was not right.

"What is Borg doing?" Vagn asked, peering up at Forkbeard perched high on his steed.

Forkbeard's throat tightened.

Fueled on Borg's adamant vow that he would have the support of the Dokkalfar, Forkbeard had heeded the words of his wife and amassed his troops. He pulled as many as he could from all of Northymbra: from Jorvik to Loden. He had left the northern reaches of Danelaw nearly bare.

"I don't care." Forkbeard grimaced. "So long as Borg upholds his end of the bargain."

The Alfar had risen back to their feet, giving Rune the time he needed to re-establish his order.

"Form ranks!" Rune commanded of the Ljosalfar as Kallan took up her sword still lying beside Astrid's body.

The Ljosalfar obeyed and fell into line as they sorted out themselves.

"Hear me!" Kallan cried with a Seidr-enhanced voice, walking through and among her kin to restore order to the masses. Slowly, the Dokkalfar repositioned for battle. Slowly, a front line formed alongside the Ljosalfar. But, almost instantly, pockets of fighting broke out again.

"Stand down!" Rune barked to his own, reasserting order among his ranks just as Kallan prepared to send off another pulse. She marched before the lines of Dokkalfar, crying out as she moved.

"Look at me!" she begged of them, sending her voice out over the thousands. "Look at me and know me!"

Silence fell among the troops as the last of the chaos dispersed and the mass quieted.

"We all have been deceived!" Kallan pleaded, hoping they would see her familiar face. "Now look at me as you once did! Look at me and know me!" Slowly, the chaos cleared and questions came as Fand's spell broke.

"Come! Rise up once more with me! Fight with me so that, should I live, I may look upon you and know you as my brother! My brother, who dared to fight alongside me this day! This day! When we rise up together in arms and fight! Not against me, but alongside me. Share this fight with me. Rise up and fight with me!

"For centuries, I have fought beside you, my brothers. Stand with me as you once did and know me again! I may not live to this battle's end, and many who stand before me shall fall. But should you fall then fall beside me as my brother. Know that if I should fall and go with Odinn into his halls, I will lift my eyes from the darkness and I will look to you with my final breath, and I will call you my brother!

"I call to you, rise up this day and fight with me! Rise up and win with me! Rise up and call me your brother!"

Kallan raised her sword to the sky, sending her voice out over the masses.

"Rise!" she bellowed. "Rise!" She turned to the west.

"Rise!" She led them on as their voices joined with hers.

"Fire." Forkbeard's order unleashed the archer's volley. It showered the Alfar as they charged over the plains of Alfheim.

Forkbeard stifled a sigh as the whole of the Alfar barely flinched against his archers.

"Again," he muttered, knowing the sacrifice he would need to make before leading the majority of his troops back to the ships.

Cursing Borg, Forkbeard witnessed the thousands charge through his arrows as if they were pellets of rain.

"Charge."

Kallan grasped her white whips of Seidr that flowed from each hand. With each turn, she met a Dani and slashed her whips around and down, exercising full control as her eyes glistened gold.

"And again," Forkbeard ordered.

Desiring nothing more than a single arrow to pierce Borg's chest, Forkbeard shifted his gaze over each face, desperate for the one Dokkalfr, who had promised him victory, to fall.

With a wide grin plastered across his face, Bergen wielded his Firstborn, swinging the blade wide with ease as he charged ahead of his troops and caught Dani after Dani with his blade. Bare-chested and brazen, the Dark One lunged into battle eagerly slashing alongside the Seidkona, who snapped her white Seidr whips.

"Once more," Forkbeard ordered as the fourth and last volley peppered the Alfar. But they remained formidable, undaunted by the barrage of his archers.

With a sick that had settled in the pit of his stomach, Forkbeard dropped the next order, despite his rising temper.

"Spearmen at the ready," Forkbeard said. "Make it look like it was worth the expense."

Vagn didn't flinch. The line of spearmen snapped their arms in unison, waiting for the command that would send them charging across the plains to their deaths.

"Advance," Forkbeard muttered.

From his seat, the Dan's Mork king watched the Alfar swallow his front line as they charged to their deaths.

A glint of a red pommel caught the sun as Rune lunged, head first, into the lines of spearmen. Alongside the berserker and the Seidkona, he wielded his sword and dagger. Slashing a spearman, Rune brought *Gramm* down across a spear then up again, plunging his dagger into a Dani. Beside him, Bergen's laugh carried over the battle as Kallan relinquished her whips only long enough to send a blast of Seidr into Forkbeard's front line. With a flick of both wrists, she restored her white Seidr whips.

Forkbeard clenched his jaw as he watched thousands of spearmen fall beneath the formidable magnitude of the Alfar. Forcing down a mouthful of curses, he delivered his last order.

"Pull back."

Vagn echoed the order as Forkbeard steered his mount around. He didn't have to look to know most of them wouldn't survive the retreat.

With a glance to the abandoned spearmen, Vagn forced his horse to follow his king.

"My lord?" Vagn asked, knowing too well the temper that brewed beneath the silence. "Will we reform and come back?

The cheers and celebration had already exploded from the battlefield behind them.

"I haven't the troops to take down such an alliance," Forkbeard said, not bothering to look back at the waste he left behind. "Not without the help of Otto."

Vagn glanced back, ensuring the Alfar too had pulled back.

"We lost many troops today," Forkbeard said.

Scowling, he followed the road back to the ships as he stewed in resentful bitterness, writhing with hate for the Alfar.

"I swear this land will pass to my son and he will inherit their land if I have to burn every last tree and scorch the earth behind me."

Vagn listened with stilled breath, wise enough to hold his tongue.

The Alfar whooped and cheered while those at the front finished off the last of the Dani. Already, the majority of the Alfar had started rejoicing, their celebrations too loud to hear Forkbeard's words.

CHAPTER FIFTY-THREE

The greens of Odinn's Riders streaked the sky with ribbons of light. In silence, they rode overhead as the Valkyrjur gathered their warriors for Valhalla. For a moment, Kallan grinned and wondered why she couldn't hear them. Soon they would send the Fallen off to sea in flame.

She could hear the boisterous drinking and merriment from Gunir's keep carry across the river as far as the vacant plains, where she stood alone with the remnants of Astrid. The Alfar had wasted no time opening the best barrels of mead and slaughtering the fattest of pigs, which seemed to cue the festivities that already had lasted for hours.

Despite the cause for celebration, Kallan's sorrow pulled her from the Great Hall as it burst with merriment. With heavy shoulders, she stood before Astrid's cold body. With ease, she mustered her Seidr, but battled against the sharp pain that stayed her hand. For a long while, she cradled the ball of white fire until, at last, she sent the flame onto him.

Alone, Kallan watched her Seidr-flame devour the stallion. The fire reached up past the tips of the trees. Flames consumed her friend and crackled as it battled back the darkness that tried and failed to swallow the light. The light of the fire glistened off her silver gown and the Valr that hung delicately around her neck. With Torunn's help, her hair was combed and pulled back to fall down the length of her back.

"From the sounds of it, the festival won't be slowing down any time soon."

Rune's voice cut in to Kallan's thoughts and she gazed from the flames to Rune. Like she, he had washed and changed. He had sleeked back his hair and left it untied.

"They've all but forgotten they once were enemies only hours ago," he muttered, coming to stand beside her.

Kallan inhaled deeply.

"It still amazes me," she said, "how much…"

Rune said nothing as he stared at the rolling fire.

"I want to cry with relief." Kallan gasped. "But my grief has left my eyes dry."

She forced her face from the pyre and Rune gazed at the golden rings that glistened brightly by the fire's light.

"Come," Rune said, taking her hand and pulling her away from the fire. "They're asking for you."

⊂⊱ ⊰⊃

Kallan felt the warmth of the Great Hall long before they ascended the steps to the courtyard. The blast of jubilation bombarded the senses as Rune led her into the glowing liveliness of the Hall packed with Dokkalfar and Ljosalfar, who passed drink and tales.

The late summer chill that swept into the Hall behind Kallan and Rune did little to deter the mood. With a boom, the Hall burst into a deafening hail that didn't die out for several long minutes. The wounded had been picked up and welcomed to share in the merriment while others, too wounded to join, had been moved to the war room where Geirolf and Torunn kept vigilant watch through the night.

The fire pit roared beneath the sweet scent of roasted pig, and barrels of mead, hauled from the buttery, rested at the ends of the tables richly strewn with candied fruits, fresh berries, pastries, sausages, puddings, and salted meats along with a large assortment of foreign vittles not even Kallan had seen in Northymbra.

Amid the merriment and laughter, Bergen bellowed and waved, bare-chested and as jovial as ever, urging Rune to guide Kallan to the table. With a grin forming at the edge of her mouth, Kallan felt the first of her spirits begin to lift.

"You're a bard," Kallan declared as she locked a disbelieving glare onto

Bergen, who beamed.

She had found a seat crammed between Roald and Bergen, who had wasted no time passing trays of meats and cheeses down the long table.

The conversation and frequent belts of laughter were deafening as they filled the Hall.

"That I am!" Bergen proclaimed with the widest of grins and the slightest of slurs. "Bergen the Bard!"

With a hearty gulp, he took down the last of the mead in front of him while Kallan pondered laughing at the entire concept.

"Would you dare look at him and laugh?" Rune asked, leaning across the table to Kallan. "If you couldn't hold your own against him, I mean."

She understood his point too perfectly.

"But why?" she asked, forcing back the bout of laughter that bubbled enthusiastically beneath her throat.

"Because," Roald interjected, staring down into his nearly empty mug of mead. "He didn't want to wait for the bards to sing his praises."

Roald threw back his head and polished off the last of his drink. He struck the table with his empty flagon.

"So he studied in Dubh Linn with the finest of Eire's Land and became a bard," Roald said. "After that, he went on to Râ-Kedet to further his studies."

"—and burn down the library," Rune said into his drink.

Bergen proudly widened his grin, clearly not hearing Rune.

"For the sole purpose of spreading my glory ahead of my time," he announced to the room, his head cocked high toward the wrought iron wheel overhead. The mead left a glossy sheen in his eyes as he gazed at Kallan. "You should hear some of my tales. I was great."

Gradually, Kallan dropped her jaw with a widening grin.

"You are *the* 'Bergen the Bard?'" she asked. "Bergen the Bard who used to perform every year at the Tailten Fair in Mide…"

Bergen obtusely nodded in a slightly drunken stupor.

"Bergen the Bard who always sang tales of the north, and of the deeds of the Dark One who fought there?" She repeated the stories back their author.

"That I am!" Bergen beamed, swinging his mug wide over the table still flooded with meats and mead.

"The Dark One," Kallan mused. "You sang of yourself!"

"Well, I couldn't very well go around singing about 'Bergen the Bold' whilst I was 'Bergen the Bard'." Bergen scoffed. "People would know."

Kallan lowered her voice, forcing Bergen silent to hear.

"This entire time we have shrieked in horror...from a bard. A bard, who coined his own name in songs he composed of himself?"

"Imagine my surprise when my little ditties caught on to the local taverns," Bergen said and tipped up his flagon.

Unable to hold back, Kallan threw her head back and laughed until tears wet her eyes.

The festivities had hardly diminished as the evening breached the first hours of morning. The kitchens proceeded to supply the constant demand for food and the first of the barrels emptied, requiring more be brought in from the buttery. An uproarious wave of enthusiasts welcomed their arrival as flagons refilled.

"Hops!" Daggon bellowed over the ruckus.

"Gruit!" Bergen barked back. "Hops are bitter and leaves the driest after-taste of tannins in your mouth."

"Gruit is piss water for babies!" Daggon hollered. "Sugared pears for children! Women drink gruit!"

"Gruit has always been, and will always be, my truest love!" Bergen said. "For there is no finer lass than Gruit, my sweet!"

Daggon sneered, grumbling into his flagon.

"Hops is a man's drink!"

"Many a lass did I impale with my longsword," Bergen announced, raising his drink to the ceiling. "But many more did I lose to Gruit, my first, my sweet."

"Hoooops!" Daggon grumbled.

"Kallan! This one is called, 'Oh, Gruit, the Dark One Comes,'" and Bergen sang, swaying a drink to his own composing:

"There, within the shadowed brink,
The Dark One comes with lavished drink,
For ne'er will a maid there be,
As sweet as my Sweet Gruit, my drink."

"Bah," Daggon scowled and chuckled into his drink as Bergen continued.

"Beyond the brink, she comes with me,
My bed that night I'll share with she.
No deeds were e'er as great as she,
Save for my sword, my tongue, and me."

Kallan threw back her head and laughed, but Bergen went on, not missing a beat.

"Within the brink and finest hour,
When fullest body, I devoured,
There it was that I deflowered,
The fruits she bore within my bower.

Ne'er mind what Daggon thinks,
Nor what lay beyond the brink,
For when I lay me down to sleep,
My coupled lass, my Gruit will sing,

Although my sword may lose its sheen,
Although sweet Gruit, she may dream,
Of sharper swords, of hops, and things,
To me my Gruit, will always be,
My first, my dearest Gruit, my sweet."

Bergen ended his song on a grin.

"That was...the most Baldr-bad...Odinn-awful song I have ever heard," Daggon said.

Bergen burst into laughter. Daggon, mid-chuckle, threw back his head and took in the last of his drink just as Bergen added a slap to Daggon's back that sent him into a coughing fit.

Shortly thereafter, in a mad scramble, they raced each other to the barrels of mead at the end of the table, stopping to pick off a bit from the pig roast before racing back to the table, each balancing a fresh pint of mead.

"You'd think they grew up together," Roald muttered. "So what happens now?" he asked slapping the table.

"What does happen now?" Bergen asked as he squeezed himself back onto the bench beside Kallan, spilling a splash or two on her.

Daggon, his mouth stuffed with roast pig, said nothing.

"Well, with the alliance, we have a lot of work in repairing Lorlenalin," Rune said, snagging a leg of pig from the table. "I imagine we'll be spending a lot of time there negotiating the treaty between our cities. There's trades to negotiate, ambassadors to assign…"

"Should probably organize a Thing for next summer," Daggon added.

"And what of Gunir?" Bergen asked, dropping his flagon to the table. "What am I supposed to do?"

"Compose a song," Kallan said. "You can call it 'The Woes of Bergen the Bore.'"

Bergen scowled at the half-eaten platter between him and his brother.

"You know how I feel about responsibility and rules," Bergen said.

"I'm sure you'll find a way to put your new position to use." Rune sunk his teeth into the meat before suggesting, "You can use it to woo your wenches."

Chapter Fifty-Four

From the window of Kallan's bower, propped comfortably in the window's sill, Rune stared through the dark of night into the distance. Pillars of smoke rose from the lake to the sky. At just the right angle, he could see the red flames engulf the twelve ships, their light reflecting on the black sheet of water. From there the flames followed the clouds of billowing smoke beneath the waning crescent moon that provided sufficient light across Gunir.

With a sigh, Kallan splayed out a gown over her bed alongside five others as the door of her sitting room opened.

"Still here, Brother?" Bergen asked as he entered the bedchamber.

Rune said nothing, not bothering to look away from the longships engulfed in flame.

"The children and Elders from the Northern Keep have settled in, and Geirolf is seeing to the children."

"How are they?" Rune asked, not moving from his place in the window.

"Tired," Bergen said. "A handful returned sick with the cold that's moved in, but overall, happy to be home. Torunn has the best venison stew on the fire downstairs."

Rune nodded in approval and stared out to the lake in thought.

"You're leaving tomorrow, then?" Bergen asked Kallan as she proceeded to straighten the dresses.

"First thing," she said.

Bergen thought for a moment as he tried to decide if he heard disappointment or relief in her voice.

"And what of you?" he asked, looking to Rune in the window. "How long before you head out?"

"There!" Kallan said as she finished straightening the skirt of her last gown. "This should be enough."

Eyeing the half-dozen gowns one last time, Kallan plopped herself over the end of the bed, arms wide, and scooped up the gowns in a single armload before dragging them to the doorway and Bergen.

"Here," she said, grinning, and promptly dumped the gowns onto Bergen.

"Wha—"

"Get them to Torunn," Kallan said. "She's waiting."

"Ugh," Bergen groaned as if Kallan had just dumped a bucket of mud onto him. "Women's work."

"I didn't ask you to sew them for the orphans," Kallan said. "I asked you to take them to Torunn."

Kallan listened with delight as Bergen sauntered off back through the sitting room and down the hall.

The heat from the hearth fire battled against the growing chill outside. Kallan glanced at the collection of herbs and spells she had already tucked neatly away with her satchel beside the bed.

"You're lost, Rune," Kallan said. "The Shadow has your mind."

Rune kept his eyes on the ships on the horizon and watched the flames lap the sky.

"The Fendinn is there," he said after a long while. "I can feel it. But it's silent. It hasn't moved since…"

Rune sighed and leaned his head back against the window frame. "I don't know if I'm relieved or worried," he said. "Maybe both. I don't know."

"What will you do now?" Kallan asked.

"There isn't much choice," he muttered. "The war is over and we have wounded here to be looked after."

Kallan nodded in reflection.

"I have a lot to do in Lorlenalin," she said. "With Aaric dead and Gudrun—"

A stale knot clamped her throat and Kallan forced in a deep breath to push it along. Exhaling, she busied her hands, mindlessly unfolding a blanket for the sole purpose of refolding it again in hopes of staving off the waves of grief that often came.

"I've been absent for nearly two moons now," Kallan said. "It will be a while before I can get back here. Maybe in the upcoming Jol after the snows and the first of the beers are brewed, I can—"

"Kallan."

Kallan forced her head down, refusing to meet Rune's eye, knowing he slid down from the window. In silence, he waited patiently for her to find her words as he leaned against the bed beside her.

Kallan sighed and gazed to the window behind him. The gray pillars of smoke filled the sky. For a moment, she contemplated asking him to come with her, and instead bit her lip for control.

"The Seidr," she whispered. "Ever since I pulled you back…"

She shook her head.

"Something hasn't felt right since." Kallan sighed, wishing Rune would leave her alone, and wanting him to stay. "I can See. I understand Aaric sealed my Sight. I understand there were things he didn't want me to See. That night when he grabbed my arm, he started to unlock what he sealed away years ago. But he didn't finish."

Rune listened quietly, recalling everything from two nights before and not daring to mention the woman they had seen with Gudrun's head.

"There are things that are still dark," Kallan said. "Things, still out of my reach. I felt something there at the core," she said, "but when I extend my Sight to See, there is only darkness."

Kallan exhaled.

"Gudrun often told me of a place buried deep within the earth where the Seidr dwells at its core." The words came quickly now. "She explained that, if I were to follow the threads, I would find the Seidr there where it all begins."

Kallan paused, giving Rune a moment to answer while she searched for the words to continue.

"I was there at the core, I am certain," she said. "But something was wrong, very wrong, and I can't find the words to call it by name."

Kallan met Rune's eyes.

"I can't even bring myself to try," she whispered and shook her head. "I don't think I want to."

⇜ ⇝

Horses were saddled, provisions prepared, and the first of the Dokkalfar moved out to begin the three day trek back to Lorlenalin. The courtyard buzzed with excitement. The constant bustle of servants led by the sharp bite of Torunn's orders accompanied her stern glare.

An unusual chill clung stubbornly to the air as the gray clouds moved from the west. The last streaks of sunlight poured into Gunir as Kallan stepped from the keep. Biting the corner of her lower lip, she studied the courtyard and felt her heart sink at Rune's blatant absence.

Gathering her skirts, Kallan heaved a deep sigh and forced a smile as she descended the steps into the courtyard where Daggon led two saddled fjord horses from the stables. Bustling servants swarmed the captain as they fastened the last of Kallan's bags to the saddles beside Torunn, who wasted no time welcoming Kallan into a tight hug as the cold bit their faces.

"You'll check in with the children?" Kallan asked.

Torunn nodded.

"Every day," she replied. "Geirolf said he wants to take a look at them and see about getting them a more permanent dwelling than the warrens."

"I've left some of the apples with him," Kallan said. "You received the clothes from Bergen?"

"I have the girls already working on them."

Torunn grinned as Kallan leaned in, dropping her voice to a whisper.

"If that isn't enough, raid Rune and Bergen's wardrobes for more," Kallan goaded.

At once, Torunn grabbed Kallan and held her tight.

"You will be missed, my dear," Torunn said. "We'll be watching the roads for your return."

With tears that glistened in the sunlight, Torunn released Kallan and took her face in her hands.

"You've filled a void here that has long been needed," Torunn said, smiling.

"And it felt good putting those boys through their own paces for once."

With a kiss to her forehead, Torunn released Kallan unto Geirolf, who warmly embraced the lady.

"Return soon," he said, taking his time in releasing her.

Kallan replied with a single kiss to his warm cheek and turned, falling almost immediately into Roald's open arm.

With a growl, he hugged her tight and lifted her from the ground.

Refusing to relinquish her to Bergen, he held her high, keeping her to himself until Bergen punched to Roald's good shoulder.

"Come on, Stumpy!" Bergen said impatiently.

Ignoring the complaint, Roald held Kallan a moment longer before lowering her to the ground.

"You'll be missed." He smiled and left her to Bergen.

"Dearest lady," Bergen greeted with a sad smile.

Kallan raised her gaze to the scar that decorated his right brow.

"Consider her a peace offering," Bergen said.

Curious, Kallan tipped her head in question as Gunnar slunk into the courtyard leading the charcoal gray mare, saddled, bridled, and ready to ride.

"Oh." Kallan clamped both hands to her mouth as the mare came to stand beside the pair of fjord horses.

"Her name is Zabbai," Bergen said. "Named for a rare...rare lady, much like yourself. She's been good to me," Bergen said. "Be good to her."

Tears burned Kallan's eyes. Unable to hold back, Kallan jumped onto Bergen, wrapping her arms around his neck.

"Thank you," she whispered into his ear, and he tightened his grip on her.

Kallan released Bergen's neck and slid back to the ground.

Eagerly, she approached the mare, allowing the horse to snuffle and sniff her hand. Slowly, Kallan pulled an apple from her pouch and extended it to the mare, who accepted it almost at once. After the horse lowered her guard, Kallan pulled herself into the saddle with Daggon's help.

"I still owe you for this!" Bergen called, pointing to his scarred brow as Kallan steered the mare toward the gates.

"Challenge me!" Kallan dared over her shoulder.

With a glint in her golden eyes, she flicked a wrist with ease and ignited a white flame.

Bergen shook his head.

"You have no idea how happy I am that you are my ally!"

"Coward," Kallan called back with a smile, then shifted to face the bailey ahead. Daggon mounted one of the two fjord horses and followed.

"Are you ready, Your Highness?" Daggon asked from atop his steed.

Quietly, Kallan gazed over the courtyard and scanned the many faces. Her hopes plummeted when she failed to see one in particular. Without a word, she nodded.

As Kallan rode through the streets, the Dokkalfar fell in line behind her, some on horseback but most on foot, as they followed her to the bridge of the Klarelfr. There, propped too casually against his horse, Rune leaned with the same bored look in his eye that Bergen often held.

"What are you doing?" Kallan asked as she came within range at the bridge.

"Do you really think you're going without me?" he asked as he hoisted himself onto his horse and readied the reins. "Besides… I can't trust you'll stay out of trouble."

"But Bergen," Kallan said. "Gunir—"

"—will be fine while we work on negotiating the details of the alliance. I'll not be gone forever. Just long enough to set things in order…until you can find time to slip away."

"And Bergen consented to this?" Kallan asked.

Rune smirked.

"Bergen doesn't know I'm gone yet," Rune said, directing his horse across the bridge to the plains. "Geirolf knows and has instructions to tell Bergen of the arrangement tonight over a pipe and flagon of hop mead," Rune called as he took the lead.

"My treat," Daggon said with a grin.

The bridge was soon behind them as they crossed the barren battlefield and pillars of dead. Ahead, the forest of Swann Dalr lay and the main road that would take them south.

Releasing a sigh, Kallan gazed up at the sky. The first of the snows had begun to fall.

Flooded with a sudden sickness, she looked to the horizons beyond the west at the brewing storm ahead.

"It's early," Rune said about the premature cold. "The harvests have barely begun."

"Too early," Kallan observed, knowing there was much more to the falling snows than she could see.

With a final glance over her shoulder, she looked down the long line of Dokkalfar that marched from Gunir's gates. From the plains, she gazed upon Gunir's keep that rose from the hill and towered over the bailey with grandeur.

Before looking back to the road, Kallan's eye lingered on the tower where Kovit still hung chained to the wall. Unease stirred her nerves. Reaching out with her Seidr, Kallan tried to See, and quickly scowled at the sheet of black that blocked her Sight. She still had a lot of work ahead of her.

ေ ၜ၁

Inside the keep, Torunn barked her orders and drove the Ljosalfar to their work. No one paid mind to a slender woman with long, ebony hair and a single slender line that marred her right cheek bone. Unseen, she slipped through the Great Hall. Servants, hunched over their tasks, didn't flinch. Warriors walked the halls as the woman ascended the steps to the second floor and up to the tower floor.

The guard on duty dozed, jerked himself awake, and failed to see the hem of a gown as the woman rounded the hall to the only occupied cell. There, Kovit hung, bleeding, broken, and half-dead.

With a creak the guard couldn't hear, the woman pushed open the door, spilling light across the floor. Her bare feet grazed the stone as she drifted into the cell and came to stop before the Dokkalfr.

Disappointment filled her golden eyes as she stared at the mass of Kovit chained to the wall.

"This is how I am to find you," she said.

Her soft voice awakened him, urging Kovit to raise his mangled face to Fand.

"Did you speak to her?" Fand asked, "Does the Drui know?"

Slowly, painfully, Kovit shook his head.

The answer seemed to please her as she exhaled and relaxed her shoulders.

"Very good," she said, and the deep red of her lips curved into a gentle smile. "And then there was one."

CHAPTER FIFTY-FIVE

Standing in a foot of white that blocked out the afternoon sun, Rune peered through the white, his arrow notched in readiness. It was there, whatever it was that Rune had seen just beyond the snows.

He shifted his position, and followed the trail of prints into the wood. The snows that had started three days ago still fell thick and heavy along the East Road, making the journey back to Lorlenalin an arduous one. Less than an hour out from the White Opal, a surge of Seidr drew Kallan's attention toward the Alfheim wood, and a tuft of fur from a fox tail caught Rune's eye. After sending the caravan on ahead, Rune slipped into the forest.

Rune closed in on the orange light reflected in the snow at the end of the trail. He slowed, bringing his bow eye-level. Staring down his arrow's shaft, he moved until he found his target. Just as he prepared to release the arrow, shock stayed Rune's hand. There, seated contentedly in the snow playing with something in her hands, sat a child encompassed by fire she wore like skin. What Rune had mistaken for a tail were tufts of red hair set aflame by the fire that failed to consume the child.

The child turned her round face toward him. Her fox-like eyes gazed sweetly up at him. There was no doubt, seeing her there in the snow, her harmlessness, her gentle curiosity and innocence.

Slowly, to not startle the child, Rune lowered his bow and extended an open palm. She paused for a moment to look at his hand, almost playfully, then jumped with the agility of a fox and fled. In two great bounds, she was gone without trail or trace.

"Rune," Kallan called from the East Road, forcing Rune to abandon his pursuit of the fox-girl.

"I'm here," he called and made his way back to the road.

"What are you doing here?" he asked as he emerged from the forest. "I sent you on with the caravan."

"Exactly," Kallan said, hoisting herself into the saddle. "You sent me on. I wanted to stay behind." Kallan pulled her overcoat tighter against the cold.

"I don't see Daggon agreeing to that easily," Rune said.

"He didn't. I used a spell and slipped away."

"Are you sure that's wise?" Rune asked.

Kallan shrugged. "We're less than an hour from Lorlenalin. I know these trees."

Rune pulled himself onto his horse alongside Zabbai.

"What was it?" Kallan asked.

Rune shook his head, unsure how to explain he was outwitted by a fox-child dressed in fire.

"Never seen anything like it," he said instead and took up the reins. "It ran off before I could get a close enough look, but from what I could see, it looked like a fox."

"There was Seidr," Kallan said, giving Zabbai a gentle nudge.

Rune gave no reply as he matched Kallan's pace and continued along the East Road toward the city.

Within moments, Kallan had resumed stretching her neck, eager to receive the city. Any moment, Lorlenalin's peaks would appear on the horizon. Any moment, through the white winter, she would be home. But the snowfall was heavy and the cloud coverage thick.

Too eager to play with Seidr threads or chat idly with Rune, she nibbled her bottom lip and thought endlessly of that evening when she would see the children again.

Kallan pulled her overcoat closed. She thought of how much the children would have changed and how long the children may have fared without Eilif. She tried to ignore the sudden rise in tears and changed her thoughts to that night's banquet when she could dive, mouth first, into a pie.

All the foods that Rune would have to try… I'll have to send some back for Bergen—

The scent on the wind changed. Kallan wrinkled her nose.

We'll have to set up trade between our cities. There is a lot to do to prepare for the new shipments that will come in from Gunir. I'll have to work out the details regarding the imports and exports with Rune.

She felt her heart flitter at the thought of trading out some of the colored glasses in Gunir with the finer weaponry.

The winds blew strong, and this time, Kallan could not ignore the stench of smoke.

"Hold," Rune said, pulling back on his reins. Kallan followed suit and peered curiously over the trees into the farthest horizon. Smoke and cloud billowed then rolled into each other. The wind rustled like wisps and spoke.

"Drui."

A distant scream carried over the trees, and Kallan whipped her reins, sending Zabbai into a full gallop.

"Kallan!" Rune cried and sent his horse galloping behind her.

Kallan steered Zabbai up the mountain, through the last of the forest and, with a sharp whinny from Zabbai, Kallan pulled back unexpectedly on the reins. Where Livsvann Falls roared, ugly masses of red flames indulged themselves on Lorlenalin, turning the White Opal red. Kallan heard nothing. Not the shrill edge of her own voice or her feet striking the frozen ground as she ran through the snows toward the fire that had encompassed the city. She had seen fire like this once before, ages ago within the mountains of Svartalfaheim, when she was but a child.

The flames consumed the last of the screams. Behind her, Rune sent his horse up the road.

"Kallan!" he cried, but Kallan didn't hear. All she saw was Lorlenalin burning.

"Drui," the wind whispered.

But Kallan was screaming.

"Kallan!" Rune shouted and kicked the horse harder until he was riding beside

Kallan. Leaning down, he slipped his arm around her and plucked her up from the road. She fought him, battled, and punched, desperate to fight her way into the city. Rune pulled back on the reins, and placed all his strength into holding Kallan from running into the fire.

"Daggon!" Kallan screamed.

A wall support cracked then bowed and broke.

"Daggon!"

The stones of Lorlenalin crumbled.

"Daggon!" she screamed, but the fire and the thunder of Livsvann's Falls took her voice and she went unheard as the wind seemed to call to her.

Drui.

Kallan clawed at Rune's arms, desperate to fight her way to the warrens, to the children, and to Daggon as she unleashed her final word, helpless to stop it.

"Daggon!"

EPILOGUE

995 years after Baldr…

Silence encompassed the world at the roots of Yggdrasil. In the distance, a single drop of moisture plunked into a shallow pool, sending off a series of high-pitched echoes amplified by the cave walls. Within its depths, through the darkest caverns, Nidhoggr slept.

Loptr raised his eyes to the snake secured above his head. The clear, thick venom swelled and slid to the tip of the fang where it began to pool. The next drop would soon fall. Loptr's rage seethed and he tightened his jaw, ready for the searing pain that would come.

The thunder of hooves pounded the ground and Svadilfari released a snort.

In a series of fluid movements, Sigyn slid from the saddle, pulled the bundle from the side satchel, and turned to Loptr fastened beneath the snake. Throwing back the cloth, she revealed the silver sheen of Laevateinn's elding steel blade secured by a tang buried in a hilt of black onyx and ordained with black pearls.

Just as Loptr caught sight of the sword, Sigyn lunged, blade drawn, and screamed.

"No!" Loptr roared, shaking the ground with his will to stop her.

And then there was silence.

Seidr light rolled down the silver blade from a hand that clamped Laevateinn's blade. Sigyn's breath beat the air.

There, standing over Loptr in flowing gowns of white, stood Danann peering down at Sigyn, Loptr, and Laevateinn.

Danann's hair, as gold as the Seidr in her eyes, hung past her waist, and her lips curved into a smile.

A drop of venom slipped from the snake's fang and Loptr's flesh sizzled. The giant howled. Rocks sliced his spine as he arched his back against the stones. Losing her grip on the sword, Sigyn relinquished the weapon as her legs gave out and she fell, sobbing, in a heap on the cave floor. The searing pain of the venom on Loptr's brow subsided and his howling faded until the caverns were quiet again.

"Sigyn." Danann's voice flowed over the jotunn.

With a sigh, Sigyn lifted her eyes to the Aes Sidhe and Danann tightened her grip on Laevateinn.

"I need your help again, Loptr," Danann said, looking upon Loptr bound beneath the snake.

Sweat stained his brow and Loptr smiled as the next droplet formed.

Thank you for your support. May the kindest of words always find you.

– Angela B. Chrysler

Congratulations! You have unlocked "The Seer's Stones." Go to angelabchrysler. com/the-seers-stones/ and enter the case-sensitive password "Runes" to access the special features reserved just for you.

Please consider leaving a review on Amazon and/or Goodreads.

About the Author

Angela B. Chrysler is a writer, logician, philosopher, and die-hard nerd who studies theology, historical linguistics, music composition, and medieval European history in New York with a dry sense of humor and an unusual sense of sarcasm. She lives in a garden with her family and cats.

News, updates, events, and upcoming releases are available at her website (http://www.angelabchrysler.com/), or you can find her on Twitter, Facebook, Goodreads, and Google+.

Pronunciation Guide

A complete list with audio is available at www.angelabchrysler.com

Alfr (Alf) Elf

Alfar (Al-far) Elves

Alfheim (Alf-hame) Elf Home

Bergen Tryggveson (Bear-gen Treeg-vay-son) Ljosalfar and berserker

Caoilinn (Kway-linn) Ljosalfar

Daggon (Day-gon) Dokkalfar

Dokkalfr (Do-kalf) Dark elf

Dokkalfar (Do-kal-far) Dark Elves

Dubh Linn (Doov Linn) Dublin, Ireland

Dvergr (D-vare-g) Singular

Dvergar (D-vare-gar) Plural See "Regarding the Dvergar" at www.angelabchrysler.com

Eilif (A-leef) Dokkalfar

Eire's Land (Air's Land) Ireland

Elding (El-ding) A mysterious metal infused with the Seidr only used by the Dokkalfar and the Dvergar.

Elding (El-ding) The age in which the Alfar reach full maturity and stop aging.

Finn (Fin) The Old Norse word for the Sami

Finntent (fin-tent) The Old Norse words for a portable teepee-styled tent still used by the Sami

Fjandinn (Fee-yan-din) The old Norse equivalent to the Christian word "Devil" used by Norsemen prior to the introduction of the Christian culture.

Freyja (Fray-ya) Norse goddess

Gamme (Ga-may) The Old Norse word for an earthen home still used by the

Sami

Ginnungagap (Gi-noon-ga-gap) The Great Gap

Gudrun (goo-droon) Dokkalfar

Gunir (Goo-neer) The Ljosalfar city in Alfheim

Hel (Hel) Loptr's daughter, Hel, guardian and overseer of Helheim

Helheim (Hel-hame) The Norse version of the Underworld where Loptr's daughter, Hel, resides.

Idunn (I-thoon or I-doon) Norse goddess

Jotun (Yo-toon) Giants

Jotunheim (Yo-toon-hame) The home of the giants

Kallan Eyolfdottir (Ka-lon A-olf-do-teer) Dokkalfar

Loptr (Lopt) The Old Norse name for Loki

Lorlenalin (Lor-len-a-lin) The Dokkalfar city in Alfheim

Ljosalfr (Lee-yos-alf) Light Elf

Ljosalfar (Lee-yos-al-far) Light Elves

Midgard (Mid-gard) Literal translattion "Middle-Earth." Midgard is the human realm.

Nidingr (Ni-thing) Literal translation: "Nothing." The status of "outlaw" given to a dishonorable coward who has been stripped of his station, property, and citizenship in Norse culture.

Odinn (O-thin or O-din) Norse god

Olaf Tryggvason (O-lof Treeg-va-son) Historically, the first king of Norway. Note: Olaf Tryggvason has no relation to Bergen or Rune whose last name is Tryggveson. The name of Olaf's father was "Trygg" while the father of Rune and Bergen is "Tryggve."

Seidr (Say-th or Seed) The life source bound to the elements and all living things and referred to as "magic" in the Deserts.

Seidkona (Say-th-kona or Seed-ko-na) Old Norse for "Witch"

Surtr (sert) Lord of the Fire Giants

Sigyn (See-gin) Loptr's wife

Svartálfr (Svart-alf) Black Elf

Svartálfar (Svart-alf-ar) Black Elves

Svartálfaheim (Svart-alf-a-hame) Home of the Black Elves

Thing (Thing) The Norwegian Parliament still in existence today in Norway.

Tryggve (Treeg-vay) Ljosalfar

Wicce (Witch) Anglo-Saxon word for "Witch"

Winter and Ash
(Tales of the Drui Book 3)

CHAPTER 1

Silence. The snow fell lightly onto the ash and stone. The birds that had long since nested here came no more. Silence of the worst kind settled over Lorlenalin's streets.

Kallan walked among the ash and snow. Her crimson gown upon the stone, the only sound. Without a word, she stepped through the ruins of Lorlenalin. She inhaled, expanding her chest against the empty chasm that filled with the silence left behind. Silence and stone. Silence. It and Kallan were all that remained of Lorlenalin.

Each footfall was like an echo that drummed life back into her. Each breath was as a renting reminder that she lived while they did not. It violently reawakened her to her solitude and she repeated Bergen's words in her head.

Dead on the cold dank shoals
Dead on the barren floor
Millions could weep no more
Silence the thousands.

Kallan stopped beside the dilapidated stone, crumbled and broken, unrecognizable, save for the location. Once the grand fountain in Lorlenalin's center, now a ruin.

It would be Jol soon. Voices would have been raised in song this day. Voices no more will sing. A shiver ran up Kallan's spine. A month ago, she would have broken to her knees and screamed. A week ago she would have dropped her shoulders and sobbed. This day, she could only stand and let the agony of grief eat through her. There were no tears left for this.

There now the children be
Those who've forgotten me
Too dead to smile for me
Silence the hundreds.

And so it was done. Kallan stepped and stopped. Her eye caught a gleam of something. Not stone or beam. Not skeleton or skull. Not this time. Kallan bent down and pulled the smooth white bracelet from the ash and snow. She knew the etchings, inscriptions, and eternal knots long before her skin went white. She clamped the elding bracelet in her hand and remembered.

Rind.

A pinch of pain found her through the hollow remains. Too clearly, she could hear Rind's little voice once more.

"Will you promise?"

She had slipped the bracelet over the tiny hand and watched as Rind spun the bracelet over once then snuggled into her and went to sleep.

"I promise," Kallan whispered and closed her voice on a sob. If there had been tears left, one would have fallen. But her heart was empty and her eyes were dry.

Once more Kallan walked through the ruins of Lorlenalin, clutching the bracelet. For hours at a time she wandered with no place to go and no one to find. She walked as if looking for someone she knew wasn't there. Regardless, she walked and looked.

She wandered for hours taking in each broken step and stone. She wandered for days. The snow only fell. She wandered for weeks… a moon passed and then another. She wandered until she could no longer count the moons. Walking and circling the steps of Lorlenalin. Maybe there was someone, somewhere. Maybe she wasn't alone. She wandered until the silence carved out the last of her heart in the depths of her solitude.

At the base of a mountain, at the shores of the sea, Livsvann's water flowed. The snows fell here, coating the gray sands with white. Rune stared into the Kattegat and waited. For moons he waited, ready for when Kallan, at last would pull herself away.

"Rune?"

Rune stared a moment longer into the sea before turning to give a weak smile to Torunn. Her cloak pulled tight on her shoulders. Though he couldn't see it he knew, she had fastened her gray hair tightly to her head beneath her hood.

"Rune, it's Jol."

"So it is."

"Come home."

Rune smiled, cold and distant.

"I'm waiting here, Torunn."

Torunn sighed quietly and came to stand beside Rune. Even the docks were left in ruins.

"Has there been anything?"

"Nothing. No clue, no sign. No life."

"Will you go to her?"

"That isn't what she needs now, Torunn. She has lost everyone. Her orphans, herfather, her friend, Gudrun, Daggon . . . Astrid . . ."

Rune shook his head.

"She has nothing left. The least I can do is stand here and wait and be here when she decides to find me."

"But it's been months. It's Jol. Get Kallan and come home. Bergen is gone. All of Gunir has felt the magnitude of this. The city is colder than the snows."

"Torunn, I love you. But I will not move a foot away from these shores until Kallan is ready to leave."

Torunn's shoulders fell. She wouldn't fight a known defeat.

"It is the least I can do for her."

Torunn nodded, but when she turned to go, Rune called her back.

"Torunn."

She gazed over her shoulder.

"Did Cook make the Jol pudding this year?"

"As always. And the halls are strung with balls of holly and pine."

Rune nodded. He could smell the cinnamon and pies . . . such comforting warmth during such a dismal time.

"Could you—"

"I can bring you a basket."

Rune smiled. Though still cold, a touch of warmth broke through.

"Thanks Torunn."

Torunn gathered her skirts and trudged back up the hill, following the waters of Livsvann and leaving Rune to Kallan and the sea.

c͛ ͛ͽ

Rune crunched the snow beneath his boot. But she didn't turn. Frail and thin, Kallan stood staring at the gray sky. Her gown fell like sheets of blood on white. The silence was deafening, but Rune stood and waited.

"I can't hear the sea," Kallan muttered. Her throat was dry and cracked from disuse." I never noticed before now. I never cared. I wish I could. It would help fill the silence."

Rune glanced at a pile of rubble buried now beneath the elements. Most of the ash was gone save for the path Kallan had worn into the snow with her pacing.

"I'm so cold," Kallan whispered. "And I can still hear them. Their voices, so clear. Their faces…I remember so clearly…" Kallan turned. Her face usually so pale, was nearly as white as the ice that clung to the ruins." It's as if they are here…in the keep, in their beds... They're just sleeping and I can see them if only I will it…If only I tried. And so, I keep walking, as if I'll turn a corner and see them. And I can reach out and touch their faces. And all will be well again. If only I bother to try…I can take their hands again…if only I bothered to look. All I have to do is call out, and they will answer. And so I walk…but there is only ever snow."

As she spoke, her breath hastened and dry tears swelled, but never fell, and a madness had taken her, leaving behind a wild look in her golden eyes.

"I have to remind myself that they're gone," Kallan said. "Even though Lorlenalin's streets lay in ruins, I have to remind myself that they're dead. And I hate it! And so much of this tastes like a lie… But if I don't… I'll forget and I will never stop looking."

Rune dared take a step closer, uncertain if Kallan would collapse as she shook.

"There is nothing I can think that doesn't remind me, nothing I can do that allows me peace. Living is a constant reminder. But I live, and they are dead... all dead. And what's worse, I don't even know why. How I want to die...to join them. How I want...to join them, if only to end this writhing in my chest..."The wave she held back broke forth." My heart has been cut from me! It's buried here among the ash! If only I look, I could find it! I can feel it!I know it's there! And I want it! If only I look...I will find it...I will find it! So I look and I wander to find my heart again."

Grief pulled her shoulders down and arched her back as Kallan buckled beneath the sorrow. But, she did not falter. She did not fall. Kallan stood and kept her feet on the ground. Rune drew near and took her and held her as she sobbed for all of Lorlenalin and the children and the Dokkalfar who lay dead there.

The snows fell silently on the streets of Gunir. A stale fear hung in the air, the kind that quelled even gossip. The horse masters barked their orders with more venom. Mothers scolded their children with more bite. But no one spoke of the unease that clouded them all. Inside Gunir's keep, Geirolf tightened his back as he hunched himself lower over his bowl of stew. The vast fire behind him barely fought back that chill. Instead, he slurped his soup, minding his own, as infected by the cold as anyone there.

Torunn's sharp step from the kitchens nipped the silence, and Geirolf pulled his fur cloak higher over his shoulder. Her chair scraped the stone floor. Geirolf slurped. She pulled her shawl closer as settled herself beside Geirolf.

"Any word?" Torunn asked.

Geirolf slurped.

She wrung her hands together, but failed to rid the cold from her bony hands.

"Not of late," Geirolf answered and slurped.

Torunn sighed and gazed up at the holly and pine trims that still hung on the wall from Jol nearly a fortnight past. Piles of dried pine needles collected along the edge of the room and the sheen has long since faded from the holly leaves. Most of the berries had withered and fallen to join the piles of dead pine needles.

"Are you ever going to them down?" Geirolf asked, shaking Torunn from her musings." They only add to the abysmal mood."

"I—"

The sudden baritone of Gunir's horn penetrated the silence causing a brief delay before either Torunn or Geirolf could determine its meaning. Exchanging a look, Geirolf dropped his spoon and stood with Torunn as they threw themselves to the double oak doors that led to Gunir's courtyard.

With a stiffness and a gimp to his leg, the horse master hobbled from the stables as men from the barracks filled into the courtyard to greet their King and Kallan. As Rune slid of his mount, Kallan lowered herself to the ground.

"Welcome back, Rune," Geirolf said slapping a hand to Rune's shoulder with a warm grin that seemed out of place. Before Rune could release Kallan, Geirolf swept her hand from Rune, and planted a kiss to her cheek." Sweet Lady."

"Tell me you have fresh mead and a hot fire inside," Rune said, catching Torunn in a hug.

"As always," she said and followed Rune into the Hall ahead of Geirolf who took Kallan's arm.

Stripping his gloves from his hands, Rune slid his overcoat from his shoulders to welcome the warmth from the fire as he made his way to the grand stairs on the Hall's North side. His gaze shifted to the empty throne briefly before leading his clan up the stairs to the second floor corridor.

"Torunn," he said as Kallan slipped her arm free from Geirolf and silently made her way to the first set of double doors on her right." Have your girls bring up a platter for Kallan."

"Certainly," Torunn said as Kallan closed her door behind her. But before she could gather her skirts, Rune grabbed her arm.

"She hasn't spoken a word in two weeks," he muttered. "She barely eats. Brew one of Geirolf's teas for her...something that will help her rest."

The key keeper pursed her lips and nodded then hastened down the stairs to the kitchens.

"Geirolf." Rune gave a nod and proceeded down the hall to the door of his sitting room that was filled with the warmth from the hearth fire.

Geirolf followed Rune inside and closed the door behind him as Rune dropped his coat and gloves to a chair and made his way to the collection of meads and ales beside a table laden with maps and parchment.

"Rune."

The cork whined as Rune pulled the flask free from the mead.

"How is she?"

Rune chugged back a long mouthful and Geirolf waited.

Slowly, Rune's hand began to shake and, pulling the bottle from his mouth, he flung the glass into the fire that shattered then ignited and settled back down in the time it took Rune to brace his hands on the table's edge. His shoulders hunched over as if buckling beneath Kallan's grief.

"Ten thousand..." Rune muttered. "Ten thousand."

Geirolf held his breath as Rune dared speak of the fear that vexed them all.

"Ten thousand men, wives, women, children...Ten thousand dead." Rune released the table and gazed at Geirolf." Lorlenalin's walls were built on the granite and stone hewn from the rock and mountain. Shipments of quartz and tungsten were brought into port. What could possibly do such a thing as to rent every last stone of the White Opal?"

"Is no one left?" Geirolf asked.

"Not a child, not a stone... Not Daggon," Rune answered and stared down at his hands." Not a clue as to what or why."

"Everyone fears that we're next," Geirolf said.

"That thought constantly plagues me." Rune sighed and rubbed his face then stared into the fire. A bit of glass glistened in the firelight." Any word from Bergen?"

Geirolf shook his head." He left early this year."

Rune furrowed his brow." Did he say why?"

Geirolf found a smile beneath the solemn mood. "You know Bergen gives no reason where Râ-Kedet is concerned."

YOU MAY ALSO LIKE

Readers who enjoyed Tales of the Drui, also enjoyed…

The Wizard Killer by Adam Dreece

From the Steampunk Fairytales of *The Yellow Hoods*, to his post-apocalyptic fantasy *The Wizard Killer*, Adam Dreece brings high energy and intensity to everything he writes.

His newest release, *The Man of Cloud 9*, takes place 70 years in the future, on a damaged Earth that has come to fear innovation. When a Steve Jobs-like inventor comes up with an idea for nano-bots living off the human microbial cloud, he finds himself challenged at every turn.

Adam Dreece lives in Calgary, Alberta, Canada with his wife, three kids, and copious amounts of sticky notes and scraps of paper.

Walking Between Worlds by J.K. Norry

Walk between the worlds of angels and devils. Explore the deeper meaning of demons, and face the beauty of the monster in all of us with author Jay Norry.

"Stumbling Backasswards Into the Light" is an uplifting memoir, the tale of Jay's decision to question the answers he had been given and discover his own deeper meaning.

Walking Between Worlds is an exciting and action-packed philosophical adventure, a dark humorous romp through heaven and hell and the deeper meaning of all the worlds we walk between.

"The Secret Society od Deeper Meaning" is currently exploring the softer side of zombies, and the deeper meaning of the archetype: could Mother Nature be saving us from ourselves?

Sign up for free "Zombie Zero: The First Zombie" short stories, and find out the deeper meaning of it all in Zombie Zero: The First Zombie.

Jay lives in Northern California with three of his favorite angels, an unending to do list and a mind full of thoughts about the deeper meaning.

The Crown of Stones series by C.L. Schneider

From a land long-divided by prejudice and fear, comes the story of Ian Troy, a magic-user bred for war. Reviled for their deadly addiction to magic, Ian's people suffer in slavery. Their once great empire lies buried, lost beneath the sand and a thousand years of secrets—until Ian unearths the Crown of Stones. Ignorant of its true purpose, Ian wields the circlet's power and brings peace to the realms, but at a terrible price.

The Crown of Stones is an epic fantasy trilogy that turns everything you knew about magic on its head. It's a time-spanning adventure filled with battles, creatures, loss, love, betrayal, secrets, addiction, and magic.

C. L. Schneider writes epic and urban fantasy for adults. She lives in New York with her husband and two sons.

Made in the USA
Columbia, SC
14 June 2018